I9

JEAN DAVIS

I9

www.jeandavisauthor.com

ISBN-13:   (print) 978-1-962708-07-4
          (ebook) 978-1-962708-08-1

First Edition: November 2025

Also by Jean Davis

Sahmara
The Last God
A Broken Race
Everyone Dies
Destiny Pills and Space Wizards
Dreams of Stars and Lies
Not Another Bard's Tale
Spindelkin
Frayed

The Narvan
One Shot at the Sphinx
Trust
The Minor Years
Chain of Gray
Bound In Blue
Seeker
Tears of the Tyrant

1

I Hate All Of You

I stared out the window at two more ships docking on the outer ring of the station, wondering what fresh hell these idiots would bring. A discordant mash of music blasted around me from the three clubs that were in full swing despite it only being midafternoon. Two women in short dresses screamed at each other. A slap-fest erupted with all the coordination of drunken fish. One of their high heels tipped sideways, spilling her onto the sticky social district floor. The other one laughed and turned to walk away. Then she caught sight of the impromptu orgy happening in the sofa-filled lounge and wandered over to poke the nearest naked ass with a pointy orange fingernail. When the man didn't seem to notice, she shook her head and moved on. I really hated the burning season on Anduvea.

With so many people flooding the station, attempting to enforce the rules was a pointless endeavor, but I figured I ought to help a fellow woman out. I straightened my security uniform and descended the stairs from my post. Weaving through the milling crowds, I made it to the fallen woman and helped her to her feet. Fights, I could let go. Trampled bodies meant paperwork. No one wanted that.

Once she found her balance on her ridiculous heels, she shook me off and then squinted to read the nameplate on my uniform. With a scorn-filled glare, she yelled over the music, "Don't touch me, Officer Stabinov. She started it. You can't charge me."

"You go on and have a really nice day then." After making sure she was steady enough to be on her way, I returned to my elevated platform where I could monitor the sea of spoiled, rich assholes.

The thick, clearplaz ring of wall panels allowed a distant view of Anduvea while providing just as much shielding as the opaque panels. The view was one of the few things I liked about this job. That and I didn't have to live with these people year-round on Anduvea's surface. My family wasn't one of the rich ones. I'd never fit in with these people even when I had lived among them.

At twenty, the minimum age for station employment, I'd been overjoyed to take this job. Despite my initial plan to save up and then hire on with the first freighter headed somewhere far from the empire of Empaetor Iradio VIII, half a lifetime later, I was still here. Leaving my parents was a step I'd never been able to make, especially now that my father had health issues.

The orgy in the lounge seemed to be breaking up, the sweaty naked bodies peeling away from one another. Who knew what they were on, but none of them seemed to care that they were standing naked in public.

"Put your damned clothes on," I yelled. A few of them picked up whatever they'd been wearing before the sex had broken out. Two slipped a shirt or dress over their heads, the rest ignored me. I'd run down later and grab what they'd left to throw in the donation bin. Some teen on the outskirts of town would love some barely worn designer clothes once the ash was out of the air. I would have swooned at a gift like that when I'd been a kid.

Burning season was in full swing on the surface of the planet below. Firestorms licked at the edges of civilization, kept at bay only by the vast plascrete swathes surrounding each city. The buildings might have been safe from the flames, but the air was thick with ash and the skies a murky grey for two months straight. The stench of smoke permeated everything. I didn't miss it one bit. And if I did, I could take a shift on the docking ring and get a whiff of all the refugees—the term *they* used—flooding in to spend the burning season up here.

I enjoyed the off season, where my level of excitement was nothing more than explaining the proper use of refuse chutes or bathroom facilities to confused trade ship visitors. Sometimes we had a thrilling moment where we had to search a suspicious ship for stolen goods or detain wanted criminals, but those were few and far between. Empaetor Iradio's empire was a well-oiled machine eight generations in. Most people were too afraid to take the kinds of risks that brought moments of thrill to my life. Justice was often banishment or death. It was an effective deterrent.

A red light went off on my terminal. I hit the button to pull up the report. Unruly behavior in the restaurant below my platform. At least it wasn't a long walk.

Back down the stairs and through the crowd lined up outside the door, I caught sight of Tino at the counter. He waved me over.

"What seems to be the problem?"

"Burning season?" he snipped.

The noise in there was so damned loud, I had to lean closer to hear him clearly.

"Fucking hell, Rita. Can't we put up a station closed sign for just one year?"

"I wish. But look at all the business you'd miss."

His annoyed tone faded to whining. "I love the business, but the people... Could they be different people?"

"At least they know where to piss. Point me to the one I need to kick out."

He gestured to a table through the crowd, where the loudest yelling emanated. I shoved my way between people to see what I was dealing with.

"No fucking way."

The other drunken fish slapper from the social district stood next to a table full of people, gesturing forcefully and slopping her drink over the woman beside her. She appeared to be trying to incite a riot over Tino being out of Saba melon. The menu said he had it. How dare he be out of her favorite melon? The nerve.

Every time she waved her fist in the air, her indecently short skirt revealed far more than I or anyone else needed to see. What I really wanted to do was roll my eyes, turn around, and go anywhere quieter on the damned station, but as a senior security officer and Tino's friend, I couldn't do that. Stupid job.

"Sit down," I ordered, giving her the authoritative stare-down that usually worked on surface-dwellers.

After a glare and a squinty-eyed examination of my uniform nameplate, she kept up with the slurred complaining, but planted her bare behind in the chair. I hoped Tino's staff would sanitize it before anyone else sat down. Why anyone would want their hoohaa rubbing all over a public surface was beyond me.

"Next time wear pants or at least underclothes when you leave your room, or I'll cite you for public indecency."

I wouldn't. That wasn't worth my time, but it made her shut up for a moment to glare at me.

"Cite da guy for false advertinizing," she slurred.

The other occupants of the table shook their fists and slurred their agreement with her declaration.

"Yeah, I don't think we can cite him for running out of a melon during burning season when the only place they grow is Anduvea. Burning season isn't good for crops, and the melons only have a one-week shelf life. But you wouldn't understand any of that because you've never worked on a farm or transported stock. I bet you've never even prepared your own food."

She shot to her feet again. "My dad will hear this. Imma report you ta him and da station commander. Would ya like that, Officener Stabbenavov?"

"Oh, that might get me a meeting with the station commander. I've been trying to get one of those for years. He owes me a raise for putting up with people like you." I pulled a bubble tab from my belt and, after verifying that I had the 'this side down' oriented correctly, tapped it lightly on her shoulder.

The containment bubble inflated instantly, knocking her chair over, and sealing Daddy's Girl in a safe, soft bubble. Semi-transparent walls silenced her ranting. The other people at the table cheered and immediately began to mock her. What a fickle crowd.

Once I had the bubble moved out of the way, I righted the chair, touching it as little as possible, because: yuck.

I contacted my team to let them know I was escorting a bubble to lockup. Not that it really mattered, we were too short-staffed for anyone to cover my station.

With the bubble floating beside me, I maneuvered through the crowded social district, getting jostled with nearly every step. The obscene gestures from tourists rolled off my back. I'd grown skilled at ignoring those.

Once out of the main public fray, we took a side corridor to the staff lift that brought us down to the level security shared with the maintenance crew. One of the narrow levels of the station, it allowed space for the gravitational rings that alternated with the hydroponic loop.

The lockup terminal was unoccupied. Sieno, who was on duty, was no doubt off somewhere supervising one of the junior members of our team. They all seemed incapable of reading the employee manual.

After signing in, I located an empty cell, deactivated the bubble, and left Daddy's Girl to her ranting behind the field that also blocked her voice but left her visible to the staff. Senio was a lonely man. He deserved a gratuitous show.

The comm pin on my collar pinged. I answered, "Stabinov here."

"Are you available to do a stock security inspection? Against our recommendation, Commander Keef granted docking privileges to a trade ship," said a female voice from dispatch.

"I know we're happy for any food stores and distractions for the tourists, but right now? Was Commander Keef not aware that we have a constant flow of incoming idiots today? They're flooding the unloading zone."

Dispatch sighed. "I know. He said, and I quote: 'Handle it'."

"Sure. Yeah. So easy. I'll be up in twenty."

"Thanks, Rita."

Since Sieno wasn't around to take my report, I sat at his terminal to enter it myself. With that finished, I hightailed it back to the staff lift and rode to the end of the station nearest Anduvea, where the docking ring currently was. I was counting the weeks until we could perform the station flip to position docking back on the far end for trade ships. We had to make connections as easy as possible for all the I'm-a-pilot fools who thought they could handle a docking maneuver just because they could park a surface transport at home.

The staff lift offered a stunning view of the stars for a quiet, peaceful twelve minutes. I had a feeling they would be the best moments of my day. Just as a sliver of the sun came into view, the lift slowed and then stopped. Back home, my parents would be sitting at the table, sipping their brewcaf while watching that same sun rise over the plas-crete expanse that had served as my childhood playground. Up here, it was a signal that my mid-shift break was in half an hour. And thanks to this damned stock inspection, I was probably going to miss it. Who needed to eat anyway?

In the hopes I could salvage part of my break, I hurried to the docking control station and checked in to see which ring sector I needed to get to. The tourists gave me little space to move as they griped about having to haul their own towering stacks of luggage onboard. We had hover-carts, but there weren't enough for everyone. They bitched about that too.

With the location attained, I headed to sector six, ramp two, dodging precariously stacked loads on hovercarts and clumps of people hauling cases nearly as big as they were. Not counting furniture, everything I owned in my staff-issued suite wouldn't have filled one of those giant cases. These people were only staying two months. Their excess sickened me.

When I spotted one of the docking staff accompanied by three people in stock crew uniforms, I knew I was in the right place. The door between the station entrance at sector six, ramp two was sealed. I hailed the docking attendant, who hurried over.

"Thank goodness they sent you. This will take half the time now."

Efficiency was one of the few positive words associated with my name. I mustered a smile in return for her compliment. "Why is the door still sealed?"

"Dock security is tied up with all the incoming refugees. We need the standard clearance search performed and paperwork checked before we can allow the *Asbodot* to unload any stock."

Ah yes, proper procedure. I guess they were still doing that up here. I wouldn't want to screw that up for them by half-assing the inspection. "You got the checklist? I don't do incomings every day."

"Sure, I'll send it to your datapad." She pulled out her own and tapped the screen a few times.

The one in my shirt pocket pinged. "Got it. Thanks."

She opened the door and sealed it behind me. I walked up the ramp, appreciating the quiet, but not so much the confined, enclosed space. Upon reaching the ship door, I pounded once and stood back. The door opened a moment later.

A short, smiling male with a balding head and big blue eyes stood waiting. He held up a slim device similar to my datapad. The data synced, relaying his port paperwork and inventory to me. That was when I noticed his very long fingers. They had an extra knuckle.

He wasn't the average Scaavo Empire citizen, but presented recognizable male features and a similar bipedal structure. Some races were very different, but many were the same, as if we'd all come from the same stock but mutated to fit our homeworlds. From the fact that he hadn't bothered to speak, I gathered we didn't share a common language. Thankfully, the datapads accounted for that and facilitated smooth translations.

The *Asbodot's* log indicated they regularly traveled our trade route, though hadn't stopped here in a couple of years. That wasn't a surprise, with Anduvea being on the edge of the empire. No one was excited about visiting an exile world and ours was fully that. Not just a family that had gained the Empaetor's disfavor, but a whole cross section of Harilax's elite, shunted out to a shitty unpopulated world.

For speaking their minds, old Empaetor Iradio VI had banished most of his advisory board and their support staff here one-hundred-and-twelve years ago. Living on a world with a two-month burning season hadn't curbed their penchant for the finer things they'd been used to enjoying on Harilax, the Empaetor's seat of power.

The original exiles and their offspring could trade and

use the station, but, for them, leaving Anduvean space was punishable by death. For me and the rest of the third generation, leaving was an option, but our family names were tainted to such a degree that Anduvea and its couple of months of inconvenience were preferable over contemptuous sneers.

Traders might not want to be directly affiliated with us, but they appreciated our credits. They even kept their disdain to a minimum as long as we didn't attempt to book travel.

The *Asbodot's* inventory listed a lot of items that would interest the tourists. No wonder Commander Keef wanted them to dock. The holo projectors were going to be used for all the wrong reasons, but as long as I didn't have to hose down those recreational spaces, that was fine by me. Anything to keep the horny morons contained. Food of any variety was always a good trade. No matter how much we stocked up before the burning, inventory always seemed to gutter out before most of the tourists returned to the surface. Assorted diversionary gadgets, as well as an impressive array of audio and visual distractions, would hopefully keep them safely occupied.

The fashions from worlds near the center of the empire were going to ignite a bidding war. I envied whichever shop owners would win that deal and then get to bask in the profits.

I sent my parents what credits I could, but it never seemed to be enough. Despite the fact that we all suffered the same exile situation, the rich got richer, and the poor grew poorer, just like on any other world in the empire. Give Anduvea another couple generations for the exile stigma to wear off and we'd be competition for some of the more popular worlds. Hell, some enterprising asshole would probably figure out a way to monetize burning sight-seeing opportunities for actual tourists.

The *Asbodot's* crew members didn't have any outstanding warrants, at least none that had made their way out here yet. The prices they were asking were reasonable and within the range that didn't require me to get higher authorization to accept the goods.

Since Commander Keef had already given his approval, I entered my code to initiate payment from the station fund and verified the checklist on my datapad. All the line items had been covered.

"Yeah, you're clear. Start unloading," I said before remembering Mr. Long-Fingers didn't speak my language. I clicked the approved button on the screen. After a moment, it translated on his pad. He grinned and gave me a quick wave.

I left and walked back down the ramp to observe the tourists and dock workers in case there were any urges to get sticky fingers. Everything would go into the station storeroom where our retailers would bid on it. Commander Keef liked to make his share of credits too. He claimed those profits went to the upkeep of the station, but we also taxed every Anduvean citizen, so it sure felt like double dipping to me. Not that the commander had ever asked my opinion. We'd only spoken in person at my initial interview. Everything since had been by message or word passed down to the security chief. That was a position I hoped to grab for myself when Yumi retired in a year or two. Maybe I'd get the Commander's ear then. Maybe I could make some changes. Someone needed to.

The first mover units made their way down the ramp with a crewman following behind. Two more loads came down, a crewman accompanying each one. One of the stock staff scanned their loads and escorted them to the lift where they'd head to the storerooms two levels below us. Another pair came down with a loaded hovercart.

"Keep close track of that on your way back." I cautioned. "The tourists will try to commandeer it." Another of the stock staff led them off, promising to heed my words.

A crowd of tourists and their luggage flooded down the sector corridor just as the first two crewmen returned with their empty movers and went inside to reload. I yelled at the incoming masses to let them through before we had a total traffic jam. Half of them listened, forming a wall that stopped further interference. Half of them didn't. They shoved their way through the knot of movers and crewmen, complaining loudly about the poor service on their flight to the station and how tired they were, how they had spa or dining reservations to get to. How they knew the commander or were a fourth-removed, distant relation to Empaetor Iradio VIII himself.

In the midst of blowing off an elderly snob who threatened to fire me on the spot, I caught sight of a man dashing down the ramp. He wasn't wearing an *Asbodot* crew uniform. We hadn't cleared them for recreational visitors. I held up my datapad and captured his face in a still frame. It automatically did a recognition scan and pulled up his ID.

Ari Leeman. Occupation: Bodyguard to the household of Empaetor Iradio VIII. Employment terminated as of thirty-eight days ago for theft from the Empaetor's private treasure vault. Wanted dead or alive.

And he thought he could sneak onto my station?

2

Luggage Handler

I grabbed the nearest dockworker and shoved him toward the crowd. "Sort this out. I have to go."

He shook his head, mouth gaping. "But Officer, I don't—"

I cut off his protest with a stern glare and took off after Ari Leeman. Catching the thief would be beneficial, but hopefully recovering the stolen treasure would further improve Anduvea's standing with the Empaetor. One could hope.

Nothing out of the ordinary had been on the *Asbodot's* manifest. Checking for illegal passengers had not been on my checklist as we didn't allow station access to visitors from ships like these during the burning. The station was full enough already.

If Ari was looking to move whatever he'd stolen, he likely had the goods on him. Visions of catching him in action and maybe also implicating some of our usual seedy station visitors added energy to my step.

The tall man stood out in the crowd thanks to the tousle of tawny hair that barely reached his ears. Maybe it was the current style on Harilax, but the prevailing Anduvean hairstyle was long and straight. The straighter and stiffer, the better. Disregarding trends, I wore mine in five thick braids that hung halfway down my back. Braids stayed out of my way, and that was far more important than fashion.

I couldn't see Ari's clothes through the crowd, but his head worked well enough for now. As we wove through the tourists, I wondered how smart he was. Ari had ridden the *Asbodot* out here to the edge of the Scaavo Empire. Was he hoping to catch another ship going beyond the Empaetor's reach to sell his goods elsewhere? At the moment, luck was not on his side, as all our docks were filled with public or private ships carrying tourists from the surface. The *Asbodot* was the first trade ship we'd made room for in days.

If finding a ride was on his mind, he'd have to hide out for another week until the initial influx of tourists had boarded and we got back to prioritizing trade. I wasn't sure I had the patience for that or wanted to take the chance he might slip through my fingers.

I offered a prayer up to the Maker that Ari would want to move his goods now. We had plenty of rich idiots currently in residence. His success would depend on what type of goods he had to move and not bragging about where he got them. No one on Anduvea was foolish enough to invite additional negative notice from the Empaetor.

If Ari was as much of an idiot as the average Anduvean, he might have simply left the *Asbodot* to find a frisky local girl looking for a wild night. I wouldn't know until he got wherever he was going.

The thief stuck with the crowd, filtering out of the docking ring sectors and into the open space where the public lifts would disperse the packed chaos throughout the rest of the station. The jostling and vying for position for the three lifts was fierce. I wedged myself through the crowd, fighting to stay close to Ari. If I lost him here, I'd have to stay on the platform and watch where the lift stopped and then contact whoever was on security duty for those floors to turn over the surveillance. In the few minutes since Ari had shown his face, I'd grown rather attached to the idea of being the one to bring him and his stolen treasure in.

When the next lift door opened, the crowd surged forward. Someone yanked their stack of luggage onto the lift, sending an older woman sprawling onto the floor. Showing no mercy, others stepped right over her as they fought for a spot. Impatient bastards. It wasn't like there wouldn't be another lift in a few minutes. Not waiting for further excuses, I took advantage of being a security officer.

"Security coming through!" I shoved my way to the front, keeping Ari in my peripheral vision. Pulling the shaken woman to her feet, I kept one arm around her. Nothing to fear here, thief, just helping someone out.

"Thank you! May the Maker bless you," the woman gushed as we moved to the front of the line without further interference. "Oh, could you be a dear and grab my luggage? I think I'll be alright on my own now." She detached herself, despite my attempt to keep a loose hold on her without being too obvious.

"Sure." Like I wanted to drag her luggage around. But, I supposed, it allowed me an innocuous reason to be on the lift with Ari. I just needed to make sure he got on the same one.

"You there," I nodded to him where he stood three people back from the front of the line. "Could you give me a hand with her luggage?"

He glanced to either side, clearly hoping I was addressing anyone else.

"Yes, you in the yellow shirt." Was yellow really back in style? I looked awful in yellow. It made my tan skin look sickly. Thank the Maker, security uniforms were a flattering deep rust color.

"Come on then. You'll get a spot on the next lift if you help," I said.

Resigned, he nodded and gathered the abandoned stack of green cases. How had the woman been hauling all those on her own? Then again, maybe that's why she'd been knocked off balance. Standing next to me, she cradled her arm.

The next lift arrived. Its doors opened. The crowd actually waited for me to escort the woman on and Ari to wheel her luggage inside before resuming their forward rush. Crammed in the back, I was at least grateful that Ari was stuck right there with me. Assuming he was going where I hoped he was going. He'd find buyers, a crew, or a party waiting to happen on the social district levels.

Once the doors closed, everyone hushed, hanging onto their belongings or children. The air turned stifling within a single floor. We were at capacity and it smelled like it. So much perfume and cologne. My eyes watered.

"Would you like to go to the med clinic to get your arm checked?" I offered the woman. Not that I had any plans to take her there myself.

"That might be a wise idea," she said.

"I'll have someone waiting to escort you at the lift exit

on level four." I side-eyed Ari, gambling on where he'd be getting off. "There's a situation I need to attend to in the social district, so I can't take you myself."

"I don't know why everyone says the staff here is so awful." She shook her shoulder-length hair. Not a strand moved.

"Me either." But I had a feeling that come tomorrow, she'd be cursing us with the rest of them. How dare we attempt to keep them safe when they were just trying to have a good time?

I pinged an escort to meet us on the services level. Since the woman wasn't an emergency case and I had little desire to push my way through the entire lift full of people, I decided we'd drop a few other occupants first. Using my security clearance and my datapad, I blocked the request to stop at the social district and instead gave all three housing levels priority. If I was going to get the thief myself, I needed fewer distractions.

We moved upward to stop at the econo-housing level at seven. While I hoped that half of the occupants had booked rooms there, I doubted that would be the case. Being just under the constant flood of noise from the business and entertainment on the lower level of the social district, there was little peace and quiet. Hence the discounted rates.

Only one young couple got out, each holding two cloth bags rather than the heavy cases the rich used. On the rare occasions during my childhood when my parents had saved up enough to allow us to escape the burning, this was the level where we'd stayed. It had its own small entertainment zone. I'd been thankful for the nearly two months of freedom from disparaging remarks, teasing, and feeling socially inadequate.

Now I was paid to be told I wasn't good enough. Not that I cared. Thanks to my job, I had the right to roam the entire station whenever I wanted to.

It wasn't until we'd gone down to the general housing on levels two and three that most of the occupants exited with their luggage. I breathed a sigh of relief and shook out my arms. Then I entered the manual command to bring us to services at the fourth level. After this stop, everything would be up to chance.

The door opened. One of the med staff waited for us, her white uniform glaring under the bright lights. No seedy or illicit action was going on here. Two members of my security team sat in a room full of vids, overseeing the whole level. Not that Ari needed to know that.

He pushed the luggage to the door, and for a moment, I tensed, thinking he meant to escape the lift with it, but he left it beside its owner and stepped back inside. He leaned against the wall, staring at the level indicator. As the door closed, I focused on that too. We went up several levels before coming to a stop.

The social district encompassed levels eight and nine. Open ramps gave access to the second floor of the entertainment district. The lift doors opened, allowing the cacophony in. One of the teen girls on the lift squealed, her eyes alight with excitement.

"Come on!" She grabbed her friend's hand and pulled her into the wide corridor filled with flashing lights, some from signs and others for ambiance. My favorite time to be here was early morning, when it was only stock workers and business owners. When it was quiet.

Three of the other occupants exited slowly, their necks craning left and right and scanning upward to the flashing displays on the second floor that advertised diversions of all legal varieties. There were a few illegal ones too, but as long as they didn't cause a disturbance or hurt anyone without their consent, we let those go.

Taking a deep breath and hoping I was making the right choice, I followed the three people off the lift, waiting patiently for them to get moving, not because I was actually being patient, but because I was waiting for the thief to follow us. The doors started to close. I swore under my breath.

A hand protruding from a yellow sleeve clamped over the edge of the door. I made sure I was busy examining my datapad as Ari slipped off the lift to my left and slunk away, mingling with the crowd. Follow you? No, not me.

I slipped the datapad back into my pocket, darted around the still gawking tourists, and tailed Ari at a distance. The flashing lights muddied everything, making his hair harder to spot. I worked my way closer, keeping my head down and lagging a few people behind. He seemed to have a destination in mind rather than meandering to see the sights. One of the gang of orphans who squatted on level five eyed up a rich jerk who was berating his female companion for bumping into him. Surely it wasn't her four-inch heels, or that we were reaching maximum capacity for the social district. She was just clumsy. Sure.

The kid noticed me just as he did a double-check to verify security was out of sight while he reached toward the man's pocket. I gave the kid a nod. He raised his brows. I nodded again and kept walking. The dick deserved it.

It was people like him who drove kids like that up here.

Half the fivers had sold whatever they had to in order to buy a ride up to the station so they could escape the same constant ridicule I'd endured. The other half had permanently ditched their asshole parents here to live life on their own terms.

Security chief Yumi and I knew they were living in the hydro maintenance on five, but as long as they didn't cause too much of a nuisance, we let them stay. I'd dropped in a few times to gift them with some clothes that had been left behind during burning season cleanup. In an unspoken arrangement with the orphans, we kept an unlocked storeroom there, where we left drinking water, food, and supplies when opportunities presented themselves. Yumi and I encouraged them to do some shifts on the hydro ring, upkeep kinds of things that didn't require much skill but gave them access to fresh food rather than the restaurant scraps they lived on when the storeroom was empty.

Whenever I met one of employable age, I hooked them up with a legit job so they could move down to level one with the rest of the staff. Our suites were utilitarian, but it beat sleeping on the floor. If they had siblings, they could bring them too. We'd been keeping the orphan population under Commander Keef's radar that way. I hoped my lenience this one time didn't encourage them too much in the wrong direction.

Ari Leeman headed for the first ramp to the second floor. I let him get all the way up before I followed. The press was pretty heavy up there. He wasn't getting far fast. The adult-centric amusements were on the upper floor. I exchanged nods with the attendant at the top of the ramp, causing only a momentary distraction from her bored scanning of everyone's ID chips to verify they were over twenty. The thief was, and the attendant apparently had no inclination to look at any further details because that would have required effort and enthusiasm. Ari walked onward and so did I.

He traversed a quarter of the upper walk before squaring his thick shoulders and heading into the Sector Nine club.

3
Free Drinks Come With Consequences

As far as clubs went, Sector Nine was a quiet one. If you wanted to hold a conversation, you could do that with varying degrees of ease depending on how far you sat from the dancefloor. The spinning kaleidoscope of lights washed everyone in color. For a moment, I lost Ari when his yellow shirt blended with everything else. When I spotted him again, he'd taken a seat at a tall table against the wall. He checked out the other patrons as if he were wedged in a covert bunker.

Having lived here for twenty years, I knew where to stand to have a good view of the room while actually remaining out of sight of the crowd. Despite the yellow shirt and curly hair, no one paid any attention to Ari.

Music thumped around us. A gaggle of young men and women gyrated on the dancefloor. The older crowd sat at tables, pounding down drinks, smiling and laughing. Everyone appeared to be having a good time. Was Ari waiting for someone or looking for someone?

One of the servers, Tessy, according to the nameplate on

her tight but tastefully cut shirt, spotted me. She mouthed, "Everything okay?"

I nodded and waved her off.

A bright smile broke out on her generous red lips as she noticed Ari waiting for service. Her heels may have clicked on the tile floor, but I couldn't hear them over the music. She stepped with purpose, swaying her ass and working each step like it was a paying customer.

Ari offered her a smooth smile while she looked him over with appreciation dripping out of her perfect twenty-something pores. In keeping with his line of work, Ari appeared to be packing a full body of defined muscles beneath fitted black pants and that hideous shirt. They spoke for a moment, and then she left. Her ass sway was even more pronounced on her way to the bar. Sadly for Tessy, he wasn't watching her show. He was busy scanning the crowd.

When she returned with his drink, he waved a credit chip over her reader and must have tipped to her approval because Tessy was all smiles when she walked away. I imagined a man who had stolen treasure from the Empaetor had deep pockets.

Looking determined, Ari carried his drink over to two men sitting at a low table. From their smarmy appearance, they were off-world dealers out to make a comfortable living off the next year's-worth of sales crammed into the two burning months.

The men cut off their conversation and watched Ari approach with interest. From my hiding spot, I couldn't hear them, but Ari's lips said something about looking for transport out of the system. Thinking him one of us, they gave him the disdain-filled look they gave any Anduvean asking to travel off-world and shook their heads. Ari, with his drink in hand, moved on to another table, this one with a couple who looked more business than pleasure.

They seemed receptive and asked him to sit. No one's face was visible enough for me to read lips. After ten minutes of chatting, no deal appeared to have been made. Ari went back to his table, where he surveyed the room and finished his drink.

I hoped to have him secure a ride or buyer so I could turn them in as conspirators. More favor for Anduvea. Admittedly, I was also curious to learn what he'd stolen and why. Bodyguard of the Empaetor had to be a pretty cushy job with enviable pay. What would drive a man to betray the one he'd been watching over for years? Not that I blamed him. Empaetor Iradio VIII was just as much of an asshole as Iradio VI. In fact, according to the history we were all taught in school, every Iradio, all the way back to the first, was a bastard to some portion of the ever-growing Scaavo Empire. Depending on what colony or station or world was asked to rate his popularity, one would get wildly varying answers.

Tessy watched with a dismayed pout as Ari set down his empty glass and headed to the exit. I lagged behind but kept him in sight.

He walked two doors down to another club. This one had dancers on a stage. While Ari went to the bar to order an overpriced drink, I nodded to the pair of bouncers near the door and jutted my chin toward the yellow shirt. They waved me inside and wished me luck.

Ari surveyed the room, leaning against a wall here, a

table there. He stopped to feel out a ride or buyer for a sip or two before moving on. After half an hour, his drink was empty. Just as he was headed to the bar, a pair of young men waved him over. They both sported short, spiky hair and the facial tattoos of the Da'Adio clan.

I caught myself shaking my head, trying to warn Ari off. No one did honest business with the Da'Adio, but that was profitable for some. Others ended up indebted, enslaved, or just plain dead. The brothers, I guessed by their similar faces, were probably looking to work over the tourists for profit or pleasure like every other off-worlder who'd ensconced themselves on the station before our non-Anduvean intake cut off.

The brothers smiled and waved a server over. A round of drinks arrived in short order. What appeared to be friendly conversation continued through another round of drinks. The Da'Adio brothers paid both times, one of them handing the drinks around. I didn't doubt the likes of Ari Leemen could take care of himself, but I kept an eye on him anyway.

One brother pulled out a datapad, set it on the table, and pointed at it.

Ari spun it around and looked it over. He shook his head.

The brother pointed adamantly at the screen.

Again, Ari shook his head. He slammed the rest of his drink and pushed his chair back.

The brothers scowled. One of them glanced around. The other reached into his dark green coat.

My hand went to my stunner at my side. I took a step out of my hiding spot and drew my station-authorized weapon.

Ari stood. His first step wavered. He grabbed the edge of the table.

In the next second, one brother nodded. The other drew a death toller pistol. They weren't allowed on the station. I was going to have to do an investigation to find whoever had scanned their goods and probably took a bribe to allow them through with such a deadly weapon.

The din of conversation died off as other patrons realized that something bad was happening. People leapt from their chairs and backed away. The bouncer by the stage sent the scantily clad dancers to safety behind the shimmery backdrop and craned his thick neck, looking for the culprit in the crowd.

Ari stared at the pistol and tried to take another step. One leg buckled. His head lolled drunkenly. He flopped into the chair he'd vacated.

Darting out of my cove, I headed for Ari and the brothers with my stunner in hand. The moment I had a clear shot, I fired. So did the Da'Adio with the toller pistol. I fired again.

Patrons ran screaming from the bar. The staff, shaken and staring, stayed on the other side of the room, as per procedure.

Both stunned brothers dropped harmlessly to the floor.

Ari sat in the chair, looking down at the gaping hole in his stomach.

I quickly slid the dropped death toller under my belt and applied a bubble to each brother so they would be contained when they woke up in ten minutes. While I could have pinged medical, the size of the hole in Ari's stomach said he wouldn't last until they arrived. The emergency supplies I had on me wouldn't hold him over either. Thankfully the reward had stated dead or alive.

"You," he said, meeting my assessing gaze.

"Indeed." I pointed at the hole in his stomach. "Sorry, I wasn't planning on turning you in dead."

"I need help," he said weakly, holding onto the table with one hand and the seat of the chair with the other.

Propping himself up wasn't doing him any good. I might be jaded, but I did attempt to be a decent person. "Come on, let's at least get you comfortable. Ish. I mean."

I pried his hand away from the table and eased him off the chair. Gravity and his slow slumping backward did the rest. His ass landed on the floor. I helped him down from there.

One of the staff hurried over with a clean towel. She handed it to me and darted back to the emergency staff cordon. I pressed it to his stomach. It wouldn't do anything other than comfort him a little.

"Medical is on the way," I lied.

He nodded without a lot of conviction. We both knew the inevitable wasn't long off.

Ari turned his head from side to side. "Are we alone?"

"If you're going to tell me where the Empaetor's stolen treasure is, then yes, no one is close enough to hear you. If you're asking if there's anyone in the room with a spare stasis tube we could toss you into until medical gets here, the answer is no."

He smiled weakly, his skin growing more ashen by the second. "You're a funny one. He'll like that."

"I don't care what the Empaetor likes as long as he pays me the reward."

"No. You can't go to him. You can't." He coughed.

I glanced over my shoulder to make sure the containment bubbles were still there. Not that they should drift around on their own, but if they were resourceful enough to get a toller pistol onboard, I couldn't put it past a member of the Da'Adio clan to have figured out a way to manipulate a bubble.

Momentarily assured that both brothers were still secure, I turned back to Ari. The front of his shirt had turned red. Damned death tollers, they killed too many, too fast.

Ari grabbed my arm, his fingers squeezing hard, twisting my skin. "I'll give you the treasure if you promise not to return it to the empire. It can't fall back into the Empaetor's hands. Do you understand me?"

"I don't need you to give it to me, though that would be easier. I can just get a warrant to search your belongings on the *Asbodot*. If I need to, I'll hold them over until I go through every inch of that ship. It's my duty to the empire."

"Please." He squeezed my arm again, weaker this time. "You can't sell it or trade it. You must keep it safe."

Had the Empaetor gotten his hands on a terrible new weapon? Was the stolen treasure not riches but tech that could kill millions? The whole Iradio line had always been fast to punish. My ancestors had been fortunate to be banished here considering other offenders had been wiped out or had their worlds devastated by disease or environment-altering weapons. In his lifetime, Empaetor Iradio VIII had turned a colony world's densely populated continent to ice, and rumors said he'd plunged another world into a perpetual flood.

"You can't have any love for the empire. You're Anduvean, yes?"

I nodded, wondering if making a deal with the dying man to ease his mind would also ease my conscience about not acting a few seconds sooner. Once he was dead, it wasn't like he could do anything, whether I honored the deal or not.

He tried to sit up. I gently pushed him back down with my arm that he held.

"Promise me you'll keep it out of his hands. You'll be saving lives. So many lives." Ari let me go and thrust his hand into his pants pocket.

Something small then. A weapon. That's what it had to be. A chip holding the instructions for an awful bioweapon. Plans to embark on a war to expand the empire that none of us wanted to take part in.

If it were any of those things, I would incinerate it rather than return it for a reward. Ari wouldn't be a traitorous thief. He'd have acted as a bodyguard for all of us. It was a shame he was dying, but he should have just destroyed whatever it was rather than trying to run off with it.

I couldn't see a way this would have ended any neater. We'd all be safe, and I'd have Ari's body. Surely that would be enough to gain the Empaetor's favor for Anduvea.

4

Bubbles For Bad Guys

"You can't sell it," Ari implored. "Keep it for yourself. Safe."

Keep the Empaetor's treasure, whatever it might be, for myself? Well, if Ari insisted.

"I promise."

Ari handed me a smooth red plas rectangle with a number engraved on one side and the *Asbodot's* logo on the other. A storage claim ticket. Alright, so not something small.

He coughed again. I caught a hint of blood at the corner of his mouth. His eyes took on a distant gaze and then his arms went limp. Well, there was that then. Whether he was a hero or villain would remain to be seen, but either way, Ari's body would be heading back to Harilax.

Before he went anywhere, I did a quick pat down to see what else Ari might have on him. Two credit chips, one nearly empty, the other containing a year of my salary. If this was what he openly carried on him, I had to believe security for the Empaetor paid well. Other than the chips, his pockets were empty. He hadn't even been armed. Though, I supposed, the Empaetor's bodyguards were well trained in ways to be deadly that didn't require weapons.

If I was going to ask the empire to trust me, and by example, all Anduveans, I regrettably had to leave both credit chips with the body. I made a note of the amounts to add to my report later in case medical or anyone else got greedy.

I pinged medical to send someone up to collect the body with instructions to store it as it was found. Next, I pinged the sanitation dispatch to take care of the blood on the floor.

Pocketing the ticket, I approached the staff. "You're free to return to business. The body will be removed and the mess cleaned up shortly. Sorry for the interruption. I'll get these two out of here. Have they paid their tab?"

A young man stepped forward to check his terminal. "They have not."

"I'll make sure you get a chip to charge and don't forget to tip yourself nicely for the trouble."

He grinned. "Thanks, Rita."

I guided the Da'Adio brothers out of the bar and to the staff lift. Two bubbles would be a tight fit, but it beat trying to get them both down to the larger main floor public lift with the hoard of tourists clogging the traffic flow.

Business was hopping at the other clubs and shops along the arc. When I passed the second-floor security post, the officer on duty nodded. He was one of the newer members of the team. His first on duty burning season. Poor guy.

Getting the prisoners down the ramp and through the bustling first floor crowds took all my patience and more time than I would have liked. Staff from both medical and sanitation passed me on my way out. I noted their speedy response for the incident report I'd need to fill out later.

The staff lift took its sweet time arriving. When it did, I herded the two bubbles in. The exterior view was less spectacular when viewed through a sliver of space between two criminals.

On a typical shift during the burning, I'd be making this trip about three times. This was my fourth run. That didn't bode well for the rest of my day.

Senio was at his desk this time. He waved me in and shook his head. "That woman you brought in, she's a pain in the ass. Already threatened my job twice."

"Did you process her ID?"

"Oh yeah." He whistled softly. "One of those execs from the surface. Granddaughter of Iradio VI's financial advisor."

"She's awfully young for a third gen." I checked the open cell display on his desk over his shoulder.

"Daughter by a third wife."

"That explains it. Money *does* buy love."

"Didn't buy you mine." He clapped his hand over his heart, winking.

"Your salary is even less than mine, loser, and seriously, one of these years, you're going to thank me for not giving you a second chance."

"Still wounded, Rita." Senio laughed and shook his head as he nodded toward the cell where I'd left Daddy's Girl. "I figured it would be wise to only keep her for the minimum. Don't need her father to follow through on her threats."

"Fair point." I pushed the two bubbles toward the corridor on the left. "These are Da'Adio's. Different kind of threat level. One of them just killed a guy on Prom-two. He's going to need longer term facilities."

"Got it. I'll follow you and get their IDs when you transfer. No way I want to go in alone after you leave.”

"Wise." I pushed one bubble to Senio. If he was going to follow me, he might as well be useful.

We dropped the bystander brother in one of the front cells. As I disengaged his bubble, Senio held out his reader and scanned the embedded arm ID. He also did a facial ID. I was surprised both matched.

Once the cell was sealed, I peered at Senio's datapad. "Huh, a Da'Adio with no record beyond a couple of minor offenses as a teen?"

"Oh, don't worry, I'm guessing Mr. Murder will make up for it," Senio said, double checking the seal on the door.

"When you get a chance, they have a tab to pay." I gave Senio the club information.

The young man inside watched us guide his brother away with a dismayed scowl. Maybe he'd been tasked with keeping his brother out of trouble. If that was the case, Papa Da'Adio wouldn't be pleased with them. He liked his people available to do his bidding.

We got the second brother secured, searched, scanned, and then headed back up front with his confiscated belongings in hand.

"Tell the team to take it easy on the arrests today, will you? We've got thirty cells open, but seven more weeks of this shit. Unless they're all overnighters, we're going to be issuing early releases out of necessity."

"Nah, we'll ship the long-terms back down to the surface. No need to clog the system up here. Don't worry, Senio. Chief Yumi and I have been doing this for a long time. We know how to make this work."

"Glad someone does. I hate this time of year." He sat

back down at his desk and resumed his perusal of the cell vid feeds.

"I'll be seeing you soon, I'm sure."

"Let's hope not," he said as I headed for the door.

Throughout the rest of my shift, I let several smaller incidents go in favor of keeping cells open, but I saw Senio twice more. I added making a list of long-term prisoners for deportation to my tasks for tomorrow and signed out for the evening.

While I waited for a public lift to my suite on level one, I toyed with the claim ticket in my pocket. As much as I wanted to go see what Ari had left me, I needed to deal with the bigger issue of his body and turning him over to the empire. I was anxious to know what this would get me. Well, me, the station, and Anduvea, of course.

The first two lifts were full, and given I'd missed my mid-shift meal, everyone in my vicinity owed me their undying gratitude for not verbally exploding. I was considering slipping into the maintenance tube to make my way down when the third lift arrived with enough room for me to squeeze into.

We went all the way up to the docking ring and every stop in between. And then we had to stop several more times on the way down. Had I still been on duty, I would have dared to take manual control again to get myself home, but I wasn't. It's like the universe knew I was in a hurry and was just screwing with me.

When I stepped out of the lift, so did one of the other staff members. We had so many new hires prior to the burning season, I'd yet to learn all of their names. A perky woman with her perfect long, straight hair and a body that filled out her uniform with enviable curves stopped me to chat. Like I had nothing better to do. Yumi wouldn't like getting yet another call about my questionable social skills with our staff. I put on a half-assed tolerant smile while she rambled on about her day and how stressful it was with the surge of refugees.

My empty stomach growled as I played with the ticket in my pocket. "We call them tourists."

She paused. "They're not here by choice. Not on a vacation."

"A hundred years ago, I'd have been more agreeable to that term. However, we now have the plascrete fields. We have top-notch fire suppression systems in the city. There's plenty of air filtration as long as people stay inside. Nothing is making them come up here. Nothing except the excuse to take a vacation so they don't have to look out their windows at dark skies until the winds whip up enough ash that the windows are too dirty to see out of."

"They warned us that you older people were out of touch. I see they were right." She huffed and walked away.

I was the one out of touch? Shaking my head, I hurried to my suite, grabbed a snack out of the kitchen, and ran to my terminal, unable to take the delay any longer.

Filing the incident report and then all the proper forms to document Ari Leeman's death took an hour. Were he an Anduvean who died on the station, I would have wrapped it up in fifteen, but off-worlders were a more complex situation. As expected, submitting those forms to the greater empiric system triggered alerts. One of those contained contact information for Empaetor Iradio VIII's security advisor.

I sent out a request for a call, knowing I'd likely get a delayed voice message instead. Harilax was too far away to sustain a vid call, but one could hope.

Trying to contain my excitement was futile. It was one thing to aspire to be chief security officer on this station. That was the highest rank I could attain without leaving what I considered home. But in the dark hours when I dared to dream, I stood on the faraway world of Harilax as part of the palace guard, a job that I might have had the remote possibility of holding had my people not been exiled out here three generations ago. That would only ever be a dream, but today, I was talking to the Empaetor's security advisor, the man who could be my boss if that dream ever came true. And what thing would ever make someone like him take notice of someone like me? Capturing Ari Leeman. I grinned, laughing to myself.

5

I'm Not Hiding Anything

A lined, solemn face filled my vid. I tried to tone down my giddy grin, but it refused to abate.

"I hope your interruption of our search efforts is worthwhile," he declared.

Search efforts. Of course, the Empaetor would send out a force to find his heir. The speed at which he had answered my vid request meant he must have been on Ari's tail somewhere outside the center of the empire.

"It's an honor to meet you, Security Advisor Tekka. I believe I have a body you will be interested in."

He didn't blink. "And you are?"

"Senior security officer Rita Stabinov. Anduvean station."

"Oh. Anduvea." His upper lip curled.

Dammit, I was losing him already. "Ari Leeman. I have him."

His eyes lit up. "His body, you say?"

"Yes, sir. He was trying to make a deal with the wrong people and was shot."

"What kind of deal?" He leaned in closer. His white,

slicked back hair disappeared, giving way to an up-close every-pore view from forehead to chin.

"Looking for transport out of the empire or a buyer, I'd imagine. He was meeting with a couple members of the Da'Adio clan, if you're familiar. I have the man who killed him in custody as well. He's slated to be deported to Anduvea to serve his sentence, but I could interrogate him beforehand if you'd like."

"That won't be necessary. What did Ari Leeman have on his person at the time of his demise?"

Definitely not a stock ticket for a mysterious item I promised to keep from you and the Empaetor.

"Just two credit chips, sir. I've not yet searched the *Asbodot*, the ship on which he arrived."

"There is more. Search the ship. If you find anything, let me know immediately. Hold any evidence. Yourself. Trust no one else with it." His pale blue eyes stared into me.

My palms began to sweat. Did he know I was hiding something? That was some next level interrogation eye drilling. Good thing I had experience in that arena as well. Not that my gut wasn't churning or that the urge to come clean wasn't working its way up my throat.

The Scaavo Empire owed Anduvea, I repeated silently to myself. It owed me.

I nodded like a good citizen. "Of course."

His gaze left my face to scan up and down beside the vid, likely skimming my report. "I see you've noted the vessel's information. If I need to search further, I can call them in."

His attention returned solely to me. "I will send out one of my agents to interrogate your prisoner. See that he goes nowhere until my agent arrives."

Well shit. I didn't need an empiric agent digging around on my station while I had Ari's stock ticket on me or whatever the ticket claimed. My gut churning notched up a level. Maybe I should mention the ticket. But how was I going to work that into the conversation now that I'd said I'd found nothing? My mind whirred. The Da'Adio brothers. I could magically find the stock ticket on one of them later if whatever it led to wasn't worth my time. If I knew how much time I had.

I took a deep breath to calm my nerves, hoping the agent took it as me working up the gumption to question him. "May I ask when the agent will arrive? We'd planned to deport prisoners in the next day or two."

"By the end of the week, jump gate availability willing. Six days at the latest."

That didn't give me a lot of time to work with, and I wasn't excited about the uncertain timeline.

"Got it. I'll make sure that prisoner remains aboard. His brother was also present for the conversation but is slated to be released tomorrow. Would you like him detained as well?"

"Yes."

Papa Da'Adio wasn't going to like that, but he could take it up with the empire.

"You will preserve the body of Ari Leeman and collect all his belongings. My agent will retrieve the body and all items and interrogate your prisoners. All that I require from you is to search that ship for everything he left on it or had with him on your station if he secured a room there. Can I depend on you for that rudimentary task?"

"Yes, sir."

"Good. Your reward will be processed once the body is in my custody."

I raised my hand. "About the reward..."

"The empire thanks you for your service." SA Tekka gave me a stern nod and ended the vid call.

While the posted reward would mean a significant financial boost for me and my family, I'd hoped for something a little more, I don't know, personal. A smidge of recognition wouldn't have cost the Empaetor's security advisor anything. Should I have been more assertive? Asked for forgiveness for all of Anduvea? It was too late now to do anything more than kick myself for not saying more. Fucking star-struck, tongue-tied idiot.

At least searching the *Asbodot* would give me an excuse to turn in the stock ticket. I wanted to go immediately, but I was off duty and showing my face after hours would make the rest of the staff curious. They all knew I rarely went anywhere after my shift, especially during the burning. I collected enough contemptuous remarks during duty hours.

The *Asbodot* wasn't cleared to leave until late tomorrow. I'd hit it up first thing in the morning and figure out if whether whatever Ari was hiding was worth the risk of possibly getting caught by the Empaetor's agent. I cringed, considering what that might mean, not only for me, but for the station, or even all of Anduvea.

Or Ari's treasure might change everything for the better. I prayed to the Maker that was the case. Tomorrow, I'd find out.

6

Your Illegal Goods. My Stolen Goods. It's All Good

The night passed in a restless attempt to sleep. As soon as the time display hit a reasonable hour to get out of bed, I showered, threw on a clean uniform and then contacted Chief Yumi. He answered my vid call almost immediately. Apparently, I wasn't the only early riser.

"I'm following up on the Ari Leeman case under direct orders from the empire. I may be late for my shift."

His bushy brows lowered over his wrinkle-lined eyes. "You could have come to me with this. As the chief security officer, I should have been the one to contact the empire about the arrest on our station."

Yumi and I often saw eye to eye on day-to-day matters, but today wasn't one of them. "I tracked the felon, and I filled out the paperwork for his reward. Yumi, I'm not trying to go over your head on this. Your family is on the station. I need that reward to support my family on the surface. I will make sure any other goodwill that can be gained from this reflects on the station and Anduvea."

He scoffed. "It's no secret you want my job, Rita. I can't

say as I blame you for wanting this for your resume."

"Yet you're still pissed about it." I shook my head. "I don't want your job while you still have it, Yumi. Only when you're done with it."

"Once Commander Keef gets word of your status with the empire, I have a feeling I'll be done with my job faster than I'd planned."

It wasn't like Yumi was young, and neither was his wife. He'd been working long hours at a thankless job for the past forty-seven years. He deserved some time to spend his credits on things he enjoyed before he went to meet the Maker.

"Not that I'm angling for it, but would an early retirement be so terrible?" I asked.

He smiled sadly. "As long as I'm compensated for it, no, I suppose not. You remember that when Commander Keef calls you in."

"Nothing is going to happen that quickly. Relax, Yumi. Have a good day."

"You too, Rita." He ended the call.

I grabbed a quick breakfast and then headed straight for the staff lift. I didn't have the patience to take the public one today, not with an empiric agent on the way and a treasure to discover and deal with before they arrived. The exterior view along the way gave me twelve minutes of serenity that I sorely needed.

When I arrived on the docking ring, a herd of geppas ran in front of me, darting between the movers with panicked squeals. Their keepers scrambled after them, yelling and waving their hands. The shaggy, white, six-legged animals tried to find somewhere to hide and re-congregate.

There weren't many places on the open docking ring where thirty-some, waist-high creatures could hide on their own, let alone as a group. Mostly, they were just going to shit everywhere and leave ropes of stinky white hair for the sanitation crew to clean up.

"Get those animals back into containment!" I yelled, as if that wasn't what they were trying to do, but duty prodded me anyway.

While importing live animals from the surface created issues, this being the primary one of them, the meat tasted better fresh. This flock would serve us a week at most before we'd be going through this again. Within the hour, Tino and the rest of the food vendors would be clamoring for their share of the herd to add to their menus.

The herders tapped bubbles on multiple geppas whenever they got within reach. Their bubbles were far inferior to ours, but they were suitable for stock who didn't know how to squirm out of their looser hold. I sidestepped a clod of pungent geppa dung and made my way to the *Asbodot*.

I happened upon a crewmember maneuvering a mover full of stock up the docking ramp. "Found something to buy, I see?"

He looked at me blankly. I noted his long fingers. Another of the crew who didn't speak my language. I waved him onward and followed the slow climb of the encumbered mover.

When we got to the ship, the door was open. I followed him inside. He again turned to look at me. I pulled out the claim ticket. The crewman nodded and held up his hand, indicating I should wait.

I waited.

Feeling as if each minute was speeding by, bringing the empire's agent ever closer, I fidgeted with the ticket, shuffling it between my fingers until the smooth plas grew warm from my constant touching.

Another crewman came up the ramp behind me and entered the ship. He had a box in his hands, which he tucked under one arm as he approached.

"How can I help you, Officer?"

Thank the Maker, someone who spoke my language. I held up the ticket.

"I need to retrieve this item."

He pulled a scanner from his pocket and held it up to the ticket. Then he consulted the screen. "Storage bay three. I'll take you there."

"I will also need to examine all accommodations used by the man who purchased this ticket."

He glanced at the box he held. His forehead glistened.

"We both have bigger problems than whatever illegal goods you might have in that box."

The crewman smiled weakly. "What kind of problems?"

"Ari Leeman, the man this ticket belonged to, is wanted by Empaetor Iradio VIII himself. I'm to seize whatever belonged to Ari Leeman and hand it over to the empiric agent that will be headed this way in a matter of days."

"Wanted by the Empaetor?" He audibly swallowed.

"Indeed. And you were transporting him. Unless you'd like a visit with the Empaetor's personal security team to discuss what is in that box or elsewhere in your bays, you'll give me what I need and then be on your way with all due haste."

"Yes, Officer. Thank you. Right this way." He brought

me to the common housing area. As a bodyguard of the Empaetor's household and knowing how much Ari had on a single credit chip, I was surprised to discover that he'd settled for a standard rack rather than a private suite.

"Row one. Third one up on the left." The crewman pointed to a faded label with three symbols that I assumed indicated the rack assignment he'd given. I climbed the ladder mounted against the scratched-up metal surface and crawled to the rack bunk. It smelled like sweat and dirty clothes, a rumpled pile of which sat at the foot of the sleeping pad. The bodyguard must not have been accustomed to using a laundry unit. I'd seen an easily accessible one against the far wall of the housing room.

A search of his clothes came up empty. Beyond those, there was a nearly flat pillow that had seen better days, a blanket that looked fairly new, and a small bag with a sturdy clip that would have likely been worn on a belt. The blanket and pillow were free of surprises.

Positioning my body to block the view into the rack from below, I loosened the fastener on the bag and lifted the top flap to dump out the contents onto the mattress: three credit chips and an ID card. The card had Ari's picture, but the name said Hedvick Shadar of the inner empire world of Jeruit. From what I recalled, the height and weight matched. It seemed the *Asbodot* was willing to bypass implant ID scans and work solely from an ID card. I could use that if I needed to foist the threat of a procedure violation upon them to throw any suspicion off of me. Not that I'd done anything an empiric agent would be suspicious of. Yet. I eyed the credit chips.

It wouldn't hurt to check the balance on them, right?

For my report, of course. I scanned them with my reader and grinned. Well now, there was a nice bonus beyond the empire's advertised reward payment. The three chips each bore the amount of the large one I'd found on Ari's body.

I ran my fingertips over the smooth surface of one of the chips, marveling at the comfort of sudden financial security. My parents would be taken care of for the next couple of years. Maybe I could take a short leave and spend some time on the surface with them once the burning season was over. Or travel. By the Maker, I hadn't been anywhere other than Anduvea or the station in all my life. I could visit some of the worlds traders had mentioned, maybe ask some of the ones passing through for advice on the best places to go for a vacation. Screw the exile stigma, I was used to scorn-filled glances and people not liking me. I could get the hell out of here for a little while.

Holding one of the chips up to the light, I grinned. Freedom rested in my hands.

I clipped the bag to my belt and then ran my hands over every crevice, feeling for any loose panels that might be hiding additional clues. Nothing. I upended the mattress with a thorough pat down, but found nothing inside or underneath. Well now, that was disappointing.

Resolved to turning over the clothes and ID card to the empiric agent but making sure Ari's credit chips were never seen again, I climbed out of the rack bunk and carefully made my way down the ladder with a wad of dirty clothing under one arm.

My cooperative guide awaited, though I noted that he no longer had the box in his possession and he seemed more at ease for it. "Find everything you needed?"

"This was all that was there, so let's hope so. Other than the stock ticket, does he have anything else on this ship? Anything at all? Think carefully, because I assure you, I am much more pleasant to deal with than the empiric agent will be if they have a reason to call you in for a full investigation."

That hint of ease evaporated. "Let me double check our records." He went over to the public terminal in the main area of the room and entered his personal codes. I stood over his shoulder as he accessed the *Asbodot's* records. I might not know their language, but I understood the blank space after Ari's name other than the one stock ticket and the rack rental.

"Nothing physical on file." He craned around to look up at me. "There is one communication. It's encrypted, but I'm guessing as a security officer, you have ways around that?"

I nodded and fished out my datapad with my free hand. "Transfer it here and then erase it from your system. You can put my authorization on that in case you suffer an investigation."

"Thank you." He did as I asked.

As soon as I verified the file transfer, I put the pad away. The crewman led me through the corridors to a set of wide double doors. He pressed his palm to the reader panel and then entered a code. One door opened to allow us inside and then closed.

Inside, the bay was just like any other I'd searched. Rows of shelving with smaller items and rows of crates, tubes, tanks and containers of all sorts. Everything was neatly labeled and stored. There were a good number of empty spaces that assured me that our storerooms were looking better than before their arrival.

"I hope this stop was beneficial for you?" I asked.

"Likely not as beneficial as it was for you," he remarked with raised brows.

"I can safely say it has probably caused headaches for both of us, but I hope we both come out better for it."

He nodded eagerly. "We can hope."

We wove through the rows until he stopped at a large opaque black plas case easily as tall as me and half as wide.

"That looks heavy." My mind spun with glittering visions of what might be inside something that large. This was no little treasure chest and far too large for a chip loaded with secret evil plans. Just what had Ari stolen?

"I can have one of the crew deliver it, if you'd like."

While I knew the basics of operating a mover unit, the deft maneuvers it would take to load a case that large into my suite without denting every wall and doorway between here and there was beyond my skill level. I wasn't even sure it would fit through my door. It was going to be close.

"That would be much appreciated," I said.

"I'll get someone on it and have them follow you."

With the claim ticket in his hand, he started back through the rows. I gave the large nondescript case one last look and then followed him.

"If you want to wait out on the ring, I'll send someone out shortly."

I considered just giving him my room number, but leaving the stolen goods to travel through the busy station without my supervision felt like pushing my luck. If it was luck. Only the Maker knew if what was inside was a blessing or a curse.

While I waited against the wall, trying to stay out of the way of the latest batch of arrivals bitching about having to carry their own luggage, I pondered my criteria for keeping my word to Ari versus gaining Scaavo favor.

If the case contained a weapon, the Empaetor didn't need more of those. He and his entire line had been employing them to expand and keep the empire in line with a heavy hand since Iradio I. I'd be doing the universe a favor by keeping additional destruction out of his hands.

Should it be treasure in the traditional sense, I'd ogle it for a few days until the agent arrived, maybe try on a few things, drink out of a fire-gem-embellished cup or wave a jeweled blade around. One or two small things might be written off as Ari pawning them on his journey, but holding onto the rest would be impossible. At least being on the edge of the empire, finding a buyer, should I want to sell anything, might be possible.

About to crawl out of my skin with anticipation, I let out a loud sigh of relief when a heavily encumbered mover crept down the ramp. Once it was out of the ramp and into the larger docking ring corridor, I hung back, fussing with the clothes under my arm while I waited to see who I was dealing with.

A female who could have been a copy of the male who had just helped me smiled. "Where are we headed?"

"Level one."

"Another storeroom? We delivered everything else to eleven."

"My suite. I'm holding this for an empiric agent."

She grimaced, eyeing the size of the case. "That will be tricky."

"That's why you're driving that thing instead of me."

"Great," she said with little enthusiasm.

"Don't worry, the station has plenty of dings and dents already. A couple more won't be noticed."

She chuckled. "Good to know. After you."

I walked ahead of the mover, clearing a path. Thankfully, it was early. There was only one group of newly arrived tourists clogging up the lifts. The geppa had been removed to their pen on five where their droppings would be composted for fertilizer for the gardens. Other than a few brown stains and tangles of white hair on the floor, no other evidence of them remained.

Two of us and the case took up the entire lift. The ride down passed in silence until she turned to me and asked, "What's inside?"

"Your guess is as good as mine. Not my problem. I'm just holding it."

At least, that's what I wanted her to know in case the empiric agent did hunt them down to ask questions. What I would actually do was still undecided. After all, SA Tekka never said I couldn't open anything. Not that I told him that there was anything to open, but still. His mistake.

The staff housing corridor was empty by the time we got there. Morning shift had officially started, and anyone not having to get up that early was blissfully still asleep.

"This one." I pointed to my door.

The mover hummed along and then let out a pneumatic sigh when the guide brought it to a stop. It beeped loudly as she turned it sideways to face the door.

The door down the hall opened. "Good morning, Rita," called my neighbor, Brenna. "What do you have there?"

"Nothing exciting."

Not a stolen treasure or any evidence on my belt or under my arms. Nope. I often walked around with a wad of men's clothes and held evidence in my suite. Didn't all the security officers?

"Sorry to wake you," I said.

"Oh, you didn't. I was getting ready to go for a run when I heard all the commotion."

"Have a good run. If you catch the lift to four now, you'll beat the rush."

"Thanks. Gotta keep this body in shape. You know how it is." She winked and then jogged off down the corridor with a bouncy step.

I glanced down at my blocky uniform covering my healthy and strong but no longer twenty-something body. Oh yes, I knew exactly how it was.

"Enjoy it while you've got it," I muttered to her fleeting form.

I opened my door and hurried inside to set Ari's clothes on the kitchen counter and shove furniture around. Take that Brenna. I might not be lean and trim, but I could wrestle furniture and criminals that would snap her in half.

Shifted to its lowest setting so the crate would fit through the doorway, the mover advanced at an agonizingly slow pace. Only a sliver of light showed all the way around the frame. I held my breath as the guide worked. She only bumped the frame once, and impressively, hadn't left her mark anywhere else on the station. When the crate was through at last, the next challenge came. Where to put it that wouldn't be in the way?

I laughed out loud. Something that large would be

in the way no matter where it was. My single-sized suite wasn't that big.

"Just set it over here." I gestured to where the couch had been. It now sat only a few feet away from the vid wall, far too close for viewing anything. I'd have to watch the news feeds on the terminal in my bedroom.

The guide got the crate positioned and then extracted the mover. She backed toward the doorway.

"Anything else?" she asked.

"No, thank you, and by the way, you're a master at driving that thing. Best of luck with avoiding an empiric inquisition."

"Thanks." She offered me a nervous smile and left.

Rubbing my hands together, I prowled the perimeter of the plas case.

7

You Did This To Yourself

Locating the opening mechanism was an unexpected challenge, but it wasn't like I could have asked the guide where it was. I hadn't wanted her to know I was going to open it.

A quick lookup search on my datapad provided the instructions. The end of the crate swung open like a door, inviting me inside. Using my datapad for a light, I took a cautious step forward. There was something long and solid, rectangular with a domed top, that filled the crate from front to back, leaving just enough room to stand sideways between it and the wall. Straps attached to the wall and floor held whatever it was in place.

My light glinted off the domed top, revealing frosted clearplaz. I leaned closer to look inside, to see what Ari Leeman had stolen. The datapad nearly slipped out of my sweaty hand.

I made out the hazy shape of a male figure inside. Ari Leeman had stolen a person.

My throat went dry. I coughed. Who in the name of the Maker was this?

So, this was what a stasis tube looked like. We had two on the station, but I'd never seen them in person. According to the station population records, both had been occupied since I was a child. They resided in a storeroom on level four in the medical zone. Doctors were supposed to be finding a cure for whatever ailed the people inside, but for all I knew, they were forgotten, shoved in the back with supplies piled on top.

If I wanted to know more about the occupant of this one, I had to get him out into the light. I could always put him back.

The stasis tube was mounted on a wheeled base. I took a quick still frame of the way the straps were configured so I could replace them later.

Releasing them, I freed the stasis tube. I set the lit data-pad on top and pulled as hard as I could. The tube resisted all my efforts. The wheels were locked. Swearing under my breath, I squeezed back into the crate and kicked the release on each leg of the base. The whole thing pulled out with ease.

Who would Ari have abducted, and why? The indirect light outside the crate made it even harder to see through the frosted surface. I grabbed the datapad and searched for how to access a stasis tube. It wouldn't hurt to open the top for just a few minutes as long as I could do that without reanimating the occupant.

As my search for knowledge on stasis tubes led me down several time-consuming trails, I started getting notifications from my team that I was needed. Dammit, I was busy doing things I shouldn't be doing, and I'd told Yumi I'd be late. I should have asked for the day off.

With great reluctance, I saved my searches and put the datapad in my pocket. As I ran my hands over my uniform to straighten it after all my exertions, I realized I still had Ari's bag clipped to my belt. I glanced around my suite and decided to stash it in my undergarment drawer for now. After double checking the lock on my door, I went to work.

Foremost of my needed duties was dealing with a vid call from the leader of the Da'Adio clan.

"Shouldn't you take this?" I asked Yumi, glaring at him over his desk in his office.

He raised his white brows and shrugged. "You want my job? You'll need to know how to deal with these types of situations."

"Wouldn't proper procedure be to escalate this to Commander Keef's attention? Shouldn't he deal with it?"

Yumi chuckled. "If Keef were a better man, sure. But we both know he's not. Personally, I don't want to see our home, especially when it's packed with tourists, come under attack from a well-armed madman throwing a fit. Do you?"

Talking to Papa Da'Adio was like dealing with a low-budget version of the Empaetor. I shifted uneasily in my chair across from Yumi, wondering what kind of fit the Empaetor would throw over the man in the case in my suite.

Play it cool, Rita. Don't give Yumi any reason to ask for details in Ari's investigation.

I sat up straight and took a calming breath. "Think of all the paperwork from the body count. Yeah, no thanks. But if you're saying I would be better at diplomatically deescalating this situation with Papa Da'Adio than Commander Keef, I urge you to recall the many citations filling my file."

"I know your file by heart, Rita." Yumi reached into his

drawer and pulled out a protein bar. He held it out to me. "Have you eaten lately, Stabby? We all know you're much more, shall we say, diplomatic, when you're not hungry."

Taking the bar, I ripped open the wrapper and bit off a mouthful. "You're serious?" I said around the food in my mouth.

"You put yourself in this situation, calling in the empire. Unless you want to involve Commander Keef in whatever reward arrangement you've got?"

"No," I said without hesitation. "But what if this call goes poorly?"

Yumi glanced around his office filled with dusty mementos of a lifetime of trips down to the surface with his wife. "Then you cut your losses on the reward and drop this in Keef's lap. He'll be annoyed with both of us, but the reward should keep you in his favor enough to get my job in a few years. You know, once he forgets that you put us all in empiric crosshairs."

"I didn't..." Alright, maybe I did. I could have alerted SA Tekka of Ari's arrival and apprehended him immediately before he ever met the Da'Adio brothers. I could have told him about the storage claim ticket. Either of those options would have kept me and the station clean and happily rewarded. Then again, we could all be reading about another colony being wiped out next week if the Empaetor used whatever the man in my quarters knew, had access to, or created.

Maybe I was doing the right thing.

I sighed. "Fine. You have pointers, I assume?"

We spent the next hour going over what Yumi thought I should say and what he expected the Da'Adio head to demand. Then I made the call.

Papa Da'Adio was no more pleasant than the two times I'd met him in person on the station. Both times had involved Yumi, Senio, and me escorting him and his people back to the docking ring. Commander Keef had sat safely in his office after handing down the eviction notice due to too many complaints. The rest of our security team had shit themselves at the thought that they might be left in charge should something happen to the three of us. I had scars courtesy of Da'Adio's people having—thankfully—poor aim, but we'd all lived.

"You'll return my nephews immediately," the fuming man on the vid demanded.

"They killed the wrong guy. Someone under empiric investigation. Which now means your nephew Kiyun has a date with an empiric agent."

Yumi, out of view of the vid, signaled me with his hands. Right, be diplomatic.

"If it were up to us, we'd simply expel your nephews from the station and ban them from returning. Kiyun, anyway. Sorry, we can't overlook murder. Kasuni would be subject to the usual two-year restriction you're quite familiar with. Unfortunately, an empiric agent is already on the way."

I wondered what techniques I might learn from the empiric agent. Assuming I could somehow ingratiate myself enough to be allowed to watch Kiyun's interrogation. If nothing else, we'd record it. Even if I never got off this station, having an empiric agent here was a highlight we'd all brag about for the rest of our lives. Watching them work was a learning experience I was loath to be left out of.

"How soon?" Da'Adio asked.

Behind those dark, calculating eyes, plans were surely forming. I didn't doubt that his fingers were busy silently tapping orders just under my view of his lined, gaunt face.

"One to six days." I stared the clan leader down, hoping to emulate SA Tekka's unnerving technique. "In the interest of avoiding further empiric investigation for your clan, it would perhaps be best to trust in the interrogation evasion training you've no doubt instilled in your nephew."

Yumi had authorized a bargaining measure to avoid serving time and instead turn both brothers out immediately after SA Tekka's agent finished with them as a gesture of goodwill. The Da'Adios did a good amount of legit business with the station. While murder was murder, Ari Leeman wasn't one of ours.

"Assuming the agent leaves your nephew to serve a sentence here, we will release Kiyun as soon as the empiric interrogation is complete. If the empire demands justice be served on their terms, there's nothing we can do."

Papa Da'Adio kept up the game for an impressive, ominous couple of minutes before his gaze dipped. "I will expect my nephews in front of me, alive and well, within seven days."

I nodded and ended the call.

Yumi let out a loud exhale. "At least I know my job will be in capable hands. Not that I ever doubted it."

"That's a load of geppa shit." I threw the empty wrapper from the protein bar at him.

"Don't make me add a citation for assaulting a senior officer to your file." He grinned as he stood, signaling my dismissal.

My patience, even with the quick meal, was going to be

strained if I couldn't get back to the stasis tube conundrum in my suite for another eight hours.

"I don't suppose I could get a day off?" I fake coughed.

Yumi offered me a deadpan stare.

I grumbled my way to the door.

"Rita," Yumi called, "I meant it, nice job with Da'Adio. I just might be inclined to lose a few of those citations and insert a commendation in their place."

Given the sudden lump in my throat, I nodded and closed the door behind me.

It was going to be a long eight hours.

8
What Did I Owe A Dead Man Anyway?

My shift crawled by in an endless monotony of witnessing the stupidity of tourists, filing reports, composing a prisoner list to deport to the surface, and taking a few trips to lockup to deliver people to Senio. When it was finally over, I couldn't get inside my suite fast enough. The moment the door closed behind me, I darted along the narrow path through my rearranged furniture. I pulled out my datapad to resume my search for instructions on opening the tube.

Once I'd gone over the opening procedure several times and felt confident I could do it without causing damage to the body inside, I approached the controls on the side of the stasis unit. The panel didn't exactly match the instructions I'd found, but it was pretty close. No doubt there were countless models of these things running around the known universe. At least the controls on this one were in a language I knew and not something off the trade vessel that had transported it.

I entered the opening sequence, double checking the steps on the datapad just to be safe. If Ari went through the trouble to abduct this person or steal whomever it was from the Empaetor, I didn't want to be the one to screw anything up. All I wanted was to open the top to run a facial scan to ID the occupant. Because at this point, I needed to know.

But what if this man was contagious? The idea of weaponizing a sick man wasn't out of the realm of possibility, especially not where the Empaetor was concerned. I grabbed a mask out of my work triage kit and slid it over my face. The med assessment program on my datapad should be able to scan the body once it was out of the tube to tell me what I was dealing with. Hopefully nothing more than a man and not a weapon to terrorize the empire.

By the Maker, what if he was a terrorist, ready to be aimed at the Empaetor's next target? Or some maniacal scientist with a head full of plagues or weapon plans? The med assessment program wouldn't tell me any of that.

I clutched my datapad and paced the little room left in my suite. What the hell was I doing? I should put him back, close the crate, and wait for the empiric agent to take this all off my hands.

Except I had made a promise not to do that.

What did I owe a dead man anyway?

Fucking Ari Leeman. Why couldn't he have stolen a crate full of gems or credit chips? A couple of those going missing wouldn't be too noticeable. One person? Yeah, the empiric agent was going to figure that out real quick.

The top of the stasis tube made whirring noises. Lights blinked on the control panel, indicating the unsealing. I'd just do the ID and med scans, then close it again. It wasn't like I was going to reanimate the guy. I just wanted to know who Ari had foisted upon me.

After ten minutes of waiting, the tube vibrated, and the whirring grew louder. A hiss and a cool puff of disinfectant-scented air accompanied the release of the seal. The whirring stopped.

The top separated from the base and slowly lifted until the door stood upright on the long back hinge. With my heart thudding loudly, I leaned over to peer into the open tube.

Inside lay a man in a light blue body-hugging suit that covered him from ankle to neck. His hands and feet were the deep bronze skin color common to inner empire worlds. Loose curls of black hair rested on the pillow, cut just above his shoulders. His eyes were closed, but something about that face tickled my brain. The tickle turned into a tingle that amplified to an electric shock of recognition.

Ari Leeman had stolen a younger version of Empaetor Iradio VIII.

Belatedly remembering that I had my datapad in hand with the ID scan ready to go, I held it up and activated the program. The results screen blinked. Nothing was happening. I banged the edge of the datapad on the tabletop. It didn't help. What was going on? Results were usually instant.

I tried the med assessment program. There didn't appear to be anything physically wrong with him. No known contaminants registered.

Pulling off my mask, I backed away from the stasis tube. Was this a clone? A twin brother kept in stasis for half a lifetime? His son? If Ari was bodyguard to the Empaetor's household, he'd have access to any of those options.

Why the fuck had Ari Leeman stolen this person? And

what was I going to do now that I had him in my suite?

Ari was trying to get him far away from the Empaetor's grasp. Was it because he was a threat? Was he in danger? Without waking him and asking questions, I'd have no way of knowing, and not knowing, I didn't know what to do about the agent who would be here in a matter of days.

If that agent came to my suite to collect the giant case, they'd have a warrant to get anything they needed from me and the station, including my personal items...like the datapad I'd used to research how to open the stasis tube. Dammit.

I rubbed my hands over my face and groaned. How was I supposed to explain this to the agent?

The datapad. Ari's encrypted transmission had been transferred to it. Maybe there were answers there. Feeling a little more hopeful about the situation I'd created for myself, hesitantly stepped away from the sleeping man in the open stasis tube. I sat down at the table and got to work.

None of my standard crack programs worked. None of the non-standard ones did either. I swore, fighting the urge to smack the useless thing on the tabletop. As if that would teach it to cooperate.

Before I had to explain why I needed a replacement for my shattered datapad, I set it down and pressed my hands to my temples instead. Of course, Ari would have access to super secure communication. He worked for the Empaetor, for fuck's sake. The empiric agent could probably read it, but it wasn't like they were going to let me in on the secret.

If I wanted to know who this was and why Ari was on the run with him, I'd have to find my answers another way.

The projection clock informed me it was time for dinner, but my stomach was in too many knots for that. The clone, or whoever he was, would be disoriented after waking, perfect for questioning. If he turned out to be a threat, I could stun him and put him back under. I had the instructions right there on my datapad.

I'd come this far. Why the hell not dig myself in a little deeper?

9

You Know Who I Am

After entering the last few commands, I stood back with one hand on my stunner. An eyelid twitched. And again. His lips parted. The display on the stasis tube showed his heart rate was increasing. Yet, he didn't wake. I glanced at the instructions again. I'd followed them all.

Keeping one hand on my stunner, I leaned over the open tube to give the man's shoulder a gentle shake. One eye cracked open, revealing more white than iris.

"Hey, can you hear me?" I asked.

Both eyes opened a little more. He let out a soft moan.

According to the instructions, he was supposed to wake within minutes and without discomfort once the chemicals stopped flowing into his system. What if he really was injured or sick and this process was harming him? I tapped the key on the terminal that halted the chemical waking process. The command line flashed and went blank. Too late to go back now.

The half-conscious man said something. I leaned closer.

He lifted his head and glanced around. "Ari?" He blinked a few times and spotted me. "Where's Ari?"

"He's not here." I kept my hand on my stunner but reached out to pat his shoulder in what I hoped was a calming manner.

From his face, now more animated, I guessed him to be somewhere between thirty and fifty. It was hard to tell with the more privileged members of society and their access to health and beauty treatments. If he came from Harilax, he definitely had access to those.

"Where is he?" Worry clear on his groggy face, the man tried to sit up.

"You need to wait there for twenty minutes. If you get up too fast, the instructions say there can be adverse effects on your heart."

He settled back, but didn't appear pleased about it. "Who are you?"

Seeing that he wasn't slipping into a wild panic and he didn't appear to be in immediate danger of dying, I stepped back to a better stunner range. If anyone was going to get answers, it was me.

"Let's start with: *who are you?*"

"You know damned well who I am." He glared, looking more awake by the second.

I knew who he looked *like*, but that didn't answer my question. "Do I? Why would you assume that I know?"

I watched him closely, not bothering to hide my curious examination of his familiar but slightly different features.

His brows drew together as silence stretched between us. "Where am I?" he asked.

Again with the questions. He was on my station. In my suite, for the Maker's sake. He owed me answers, not the other way around.

"Where were you heading?" I asked.

His glare returned. An aristocratic air illustrating his affront at being questioned slipped over his face and found a firm hold on his voice. "Where are we?"

So much for holding the upper hand. I sighed and surrendered my quest for leverage in favor of possibly gaining goodwill rather than punishment. "The trade station over Anduvea."

His brows scrunched low, and I could almost see him processing the information. "Where is Ari? Why am I here?"

"Ari Leeman is dead. He chose the wrong people to ask for a ride to wherever he was going to take you. The good news is that you're free to return home now."

"Return? I need to see Ari."

"I told you, he's dead."

The man sat up slowly and gave me an order in a voice every bit as imperious as the Empaetor himself, "In the name of my father, Empaetor Iradio VIII, you will take me to him right now or you and all your people will suffer the consequences."

His father. By the Maker's grace, I had the fucking heir to the Scaavo Empire in my suite? No wonder the Empaetor was adamant about wanting this treasure back.

SA Tekka knew what Ari had stolen. He knew I might find it in my investigation. And I had. And he was pissed.

So much for gaining goodwill.

In the hopes of not making things worse for Anduvea or myself, I nodded. "If you wish, but perhaps it would be safer for you to remain here in my suite. I will bring Ari's body to you."

Not that I was excited about having the Scaavo heir here.

How embarrassing was that? The heir to all the empire in the haphazardly decorated personal suite of a tired, disagreeable senior security officer on a cheaply built station on the edge of the empire over a world full of exiles and their offspring.

And who was going to protect him? Me? I laughed to myself. The Empaetor employed a team of top-notch bodyguards to watch over his consort, his heir, and himself. This wasn't a task I was prepared for and certainly not while the station was filled with bored, drunk, and high Anduvean exiles who had little love for the Empaetor who put them there.

"Was Ari alone?" he asked.

"Yes. May I ask why you were traveling in stasis?"

"In stasis?" He examined his immediate surroundings and frowned.

I wracked my brain for how I was supposed to address him. Other than a few public appearances throughout the years, the Empaetor kept his family private. I didn't blame him. It was safer that way.

"Forgive me, but how should I address you?"

"Iradio Octao Laurent Scaavo IX."

If that wasn't a mouthful. And here I was with my sorry little two names.

"I'm Rita Stabinov, one of the senior security officers on the Anduvean station."

He nodded. "Thank the Maker for security. Laurent will do."

Laurent would do, indeed. My gut clenched at the realization I'd just found myself on a first name basis with the heir to the empire.

If I could deal with Papa Da'Adio, I could attempt to be diplomatic with the heir. Couldn't I? I had the sudden urge to find a protein bar and maybe a still frame of Yumi so I could get myself under control.

Putting Laurent at ease would be a good first step toward getting back to the goodwill portion of my plan.

I checked the time. We had a few minutes to go, but he was looking livelier by the second. And more annoyed. "Are you feeling alright? Good enough to get out of there, anyway?"

"That would be better, yes." He started to get up, but then pinched his eyes shut and rubbed his palms on his temples.

"Maybe I should get medical in here to make sure you're alright." I gave up my hold on the stunner and went to his side. It wasn't like I was going to stun him. Not if I wanted to live long enough to enjoy Ari's credit chips.

"Just help me out of this thing." He held one hand out blindly.

I released the latches that held the end panel in place, allowing him room to get his feet and then legs over the edge.

"Take it slow."

He reached out again, keeping one hand on his head. "It feels like my brain is being crushed."

"I'm definitely calling medical." Was he expecting me to take his hand? Was I allowed to touch him? I didn't know what the proper protocol was. We didn't get visitors of any significant rank out here.

He grabbed my shoulder and pulled himself forward until he had both feet on the floor. His first step faltered. So did his second. I disregarded any attempt at protocol and put one arm around him to keep him steady while resting the other on his chest to make sure he remained upright. To my relief, he didn't seem to object.

I led him over to the chair that normally sat beside the couch. It was now crammed against the wall thanks to the giant case and the stasis tube filling my suite. He slumped into the chair, keeping one hand on his head and making gagging noises.

Laurent's vomit on my floor was not the kind of royal souvenir I wanted to find a market for, though there was likely an audience for it. The empire was vast and its dark recesses many.

The gagging grew louder. I ran to the kitchen to grab the waste receptacle and shoved it into his lap.

He utilized it a minute later. After making sure he wasn't going to vomit again, I left him to grab a hand towel from the kitchen and a cup of water. He traded those gratefully for the stinking waste receptacle. I went to the kitchen to dispose of the contents and then sat on the arm of the couch near him.

"Feeling better?"

"A little, yes. How did I get here?"

I explained about the ship Ari had booked for them and the case Laurent had traveled in.

"We trusted him. I trusted him." Laurent shook his head. "The last thing I remember is Ari standing behind me while I was dressing in the morning. Drugging me and shoving me in a stasis tube to sell to the highest bidder or blackmail my father is not something I expected of him. He'd been my guard for twelve years. Why would he do this?"

The hurt in Laurent's pale blue eyes was impossible to miss, even only knowing him for a few minutes. As much as I didn't like his father, I felt bad for his heir.

"I don't know, but Ari was very clear that I was not to sell you or let any harm come to you. He was adamant that I keep you out of your father's hands. Any idea why?"

"No." He sounded tired and deflated. "Why would Ari bring me out here? Where was he trying to go?"

"Outside the empire. Away from your father. That's all I overheard before he was shot. Was your father going to do something? Punish you maybe?"

If one Empaetor had exiled his advisors and others had handed down equally heavy-handed punishments for other subjects, business-partners, and friends, who was to say that Iradio VIII wouldn't do something rash to his own heir? There were whispers of the Empaetor flying into unexplained rages and odd behavior, but no one was privy to what was going on behind the scenes on Harilax. What seemed outrageous might be fully justified and rational to someone with all the pieces in hand.

I definitely did not have all the pieces. To any of this. In fact, I felt just as lost as Laurent looked.

"He was going to step down soon. My father. I'll be sitting on his throne before the new year. That's what he said."

"And here you are in my chair instead."

He let out a quiet snort that might have been amusement or annoyance.

"I was supposed to go into isolation for my final training. That's what I was preparing for this morning." He rubbed his hands over his face and shook his head. "If we're out here, that morning... How long was I out?"

"Ari's warrant was issued thirty-nine days ago."

Laurent grimaced. He stared into his lap. "Why would Ari want to keep me from becoming Empaetor?"

"I don't know, but he wanted you as far from your father as possible."

"We were friends. I mean, he worked for my father, but I thought..."

"Maybe you thought correctly. I really don't know." I stood. "What I do know is that an empiric agent will be here in a matter of days to take you and Ari's body back to your father."

"Why would an agent be coming to retrieve us if Ari was trying to get us away?"

"I contacted him. Your father had issued a warrant for Ari. He said he'd stolen treasure from the Empaetor himself."

Laurent smiled. "Treasure. He would have never called me that to my face."

I pointed to the giant black case that had held the stasis tube. "A case full of treasure stolen from the palace is more likely to be returned for reward and favor than saying someone kidnapped his heir. That would only lead to blackmail or ransom."

Laurent studied me. "The blackmail and ransom bit would have been easier before you woke me."

I might have my moments of questionable morals, but that was a big leap. One that certainly wouldn't go well for me or the inhabitants of Anduvea. "Then it should be clear that neither of those are my intention."

He kept up the stare, but nodded. "Why did you open the case?"

"Because Ari was so adamant about what I should and shouldn't do with it. I was curious about the contents."

"Even knowing my father's agent would learn that you accessed the case? That you found me?"

"I wasn't expecting to find you. I was more expecting a secret weapon. Keeping that out of your father's hands would be doing the known universe a favor."

"Anduvea? You said?"

I nodded.

He drank the last of the water in the cup and set it on the floor at his feet. "Your ire is understandable then, I suppose. But as you can see, I'm not a weapon. How do you plan on explaining this to my father's agent?"

I met his gaze and kept my voice level like I did when dealing with the spoiled tourists. "At first, Ari made me promise to keep the case out of the Empaetor's hands, but with his dying breath, he divulged what he'd stolen and that he regretted taking you from your father. He instructed me to wake you."

Laurent stared me down. "It would work if you can maintain that delivery."

"Why wouldn't I be able to? It's the truth."

"I don't think so."

"You weren't there. You have no proof that I'm lying."

He licked his lips and finally blinked. "Anduvea has no love for the empire, and rightly so, in all honesty. You were looking for small treasure to skim off the top while returning the rest to my father's agent to buy goodwill."

"Returning his heir would gain me more than any treasure would."

The calculating gleam in his eyes made me stand and

slip a hand onto my stunner. I took one step back, putting enough room between us to take action if needed.

He shifted forward in the chair, both hands on the arms, ready to push himself onto his feet. "Rita, you *are* going to help me get back to my father, aren't you?"

If Ari had given his life to keep Laurent out of his father's hands, was returning him the right thing to do? Hell, had Ari expected me to be Laurent's keeper now?

"How about I get Ari's body in here for you to do whatever you need to do and then we can decide together whether you're going back with your father's agent or not."

He stood slowly. I took a few more steps until my back hit a wall. While I really didn't want to stun the Scaavo heir, there was too much unknown for my conscience to be alright with letting him go home without answers. I kept the stunner aimed but my finger light on the trigger.

"You believe him? That Ari was keeping me away from my father for a good reason?"

"He died to get you away, so if he was really your friend, then yes, I think he had a good reason."

"My father and I..." he shook his head. "We're not close, but I can't think of any reason he'd want to hurt me. He was quite clear about needing me to take on the role of Empaetor in light of his health."

I shrugged. "All I know is what Ari told me, and that wasn't much. Do you trust him?"

"I need to see his body," Laurent declared.

"Alright. Have a seat. It's going to take a bit for him to arrive. We're halfway across the station from medical."

Laurent studied me a moment, his gaze lingering on the stunner in my hand. Trusting that I could draw it faster than he could rush me, I slid it back into the holster. That seemed to be what he'd needed because he returned to the chair.

I pulled my datapad from my pocket and tapped out a delivery request to medical, explaining that I needed to do a private exam via vid with the empiric agent. That, as I expected, received an immediate affirmative response. As long as I had the looming threat of an incoming agent to throw around, I had power.

A few days of power wouldn't be so bad. And if I could get Laurent on my side? Cooperating with the incoming Empaetor surely boded well for my future. After all, he now had an opening in his bodyguard staff. I found myself grinning at the thought.

Laurent's attention snapped to me. "Something funny?"

Just the absurdity of dreaming I'd get to work for the royal family directly. That pay rate would fulfill my wildest whims. I could afford to do a job I wanted and still visit my parents.

Laurent was on edge, half-smiling one minute and snapping the next. I imagined that was the burden of being Empaetor, or the looming burden, in his case. Perhaps it was the default family disposition. Or maybe, I dared to hope, it was because he'd woken to find he'd been abducted in a stasis tube and his trusted bodyguard was dead.

"No, not funny. Sorry. Nerves. Ari's body will be delivered within the hour. They'd just installed him in a preservation bag."

"I'll be able to touch him?"

I supposed being an heir to the empire didn't involve much contact with dead bodies in preservation bags. Then again, knowing his father's reputation, maybe that was part of the final training Laurent hadn't gotten to yet.

"Yes. We will have full access to his body. We will want to keep that access brief to prevent further decay of the flesh. A body can remain in a sealed bag indefinitely, but open, decay happens at a normal rate."

"Understood." Laurent grew quiet, dropping his gaze to stare at his hands in his lap.

"Are you hungry?"

He didn't respond.

Still considering contacting medical, I went over to crouch in front of him. His breathing sounded normal, his skin tone stable, no sheen of sweat on his brow. It was odd being so close to someone, someone I probably shouldn't be close to at all, and still have no reaction. It was like he'd pulled deep inside himself. Like the shock of waking up here was wearing off and reality was pulling him under. I'd had plenty of experience working with people who were going through traumatic situations. Hazard of the job.

I shook his knee gently. He picked up his chin a few degrees, but didn't look at me.

"Why don't you go use my bed for a little while? I'll let you know when the body arrives."

He stood as if on autopilot, following me to my bedroom in my little suite that must seem like a pathetic hovel to him. Thank the Maker, I'd cleaned a few days ago. My room wasn't the full mess it became between cleaning urges.

Laurent didn't remark on my unmade bed as he sat down on it. The tangle of blankets and the askew pillow didn't faze him when he stretched out on his back to stare at the ceiling.

The heir to the empire was in my bed. A bubble of laughter threatened to spill out again. I turned out the light, left the door half open, and ducked into the bathroom, sealing the door behind me before letting the laughter free.

I imagined sitting down to dinner the next time I visited my parents on the surface, telling them how I had the heir, Iradio Octao Laurent Scaavo IX himself, in my suite. The laughter spilled out until tears rolled down my cheeks.

I had Iradio Octao Laurent Scaavo IX in my bed. I laughed even harder, imagining the tales I could weave out of that tidbit the next time Yumi, Senio, and I got together for a drink.

The ache in my sides sobered my thoughts.

Laurent would be with me for days until the agent arrived. I was responsible for the heir to the empire. Me. For the heir. To. The. Empire.

Amusement turned to panic. I wiped the tears on my sleeve and forced air in and out of my lungs at an even rate while my heart tried to pound its way out of my chest. Fucking hell, I wasn't qualified for this.

10

Bring in the dead guy

My door chimed. I glanced toward the bedroom. The light was still off and Laurent hadn't made a sound. I figured it was safe to let medical in with Ari Leeman's body.

"Thank you for bringing him," I said once we'd maneuvered the cart bearing the man-sized preservation bag into the last of the open floor space in my suite.

The woman from medical eyed the plas case and the stasis tube. Her mouth hung open.

"Evidence I'm holding for the Empiric agent. They want everything under guard until he gets here. I'll be stuck in here for days with the damned body, but who am I to argue?"

She nodded and backed out the door. I closed it and made sure it was locked before going to wake Laurent.

The heir was on my bed exactly as I'd left him, eyes open, staring at the ceiling. Good Maker, please don't let him be dead too. I reached out to touch him. His head turned to me and he blinked. Alright, good. Not dead. Relieved, I retreated to the doorway to give him space.

"They brought Ari's body. Whenever you're feeling up to—"

"Now is fine." He sat up and swung his legs over the side of the bed.

I realized Laurent fit in the exact indent I usually occupied on the mattress. I'd always imagined the Empaetor to be a towering, immense figure, but Laurent was just like me. Well, at least in size and shape, but that probably wasn't complimentary in my favor as a female. I bit the inside of my cheek to keep from laughing again. Like I needed to be concerned with what the heir might think of me beyond a guard to keep him safe until the agent arrived or he figured out what Ari had been up to.

Laurent marched over to the silver bag on the cart pressed against the one bare eight-foot section of wall I had left in my suite. I might as well be living in a storage bay at this point. All semblance of my cozy little collection of mismatched, comfortable furniture and random fanciful trinkets had been eclipsed by the ominous bulk of Laurent and Ari's arrival in my life.

His hands rested on the edge of the metal cart as he peered into the clearplaz square at the head of the bag. "It looks like he's sleeping. I don't know what I expected."

I walked over to stand beside the heir. "The injuries were to his stomach. Once I open this, you'll see them. Are you prepared for that?"

He shook his head. His fingers curled around the side bar of the cart until his knuckles turned white. "He was my best friend. My only friend, really."

Was I supposed to comfort him? Was I allowed to? I'd already touched him a couple times, but I didn't dare chance offending him now that he was more alert.

"I'm sorry to hear that. How about we only open the bag

at the top so you don't have to see his injuries?"

"I need to..." He went pale.

I dashed over to grab a chair from the dining table and slid it behind him. "Please, sit."

The last thing I needed was for him to keel over and get a head injury I'd have to explain. It also wouldn't look good if I was hoping for any sort of recommendation for advancement in security from the agent, or by the Maker's miracle, from the heir himself.

Laurent sat without argument and stared at the silver side of the preservation bag with tear-filled eyes. "What was he doing all the way out here? Why couldn't he just talk to me if this wasn't a bid to get something from my father?"

"I wish I had answers for you."

Ari's dead face offered nothing helpful. His clothing had been removed and would be folded in a stack next to his feet, in keeping with processing procedure.

"You can get what I need. I don't think I can," Laurent said.

"While I appreciate your confidence in me, I'm not sure I'm qualified to assist you."

"Open it." He pointed at the bag.

"While he was processed fairly quickly, there will probably be a smell once the bag is breached. Are you ready?"

"No," he whispered.

I went to the kitchen, grabbed a clean towel and handed it to him. "Put that over your nose and mouth."

He followed my instructions without question or complaint. I wasn't used to that. It was quite nice.

Unzipping the bag, I curled the side in front of Laurent down so he could see Ari to just past his shoulders. As I'd guessed, they were wide, muscular shoulders atop well-defined muscular arms. Admittedly, I was jealous. Though I spent a fair amount of time in the gym, I'd never achieved that sort of body. I appreciated a good meal too much. At least, that's what my mother said. Maybe I just wasn't genetically inclined toward it. At this point in my life, I'd accepted that I'd never be anything other than solid and sturdy.

I was about to sit beside Laurent to keep him company while he mourned when he caught my arm.

"I need you to look for me."

"Look for what? Where?"

He nodded toward the bag. "Inside him."

"I'm sorry, what?" While I'd been around enough dead people to not be squeamish about it, rooting around inside them was not in my skill set. "I can call someone from medical in if you need him to undergo an exam."

"You do it. I don't want to get anyone else involved."

"I already went through his clothes. He had nothing on him other than a couple of credit chips and a false ID card."

I neglected to mention the other loaded chips I'd found. I wasn't walking away from all of this empty-handed if the agent went ballistic that I'd released Laurent from the stasis tube.

"Did they...look inside him?"

"Medical? Probably not. His cause of death was no mystery. I only asked them to preserve Ari for the incoming agent."

"Good. Then maybe there's something there."

My stomach did an uncomfortable heave. "I'd rather not."

"You will," he ordered. Laurent rubbed his face with both hands. They came away wet.

Well fuck. "I'm not a surgeon."

"He's dead. You can't hurt him." He let out a shaky sigh. "There has to be some clue why he did this. If he was trying to get me away for a good reason, he would have some way of letting me know what was going on if something happened to him."

Not that I was on board, but I was curious to know what methods his private guards might employ. "Like what?"

"A hidden chip? Something under his skin? Something he swallowed? I don't know. He'd leave a message somehow."

A private encrypted message. One someone like Laurent could open. Oh, thank the Maker. I closed the preservation bag and zipped it shut.

He shot to his feet. "What do you think you're doing?"

"I think I have what you're looking for and it won't require a scalpel." Using my datapad, I pulled up the message. "Ari sent it from the *Asbodot* before he arrived here. I couldn't open it, but I'm guessing you can."

"Do you have a terminal I could transfer this to? That would be easier."

From the hope beaming in his eyes, I guessed he knew what he was looking at.

"Sure. You can use the one in the bedroom. But before you lock yourself in there, let me use it to make a quick call so we're not interrupted."

Laurent didn't look happy about the delay, but he nodded.

I ducked into my bedroom and closed the door before

contacting Yumi. He answered immediately.

"Rita? You're not on duty for—" he checked the time.

"Not for you, no, but I am for the empire. They've got me until further notice. Sorry to throw off our schedule."

His lined face crunched in a tight scowl.

"Sorry, the empiric agent wants me to guard evidence until they get here."

"Rita, we're swimming in tourist shit. I rely on you to take your half of this workload."

I didn't get paid half his salary to do half of his job, so while I did like Yumi, taking this time off didn't bother me. It wasn't like I was going on vacation. I was now solely responsible for the Scaavo heir for several days. Making sure no one knew he was here would make my job easier.

"Be happy it's not you stuck in your suite," I said.

He scoffed. "Oh, I'm sure you're suffering terribly. The rest of us will deal with the station full of chaos while you kick back in peace and quiet behind closed doors for a few days."

I prayed to the Maker that Laurent and I had a peaceful and quiet few days together. Except that meant being one on one with the heir. For days. My breath started coming faster, and my mouth went dry. I was definitely going to screw this goodwill thing up by saying or doing something. I lived alone for a reason. With very few exceptions, I didn't like people, and my interpersonal skills, according to the file in Yumi's office, were not great.

I swallowed my panic and attempted a weary smile. "Thanks for understanding. I'll make sure the empiric agent compensates the station for the hours they're keeping me occupied."

"You do that, Rita. You do that." He shook his head and ended the call.

After taking a moment to compose myself, for what that was worth since my hands were still shaking and my breathing seemed restricted to jagged bursts, I left the bedroom. I was just finding my rhythm as I walked past the bathroom and kitchen when I spotted Laurent standing over Ari. Tears streamed down his face.

Hoping to distract him, I said, "I'm finished and the message should be transferred now, if you'd like to use the terminal."

Laurent nodded, but kept his face averted. He ambled to my bedroom as if his legs were half-asleep. I heard the chair by the terminal creak and realized he'd left the door open. He tapped the terminal keys. I didn't realize how loud they were. Then again, I was never outside the room listening to myself type.

Minutes later, Ari's voice came from my room. He wasn't exactly whispering but talking quietly, like he didn't want to be overheard.

I stood in the hallway listening to the sound of Ari's voice but unable to make out the words. The chair creaked again. Was I invading Laurent's privacy or posting myself nearby to keep watch on him in case he needed me? Mid-debate on that, he called my name.

Was I supposed to pretend I wasn't near enough to hear him, or should I answer right away? We were going to need to establish rules for me to follow so I didn't overstep myself.

"Yes?"

"Join me."

There he went ordering again. Unsure if I preferred the definite bounds of an order from the heir or the ambiguousness of a stranger mourning his friend, I cautiously entered the bedroom.

His hair was a mess, like he'd had his hands tangled in it, and his eyes were red. Laurent didn't appear to be up to ordering anything. I supposed the tone was habitual, being heir as he was.

He gestured to the bedside behind him. "We're stuck together for the next few days. I have zero friends or advisors to lean on, and I find myself in an uncertain position in an unknown place."

Whatever this message was, he had to be desperate to sink to confiding in me. "Sure. What's going on?"

"I wish I knew."

From the disturbed look about him, I gathered the message hadn't been a simple answer to his situation. "I'm assuming Ari wasn't selling you out?"

"No, he wasn't. Sit."

I settled onto the edge of the bed. He replayed the message.

The man I'd met the day before leaned in close to a camera. He glanced to either side before he spoke, pitching his shaky voice low.

"I9 is safe. I've done as you've asked, but I haven't been able to get us outside of the empire. No one wants to cross the Empaetor by helping me escape. That damned warrant isn't helping. Is there anything you can do?"

Ari glanced around and behind him before again leaning in. "I have enough credits to set us up for as long as it takes for the Empaetor to die. We won't return until we hear from you. I'll keep my promise as long as I'm able, Marishka."

He let out a weary sigh. "Laurent, if you're watching this, if I'm gone, stay away until your mother says it's safe to return to take your place. I'm sorry it had to go this way. We had little warning. Live long, my friend."

The message ended.

"I9, that's you?"

He nodded. "Iradio the ninth. To be my name once my father is finished with it."

His mother's name was not known to us. She was only the Empaetor's consort, the heir's mother. I imagined it was known to some, but the seldom seen consort was far overshadowed by the man who held our lives in his hands.

"Your mother didn't give you any indication of trouble?"

"We rarely speak. My father prefers it that way, and she says nothing to oppose him. Spineless." His hands curled into fists. "She gave me up to his whims when I was seven. We only see one another when my father decrees it socially necessary."

"It sounds like he runs your family much like the empire."

Laurent shot me a look that immediately reminded me to keep my thoughts on his father to myself.

"Is there something going on with the Empaetor that us lowly vagrants at the edge of the empire are unaware of? Ari makes it sound like either his days are numbered or your mother is going to murder him. Or did Ari plan on staying in hiding with you for a long time until nature took its course?"

"He's terminally ill. No one can know, Rita. He'll make the announcement in his own time."

He was supposed to be sitting on his father's throne by now. "He's ill enough that he was ready for you to take his place before your mother had Ari whisk you away?"

"Yes. He said he would guide me for as long as he had left."

Part of me longed for a work shift in the social district where I had nothing but tourists to deal with. Their idiocy was normal. I understood it. Palace intrigue wasn't in my training, and though I'd dreamed of joining the palace security force, I'd imagined the dangers would be more of the usual variety, not familial problems.

"If Ari was under orders from your mother, perhaps you could contact her so we know what to do about the incoming Empiric agent?"

Laurent grimaced but nodded. "Can I get a secure outgoing channel from here?"

"Yes, but don't expect an immediate vid conversation from Harilax. We're too far from the center of the empire for that."

Laurent turned his attention to my terminal.

"I'll leave you to it while I find something for us to eat."

He nodded absently as his fingers tapped out his message. I went into the kitchen to heat whatever had two servings in the cold storage.

The key tapping ended, and then the chair creaked. Laurent emerged from my bedroom. His gaze skimmed over my suite as if he was just now taking it in. Standing beside me, he stared at the preservation bag on its cart.

"Have a seat. This will be ready in a few minutes." I nodded toward my tiny table and the two chairs on either side of it.

He went to the table and sank into the chair facing me rather than Ari's body. "You talked to him? Ari?"

"Only briefly. Sorry."

Laurent rubbed his fingers over the tabletop. Was he feeling for grime? Playing with crumbs? Wondering if the palace tables were the same plain grey plaz under the fine coverings he was used to?

"Sorry," I said again as I set a steaming plate of cream covered cooked grains and roasted mushrooms in front of him. I wasn't sure which part I was apologizing for: being stuck with me, my suite, the food, or his situation.

He watched me sit, pick up my fork, and raise a bite to my mouth. Was I supposed to wait for him to eat first? Did the food offend him? "If you don't like mushrooms, I can find you something else."

"It's fine." Still, he made no move to pick up his fork.

"Is it?" I glanced at the preservation bag. The heir was used to having a bodyguard with him at all times. For now, that meant me. "Did Ari eat with you?"

"When I was on my own, yes."

"As part of his duties."

Laurent nodded, licking his lips and eyeing the steaming grains on his plate.

"I've already had one portion from this box and Tino's cooks are pretty good. I can assure you this is safe to eat." But to put him at ease, I placed my paused bite into my mouth and chewed. And swallowed. "Like I said, safe."

Laurent dug into his meal. Within minutes, the plate was empty.

"Are you still hungry? I could find you something—"

"I'm fine." He shook his head. "No. I'm not."

"Ari?"

Laurent nodded. "The room feels empty without him lurking in it. I keep glancing over my shoulder, expecting to see him. He was always cracking jokes under his breath, trying to make me smile at inopportune times. Calling me silly names when we were alone to get me to relax. I miss his voice as much as his shadow."

The big guard and the heir had a relationship that made me envious. I'd never had someone like that, someone I wanted beside me all the time. I liked my space, and while Yumi and Senio called me Stabby now and then, it wasn't exactly an endearing nickname.

I couldn't afford to be irritable or short-tempered with the heir. After a deep breath, I considered what a friendly person might do in this situation, someone like Senio or Tino. They had lots of friends. People liked them.

"You might as well get some sleep while we wait for answers from your mother. Take the bed. I'll take the couch."

He didn't argue. He also didn't take care of his plate. Laurent merely stood and headed back to my bedroom. This time, he closed the door.

Damned royalty. Like I'd expected him to be a regular person just because he was staying with me for a few days? I added servant services to the bill I was compiling for the empiric agent.

I spent the next eight and a half hours on my couch, secure in knowing that Laurent was safe in my bedroom. Attempting to gain some goodwill with Yumi, I used my datapad to work with Senio to file a raft of reports we'd been behind on.

Laurent burst out of the bedroom. My heart skipped a beat as I leapt up and rushed to him. He staggered into the kitchen and steadied himself, leaning over the table with both hands pressed to the surface.

"What's wrong?"

His sides heaved as he drew a ragged breath. "My mother. She's dead."

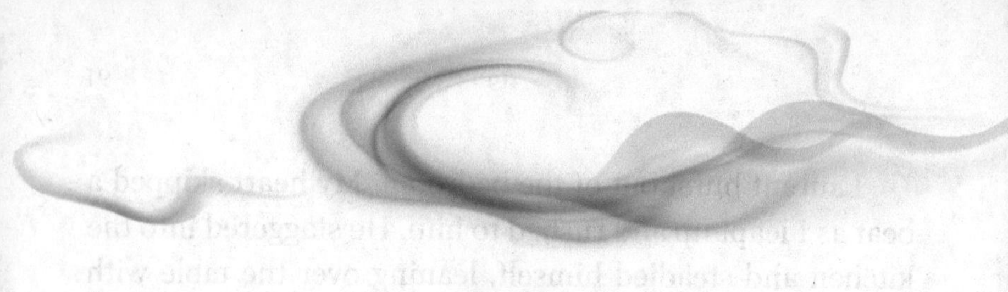

11

Implications

I sat across from Laurent at the kitchen table. He held his head in his hands, his elbows bracketing the plate and the remains of the simple breakfast I'd made. He'd eaten methodically, saying nothing.

"You received a reply then?" I asked, realizing as I spoke how stupid that sounded. His mother was dead.

"An automated reply. To Ari. To me. The message came from her private address."

I'd done a little research in my hours on the couch between attempts to sleep. Laurent was thirty-eight, two years younger than me. His parents hadn't been young when he was conceived. If the Empaetor had a terminal illness, maybe his mother did too.

I took a minute to nonchalantly push the few visible crumbs off the table. "Natural causes?" I asked with forced optimism.

He shook his head, still in his hands, his hair bunching up between his fingers. "She said my father was watching her. Said he knew she'd had a part in my abduction. If I was getting this message, she said she was dead."

For not being close to his mother, he appeared as upset about her demise as Ari's. Then again, it could have been the two losses in close succession. Or the lack of answers.

Surely the Empaetor wouldn't have had Laurent's mother killed. However short-tempered and heavy-handed he might seem to the rest of us, this was his family.

"Maybe she's just being held somewhere. There hasn't been a public announcement. You'd think the death of the consort would warrant a memorial of some degree?"

"Maybe," he said without conviction.

Laurent sighed and lifted his head. His gaze roamed around my kitchen.

"One thing is for certain. You need to get off this station before the empiric agent arrives. You're going to stay hidden until I get some answers."

Laurent stabbed at the tabletop with his fingertips. "I could try to get some from my father."

I couldn't imagine that aggressive tone would get him far with the Empaetor. It was the first time I'd heard him sound threatening, like his father. Too much so. Laurent, the man caught up in uncertainty since waking from the stasis tube, was also I9. He might need me now, but as soon as he was on the throne, he could squash me and all of Anduvea out of existence with a simple command.

"After Ari and your mother died to get you away from him? I wouldn't recommend confronting your father. Yet," I said, trying to phrase my knee jerk 'oh hell no' reaction to something that sounded more like advice Ari might have given him.

He glanced up from his table stabbing to regard me with an icy glare. "I don't recall asking for your recommendation."

"True," I said, going for contrition, but not willing to demurely back off. Laurent, whether he liked it or not, was my ticket to advancement or recognition, or whatever the hell I could get. All I needed was some time to find my footing with him and for him to understand that, at least for now, he needed me.

"We don't know why you're here instead of there. Maybe it was a threat to you as the rising heir, or maybe to your whole family—that might be what happened to your mother." I grimaced as my mind flew through a raft of potential threats. "If your father knows about whatever it is, you're safe here and he has an entire empire's worth of resources at his disposal. And if he's the threat that sent Ari running, he's got," I licked my suddenly very dry lips, "an entire empire of resources at his disposal."

"And all I have is you," he said flatly.

That might have been what I was trying to point out, but still, ouch. Keeping my wince internal, I forced my tone to neutral. "At the moment, yes."

I pondered my options, which were now *his* options. "We need to get you off this station. I know just the place to hide you until we can figure out what to do."

"*We*, is it?"

Would Ari have let him do whatever he wanted and done his best to protect him from the consequences or stood his ground? I hadn't known him long enough to guess.

Sitting back in my chair, I rested my hands on the table. "If you'd rather go at all this alone, I'll step aside, but if you'd like help, then yes, we're at *we*."

Laurent held my gaze for a long moment and then

jabbed his finger toward the open stasis tube. "How do you plan on explaining that to the agent while *you* attempt to get answers?"

"I'll figure something out."

He shook his head. "You'll be implicated."

Time to figure out where I stood. "Does it matter to you if I'm implicated?"

"Does it matter?" Laurent scowled, but then a sigh escaped his tight lips. "You've been helpful so far. Trust has not been fully established, but I'm guessing it can be bought. We both know I'm short on options. Name your price."

I already had Ari's credit chips. What exactly did I want from the man who would be Empaetor should he live to take his father's place? More importantly, if I had any scant amount of control over the outcome and I8's days were numbered... Did I want Laurent to become the next Empaetor? Was this the moment that the Empire had been whispering about for so long, a window of opportunity for change?

Not only could I do something for Anduvea, but maybe the entire empire. I needed time to get to know Laurent, to talk to him. For him to be safe while I took the few days I had to figure out which path I wanted to commit to.

"We can discuss payment later. We need to get you somewhere safe first."

"So there is a price." He smiled faintly.

"We're not exactly all 'duty to the empire' out here. Your father and those before him saw to that."

Laurent nodded. "Alright then. As a show of good faith on that future discussion, I'd prefer you weren't implicated in whatever Ari and my mother were attempting to protect me from. Wherever you're hiding me, come with."

"I can't. I already sent a detailed report on Ari's death and have a witness and the murderer in custody."

Laurent winced.

"I need to remain here. If I run, they'll know you're nearby."

He raked his hands through his hair again and pointed to the stasis tube. "They'll already know I'm close."

"Not if I play this right."

"This isn't the time to play anything, Rita. That agent is going to dig deep and hard. You'll end up either tortured, in prison, or dead. You have to hide with me."

For a second, I thought he cared about my wellbeing, but then logic informed me that he was just desperate to keep a bodyguard at his side. I had a job to do, and I couldn't do it hiding on Anduvea.

"I need to talk to the agent to get answers so we know who to trust." On the inside I was shaking because I knew he was right, but on the outside, I shrugged. "Just doing my duty for the good of the empire, right? This one time, I mean. Not like I'm pledging to make a habit of it."

He shook his head. "Only if I live. Otherwise, no good is going to come from any of this."

"Well then, I better make sure you live." I stood and started for the bedroom. "I need to make a vid call."

I felt him watching me, but he didn't voice an order or protest, so I left him to his thoughts and focused on gathering my own.

After closing the door behind me, I sat down at the terminal and placed a call to my parents.

My father's face filled the vid. Then he sat back. Warm, welcoming oranges and browns of home surrounded him. The still frame of our family from when I was a teen hung on the wall just over his left shoulder. The window on the right was closed and shuttered against the smoke from the burning. I'd hoped for a glimpse of sunlight gleaming off the expanse of plascrete so I could pretend to feel its warmth, but thanks to the fires, I was stuck with memories.

A smile lit his face. The man in the still frame had high cheekbones, blonde hair, and a pointed chin. His hair was greying now, and his face had gone soft, the definition lost. The lack of sun left him pale, and the artificial lights in the house cast heavy shadows, making his eyes seem sunken.

"Rita! How are you?" His cheery tone belied his appearance. "Are you surviving the antics of the idiots up there?"

"I'm well enough for the moment. So many idiots, Dad, so many." I shook my head and chuckled. "Hey, I have to escort prisoners down to the surface today and thought I might stop in for a quick visit."

I really wanted to mention that I'd have Laurent with me, but I needed a clean record of this conversation for the empiric agent to explain my trip to the surface. If my father caught any hint of a crack in my demeanor, he didn't comment on it. Thank the Maker for that.

"Will Mom be around?"

"She's at the store, picking up food for the week. I wanted to go with, to get out of the house, but you know how she is with treating me like a baby during the burning."

"Dad, your lungs are scarred. You have to take care of yourself and stay inside. Do you need more breathing tanks? I can bring a couple down with me."

His deep cough answered my question. "You're out, aren't you. Dad, you've got to do your breathing treatments, especially during burning season."

Now that I had Ari's credits, I could afford to buy them a better air filtration unit for the house. However, that was going to have to wait until the agent had come and gone and all eyes were off me. A sudden spending spree would raise suspicion.

My father recovered from his coughing fit. He looked at the bottom of the vid instead of me. "If it wouldn't be too much trouble, a tank or two would be helpful."

Asking for help wasn't something he liked to do. Neither of them did. I inherited my independence from both sides.

"Not a problem, Dad. I'll see you soon, and I'll bring dinner."

I ended the call before he could argue about the free meal and went back out to check on Laurent. He was still sitting at the table.

"You're going to want to change. That blue suit is too memorable."

Laurent's cheeks colored. "I wouldn't mind some clothes if you have anything. I don't usually sit around wearing only my armor."

That explained the second skin look of the bodysuit. Of course, he would wear armor at all times. The Empaetor likely did too. And here I'd been sitting around chatting with the heir to the empire in his underclothes. I smothered a snicker with a rough cough.

"Ari had some extra clothes with him. I'll wash something for you and then we have to go."

I rifled through the armload of clothes I'd brought back from the *Asbodot* and selected a shirt and pants that would blend in on the surface. Getting him onto Anduvea without attracting attention was my next problem.

I tossed the shirt and pants into the laundry and set it for the quick cycle. Then I headed back to the terminal in the bedroom to call Yumi.

He answered, looking just as disgruntled as before. "What?"

"I'm going to accompany that prison transport down to the surface. My dad needs a delivery of breathing treatments. It's an emergency. Figured I'd make myself useful."

"What about the oh-so-important empiric guard duty?"

"Yumi, it's my dad. I'm just going to run down, unload the prisoners, stop in to check on my parents, and I'll be right back. I can pull the long-terms out of the cells with one of the new trainees. That way, you don't have to pull a couple decent officers off duty. Senio says they're almost full up already. I won't tell the agent I left if you won't."

Yumi grinned. I knew the idea of screwing over the empire would get me on his good side.

"My lips are sealed. Thanks for helping, Rita. I hope your dad is alright."

"Thanks, Yumi."

The call concluded, I dressed for work and set out an extra uniform for Laurent. He still hadn't moved from the table. It occurred to me that other than my bedroom or the bathroom, there wasn't really anywhere else for him to go. The tube, crate, and my maze of furniture clogged up the one comfortable seating area in my small suite. Thankfully, he wouldn't need to be here much longer.

"I'm going to need you to help me load up a transport full of criminals to bring down to the surface."

He regarded me with a blank stare.

"I set out a uniform for you. We're roughly the same size, and as you can see," I pulled out the shapeless fabric that hid what figure I had, "they're quite roomy. It should be a decent fit. You'll have to squeeze into my spare pair of boots. Ari didn't have extra shoes on him, and I can't give you his."

"Why a uniform?"

"You're going to act as one of my trainees for this run. It's the best way to get you to a safe place."

He crossed his arms over his chest and stared at his stocking-covered feet.

"Anduvea is safe? The people there hate the empire."

"Which makes it an unlikely place for Ari or you to go for help, doesn't it?"

He nodded uncertainly. "Exactly."

"Sorry, it's the best I can do. You can change in the bedroom. I'd offer you a shower, but I have a single person water allotment."

The blank stare returned.

"Limited water supply on a space station. Everyone has an allotment to allow for proper recycling and purification before reuse."

"And if I'm thirsty?"

"I have saved water rations in the cold storage. Help yourself." As the words left my mouth, it occurred to me that the heir had likely never had to help himself. He had servants to bring him whatever he needed.

I didn't mind being his guard for the time being, but I

was not a servant.

"Once we're finished delivering the prisoners to the surface lockup, I'll make sure you get a better meal. I'm going to get some food ordered to take with us. The extra clothes should be cleaned by then. Are there any foods I need to avoid? Allergies or anything?"

"I don't really know." His forehead wrinkled. "I don't know what you eat here."

"We all came from Harilax once. Tino likely has something that will be familiar to you."

"Beats being helpless in stasis."

I had a feeling that being oblivious to his predicament and safely in suspension was probably much better, given what he'd woken to find himself embroiled in, but I nodded.

While Laurent dressed, I used my datapad to order a supply of breathing tanks with my newfound credits. They'd be delivered shortly. Then I ordered a wide assortment of food from Tino. He could use some of Ari's credits too.

The laundry buzzer sounded. I folded the outfit from Ari and placed it at the bottom of a shoulder bag. There was plenty of room for the feast I'd ordered from Tino and the breathing tanks.

Laurent emerged from the bedroom. The uniform fit him well. Somehow, he didn't make it look as boxy as it did on me.

"Why is this fabric so stiff? It's scratchy." He shifted his shoulders and pulled at the cuffs.

"Never noticed. I've worn the same fabric for twenty years. I will admit they don't breathe well. Hopefully, your armor underneath won't make you too hot."

"My armor adjusts for temperature." He scratched his

neck under the collar and tugged on the cuffs again, the only two places his armor didn't cover.

"That's handy. The station climate controls remain the same all year, but during burning season, there are a lot more people than usual. All the bodies create hot zones when they cram into the social district or individual shops. The station infrastructure isn't exactly top of the line out here."

He looked at me like I'd lost my mind. "But this is the last station. It should provide a stunning first impression of what incoming visitors can expect from the rest of our space."

Anduvea as a showcase of the empire, I stifled a chuckle. He seemed quite serious. Did he really not understand how his father and the Empaetors before him ran things? Just how in-depth was this training he was supposed to have been undergoing?

"Should, maybe. Anduvea is an exile world. There's nothing stunning out here. Unless you like flames and smoke. We specialize in those."

Laurent scowled, his posture stiffening.

Dammit, I had to remember to watch my tone.

"If there were a way to disguise your face, you'd be better off. As it is, we're going to have to be careful to not set off any ID scanners before we get you on the transport. For your own safety, you'll need to keep your face down."

"I don't have an ID implant. That should help?"

So it hadn't been my datapad malfunctioning when I'd tried to scan him before.

"How? Everyone gets them at birth." I stopped myself and wished I could backtrack my stupidity. "Right. Royal family. Got it."

"My mother had one. Only my father and I do not."

"In this case, that is fortunate. I'm still going to ask that you keep your face down." Now that he was more animated, he was also more recognizable. "We'll stop by Tino's first to get the food. Then you'll need to come with me to load the prisoners onto the transport. After that, you should be safe."

"What if one of the prisoners recognizes me?"

"We'll need to bubble them for transport. They will be too busy bitching about that to pay any attention to you." I hoped that was true, anyway.

He used the few minutes before we left to cautiously approach the cold storage and open it, looking inside like he'd never seen such a thing before. Just as I was about to turn into my father and chide him for keeping the door open too long, he leaned in and came away with one of the water storage bottles in his hand. He opened it and drank deeply.

"Use the bathroom here if you need to. It will be hours before we'll have access to another one."

"Surely there's one on the transport," he said.

"Security officers are on duty in the transport, supervising the prisoners. Once the prisoners are secured on the surface, our duty will be completed and we can go about our business."

"How long is the trip to the surface?"

"A couple of hours, plus escorting the prisoners to the prison and transferring them and their files to lockup.

Laurent regarded the half-empty water bottle with regret. He wisely chose to use the bathroom before we left.

While he was in there, I wondered how much of a pain in the ass it was to remove his armor or if it had an easy-access flap. I was mid-pondering that, and chiding myself for even concerning myself with said possible flap, when the breathing tanks arrived. I answered the door and was loading them into the pack when Laurent emerged from the bathroom.

"All set?" I asked.

He nodded. "What will I need to do? Other than keep my face down? I've been around guards all my life, but I've never pretended to be one."

"All you have to do is not be offended. I'll explain all the procedures to my new trainee as we work. My coworkers tell me I'm brusque and hard to please."

"Sounds just like my father. I'll survive."

I chuckled. "Yes, well, I'm not him, and I'm not pretending to be. I'm just being me, as anyone would expect me to act around a trainee, for the sake of maintaining your cover. If you're angry about it, save it until after we've delivered the prisoners and we're alone."

"Understood," he said tightly.

I appreciated his willingness to go along with my plan and his acceptance of his role, but I couldn't shake the feeling that I was going to be berated once he didn't need me to get him to safety any longer.

12

Who Do You Think You Are?

When the staff lift arrived, three people exited, none of them paying us any attention as we got on. We were security. Unless there was a problem, everyone tended to ignore us.

"The social district will be busy. Don't make eye contact with anyone. Don't do anything to attract attention. Just follow me."

He drew his lips into a thin line and nodded. Laurent got distracted by the view of Anduvea from space. I tried to focus on the distant stars, taking deep breaths in and out and enjoying the calming, quiet hum surrounding us.

The lift doors opened on level eight. The noise level hit my ears like a hammer. I winced. Laurent's hands went to his ears.

I tapped his arm until he dropped his hands. "You'll get used to it."

A thumping beat penetrated my body as we walked past a club. I paused to yell at a teen who was walking on the second floor railing above us. Maybe I should have let the idiot keep walking and slip and fall, but that would mean filing reports for whoever was supposed to be watching this zone, and I was trying to be nice to my coworkers. Except when I spotted said coworker, one of the new ones just off trainee rotation, chatting with a woman old enough to be his mother. Her nipples were barely covered by her low-cut shirt.

With Laurent behind me, I marched over to them.

"Have they stopped manufacturing actual clothing on the surface?" I yelled to the woman.

She turned to me, her bright pink lips expressing disapproval of my snide comment. "Excuse me? Who do you think you are?"

"His superior officer. Do you have a security concern?"

"Well, no, I was just..." She waved her hand in the air.

This close, I could smell the alcohol on her breath.

Laurent's uniform rubbed against my arm, the crowd pressing him close. Or maybe he was sticking close because of the crowd. I ignored him. He was a trainee, and he would be shadowing me, not asking questions, not expecting explanations.

"Move along then. Oh, and have a nice day." I shut the woman out of the conversation and turned to the flushed young man. "You belong on that platform." I pointed to the post he'd deserted. "Your eyes should be on the crowd and that idiot kid over there with a death wish, not a pair of tits. Save that for your off-duty time. The lonely drunk ladies will be here for weeks. Just don't impregnate any of them. Your salary won't leave you with living wages after child fees."

"Yes, Officer Stabinov." He scrambled up the steps to his post and shouted at the kid on the railing.

"That's her second warning," I yelled up to him. "If the kid ignores you, bubble her."

"Yes, Officer Stabinov."

We continued on our way, weaving through the crowd. Laurent matched my steps until a man too busy ogling all the flashing lights slammed into him. I grabbed Laurent's arm to keep him from sprawling onto the sticky, filthy floor.

"Watch it," I yelled at the light-gazer.

He turned slowly, blinking even slower. "Huh?"

Who knew what this one was on. "Go find a seat somewhere before you hurt someone." I pointed him toward the nearest lounge that was only moderately occupied at the moment. Thankfully, everyone had at least some clothing on. I didn't want to have to explain spontaneous orgies to the heir of the empire. Except, hell, maybe that was normal at the palace. These morons all originated from people who frequented that place. They had to learn this behavior somewhere, didn't they?

Having the life of the Scaavo heir on my shoulders and Ari's dead body in my suite made me even less tolerant of their behavior. I shoved my way through the crowd, arriving at Tino's with Laurent on my heels.

"You make an excellent battering ram," he stated when we came to a stop.

"I'll add that to my resume." At least he wasn't chewing me out in front of everyone and breaking his cover. I plastered a smile on my face and attempted an apologetic tone. "Stick close. I'll get you out of here as quickly as possible."

Laurent nodded, watching everyone around us warily.

Tino, standing behind the counter, noticed me right away. He gestured for me to skip the winding line of customers waiting for a table.

"Don't you get sick of constantly training people?" he

asked, nodding absently toward Laurent.

"Yes, but it's better than trying to man all the security posts by myself."

He grinned, hefting a bag bulging with small boxes onto the counter. "You could do it, though. I wouldn't want to be near you, but you could do it."

"No thanks." I held up one of Ari's chips for Tino to scan.

"At least this one is a grown man. Why does that chief of yours keep hiring all those kids who are barely a day over legal working age?"

"The adults don't want a job, Tino. They want to spend their days here eating and sucking down drinks until the burning is over and they can go back to making lives miserable for the working-class on the surface."

"Their credits make me less miserable." He set his reader down and looked past me to Laurent.

I stepped in front of him to block the heir from further scrutiny.

"What possessed you to train for this job during the burning?" Tino asked Laurent over my shoulder.

"Family trouble. Needed a fresh start," he said, keeping his head down as instructed.

"Nothing fresh up here. Other than my food." Tino winked at me. "Delivering some of this tasty goodness to your parents, Rita?"

"Gotta spoil them a little. They're stuck down there in the smoke while I have all your good cooking and endless fresh air up here."

Tino laughed. "True. True. Have a good visit. And good luck to you. We'll see if you survive the rest of the week," he said to Laurent.

Not if he stayed on the station. We needed to get moving before anyone more observant than Tino got a good look at him.

13

Do Any Of You Even Read The Manual?

I loaded the food into the shoulder bag and handed it to Laurent.

"This should keep you busy."

He regarded the bag in my hand with confusion.

"Carry it."

Laurent took the bag and slowly slipped it over his shoulder, as I had been carrying it when it was much lighter.

Deep inside, I laughed to think the heir to the empire had likely never had to carry anything he hadn't wanted to. Though Laurent hadn't shown himself to be a terror like his father—so far, anyway—subtly disrespecting the empire was ingrained in my genes. Closer to the surface, I prayed that he played along and didn't have a royal snit.

We'd made it a few businesses down before two tastefully clothed women with their straight, stiff hair halfway down their backs glanced up from the rack of artistic still frames they were shuffling through. One of them locked her gaze onto my trainee. She smiled and elbowed her friend.

"Look at this one, Nedra. He has to be related. I mean,

look at that face."

Nedra slipped the still frame she'd been holding back into the stack. "Great Maker, you're right. Think he could get us an invitation to the palace?"

"I'd settle for an invitation to any other civilized world in the empire but this one." She pulled her friend's arm away from the rack and took a step toward us.

"Let's go. Get moving," I yelled at Laurent. "They always stick me with the fucking worthless trainees so I can whip you into shape. I said go!" I pointed him toward the staff lift we'd taken, hoping he remembered where it was.

He ducked his head low, gripped the strap of the bag across his chest, and hurried several steps ahead of me.

"Hey," one of the women yelled.

I ignored them and followed Laurent, who was making excellent time through the crowd toward the lift until he crossed paths with a knot of twenty-something youths who started yelling obscenities at him and making lewd gestures. They spread out to block his path and surround him. One shoved his unencumbered shoulder. Another grabbed for the pack. The seven youths taunted the heir to the empire, who did nothing to defend himself.

Whether he could or not, that was my job, even if we'd yet to negotiate payment. I drew my stunner in one hand and swiped a bubble tab off my belt with the other.

"What the hell do you assholes think you're doing? Impeding the path of a security officer is an automatic one-day incarceration." I slapped the bubble on the closest idiot.

His yelp of surprise was cut short as the bubble enveloped him. I snagged another one off my belt and held it ready.

"Trainee, do you remember the proper procedure for escorting a bubble?"

Laurent cast a disgruntled glance over his shoulder at me.

"Of course you don't. Do any of you even read the damned manual?" I shook my head. "Hands on the bubble. Now, trainee!"

The youths who had been around Laurent melted into the crowd, leaving their friend behind. The gaggle of tourists who had stopped to see what was going on still watched us intently.

Laurent glanced at me again.

"I said, push the damned bubble! Come on. Let's go." I gestured forcefully toward the staff lift.

Laurent gave the bubble a tentative push. It glided just ahead of him. The drama hounds lost interest and dissipated.

We made it to the staff lift without further incident. When it opened, two maintenance workers were already inside, one holding what looked to be a heavy bag of tools.

Whatever Laurent might want to say to me would have to wait.

"Hey Officer Stabinov," said one of the workers. "Busy day?" He nodded to the bubble taking up every extra inch of the lift space.

"Just like every other stinking day until the tourists go home. They keeping you busy too?"

He rolled his eyes. "Broken bed, two chairs, a door stopped working, three suites were too hot and one too cold, and the floors in the social district... Have you seen them? It's barely week two and I don't think they'll ever come clean again. We may have to resurface them.”

“And the day isn't even half over,” grumbled the other one.

“Job security?” I offered.

He gave me a pained smile. “Thank the Maker the burning isn't year-round.”

“Indeed.”

Laurent remained silent, having tucked himself into the corner behind the bubble. Thankfully there was only one bubble because we wouldn't have all fit otherwise.

The lift dinged, announcing our arrival. I let the maintenance workers leave first and then took control of the prisoner.

“Come on, this way,” I said, leading Laurent in the opposite direction.

We entered lockup, pushing the bubble before us. Laurent stuck to my side, the pack on his shoulder between his face and Senio, who sat at his desk.

“Rita, please tell me this one deserves it because we're running out of room.”

“This one had no respect for authority—was harassing my trainee. We can't have that. Be happy I only nabbed one to make an example of him instead of the whole gang.”

Senio sighed, opened a drawer on his desk and passed me another bubble tab. “Does he need another one? They always mess up the first one. Or did you actually read the instructions, newbie?”

“He didn't even think to use one.” I shook my head. “Someday I'll get a trainee who actually reads and comprehends the manual.”

“I don't think that trainee exists.” Senio chuckled, pointing at the cell map on his terminal.

"If it makes you any happier, I'm ready to pick up that load of prisoners to take to the surface."

"Thank the Maker," Senio said.

"Is our transport standing by?" That would be just my luck. I tried not to let my panic show.

"Like I'd trust anyone other than you, me, or Yumi with it? And no, the chief isn't out for a joyride. It's all yours as long as you don't let that trainee touch the controls."

"Hell no. I value my life, thank you very much."

"Good to know the tourists haven't pushed you over the edge yet, Stabby."

"Shut it in front of the trainee."

He laughed and sent the cell numbers of the list of deportees to my datapad.

"Come on, trainee."

We deposited the kid in a cell, and then Laurent followed me to the first prisoner on the list. I loudly explained how to deactivate the cell well, approach the prisoner, activate the bubble, and where to push them for staging. He remained silent, staring at his feet and gripping the pack strap with one hand while clenching the other into a fist. He was likely envisioning punching me in the face by the time Senio joined us.

"The transport is ready, and I activated the auto check for you. It should be ready to launch when you are." Senio handed me two lengths of plas chain. I passed those to Laurent.

"Don't drop these. They turn into instant knots. Don't ask how. That's just how the universe works."

At least if he was holding the chains, he couldn't hit me.

With Laurent's hands suitably encumbered, we headed off to the next cell.

It was an hour and a half later that we had twenty-three bubbled prisoners strung together with the two lengths of plas chain. I showed Laurent how to hold the lead end and pull it at just the right speed to keep them flowing evenly. We marched them to the public lift. It was the only one big enough to handle twelve bubbles at a time.

"Make sure you enter the docking ring. I can't ride with you. We won't all fit. I'll go first. If there's a problem between when my lift leaves and the next arrives, run, do not walk, back to Senio. We take care of our own."

"I'm not one of you," Laurent said tightly.

"You are as long as you're in that uniform. Use it."

He nodded, but his fingers white-knuckled the end of the chain, and his jaw looked tight as hell. I wondered if he'd ever been left on his own before. Did he crave independence? Was I smothering him? Or was he terrified of having no one at his back? I'd have to wait until we were safely on Anduvea and alone before I could ask.

14

Load Them Up.
Move Them Out.

When I arrived on the docking ring, I tugged the chain of prisoners toward me, uncoiling the contents of the lift until the bubbles floated in a clump beside me. Traffic was blessedly light, but the few people waiting for the lift gave me and my charges a wide berth, as if the space these dregs occupied was tainted.

After what seemed like far too long, Laurent arrived. Maybe I was nervous about someone recognizing him, or losing him, or... My lofty dreams of working at the palace had never included the heart-in-my throat panic of being solely responsible for the heir to the empire.

In his smooth, brown-skinned hand with neatly manicured nails, the chain looked ridiculous. I glanced at my own hand. It had never enjoyed expensive lotions or spa treatments but appeared perfectly at home guiding prisoners. Suddenly self-conscious of the state of my skin, I kept any of the normal ragging I'd give my trainee to myself and let him wrangle his bubbles out of the lift in peace.

The docking staff in the main area started to pay attention to us with our two long strings of prisoners.

"Let's go, trainee, they aren't going to load themselves," I said, attempting to regain my usual grumpy level of authority for the sake of keeping the docking crew away.

The security transport was ready and waiting, just as Senio said it would be. Outside of burning season, only trusted members of the security staff used it to visit our families on the surface.

I nodded toward the back two-thirds of the transport, which was an open space with a few anchor poles. "We'll put them in here."

After stashing the shoulder pack up by the cockpit door, I detached the chain from my twelve bubbles. Laurent did his best to stay out of my way while I anchored the prisoners on pole hooks. Once mine were secured, I detached his and started on those. He managed to get a third of them installed in the time it took me to do the rest.

"Good job." I said, double checking that everyone was secured.

Laurent scowled.

"That wasn't sarcasm. You're faster at picking that up than many of my trainees."

Everyone appeared to be ready for the trip.

"Let's get strapped in up front and moving. Tino uses quality packaging, but I don't want to push my luck. My dad likes his jari puffs crispy, not soggy."

"As he should. Soggy puffs are disgusting." Laurent settled into the seat next to me at the front of the transport.

Three others sat open. I'd only flown once with a full crew. We had become efficient enough to handle a full load of prisoners with two of us. That was usually all we could spare when we had a full staff during the burning. Off season, our staff was half the size, but we also had a lot fewer offenders. It all worked out.

He eyed the controls. "I hope you know how to pilot this thing?"

"Yes, but it's fully automated between the station and the surface port. We're here in case something goes wrong or the programming glitches."

He craned his neck to look at the surrounding blackness outside the viewport above us. "Let's hope that it doesn't."

"Should be a smooth ride," I assured him.

Laurent opened his mouth, but I shook my head.

"For everyone's safety, all activity on the prison transport is recorded. You might be inclined to relax away from the station, but we are required to maintain staff standards while on duty, no matter where we are."

"Got it." He sat back but watched me intently.

I checked the auto preflight and then contacted docking control for launch. Receiving the clearance in mere minutes, I waited for the clamp release by taking quick stock of the controls. It had been a few months since I'd flown the transport, and I always found a little comfort in assuring myself that I could take over if need be. The knowledge that the Scaavo heir was sitting next to me made the need for the assurance greater than usual.

"You should familiarize yourself with the controls. Just in case something happens to your superior officer during the flight."

Laurent cast me a worried glance. "You said it was automated."

"It is. Systems glitch. Especially out here on the edge of

the empire. It's better to be self-sufficient than to expect someone else to save you."

Now he looked really worried. I gave him a quick run-down of the basic controls. A shudder passed through the transport. Laurent's eyes went wide.

"That's the clamps readying for release." I switched the auto flight to on.

Four loud clicks later, we were pulling away from the station and watching the docking clamps retract. The transport engines engaged, filling the cockpit with a vibrating hum. Within minutes, we had come around, and Anduvea was in view far below us.

"It's so grey," he said.

"Smoke. It will look just like you're used to when we get down into the atmosphere."

It took him a drawn-out moment to catch on that he should know what the world looked like if he was from the surface. "Oh, right."

It was clear the heir to the empire was not used to having to lie about who he was. And why would he be? Hell, if I were the heir, I'd make sure everyone knew it too.

To pass the time and keep Laurent from either voicing his opinions on my management style or asking questions that would blow his cover, I gave him a rudimentary flight lesson. He asked intelligent questions and seemed to be taking in the answers rather than acting like the bored aristocrat I feared he might be.

"Not that you'll likely need to know any of that, but just in case. For the future," I said as we neared the landing zone on the surface. The ship shivered as the automated landing sequence took over, syncing with the ground systems.

"Good to know. Just in case." He sounded less worried than when we had left the station.

I eyed the cockpit camera before turning back to Laurent. "Do you think you can handle monitoring this while I prep the prisoners for departure?"

His gaze swept over the controls we'd been discussing, then to me and back again. "I suppose so?"

"If any of that starts blinking red or control has something to say beyond the chatter we've heard so far, let me know."

He nodded, looking more confident.

It took me half an hour to release and restring the prisoners back onto the two lengths of chain. It might have gone twice as fast if I'd had Laurent help me as I would have any other trainee, but my nerves were more at ease with him safe in the other room out of even the blurred view of the occupied bubbles. The two women in the social district had recognized him too fast. I didn't trust that bored prisoners, waiting while I chained the others in the room, wouldn't take the time to pin their squinty focus on the new guy.

With the last prisoner secured, I laid out the chain for easy transport and rejoined Laurent up front.

"What took so long?" he grumbled. "Control has been muttering about our delayed departure for ten minutes."

"Have they now?" I pushed the transmit button, interrupting the distant muttering. "Chuey, do we have a problem?"

"Officer Stabinov," Chuey's polite tone replaced the two male grumbling voices. "Not a problem, no. Not exactly." He cleared his throat loudly. "It's just that we were wondering how long you'll be on the surface today. We got word that we're to have company shortly and they need the space clear."

"What sort of company?" I hadn't received word of any inbound important station guests. No one stepped foot on Anduvea itself during the burning if they could help it.

"An agent sent by the Empaetor himself. Maybe we've done our time and can get back in his good graces? Be nice to have some empiric assistance with this burning nonsense, wouldn't it?"

I gasped, having forgotten how inhaling worked. "I'm sorry, did you say an agent would be here on the surface? Today?"

"That's the rumor. They want the landing zone clear when they come in."

"Can you give me a couple of hours? I need to get these prisoners into lockup and then make a quick delivery to my parents before heading back to the station."

"As long as you make it fast, I can cover for you. Seeing as it's official security business and all. From what I understand, he'll be focusing on Anduvea today and staying on his ship tonight. Then he'll be paying a visit to the station tomorrow. Would you like me to relay the agent's proposed schedule to Yumi, or do you want to take care of it?" Chuey said.

My heart raced wildly. So much for having a few days to get to know Laurent so I could decide how I wanted to play this. Any of this. Damn the Empaetor and his apparently nearby agent to hell.

"The agent will be meeting with me on the station. I'll take care of the notifications on our end. Thanks for the heads up."

"Did Yumi retire and you get a promotion? Thought I would get an invitation to that party, Rita. We've known each other long enough."

I couldn't tell if he was annoyed and meant it or if he was just giving me shit. We were on friendly terms due to my frequent trips to the surface over the years, but it was hard to tell from his voice alone. If the agent was on his way, I didn't have time to screw around with an in-person visit with Chuey.

"Yumi's still on duty. Just a special assignment on my end. Good luck with your visitor. I'll make this as quick as possible."

"Thanks Rita. Good luck to you, too."

"Thanks." I released my rigid, stabbing hold on the button and massaged my finger as I hurried over to Laurent. "We've got to move fast."

He nodded, eyeing the control console with wide eyes. "I thought you said..."

"No complaints, trainee," I snapped, hoping he remembered that the interior of the ship was under recorded observation. "Let's go." I waved him out into the bay filled with bubbles. "Grab a chain and follow me."

Laurent did as I ordered, but looked none too happy about it. The moment we stepped out into the hazy air, he coughed. "What is that smell?"

"Smoke. The burning, remember? Did you get spoiled with the clean station air?"

"It's disgusting." He coughed again.

"Sure is." I wished his father was filling his lungs full of it rather than Laurent. Maybe he'd take pity on us and do something about it.

We floated the prisoners out of the transport and across the landing field. By the time we'd passed through the port doors, and I'd gotten all our prisoners logged into the surface registry, the heir to the empire looked ready to explode.

"We'll be on our way shortly. Then you can have a break," I said in as mollifying of a tone as I could get away with while in the company of port workers who knew my surly reputation.

He glared at me but did nod. Maybe having limited time to interact with him once we were done here was a blessing. I was regretting my plan to leave him with my parents though. They didn't deserve to suffer whatever temper tantrum he was about to throw.

"You're cleared to transfer the prisoners," one of the port staff informed me after consulting the datapad in his hands.

"Thank you." I gave a tug on my chain to get the bubbles moving. "We'll go single file down the corridor." I instructed my trainee.

We made it through the port and out the rear entrance in record time. The perspiration under my uniform suggested I was moving faster than usual. The day an impending temper fit outweighed the importance of a multi-prisoner transfer was not one I'd ever imagined finding myself living, yet here we were.

"Are we—"

"No," I said firmly. "Half an hour and then you'll have some free time."

He glanced around the empty back lot where we stood surrounded by bubbled prisoners. What sounded like the start of my name came out of his mouth. I shot him a look that had sent younger trainees straight to tears. Laurent swallowed any additional syllables.

"Half an hour," I reiterated by way of apology.

My pace to the prison was even faster than our march through the port. The normally ten-minute walk was over in six. The gate attendant waved us through. As soon as we entered the processing room, the intake clerk already had his datapad in hand. He set about scanning prisoner ID chips.

I unclipped bubbles from my chain as guards came to claim them. Once mine was done, I handed the empty chain to Laurent. "Coil this. I'll get these unclipped and then we can be on our way."

He pressed his lips into a tight line that matched the tension in his jaw.

Once we had nothing but two coiled chains and the shoulder bag left to deal with, I high-tailed it out of the prison with Laurent hot on my heels. One of the automated, bullet-shaped public transports pulled up to the curb. The elites had their own, but I'd been using these all my life.

A woman with a small child exited, leaving the door open for us. I slid onto one of the two padded bench seats, motioning for Laurent to take the other. He sat and took in the worn, faded green interior as though he'd never seen such a thing. Six people could squeeze in, but four fit comfortably. I shut the door to keep it at two and then entered my parent's address.

Before he could talk, I said, "Your break consists of standing outside my parents' house while I drop off supplies. Then we'll head back to the station. I don't want to hear any complaints about breathing smoke. You'll get no sympathy from me." I shook my head. "Until then, you'll be silent so I have time to think."

Whatever he'd been about to throw at me was now lodged behind a glare that promised a verbal lashing of epic proportions.

The ten-minute ride did not give me enough time to reach any conclusions about whether I wanted Laurent to be the next Empaetor. And if I did, how would I help make that happen? More immediately, I didn't know what I was going to say to the agent who would be on the station tomorrow. By the time we arrived in front of my parent's house, my thoughts were reduced to a stream of fucks.

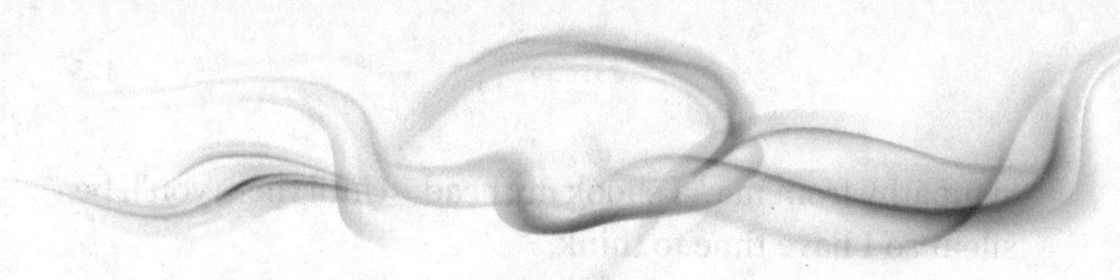

15

A Dinner Knife Can Be Deadly

"This is where you grew up?" Laurent asked as we exited the transport with the chains and pack in hand.

I blinked, trying to decipher his question through the panic swirling in my brain. "What?"

He waved his free hand at the single-story rectangle of plascrete sporting three small grime-covered windows and a utilitarian door.

"Not exactly a palace, but it's home."

The sky was an ominous dark grey, and the stench of a nearby firestorm made my nose twitch. I missed the clean air of the station already.

Laurent leaned in close. "Is it safe here?"

"Yes, we're on private property. No more possible vid bot coverage, other people, or public transport logs to worry about." I braced myself.

Like a switch had been flipped, he exploded. "You will never speak to me like that again! And placing me in the midst of criminals? Have you lost your mind? No wonder you serve as a guard out here." He jabbed his hand skyward.

"And your grand plan is to leave me with your parents on this Maker-forsaken, smoke-filled cesspit of a world?" His voice grew louder with every word. "What training do they have? Do they even own a weapon beyond a dinner knife?"

"I'll have you know a dinner knife can be deadly in the right hands," I snipped.

Laurent stood a single step away, yelling to the point he was near sputtering with rage. He looked every bit like the Empaetor in the newsfeeds when he was about to inflict his version of justice.

"Their hands, Rita. We're talking about your parents. Look at this place. Clearly, you do not come from a distinguished line of guards. You may be all I have, but this is unacceptable. I cannot stay here!"

Hot wind blew across the plascrete expanse. Sweat built up under my uniform, encompassing me in a sauna of discomfort beyond what Laurent was already inflicting. Caution said I should let him vent, apologize profusely, and pray that he didn't contact his father at the first opportunity to blast me, my family, or all of Anduvea out of existence. But this was my home. I was helping him out and putting my parents in danger for him. Like hell was I going to stand mutely and take this.

"No one knows you're here. As long as you keep your voice down, you can keep it that way," I yelled back at him. "We wouldn't be on this cesspit of a planet had your grandfather not exiled us here. And you wouldn't be here if your father hadn't done whatever the fuck spooked Ari and your mother."

Laurent opened his mouth to retaliate, but instead, inhaled a big gulp of smoky air and started coughing.

"If not for the Empaetors before you, we'd both be living happily on Harilax. You going about your life of privilege, and me serving one of those rich assholes just like my grandparents did," I repeated his jab at the sky motion. "The two of us should never have met. But no, Ari threw you into my life. You don't want to be here. I get it, but how about you keep your fucking voice down, be grateful, and maybe help me figure out this mess?"

"How dare you?" he rasped as he drove a finger toward my chest, his rage-filled gaze clearly wishing it was something sharper. "I could have you and your entire world—"

The door opened to reveal my parents. Laurent froze just as his finger met my uniform over my heart.

I forced a smile and knocked his finger away. "Mom, Dad, this is Laurent, the heir to the Scaavo Empire. Laurent, my parents."

Their mouths hung open, gazes darting between Laurent and me.

"I need him to stay here for a couple of days. Would you mind lending him my room? I've brought dinner and a few extra meals to help with the expense of another mouth to feed." I added, hoping Laurent got the hint that he was imposing and maybe behave like a decent person.

The heir straightened himself, hand dropping to his side. His fists melted away. "Hello. Nice to meet you."

"You're..." my mother attempted to speak coherently.

"Mom, no one can know he's here. Can we please go inside?"

My parents nodded mutely and stepped aside. I waved Laurent in before me and closed the door behind us.

"Rita?" my father finally uttered in a much higher than

normal pitch as he discretely motioned to Laurent with a frantic glance.

"It's a long story. Laurent can explain if he desires." I brought the food-laden bag over to the wooden table marred with three generations of use. "Dinner is on me. These for you." I handed the breathing tanks to my father. "I can bring more as needed. Please let me know when you need them and don't cut your therapy short." I aimed that at my mother, who was more likely to let me know if he was running low. Ari's credits would take the pressure off the expense, but I couldn't mention that windfall with Laurent present or until after I was hopefully in the clear with the empiric agent.

"I'd love to stay and visit, but I need to get the transport off the landing zone to make way for an important visitor. One that Laurent is evading, and I'll be meeting with tomorrow."

"Rita, what is going on?" my mother asked.

"Are you in trouble?" my father added to the worry-fest.

"You're sure you want to take that meeting?" Laurent asked.

After everything he'd just thrown at me on the doorstep, now he acted concerned? I didn't appreciate his doubtful tone or the fact that both of my parents now looked even more out of sorts.

"I'll take care of it," I said with as much confidence as I could muster. "I won't be able to swing a valid reason for a visit until next week. We'll have another batch of prisoners by then, because blessed Maker, the tourists this year..." I blew my exasperation out in a noisy huff. "Until then, please get along and stay safe. Laurent, you will stay inside and not use any outside communication. Mom, Dad, if you need me, call, but do not, in any way, mention your visitor. Is that clear?" I drilled the importance of that order in with a hard stare.

"But what if—" Laurent started.

"No ifs."

There were so many ifs. I kept my anxiety to myself, but inside I was praying his being here wouldn't blow back on my parents. The agent possibly coming down on me was one thing, but they hadn't asked for any of this aggravation. I'd thrust it upon them just like Ari had foisted Laurent on me.

As long as I could adequately answer the agent's questions, reap any reward, and get him on his way, we'd all be fine. I could do this. I *had* to do this.

"You're here until I can figure out our next steps. It's not what you're used to. We all understand that. Maybe use this time to consider how you'd like to do things differently than your predecessors, and perhaps how you could improve your popularity rating in the near future."

My parent's mouths gaped again.

Laurent snorted and shook his head. "She's a subtle one. Good job on the upbringing."

They became impossibly more mortified.

I glared at Laurent. "We can continue with your tirade when I return. Until then, please attempt to be kind? They didn't ask for this either."

He let out a huff that rivaled my earlier one. "I will."

"Thank you."

I hugged my parents, whispering apologies in their ears as I did so. After an awkward nod to Laurant, I slipped into the waiting public transport and escaped back to the port to board my ship.

Chuey thanked me for my hasty departure and sent me on my way with a highly abbreviated version of our usual departure procedure. I wasn't the only one on edge about our impending visit with the empiric agent.

16

Innocent Idiot

I'd been pacing in my suite, going over what to tell the empiric agent, when the ping finally came that he had docked on the station. One more walk-through assured me that I had Laurent's fingerprints cleaned off everything in sight and any sign of another person in my home eradicated. After straightening my uniform and taking a deep breath, I headed to the lift.

The mostly sleepless night hadn't done my wits any favors. I'd tossed and turned, wondering how my parents were doing with the Maker-forsaken heir to the empire in their house. I felt terrible for springing Laurent on them and dragging them into a potentially messy situation with the empiric agent.

Was Laurent behaving or devolving into the aristocratic monster his father was? He'd been tolerable since waking from stasis, but the glimpse into his true feelings on my parents' doorstep still rang in my ears. Now he'd had even more time to consider his situation.

The ride up to the docking ring was far less relaxing than usual given everything tossing around in my head. I'd never related so fully to the burning world below as I did just then.

I was mostly sure I'd managed to deliver Laurent incognito, but blessed Maker, what if I hadn't? If something happened to them because of this, I'd never forgive myself. And if something happened to Laurent, the empire wouldn't forgive me.

Getting the agent taken care of was the first priority. Once he was off my back, I could call my parents and check in and deal with whatever that situation had morphed into.

When the lift came to a stop, I wiped my sweating hands on the rough fabric covering my legs, took a deep breath, and walked out into the late morning chaos of the docking ring.

The influx of tourists was finally slacking, but the more spoiled were up here to accept resupply shipments of fresh wardrobe choices, private stocks of liquor or drugs, and whatever else their rich asses felt they needed to compete for superiority amongst their spoiled peers.

My foot sank into a squishy pile. More geppa already? "Get this shit cleaned up!" I yelled to the docking staff. At least this geppa shipment must have been under control, because I didn't see any stray beasts creating chaos.

I was mid scraping my boot on the floor when a stern-faced, lanky man in a dark blue uniform approached me. "Officer Stabinov?"

"Yes." I gave up on my boot and hoped I didn't track geppa dung all the way back to my suite.

"Agent Andover," he announced.

"Welcome, Agent Andover. Can I get you a tour? A meal, perhaps lodging? Or would you prefer to get right to examining the evidence I've been holding for you?"

He scowled at the mess by my feet. "Let's get right to the evidence, shall we?"

"Of course. Please follow me." I stepped as lightly as possible on my shit boot and led the way back to the staff lift. It was blessedly empty and waiting.

"Security Advisor Tekka was fortunate that I was nearby, following a lead on a sighting of Ari Leeman. I understand you have his body?"

So fortunate. I wondered if Andover would have caught up to Ari here or if Ari would have been able to smuggle Laurent out of the empire's reach had he not met his end at Da'Adio hands.

"I do. It's in a preservation bag."

Seeing that Andover wasn't the least bit interested in the view of Anduvea from space, I used the rest of the lift ride to reiterate that I also witnessed his death firsthand and had his killer in custody. No doubt he'd read my report, but I felt the need to fill the time with something other than tense silence.

He didn't tell me to shut up, so I took that as a favorable sign. The rest of the lift ride did pass in silence. I considered various ways to break into a conversation, to feel this agent out for any possible goodwill. Did you enjoy the burning? How was the level of smoke during your visit? What sights did you attempt to take in only to find everything closed beyond the self-contained towers where the elite live? How about that port staff? None of my options would lead anywhere positive. By the time we stopped and he followed me toward my suite, still not speaking, all thought of favorable anything had vacated my mind.

At my door, he finally said, "SA Tekka sent me your report. It was pleasantly thorough."

A compliment. That was progress in the right direction. Maybe he was just naturally brusque like me.

"Thank you. Did you have any further questions I might be able to answer?" I asked, gesturing him inside. "Sorry for the confined space. We don't typically use suites for storage in this capacity."

He shrugged. "Better to have these contents guarded than under scrutiny by the entire station or security staff."

Andover wasn't smiling, but neither was he scowling. I took a moment to remove my boots, setting the soiled one upside down for future cleaning. "The ship Ari Leeman had been traveling on had this in storage." I pointed to the large case.

"And this was inside?" He nodded to the empty stasis tube. "SA Tekka's transcript of your conversation with him specified that you were to hold any evidence. Not touching it was implied."

I took a calming breath, regulating my pulse. "Admittedly, we have little love for the empire out here, exiled as we are. I needed to see what Ari had stolen, whether it was a weapon that would be better kept out of the Empaetor's hands."

"And this wasn't the weapon you were expecting?" He cast me a wary side-eye.

"No. I don't know what Ari Leeman was doing with an empty stasis tube. Throwing his life and career away to help a terminally ill relative?"

Agent Andover stared through me much like SA Tekka had, digging into my visual soul. Keeping my breathing even, I met his gaze.

"I'll need to examine this."

I gave him what space I could by taking my boot into the kitchen to clean it. By the time I had scrubbed the filth off and set my boot to dry, he slid his hand-held scanner back into the pocket inside his uniform coat.

Agent Andover's gaze drilled into me again. "Were you aware that there had been a body in the stasis tube?"

"Recently or at one time?" As the words came out of my mouth, I kept my gaze steady, rather than where my memory wanted to be, replaying watching the heir to the empire wake in my lowly suite.

"Recently."

As much as I wanted to just blink vacantly, if I ever hoped for a promotion to somewhere outside of Anduvea, having 'innocent idiot' tied to my name on a report wouldn't work in my favor.

"Did Ari Leeman smuggle someone out of the palace?"

Now Agent Andover played the biding time staring game.

"Has anyone been reported missing?" I asked.

"Yes," he said reluctantly. "Someone important. Did Leeman mention anything about a travel partner?"

"No." And that was no lie.

"The crew of the ship they'd been on, that you interviewed, none of them mentioned Leeman spending time with another person?"

"They did not. According to the manifest, Ari boarded alone. He had a single rack accommodation. Nothing I observed led me to believe he was traveling with anyone else."

Agent Andover nodded, glaring at the empty stasis tube. "That is unfortunate. You said he was speaking to someone about booking further passage?"

"The men who killed him, yes. Members of an organized family enterprise with legal and not so legal arms. They obey enough rules and pay the proper fees that we allow the Da'Adio family on the station. That is to say, murder is not a common practice here."

"I would hope not."

"If you're ready, I can take you to the Da'Adio brothers."

"I'll find my way. Please remain here. I'll be back." He pulled a datapad from another pocket. I glimpsed what appeared to be a map of the station.

"Level six. Off the lift to your left. Officer Senio should be on duty to assist you there."

"Thank you. You've been helpful so far, Officer Stabinov. I hope you remain so."

Unsure how to reply, I stepped aside. Even after the door had sealed behind him, I stayed locked in place, not daring to let out the sigh of relief begging to escape. It was minutes later before I finally gave in.

I used my datapad to ping Senio with a warning of agent Andover's arrival. There was little else to do but pace until he returned. It could be within the hour or he could take in a meal or the sights or the Maker knew what else. There were plenty of options for a man wanting a little relaxation away from the watchful eyes of any superiors. It's not like any of us had the authority to report him.

A message notification snapped me out of replaying our conversation for the fourth time. Had he bought my story? I was going to need a strong drink or three when Andover left. My heart thudded heavily. Assuming he didn't drag me back to report to SA Tekka in person. Great Maker, what would Laurent do on Anduvea, stuck in my parent's house for weeks? The notification beeped again.

I activated the datapad to find a message from my parents. Already. My teeth ground together. Please let them have kept this message clean.

Rita,

Thanks for dinner. Tell your friend Tino we enjoyed his food. We appreciate the breathing tanks too. We're hoping you can visit again soon, and maybe stay a little longer to help with some troublesome things around the house that we have little experience with. Let us know if we should send a list so you can look up any answers or instructions before your next trip.

Hope to see you soon,
Mom and Dad

Well fuck, that call for help took even less time than I'd feared. If Laurent thought he could be an ass to my parents in my absence, heir or not, I'd let him have it for real.

17

Everything Is Just Fine

Agent Andover arrived back at my door four hours later. His scowl didn't bode well for me.

"That was a waste of time. And the food here? Atrocious." He strode in and planted himself in one of my kitchen chairs without invitation.

"I could recommend some of the better food establishments if you plan on another meal here."

He waved my offer aside with a stiff gesture. "I'd rather starve. That Tino's Place was a nightmare."

If Agent Andover thought Tino's food was that bad... Was Laurent also pitching a fit over what I'd supplied for him? I prayed that was all he was complaining about.

"Sorry about that. The Da'Adio brothers had nothing helpful to offer, I take it?"

Andover pointed to the giant case. "Ari Leeman was trying to move that outside the empire. He'd have no reason to move an empty stasis tube outside our space. That would only make sense if it was still occupied. But it isn't, and he was killed trying to make that deal, so he wasn't the one to free the occupant."

Fuck. I kept my hands still and relaxed at my sides as I joined him at the table. "So, either the stasis tube is hiding something that he still wanted to move, he was sending it off as a decoy, or he had a backup plan in place with someone on that ship who then released the occupant."

It certainly wasn't me. No, sir. Wouldn't even dream of it.

"I'll need a copy of the full manifest of that ship." Grumbling, he rubbed his hands over his face. "Which means I'll need to hunt them down and do a full sweep of their ship and its occupants."

"You might want to leave immediately so they can't dock somewhere else to drop whoever might have been in the stasis tube." I pulled out my datapad. "I can get you their flight plan."

"That would be helpful, Officer Stabinov."

Feeling his heavy gaze on me, I glanced up from transferring the information to his ship.

"I'll send one of my agents after them while I examine this stasis tube further and continue my investigation here."

"Great," I said, pushing the word out through my tightening throat. "What can I do to assist you?"

He smiled, an enviously terrifying curve of his lips that chilled my insides. "You can sit right there until my interrogator joins us. She's excellent at reading people, almost like she can see right into their minds."

I nodded, escaping my acknowledgment of his gaze by forcing my attention back to my datapad like I had nothing to worry about. My fingers went about their business, confirming the data transfer and then pulling up the security reports filed by the previous shift to review. A task I would normally be doing if I weren't sitting across from a fucking agent about to bust me for freeing the Maker-forsaken heir to the damned empire.

No sir, everything was just fine.

Twenty-five minutes later, my door chime sounded. My mouth went dry. Andover stood and answered it as though he were the one who lived here. When he came back into view, followed by a second set of footsteps, I forced an easy smile. I was friendly, helpful, and eager to assist. Yep. Sure thing.

A petite middle-aged woman with a bald head covered in colorful tattoos entered my kitchen and stood beside Agent Andover. She wore a uniform like his, minus the bling. Her yellow-green eyes landed on me, head tilting slightly as she spoke in a language I didn't understand.

"You'll have to use the translator function on your datapad, Officer Stabinov. Pitari's Empiric is quite spotty yet. She recently came to us on a cultural exchange program from a distant star system. Her skills are invaluable. I'm inclined not to let her go when her term is up."

If Pitari understood that threat, she showed no outward sign. Andover was just another highborn ass who thought he could control everyone, just like all the Anduvean snobs. Which checked out, since they all originated from Harilax. I'd have to find some way to warn the woman before she found herself chained to his side permanently.

"What skills would those be, if I may ask?"

"She can see inside thoughts," he said smugly.

"That's amazing." I shoved forward any recent memory of idiot tourist behavior and squashed the thought of anyone who may have been in my suite recently. Nope, no one at all. All lonely, bitter thoughts here.

Pitari smiled, revealing tiny white teeth. Maybe they weren't tiny, as they fit the size of her little head, but wow, she had great teeth. How did she get them so white? And her uniform looked very comfortable, much better fabric and construction than what the station offered.

Datapad, yes, that's what I was doing. Not thinking of every inane detail I could observe. Pulling my datapad from my pocket, I set up the auto translate function.

"Here, I'll send you the patch for her language. We've translated most of the words since her arrival. She has some sort of implant that allows her to understand us fairly well, though there have been some hiccups."

There always were with a new language. If Andover was still enamored with Pitari, and she was still willing to assist, the hiccups must have been minor. Once I had the patch installed, I activated the translator on my pad and greeted Pitari.

She returned the phrase, watching me with interest. "Are you ready to begin?" she asked.

I glanced at Agent Andover. "What will we be doing exactly?"

"You'll start with the docking ring crew. Anyone who was on duty after the *Asbodot* docked. Your job, Officer Stabinov, is to guide Pitari to those who need to be interrogated."

That sounded easy enough. "We have a lot of incoming traffic during the burning. Do you suspect anyone in particular was in the stasis tube?"

"We know exactly who, and my preliminary examination of the tube confirms it." Agent Andover held up a still frame of Laurent and handed it to Pitari.

"What an amazing resemblance to the Empaetor," I remarked.

"He has his mother's lips and nose, but otherwise, the Scaavo line remained dominant."

"The heir?" I said with what I hoped was adequate awe.

"Yes, so you understand the need for speed and discretion."

"Certainly." I turned back to Pitari. "Shall we get started?"

As we headed for the door, I couldn't help but notice that Andover didn't follow us. Instead, he approached the stasis tube like a puzzle he was determined to solve with all due haste.

"I'll be here. I hope you don't mind if I make myself at home, Officer Stabinov?" he asked over his shoulder.

"Not at all. Please do." Just don't go snooping around. Don't. Go Snooping. I filled my head with specific personal items I didn't want anyone to discover in case Pitari was doing her job.

"Pitari, contact me if you discover anything. Anything at all."

"I will," she said in shaky Empiric.

I was nervous because I'd just learned the heir to the empire was missing. Yes, that's why my stomach was in knots and my palms were sweating. Terrible news. Absolutely terrible.

18

Good Little Citizen

Pitari and I had talked to the entire docking ring crew and the warehousing grunts. No one had seen Laurent's face. No one called him Laurent either. He was simply the 'Scaavo heir'.

While the mind reader was busy with the first of the security crew, I wondered, did it bother Laurent that no one used his name? I considered the readiness he'd exhibited upon waking from stasis to be addressed by his first name. Was Ari the only one who had used it? After hearing him describe his family dynamics, I didn't imagine either of his parents did.

Yumi nudged his elbow into my ribs. "You really weren't making all this up, huh? Now you're getting all chummy with the empiric agent. How long until you're working for him?"

"He hasn't made any offers, if that's what you're asking," I whispered back.

Four other off-duty members of our team shuffled their feet and watched nervously as Pitari spoke with the young man I'd berated for ogling tits yesterday. I asked the questions; she listened to their answers. No one had mentioned any discomfort or had gone away with even a headache as far as I could tell. I'd also never witnessed subjects offering so much information, even if none of it had to do with the subject of our search.

I understood what agent Andover meant about not wanting to let Pitari return to her people. She was damned useful, even if only used as a scare tactic.

Was that all she was? In between interviews, she'd told me that among her people she was called a Seeker. As in a seeker of truth, among other things. But did that mean she was just good at reading people or could she really see thoughts? Was I on high alert for nothing?

The threat of someone knowing secrets seemed to be enough to prod many people to confess their sins rather than be called out on them. Or was she somehow manipulating them to do so with whatever mind powers she was wielding? Great Maker, I was psyching myself out. Pull it together, Rita.

We finished with the last of the four and then it was Yumi's turn. He'd been beside me for the four interviews and knew the drill by then, but I asked the same questions anyway.

"Have you seen this man on the station?" I held up the still frame of the Scaavo heir.

"I have not."

"Did you witness or overhear rumors of any dealings with the *Asbodot* crew?"

"Other than the standard docking clearance, no. Rita did their security and manifest check."

Pitari glanced at me. I let my thoughts wander to the

strange language of the crewman I'd met when examining the manifest. Whether she saw any of that or not, she returned her attention to Yumi.

"Have you seen any reports of deals with anyone related to the *Asbodot*?"

"Other than Ari Leeman, no. They unloaded their goods, got paid, and left. Pretty easy, in and out. No trouble. I wish more trade crews were like that."

"And the altercation that ended in the shooting death of Ari Leeman, do you have any additional information on that? Has anyone come forward saying they spoke with him or to ask questions about him?"

"No. Rita was there when Leeman died and had followed him off the *Asbodot*. The only other people who spoke to him were the Da'Adio boys and the couple others he attempted to approach before them. Rita's report didn't mention their names."

"Because I didn't know their names. He didn't get far with any of them. Whatever he was asking, they shut him down fast," I clarified for Pitari.

She turned to me and spoke. The translator kicked in. "Did Ari Leeman speak to you after he was shot?"

I focused on the memory of helping him down to the floor, of holding the towel to the ragged hole in his stomach. "He was begging to be saved, but I knew medical wouldn't make it there in time. His wounds were too severe. I made him as comfortable as I could and stayed with him until he'd passed."

Pitari nodded. "And what did he speak to his killers about?"

"I was across the room, not within hearing distance, but

from what I could tell, he wanted to move something out of the empire." I shrugged. "He was drugged, so I assume they'd planned to screw him over. He was shot before any deals were made, and they were taken into custody. I don't think anything was moved."

I didn't like the way she seemed to have forgotten about Yumi and was now focusing on me.

"You did not like Ari Leeman," she stated, holding me in her yellow-green gaze. "Thankfully the reward said dead or alive," she said, repeating the words I'd thought after he'd been shot.

My breath instantly went shallow, and my muscles locked into tight mode. This little freak was the real thing, not a mere scare tactic. Though I had to admit, the scare part was very effective.

"He was wanted for a crime against the Empaetor himself. There's nothing likeable about that," I said like a good little citizen.

"You don't like your Empaetor either."

Was she smiling just a little? Did she not like him either? Had they met? Or was it because she thought she was on to something? I had nothing to hide. Nothing at all. Just doing my job.

"We are exiled out here thanks to him and his predecessors. I can't say as I have much love for that, no."

The little mind reader nodded. Her smile faded away, leaving her looking tired. "How many more members of your security team are there?"

"Eleven," said Yumi. His gaze met mine, nice and steady. "Unless you have any trainees that aren't on the roster yet?"

Did he know? Was he offering me a chance to come

clean or was he egging me on to screw over the Empaetor? I thought about the members of our team, mind flashing to each of their faces, and shook my head. "Everyone is on the schedule who belongs there."

Yumi blinked twice before nodding. "There you have it then. I'll send these four out to relieve the rest of the on-duty crew and rotate them as needed until you're able to speak to everyone. I hope you find him." He inclined his head toward the still frame of Laurent in my hands. "I'd hate to see the chaos that would befall our great empire if the people were forced into a mad power war over who would be our next leader."

"Indeed," I said with conviction. "It wouldn't be in anyone's best interest to ignite that nightmare."

But maybe that's what we needed to get out of this leadership rut we'd been in for eight generations.

"See that you find him then, Rita. I'm putting you on leave until further notice so you can fully assist with the investigation," Yumi declared.

I thought I was already on leave, but I wasn't going to argue. "Thank you."

He excused himself and took the people we'd interviewed with him, leaving me with the mind reader. I had no intention of letting her roam around in my head. That meant keeping her distracted.

"How did you come to work with Agent Andover?"

With the help of the translator, Seeker Pitari spent the next half hour answering my questions about her homeworld, training, and the exchange program brought about by a council of worlds that her people were members of. I was getting a better understanding of what a Seeker was—a mix of priest and healer—when the next batch of interviewees arrived.

The little Seeker was looking decidedly weary by the time we finished with the security staff. I led her to the docking ring and then to where the *Knaldon*, Agent Andover's ship, was docked. I wondered why he didn't use her title, and if it bothered her that he didn't. She'd seemed proud of it when she'd told me about her long years of training. Maybe by not acknowledging what she was, he was able to put aside the fact that she could read his mind too.

"Thank you for your assistance, Officer Stabinov."

"Of course. One more question, if you don't mind?"

She nodded.

"Do you know why Ari Leeman stole the heir? I mean, was he in danger on Harilax or was there a danger to the Empaetor and his family? I didn't get the impression that Leeman had ill intent, but perhaps I'm not a great judge of character when it comes to people outside of Anduvea."

Pitari cocked her head, studying me in a way that made me seriously regret opening my mouth. "I cannot speak to what kind of man Ari Leeman was or what his motivations were. I never met him. Agent Andover is under direct orders from the Empaetor to retrieve the heir, or the *stolen treasure*, as far as the rest of the crew knows. If there were dangers to the heir or the Scaavo family, they were not shared with Agent Andover."

Well now, that was an interesting insight to share. I pondered the Seeker. She'd proven her abilities legitimate, but hadn't thrown me to Andover. The fact that she could see my thoughts was unnerving, but overall, she'd been friendly. I sort of liked her.

One corner of her lips tugged upward and she may have winked, or it may have been simply a blink and my scattered nerves seeking an ally.

"You seem to be an excellent judge of character, Officer Stabinov." She stepped back and turned toward Andover's ship. "I will report my findings to Agent Andover. I don't think we shall see each other again."

What the fuck did that mean? Maybe I was being paranoid, but having been around her for hours, my nerves were in tatters. The only defense I had left was to be polite and overlook her potentially ominous statement.

"Sleep well, Seeker Pitari."

"Thank you." She meandered up the ramp and out of sight.

If only I could fall into my bed and sleep. It was more likely I'd lie awake, hyper-analyzing her every expression and everything I'd said and thought all day.

Then I remembered that I likely had Agent Andover waiting for me back at my suite along with whatever his thorough examination had uncovered. Sleep or not sleep would have to wait. With a sigh, I trudged to the lift and back down to level one.

19

Hide The Chips

When I walked into my suite, I found Agent Andover hunched over his datapad, his spine near curved into a half circle. He rubbed his eyes and blinked up at me.

"Any luck with the interviews?" he asked.

"Nothing on the Scaavo heir, but we uncovered some other issues and guilty parties."

He sat back, stretching and rolling his head from shoulder to shoulder. "Pitari has a way of bringing out the truth in people."

"It would seem so." I sat across from him, wondering how fast I could get him out of my suite so I could call my parents to find out what was going on with Laurent.

"Tell me, Officer Stabinov, why didn't you take Ari Leeman into custody when he initially left the *Asbodot*?"

Blaming his death on me? I was doing that already. I didn't need his guilt added to the mix.

"As I said in my report, sir. I was hoping to get further information to recover the stolen treasure. If he worked for the Empaetor, he wasn't going to spill anything during an interrogation. I was trying to help. He wasn't supposed to get shot. Projectile weapons aren't allowed on the station."

"Yet, there was one, and the man I need to talk to is dead."

Yeah, thanks. I hadn't put that together yet, asshole.

Agent Andover let out an irritated huff. "Tell me again why you opened the stasis tube, contaminating my evidence?"

"I was curious." That was the truth.

"About what exactly, given that you were told only to hold any evidence linked to Ari Leeman?"

"SA Tekka also said you wouldn't be here for nearly a week. If there was a clue about what Leeman had stolen in the case or in the stasis tube, I thought I could save you some time by finding it."

He reverted to the drilling gaze. "And what clue did you find?"

"Nothing. It was empty."

Agent Andover worked himself to his feet, his joints creaking as he did so. "I don't believe you."

Could I rush the older man, knock him down, and flee? Yes, but where would I go and to what end? Better to talk my way out of his suspicions.

"Since Leeman was dead, I was hoping to find something else that would allow me to recover the stolen treasure so I could maybe earn a promotion off this damned station. I'm at a dead end here."

"That, I believe." He stood up straight and crossed his long arms over his chest, looking much more like the imposing man he'd been when he first arrived at my door. "Pitari and I agree that you're hiding something. So, if you are being honest about wanting a job outside of this station, which I can offer you, you'll tell me what you're omitting from your story."

As much as I despised the empire and its leadership, Laurent was on the run from them too. Both his mother and his best friend had died to keep him away from the people this man worked for. I might not know the Scaavo heir or whether his rule would be better than his father's, but if keeping him out of Andover's hands pissed the Empaetor off, that made me happy.

Time to make a stand for better or worse.

"I can't do that."

"You realize you're throwing away any prayer of ever working anywhere other than this shithole of a station?"

"I do."

He reached down to tap his datapad. The suite door slid open. Three men in empiric uniforms marched in.

Torn between appreciating that he felt I was enough of a threat to need three escorts and mourning the death of my career, I didn't stop to consider what he might have in mind beyond that moment.

Agent Andover addressed his men. "Escort Officer Stabinov to the station's prisoner holding. Do it our way." He pulled out one of the sneering head to toe once-overs that rich Anduveans loved to use. "We haven't used bubbles on Harilax for seventy-five years. Our criminals face their crimes in clear view of their peers. Enjoy your walk."

Fucking Andover. It wasn't enough to ruin my future prospects? He wanted to shame me in front of my own people too? My reputation would be forever marred.

For a split second, I considered giving Laurent up. I needed my job even after Ari's unwilling gift of wealth. The credits I regularly sent allowed my parents to live safely on the surface. Even worse, now that I'd had the brilliant idea to hide the heir in their house, their lives were just as much at stake as his. I doubted Andover would be ambivalent toward them if I were to tell him where to find Laurent.

Laurent. He'd been a real person with emotions when he'd been in my suite, not a wrath-filled monster like his father. He was angry about how I'd spoken to him, but that was understandable given who he was. What I didn't understand was the threat that had landed him in my hands. Two people who cared about the heir had already died to protect him. That wasn't a threat I could easily dismiss, no matter that I didn't like the empire or the Empaetor.

Besides, what would my parents think of me if I handed him over? My mother had spent a good deal of my childhood harping on me to do the right thing in the eyes of the Maker. Keeping Laurent safe until we had answers was the right thing. If that took some sacrifice, so be it.

I stood up straight and kept my face impassive.

"Enjoy your stroll, Officer Stabinov. I understand you've been put on leave so you can join our investigation. How handy, now that it's you who we'll be investigating." He smiled. "We'll give you the evening to enjoy the hospitality that you've offered so many of your station visitors. I'm sure they'll be happy to see you joining them."

Oh, I'm sure they would. I did a quick calculation of who might be on duty for cell assignments. Senio's shift was surely long over. The current batch of trainees hated me. The rest of my team could go one way or the other. Some understood me. Others considered me a bitch, second only to Yumi, the chief bastard. A fine pair we made. Good for keeping people in line, not so useful when I needed a friendly face and some sympathy.

"Pitari will visit you in the morning, and this time, I'll be asking the questions."

"Great. See you then. Have a good night. Could you lock up on your way out?" I started for the door.

"I hadn't planned on leaving. A hold has been placed on your assets until I'm satisfied that you're being truthful."

"Wonderful." It wasn't the least bit wonderful. Could he trace Ari's credit chips if he found them? I hadn't anticipated losing access to my suite when I'd slid them under my intimate toys in my undergarment drawer.

He signaled one of the uniformed men. "I'll need whatever devices you might locate upon doing a search."

Before I could gather my thoughts long enough to come up with a snarky reply, two pairs of hands started a thorough pat down. One gave my datapad to the third man.

If he examined that, he'd uncover the instructions for opening the stasis tube. I'd considered erasing them from the pad, but Andover likely had the same if not far better methods of recovering hidden and deleted data than I did. Finding incriminating deleted data was far worse than leaving it out in the open. At least I'd have the night to get my wits about me and come up with a host of reasonable answers for whatever Agent Andover planned to throw at me in front of his little mind reader.

When his men had finished their pat down, I asked if I could change out of my uniform. That would make me a little less conspicuous to the tourist population. Most of the permanent residents knew my face. There would be no hiding from them.

Agent Andover appeared to be considering the same thing. "I suppose we can allow that. You have five minutes. Your terminal is locked down. Don't bother wasting time attempting to make any calls."

He'd already been through my bedroom? An uncomfortable shudder shimmied up my spine at the thought of his hands on my personal things.

I escaped my escort to slip into my bedroom and quickly strip out of my uniform and into a comfortable and nondescript shirt and pants. Using the two minutes I had left, I grabbed one of Ari's credit chips and tucked it into my sock before sliding on my boots. It was thin enough not to leave any significant outline, and if I was lucky, a trainee would do my intake body search. Their minimal effort would assure my success in keeping at least one stash of credits out of Andover's hands.

Feeling slightly victorious, I left the safety of my room to return to the care of my keepers. We left my suite without further interruption.

To my dismay, we took a long walk through the staff corridors during shift change before boarding a public lift. By that time, many of the staff members had seen me, including Brenna, the bubbly bitch across the hall. Give her half an hour and every soul on the station would know I'd been taken into custody.

We then stopped on every damned floor between one and six to pick up and drop off other passengers. No one spoke to me, but many recognized me and, from the smirks and whispers, sympathy was not on their minds.

When we finally marched into the security office, my teeth were aching from clenching my jaw, and my neck muscles were wound so tight that I had a hell of a headache blooming behind my eyes.

One of the just-out-of-trainee security officers sat at the desk, outright grinning with no doubt some cocky-ass comment on the tip of her tongue that never made it out of her mouth thanks to the door sliding open behind us.

There were only a select few people on the station who could instill that button-lipped silence. I prayed Agent Andover hadn't followed me down here to inflict a little more humiliation. My second terrifying thought was that he'd roused Seeker Pitari from her sleep to interrogate me while my defenses were in tatters.

"I'll do the intake myself. Wouldn't want any mistakes," Yumi glared at the young woman at the desk as he took my elbow and pulled me out of the clutches of Andover's agents.

"Glad to see a friendly face," I muttered.

"Keep your mouth shut," Yumi snapped before launching into a tirade that nearly sent tears down my cheeks. Damn, I hadn't had such a dressing down in a decade, and I hadn't missed it one bit, especially not from Yumi, someone I actually respected. Not one ounce of smartass remained by the time he shut me in a cell to do the intake pat down himself.

"They already did that," I mumbled, knowing he had to go through the motions anyway. Andover's goons had followed us, standing against the semi-translucent cell wall opposite mine. I couldn't tell who was incarcerated there, just the shape of a person against the wall, straining to see who was blocking the light.

"I know." He made the motions of going over my entire body without actually touching me.

A glimmer of hope lit in my chest.

"That trainee you took down to the surface... That's him?" he whispered.

No sense in lying to the one person who might be able to help me. "Yeah."

"The mind-reading freak you were with today, she the real thing?"

"Yeah."

"And you're meeting with her in the morning?"

I nodded.

Yumi grimaced. "You managed to evade her exposing you today. Any chance you can pull that off again?"

Pitari had been on my side if I'd read her wink right, but would she be willing to make the same stand I was for someone she didn't know?

"Not likely with Agent Andover leading the interrogation."

"All right then. The heir is going to owe us. He understands that?"

I grinned, never so glad to have someone on my side as in that moment. "If you can save my ass, I'll make that abundantly clear."

One quick nod was all I got before he stepped out with a firm scowl locked in place, erasing any hint of our whispers.

The cell wall snapped into place, closing me in and relegating my captors to shadowy shapes. With nothing but time ticking by and a motherlode of worry to keep me company, I sat on the narrow cot and stared at the shadows.

20

Lies

The shadows of Agent Andover's men left after an hour. I lay sleepless, staring at the ceiling until the air scrubbers switched to the night setting two hours after midnight.

My cell neighbors remained quiet. I had nothing to attempt to yell over the sound dampeners anyway. Andover showed up an hour later. My stomach and throat had an unpleasant meeting in the middle. He'd likely hoped to catch me mid-sleep cycle to make this unexpected interrogation round more productive. Too bad for him, because I was awake, over-tired, and hungry.

I sat up as he entered, hoping to see Yumi present as well, but we were alone. At least Seeker Pitari wasn't joining us quite yet.

"Not sleeping well?" Andover asked, looking more rested than when we'd spoken hours ago.

"Did you find what you were looking for?"

"As I do not have the Scaavo heir in my keeping, no. Why don't you save us both some aggravation and tell me where he is?"

Remaining on my cot, I leaned against the cold grey

metal wall dividing me from the next cell and stared up at the flat grey metal square of ceiling. The cell had little to offer for distractions. They were, however, easy to clean and repelled all defacing efforts. The most mischief I could hope for would be to splash water at him from the trickling sink on the back of the toilet. As fun as seeing the distaste on his face might be, I stuck with boredom. That always annoyed the piss out of me during interrogations.

"As I told you, he was gone before I came in contact with the case and the stasis tube."

He stood looming over me, taking up all the extra air in the room. "If that is true, why are there instructions for opening the tube on your datapad?"

"I was curious how they worked and considering selling it to a buyer on the surface before you arrived. Station pay rates aren't great."

One silver-threaded eyebrow rose. "Can you prove that with a statement of intent from the proposed buyer?"

Dammit, just accept my story. "I didn't have one lined up. You showed up days before I was expecting you."

"I want to believe you, Rita. But I don't."

I believed that as much as he believed me. By now, he undoubtedly needed someone to blame for his lack of progress. The Empaetor was not a patient man.

"Since we're both curious people, indulge me. If you had sold the stasis tube before I arrived, how did you plan to cover for its absence and protect your buyer?"

The small cell didn't allow much room, but if he didn't back up a step, I was going to get testier than I already was. Give a woman a little space to put a lie together, would you?

I shrugged. "Ari Leeman likely dropped the tube somewhere along the way and kept the case with him as a decoy."

Agent Andover cocked his head and scowled. "You delivered that lie far too easily. How can I believe anything you've said?"

Oh, the perils of being a good liar. My mother had said repeatedly that this would catch up with me. I hoped I got the chance to tell her she was right.

"Guess you'll just have to wait for your mind reader to recharge and find out."

His scowl grew more pronounced. "I'm not your enemy, Rita. I'd be happy to clear you if you could just be honest with me."

But he kind of *was* my enemy, being sent directly from the man responsible for keeping my people bound to a world on fire for months out of the year. And really, was it my fault he couldn't tell fact from fiction?

I remained silent, but it was only because I was biting my tongue. Andover let out a disgusted grunt and left. Not knowing how long I had before he returned with Pitari to blow my lies to bits, I settled back onto the cot and closed my eyes.

A hard shake brought me back to wakefulness in a gasping second. A rough hand clamped over my mouth. The lights were on the lowest dim setting, just short of blackness. The shape beside me remained silent, but let go slowly and backed up. I could just make out a gesture for me to follow. Given my impending second interrogation with Andover, I high-tailed it after my savior.

As soon as I made it into the hallway, a bubble closed over my head, expanding in seconds to encapsulate me. Either this was Yumi doing his best not to incriminate himself, or one of Andover's goons giving me a minute of hope for kicks before dragging me off to Andover's ship for a private interrogation. The odds were equally matched, and in case this was Andover's plan, I kept my hint of hope under wraps. On the off chance it was Yumi, I didn't pound on the bubble or yell muffled obscenities. Whoever it was, we moved quickly.

They had me in one of the deluxe cloudy bubbles. The kind we reserved for violent offenders. The kind Andover might sink to using to sneak me out from under Yumi's notice. It obscured my vision, leaving me with only a mild sense of traveling punctuated by brighter moments as we passed under fixtures.

A rising feeling in my gut informed me we were on the lift. The gut rise lasted long enough to confirm we'd arrived at the docking ring. We traveled onward for a good fifteen minutes before my bubble bumped against something, knocking me around as I scrambled for balance. My hidden hint of hope guttered when the lights went out, leaving me in complete blackness.

Well, hell, this couldn't be good.

21

Hangry

I woke to the realization that there was light outside my bubble. From my exhausted state, I guessed I hadn't been asleep long. The bubble jiggled and shook and then retracted, dropping me to the floor, where I barely caught myself. Like hell was I going to let Andover see me fall on my ass.

I turned around to find Tino grinning in front of me.

"Yumi said you needed a quick exit. I needed a melon shipment." He waved a hand in the air. "It all worked out."

"Did it?" I shook my head, trying to keep up. "Did you get me out or Yumi?"

"He got you to my ship, making sure I was one of four other vessels cleared for travel to the surface, all leaving within the same hour."

"Thanks."

Tino handed me a sack with some weight to it. "Yumi said you get cranky when you're hungry. I'm thinking no one needs you in a mood right now."

I was in a mood alright.

"Thank you, Tino."

He chuckled. "Better make yourself scarce. I'm due for inspection shortly. You know, making sure I'm not carrying any contagions or stowaways from the station."

"Got it." I took the sack and followed his pointed finger to the exit.

Smokey Anduvean air hit my lungs the moment I stepped out. I sprinted for the nearest ship and then to the next, working my way to the edge of the landing zone, far from Tino and anyone else I might implicate in my escape.

Entering the port would get my ID scanned. Instead, I made the long hike around the building until I reached the front walk where I hailed a public transport.

Andover would soon discover my absence if he hadn't already. My defection to Anduvea would be a logical assumption, leading to the interrogation of my parents in short order. There was no way to prevent that, so I needed to warn them. And figure out what to do with Laurent. And how to get off Anduvea with him. Fucking hell.

Having no time to waste, I scarfed down a container of creamy noodles and mushrooms that Tino had thoughtfully supplied and had barely wiped my face when the transport stopped along the street at my parents' house. I set it to standby.

Grabbing the sack, I dashed to the door and palmed the panel. Nothing happened. Of course, they'd have it locked with the heir in residence. I'd told them to keep it locked. Groaning, I stood there and knocked.

My father took far too long to get to the door. I shouldered my way inside the instant I fit through.

"We need to go. Now," I announced to the house.

My father, breathing tube attached to his nose, blinked

vacantly. My mother, sitting across from Laurent at the table... Was she having tea with the heir? They looked to be having a pleasant conversation until my sudden arrival. They both stared at me.

"On your feet. Grab your things. All of you." I shooed them out of the bucolic scene they'd been enjoying. "The empiric agent won't be far behind me."

Laurent sprinted into action, darting into what used to be my bedroom. My mother remained at the table, and my father appeared ready to join her.

"No, no. Get up, grab some clothes, a credit chip if you have one, and food. Let's go. Unless you'd like to have a one-on-one chat with Agent Andover and his Maker-forsaken mind reader?"

My father was still stuck in his blinking routine. "His what? That's a real thing?"

"Yes. I spent most of yesterday with her. She's legit."

"But Rita, where are we going?" asked my mother.

"I'm working on that. Pack. Now."

As soon as they left the table, I sat. My mother's tea was still steaming. I drank it, hoping it would calm me, even slightly.

I might be able to bluster my way through Andover's interrogation, but neither of them would last three minutes before cracking. They could be stubborn, but they hadn't built up a tough shell from twenty years of working with entitled asshole tourists.

I ran through options of staying on Anduvea. Our house didn't have a super-secret panic room or an invisible cellar. I wouldn't want to endanger any of their few friends by imposing on them to hide us. Thanks to the burning, an impromptu camping trip in the wilds was out of the question. I could use Ari's credit chip to book a suite in a hotel, but no one was staying on the surface if they could help it. There would be no blending in with a host of people booking a couple of weeks of vacation time.

Booking a flight off Anduvea would also be a challenge. Trade ships stopped at the station during the burning, but not on the surface. They found the uncertain level of visibility off-putting. But Tino's ship was still here, loading up on melons and whatever else he could find.

Would it be crazy to hide out on the station? I was pondering my options there when three bodies congregated before me with luggage in hand.

"Into the transport. We're going to catch a ride back to the station."

"Are you sure that's wise?" asked Laurent.

"I never claimed to be wise. I would, however, prefer for all of us to avoid your father's agent. He's very determined to find you."

Laurent nodded. "I'm sure my father set out good incentives or threats. Or both."

"Right. The transport is waiting. Our ride is not expecting us. We need to hurry."

I herded everyone into the transport, and we zipped back to the port. Laurent eyed the sack I'd been grasping like a security blanket.

"What's that?"

"Tino sent food. He didn't want me cranky."

"Thank the Maker for that," my mother muttered.

"I heard that."

She managed a shaky smile. "You know how you get."

"I'm well aware. Thank you."

"You've been nothing but cranky since I arrived. Have you been hungry this whole time?" Laurent asked, seemingly in earnest.

A nervous laugh escaped my father.

"You have no idea. Be thankful I ate on the way here." I shifted the sack between my legs so I could attempt to stretch out a little. "Did you have any epiphanies as to why Ari and your mother wanted you outside the empire?"

Laurent shook his head. He turned away to stare out the window as we sped through the streets. There wasn't much traffic. Smoke hugged the ground, masking much of the city from view. Only the taller structures loomed over the dirty grey, but their soot-covered windows didn't reflect any light. All in all, it was a depressing sight. Fitting, I supposed.

"Rita, dear, what exactly is going on?" asked my mother.

First off, Mom, ditch the dear in front of the heir to the empire, would you? I repressed the urge to snap at her, knowing she was out of sorts and confused. Me too, Mom, me too.

"Bad things," I said. "I can list them if you'd like, or you can trust that I'll take care of us the best I can and maybe do some of that praying you're always harping on me to emulate in the meantime."

Laurent's brows rose. He looked ready to snap at me, but then my father spoke up.

"We haven't been to the station in years. Our clothes," he shook his head, "we won't fit in at all. I suppose we can stay inside on level seven like we used to. We're not going there for a good time, right?"

The defeat on his face twisted my insides. Just once I'd love to bring them somewhere they'd actually have a good time, where they didn't have to worry about not being part of the elite crowd.

"Dad, level seven might be optimistic. We'll need to not exist. That means no rooms, no registration, no meal plan."

My mother gasped. "Where exactly are you planning to hide us?"

Being invisible meant level five. I hoped I'd made enough friends there to not have any of the orphans rat me out for a reward.

"This isn't a vacation, Mom. You'll be warm, have access to fresh food, and the air will be clean. That's all I can promise."

The remainder of the ride to the port passed in silence. When the transport pulled to a stop, I led them around the vast building to the landing strip, avoiding the security vids as much as possible and praying whoever was on duty to monitor them was doing their usual half-ass job.

We made it to the landing zone, and I'd just pointed out Tino's ship when Chuey exited the door. Of all the days I didn't want to chat with my long-time admirer. I groaned. My braids made me too damned recognizable.

He waved and called my name, jogging my way. I made no effort to shorten his trip.

Facing Chuey, I said over my shoulder, "Go. Don't run, just go. Dad, tell Tino who you are if he asks. If you can avoid being seen, find an empty crate and get in it. We'll figure out the next step when we get to the station."

"What about you?" asked Laurent, glancing between Chuey's approaching form and Tino's ship.

"Don't worry about me. Get moving before he gets a good look at your face."

Laurent ducked his head and escorted my parents toward Tino's ship without another word. I appreciated his cooperation and lack of a tirade.

Now that my charges were on their way, I took a few half-hearted steps toward Chuey. "What can I do for you?"

"One of the guys mentioned he saw you making the long trek?"

"Did he also see who I was following?"

Chuey shook his head, sending his frizzy greying curls flopping to-and-fro. He drew his tall, lanky form upward. He'd asked me out a few times, but our schedules never lined up, and I wasn't enthusiastic enough about him to make a date work. He hadn't stopped trying, but these days he was playing the long, quiet and friendly game instead of going all in. I liked this game better, but I still wasn't enthused about a date.

"No, that's why I came out to ask you. I wanted to make sure you were alright."

Like I couldn't take care of myself? "Just some kid looking for trouble. Saw him eyeing up the cameras. He took off."

Chuey smiled bashfully. "You do tend to be intimidating."

"Do I?" Good. "Hey, it was great seeing you, but I've got to get back."

"I didn't see your security transport on the log?"

Why did he have to be one of the competent ones? "Working a side security gig for some extra credits. Aging parents to take care of, you know?"

"I do. Have a good rest of your day, Rita."

"You too, Chuey."

I walked away, heading toward no particular ship until I no longer felt his eyes on me. Even then I waited to turn around, just in case. It wasn't until I caught the blinking lights on Tino's ramp, indicating it was about to lift, that I full out ran for it. The ramp was halfway up before I was halfway there. Fuck.

If they got to the station without me, would they have a clue where to go and how to get there covertly? I hadn't voiced enough of my plan to give them guidance. Well, I hadn't even formed much of a plan yet, but still.

I didn't slow down, though the ramp was still rising. It came to a jerking halt three quarters of the way up with a loud clang. Not waiting to ask questions, I dove in and rolled to an abrupt stop when my shoulder connected with a dingy plas crate full of melons. Tino held out a hand to help me up.

"I don't want to know," he said as he hit the button to seal the ramp.

"I'm not here."

"Then you better get in there with the rest of the shrieking 'wait for Rita' gang."

That had to be my mother. I prayed to the Maker for patience.

"Thank you, Tino."

He chuckled and headed for the cockpit.

I listened for any hint of which crate hid my charges. It took all of thirty seconds to locate the shoulder-high green plas container with someone banging around inside. Someone else was complaining. The door latch wasn't even flipped. Great Maker, we were doomed.

Opening the door, I peeked inside. "Seriously, that's you hiding? Do any of you know the first thing about being stealthy?"

The three of them huddled inside, my parent's bags acting as seats. Only Laurent appeared mildly abashed. My parents blinked up at me.

"Were we supposed to leave you behind? We don't even know how we're supposed to hide him. Or where we are supposed to go on level five or how to get there without being scanned," said my father.

"One of you, put the rest of this food in your bag. You'll want it later." And I was sick of holding the sack like a security blanket.

I wasn't sure how we were going to make it to a safe place on the station, let alone avoid Andover until he left, if he *would* leave without finding me, but, by the Maker, I was going to give it my best shot.

22

Bathroom Break

In the darkness of the crate, the mover beneath us beeped, jostling us into each other as it trundled down the ramp, to the lift, and then down the corridor that led to one of the large bay pods on either of the storage levels below the docking ring. I'd already had to clamp my hand over my mother's mouth twice. Warning looks in the blackness were not effective.

With my father crammed up against my left side and my mother on the other side of Laurent's feet on my right, I was uncomfortably aware of my leg rubbing against the length of Laurent's, who sat across from me in the very limited space. I'd been using mine to brace against the opposite side of the crate. The heir seemed to have the same idea. At least he was moderately better at this than my parents were.

The crate shifted drastically, pitching the three of us forward. I threw my hands out, one sideways in front of my mother's shoulders and the other forward to catch myself, which was not entirely successful due to the added weight of her body. My head slammed into a solid object with a crack. My eyes watered and expletives begged to burst from my lips.

A muffled voice shouted, "Watch it! Tino will spit in your next order if you break his stuff."

"Sorry, boss. The load was unbalanced. Tell him to blame whoever packed it on the surface."

After a deep thud, our crate settled onto the floor. The mover beeped as it backed away. The beeps had barely faded when my mother started to move. I grabbed her shoulder. My father shifted. I grabbed his shoulder. Why did they have to be so bad at this? Just sit still, for the Maker's sake.

My forehead throbbed, and I was pretty sure the warmth on my face wasn't tears but blood flowing from my nose. I hoped Laurent had fared better from our encounter.

It felt like at least an hour later before the mover didn't return with another load. I waited another fifteen minutes, listening for anyone speaking or footsteps. Still, someone might be quietly cataloging the shipment and its placement.

I whispered, "Keep your voice down and move carefully."

"Rita, I have to use the bathroom," my mother whispered.

Sweet Maker, have mercy. We don't have a bathroom in the crate, Mom. What the hell do you expect me to do about that? I drew a shuddering breath and exhaled through my aching nose that had thankfully stopped bleeding.

"Hold it," I snapped through my teeth.

Everyone must have sensed that I was on edge because their shuffling remained minimal and quiet and no one whispered a word. The air grew thick with sweat and my mother's perfume.

Hours later, when I was sure the stock staff must have left the bay, I crawled past my father to flip the emergency release clasp. The seal sighed. Fresh air rushed in. I shoved a finger through the rubbery flange to flip the outer latch and pushed on the side of the crate. The door slid across the floor with a raspy protest.

Standby lighting dimly lit the bay filled with barrels, boxes, and crates stacked neatly in their designated and labeled locations. The stock staff took their jobs seriously.

"Come on, let's go," I said, allowing only slightly more than a whisper.

My father emerged first with one of their bags on his shoulder, taking in the bay with wide eyes. "So many supplies."

"So many tourists," I muttered.

My mother came out next, her bag on her back, and her balance uncertain. Even my joints were stiff after being in the same cramped position for hours. She kept one hand on the crate and stretched her legs.

Laurent emerged last, gasping as his gaze met mine. Thankfully, he wasn't bleeding. Only a red spot on his forehead commemorated our collision.

Sensing something was wrong, my mother snapped into mom mode. "Oh Rita, you're hurt!"

"I'm fine, Mom. We should move."

Not to be deterred, she brushed at the dried blood on my shirt and then reached for my face. I caught her wrist and gently redirected her toward my father. He looked like he wanted to say something too, but at least he kept his mouth shut.

Laurent stuck close as I set a cautious trail, dodging from row to row until we reached the bay door. The access panel required proper ID for entry, but not for exiting. I waved the others to stand off to the side as I opened the door. A quick glance up and down the outer stock corridor revealed it was currently empty. However, being rounded, conforming to the central lift shaft as it did, that could change quickly.

"Let's go." I hurried to the nearest lift door, hoping we could get lost in the crowd until we reached level five.

Laurent cleared his throat and gestured at my shirt. "Won't people question the blood?"

Yes, they definitely would. Dammit.

"Bathroom break it is then."

Leaving the lift behind, we hurried to the nearest bathroom. It held no frills, being for the stock staff, but the necessary facilities were in place. I made everyone stand just inside the entrance so they were out of direct view of the corridor. While my mother used a stall, I went to work with the shitty paper-like disposable towels that disintegrated if they got too wet and barely absorbed water when absolutely dry. How did anyone create and manufacture such a useless product? It had to be from one of the rich idiots on the surface who scored a contract with the station through a buddy. That's how we got stuck with most of the inefficient and useless stuff up here.

"Rita, someone's coming," Laurent said.

"Mom, get out there and take Dad with you. Head back to the lift. If anyone questions you, say you got off on the wrong floor. If we don't join you immediately, get on and go to level seven. You'll blend in there. Wait by the lift doors.

There's a window close by. Enjoy the view."

"Getting separated sounds like a bad idea," my father protested.

I gently pushed them out of the bathroom. "All of this is a bad idea."

After a hesitant backward glance, they did as I had instructed. Two members of the stock staff caught up with them quickly. They spoke, and then all four headed for the lift.

Once they were all away, I made sure no one else was in view and dashed to the lift doors to catch the next one.

"Will they be alright?" Laurent asked.

"Better off than they would be if someone recognized me. I'm supposed to be in custody, thanks to your father's agent."

He grimaced. "Should I have gone with them?"

"Maybe, but I feel better having you with me."

"Do you?" His voice sounded different, lower.

Why was he looking at me like that? I replayed what I had said. "Things would not go well for you if anyone recognized you either. Your face is far more recognizable than mine. My parents would do a terrible job of fending off any troublesome security officers, let alone any of Andover's people. I mean, if you want to take your chances with them instead of me, I'll remember that for the next time we end up in a situation like this."

"Will there be a next time?"

Where the hell was that lift? I hit the call button again.

"Assuming we don't get caught in the next hour? Yes, the odds we will have to split up again are likely."

"How's your nose?"

I took a step away to put some space between us. While I may have joked to myself about having the heir to the empire in my bed, I knew it for the joke it was. I didn't appreciate him playing all charming royalty to get whatever twisted enjoyment his kind got out of screwing with the hopes and dreams of us common folk.

"It's sore," I said sternly. "Your head?"

Laurent brushed his fingers over his forehead. "Also sore. Let's not do that again."

"Deal."

The blessed lift finally arrived. It was full of loud, half-dressed women. Liquor fumes rolled off all of them. One belched. The others laughed. The only blessing was that none of them realized they'd picked us up on the stock floor. They were all too busy gabbing, laughing, and stumbling into one another on ridiculously high-heeled shoes.

"Don't make eye contact with them," I muttered to Laurent.

It didn't seem to matter that he was staring at my boots. One of the women squealed.

"Oh, what do we have here?"

"He's a pretty one."

"Andralu, it's my turn. You got the last one."

The gaggle of drunks turned their full blurred attention to us, continuing to bicker with each other.

I put my back to them rather than give them a chance to notice any blood I'd missed, my damp shirt, or my swollen nose or, Maker forbid, any of them be sober enough to describe me. Either of us, for that matter.

How far was this damned lift going? I checked the display and groaned. We were headed all the way to level two before we'd possibly get the chance to join my parents on seven.

The drunken floosies closed in.

"Back off. He's taken," I snarled over my shoulder. If only I had my stunner or a handful of bubble tabs. Or my uniform. Even that might have kept them in line.

"Rita?" The damn Scaavo heir caught my darting gaze. The unspoken plan transmitting between us in a heartbeat.

"Yeah, fine." It was the most peaceful of the solutions at hand. Punching a few of them would have surely worked to deter their interest, but would also bring my security team running once the women staggered out.

Laurent wrapped his arms around me and spun me around, trapping me in the front corner of the lift. In the interest of playing along, I slid one hand onto his shoulder and the other onto the back of his neck, urging him to get on with it already if this was really his plan. I certainly wasn't going to be the one to lay lips on the heir to the empire if all he intended was to make it look like we were having an intimate moment.

His firm lips touched mine briefly, as though he wasn't sure he was going to go through with this either. I didn't blame him one bit. He might have been assholishly toying with me only a few minutes ago, but now he was having to follow through. I took a little satisfaction in that, smiling to myself.

Whether he'd taken my smile for encouragement or he'd worked up the fortitude to commit to the ruse, Laurent was suddenly kissing me. For real. Or at least it felt real.

It took a few seconds for the shock to wear off enough to take in the grumbling of the other occupants of the lift.

It was another awkward few seconds before I remembered how to do this.

"If you're not that into him, step aside," called one of the women.

A round of rowdy laughter followed.

I flipped her three fingers over Laurent's shoulder.

"Screw you too, lady," my tormenter yelled.

I got distracted by Laurent's lips, which were becoming more convincing by the second. It was several breaths later before I realized we now had a pocket of space around us. The lift stopped. Half of the women got out on level three, some grumbling in our direction, the others making plans to meet up for a meal later.

Level two couldn't come fast enough. The moment the lift stopped, and the doors parted, I planted both hands on Laurent's chest and pushed him back a few inches. He gracefully retreated without further urging, yet stayed facing me. That put his back to the six people who walked in after the women exited. I caught sight of a dark blue uniform. My stomach went cold. I wanted nothing more than to escape the confined space immediately. But where would we go? If Andover's people were wandering the station, or at least it appeared a few had moved off his ship to stay in public housing, we might be recognized in any of the public spaces. I certainly couldn't risk slinking back to my suite. He had probably posted someone there or had it under surveillance.

Maybe sensing my panic, Laurent shifted closer again as the lift doors shut. Leaning in as if nuzzling my ear, he asked, "Who is it?"

"One of Andover's crew and two of my team." I sagged

against the wall, doing my best to appear shorter and maybe to disappear.

The three of them were talking in low voices. Did they recognize me? If my damned face got Laurent picked up and dragged back to his father for whatever that evil dick had in mind...

Laurent's hand was suddenly on my cheek. His shoulders blocked my view of the security nightmare sharing our ride. He didn't say anything, just watched me. I closed my eyes, blocking him out, trying to overhear what the team was saying.

One floor passed, and we were just about to the next when one of them seemed to realize neither of us was moving.

"Hey, are you alright?" asked one of my security crew.

You pick now to do your job correctly? I groaned inside.

"Is he bothering you?" asked the female security officer.

Now Laurent looked as panicked as I felt. I didn't know what to tell him. This wasn't good. Not good at all.

"We're fine," he said.

"I'm talking to her."

"We're fine," I affirmed.

Apparently, that wasn't good enough because there she was, looming over Laurent's shoulder, getting a good look at my face and the residual blood that hadn't washed out of my shirt.

"What did he..." her voice rose, "Officer Stabinov?"

Fuck.

23

My Manners Suck

There was one quick way out of this, and it wouldn't be pretty. There was definitely going to be more blood on my shirt. While I still had a heartbeat of surprise in my favor, I hit the stop button for the lift, swiveled Laurent into the corner and punched Officer Lucia in the face. While she stumbled aside, I grabbed her stunner and shot Officer Valjean and then Lucia.

I might have made a clean sweep of it had Andover's man been one of mine, but that was not the case. He kicked the weapon from my hand and grabbed my shoulder and arm with enough force to nearly dislocate one from the other. I slammed my forehead into his nose. It emitted a snap that gave me a second of glee before I drove my heel into his toes and my knee into his crotch.

Andover's man staggered in place long enough for me to scramble for the dropped weapon. It was gone. I lunged for where Valjean had fallen and had just reached for his stunner when Andover's man went still. I glanced up to see Laurent holding the missing gun.

"Nice job."

"You too." He held out the weapon.

I took it and put both stunners back on the floor. As much as I'd have loved to keep one, they had trackers embedded in them.

"We need to get out of here." I pointed to the emergency hatch at the top of the lift.

Laurent craned his head upward and read the instructions printed on the hatch. I nudged him out of the way, jumped up, and tapped the clasp to open the hatch.

He peered through the opening. "But how do we—"

"Jump, grab the edge and pull."

"I don't know if I can—"

"You have muscles. I've seen them. They're useful for more than decoration."

He glared at me. I jumped again, grabbing the edge of the opening and pulled myself up to show him it could be done. To be fair, I had years of emergency training drills behind me. He'd likely never had to exert himself beyond recreational exercising.

Flattening myself on top of the lift, I reached down through the opening for his hands. He jumped. I caught him and helped him up. It wasn't a well-coordinated effort, but he made it to the top of the lift with an undignified huff.

"I hope you don't mind sweating, because we've got some climbing to do, and thanks to the crappy station ventilation system, this tube is where a good deal of our heat gathers."

Laurent gazed up at the dimly lit shaft full of lift mechanics and then to the narrow metal ladder on the wall beside us. "Why don't you fix it?"

"Why don't you fix it?" I repeated in his haughty tone.

"Who would you suggest we have do that and with what funds?" I scoffed. "We make do with what we have, and that's not a lot, thanks to your family."

I grabbed a rung on the ladder and pulled myself up. "If you're done judging our infrastructure, maybe we can get moving? My parents will be worried by now, and the Maker knows what trouble they'll get into left to their own devices."

He studied me for a moment, eyes narrowing. "You should watch how—"

"Yes, my manners suck. Yell at me later." I left his brewing tirade behind and scrambled up the ladder to give him plenty of space to mount and follow.

By the time we'd climbed past the fifth level, the heat and the double tap on my skull had brewed into a throbbing headache. I gave myself a moment to catch my breath. My nose hurt, and my fingers weren't happy about being kicked by Andover's goon. Using them on the ladder wasn't making them any happier. My mood did not bode well for any further challenges standing between me and a few hours of sleep in a safe place where I could stretch out.

Laurent lagged below me by level six. That being the security floor, I couldn't exactly pop out of the lift shaft access there. We needed to keep moving, and quickly. One of the maintenance crew had likely been dispatched to check the stalled lift by now. It wouldn't be long before security was swarming up the ladder behind us. Within a few minutes, the three stun victims would wake and identify me. They might not have identified Laurent, but Andover would put their description of him with the name in seconds. We needed to be embedded wherever I could find to hide by then.

"Rita, wait," Laurent called from the shadows.

"Climb faster." With renewed purpose, I forced my sore fingers back into action.

The faintly lit outline of the level seven access door was in sight when a clang sounded below us signaling the re-opening of the lift emergency hatch.

There was no time to pause and listen for a quiet gap in foot traffic outside the access shaft. I rushed up the last rungs and threw the door open. The immediate area was clear, but I could see several couples and a group of small children at the edges of a milling crowd just around the corner, waiting at the lift door. They were grumbling loudly about the long wait and were blaming it on the fact they were on the economy level, naturally assuming they were being snubbed.

It wasn't often I prayed for a minor riot, but today was a special occasion.

Laurent wasn't far behind me. The moment he emerged, I sealed the door and grabbed his arm, towing him alongside me. Ruse or not, we'd kissed, so I threw all thought of protocol out the airlock. Boundaries could be reestablished after we were safe.

We joined the edge of the crowd, slowly weaving our way through the mass. I took the opportunity to encourage their ire with as many hurried comments about unfair treatment as I dared.

When I spotted my parents, hands fidgeting at their sides, plastered against the wall by the window that I'd mentioned, I pulled Laurent toward them. The crowd was growing fast. The group, now having taken up chanting, drew people from nearby rooms at an alarming rate. I didn't envy the security officers on duty today.

"Where have you been?" chided my mother in the same tone she'd used when I was eight and had been outside playing too long. She glanced at Laurent. Whatever she saw on his face brought about an abrupt closing of her mouth.

Having him beside me had benefits.

"We ran into some trouble. Speaking of which, we need to keep moving. We're going down to level five, but we can't use the lift."

Laurent clamped his hand onto my shoulder. I resisted the instinct to shake it off. He'd likely been pushed to his limits today too.

"We can't go back in there." He nodded toward the lift access shaft. "Your parents can't climb that."

"We're not. Come on." I hustled the three of them farther from the amassing, seething crowd. People filled the corridor, making travel upstream a challenge. I lost sight of my parents twice, but then they were behind Laurent again. I pulled us out of traffic at a secured door labeled employees only. The door's control panel taunted me with its cheerful yellow blinking lights. And me without my staff ID.

"Where does this go?" Laurent asked over my shoulder.

"Station systems maintenance tubes. We can travel between floors."

"If you can get inside," he stated doubtfully.

"Give me a minute." I'd learned early in my security career that there was more than one way to activate a control panel. Losing one's ID led to creative solutions until it turned up again.

Using the few longer nails I'd yet to break this week, I

worked the panel cover off and examined the inner work-ings.

"Do you know what all of that does?" Laurent asked.

"No, but I know what these four wires and this trigger switch are for." I pulled one end of each of the four wires out, swapped them, and then pressed the switch. The door opened. The alarm didn't go off.

"That seems awfully easy to circumvent," he said.

"Only if you know what you're doing. And also, it's a maintenance shaft. It's not like we get a lot of terrorist activity out here. Tourists have no interest in going places that are dark and dirty."

"More dark and dirty. Wonderful."

If he wasn't wild about our current level of discomfort, he was really going to love where we were going. I laughed to myself.

I held the door open so the three of them could enter the tube and then wedged my foot in the opening. Once I had the control wires replaced and the cover reattached, I ducked inside and let the door close behind me.

There were no lights here, dim or otherwise. We stood in the blackness for a moment while I got my bearings. I'd been all over the station, inside and out of public areas, for most of my career. This was the first time I was thankful for being made to memorize the tube system and all its access points. However, I'd always had a light on me. I prayed I didn't get turned around now.

"Rita?" my father called out.

"Keep your voice down. I'm right here. Everyone is going to have to put their hand on the shoulder of the person in front of them. If you get detached, say something. Quietly.

I do not want to have to come back to find you."

It was one thing to be in charge and give orders to the security staff under me, but quite another to be ordering my parents around. Though, I supposed, no less unsettling than everything I'd been slinging at the Scaavo heir since he'd come into my life.

Laurent's hand returned to my shoulder. Thankfully, with a less aggressive grip. My parents followed behind him. I hoped they were up for the hike we were about to undertake.

Setting an easy pace would have been ideal, being in the dark and considering who I was traveling with, but that's not how the day was going. Even remotely. I held one hand out ahead of me and the other against the wall, brushing my sore fingers over the conduits and wiring fastened there. There were several places where the tube would narrow thanks to a poorly planned ventilation shaft. I opted for a cautiously speedy pace. My face didn't need to forcefully meet anything else today.

We were nearing the pole that would take us down to level six when I could no longer ignore my father's labored breathing. He got a few moments of respite due to only one person being able to slide down at a time, but it was all I could offer. The air might be cleaner on the station, thanks to all the scrubbers and the lack of smoke, but his lungs were still impaired from the long-term damage he'd suffered living on the surface.

He didn't sound any better when we regrouped on six and set off toward the pole that would take us to five. Guilt tugged at my gut. I should never have dragged them into this.

My head informed me that Agent Andover would have had no qualms about using my parents against me if his interrogation had continued. At least this way, I had some control over their wellbeing. Small consolation that was, given the huffing and wheezing going on behind me.

"How much farther?" Laurent whispered close to my ear.

His close proximity reminded me far too much of our kiss in the lift earlier. The urge to put space between us was strong, but not wise, given our blind situation.

"This far again and then some."

"They need to rest. Can't you hear them?"

No one had said they needed to stop. "What, their breathing?" I asked, glaring at him over my shoulder as if he could see my annoyance in the dark. "Would either of you like to tell his highness why your breathing sounds so rough even just walking as we are?"

Silence, other than said breathing, answered me. I guess I was the only one willing to spell the truth out for him. Or they were mortified both to be heard struggling and of my smart mouth. That was probably more the case.

"Much of the working class can't afford to escape the burning by coming up here or living in one of the luxury plexes. They're stuck breathing shit air for two months out of the year. It does a number on throats and lungs over a lifetime. And why are we all here, breathing smoke and volcanic fumes? Oh yes, some advisor said something your grandfather didn't like. It wasn't even us. It was some elite asshole who couldn't go into exile without staff to care for him."

"Rita, that's enough," my father scolded.

"It was eleven advisors, actually," Laurent snipped. "But

I see your point."

"Five minutes of rest," I also conceded. "Then we have to move."

24

Riots Make Great Distractions

We were making decent time toward the pole until alarms sounded above us. All around us. I clamped my hands over my ears. From the lack of a hand on my shoulder, I guessed Laurent was doing the same. The next thing I knew, my parents were crammed against me, and Laurent was nudging me downward with his elbow.

As far as I could tell, we hadn't set the cacophony off. Maybe he was right. Holding in place for a short break would be a good idea. I couldn't concentrate on my memorized map with all the noise bouncing off the metal tube anyway.

Feeling the wall behind me, I made sure I wasn't leaning on anything that could be disconnected or damaged as I sat down. Resting my back and stretching my legs felt damn good. It wasn't the safe haven I'd been aiming for, but at the moment, with my head pounding and the lack of sleep the night before, I'd take advantage of whatever respite the Maker offered.

"What set them off?" Laurent yelled in my ear.

There weren't any voice warnings to seek emergency shelter, so we weren't under attack. I couldn't make out anyone yelling orders within the nearby tubes, or see any lights from people searching for us. "Probably the riot we saw forming. We're safe. For now."

I tried not to think of whatever dust and dried puddles of previous fluid leaks I might be sitting in. Then I shut my eyes and did my best to ignore the sound. It wasn't easy, but apparently I'd been successful because I woke to find I'd nodded off for a few minutes on Laurent's shoulder. The alarms were still going off. Whatever those angry econo folks were doing was an impressive distraction. We needed to use the rest of it.

I reached over to tug Laurent up and felt him passing the message along. We'd made it to the pole to five when I caught the glint of lights flashing off the tube walls behind us.

"The sensor at the last intersection was tripped, sir," said a distant voice I didn't recognize, probably one of the maintenance crew.

"Could it have been vermin?" asked a male voice. "When will they shut those damned alarms off?"

I left them to their investigation and hurried my parents down the pole. Laurent went next. I'd just gotten my legs wrapped around it when the light beam grew wider. Dammit, they were close.

"Take your shoes off," I whispered to Laurent upon reaching the floor. He passed the message along. Our footsteps might have been quiet under the alarms, but they had to be nearing the auto shutoff time limit if whatever had set them off wasn't resolved soon. People outside the tube certainly wouldn't hear us walking, but we had a tail inside and they would.

Stocking-footed, we hurried through the tube, weaving around the more plentiful ventilation shaft interruptions where they branched off to offer more thorough coverage to the elite living

quarters on the lower levels. The labored sounds of my father's breathing sent spikes of guilt through me.

Everyone remained quiet, but I could feel the impending weight of their questions and doubt. How long would we be here? What will happen if we get caught? When can we go home? I didn't have answers. All I could do was keep moving forward and hope for the best.

The door I'd expected to find near the geppa pen wasn't where it was supposed to be. I slowed to a stop.

"What?" whispered Laurent.

"I must have made a wrong turn."

"What are we going to do now?" my mother's panicked question was the straw that broke my patience.

"I don't know," I hissed back. "Give me a minute."

Something let out a loud clang in the tube in the distance. The maintenance crew was still in here somewhere. I swore under my breath.

"Would we be better off outside?" Laurent asked quietly.

"I don't know."

Scraps of a distant conversation echoed our way. Something about smudges and footprints.

Maybe taking our chances in the corridors of level five would be a risk we needed to take. I took a slow, deep breath and tried to concentrate on the map in my head, but because I'd missed a turn, I didn't know where we were or where the nearest exit was. My heart raced. I rubbed my aching temples. There was nothing more to do than keep going until we came to a door.

Gauging where I heard his breathing coming from, I felt around for Laurent's arm. I grazed his stomach and what I hoped to the Maker was his hip before I found his hand. I placed it on my shoulder. He squeezed it, and then I could feel him twisting to reach backward for my parents. He squeezed again a minute later. Hoping I interpreted that correctly, I headed off slowly, feeling the wall as I went.

The noise stayed behind us, but there were two voices and maybe three sets of footsteps. Maybe. It was hard to tell with our shuffling feet and my fingers running over pipes and wires and occasional smooth patches of tube wall, seeking blindly for a door seam. My concentration was shot, thoughts a tumble of worry over being caught, of losing Laurent to Andover, of having my parents interrogated and whatever punishment Andover might see fit to assign them. I'd brought this down on them. On Laurent too. I should have just left him in stasis. Should have minded my own business and turned him over, still locked in his case, and been happy with my little reward. He wasn't my problem.

Except that he was. If I could figure out this threat and confirm his safety, the next Empaetor would look favorably upon Anduvea. Maybe on me. Financially. The very vibrant memory of our kiss in the elevator was nothing to dwell on. Nope. I shoved that little pipedream back into the shadows so I could concentrate on my raw fingertips and getting us out of the maintenance tube.

My hip slammed into a ventilation shaft I'd missed feeling. Dammit. I prayed the dull thud didn't carry. Laurent squeezed my shoulder again. Just as I was about to turn to ask him what he needed, he gently pushed me forward.

Right. Keep going. I was tired of going, of everything resting on my shoulders. Why couldn't someone else be in charge for a few minutes? I slowed a little more, feeling ahead of me and to the right while keeping my other hand on the left wall. There had to be a door here somewhere. They were scattered throughout each level, allowing the maintenance crew to infiltrate integral systems at multiple points.

The wires and tubes and bumps and lumps of every other minimally covered system interface panel my fingers skimmed over were blurring together into a hopeless muddle. We were never getting out of here. Andover's people had lights. They might not hear us, but they could see our smudged tracks and where we stopped. They'd know we were on level five. Somewhere.

My fingers skimmed over a maze of water tubes and power casings and then bare wall. Another two feet of bare wall. And finally, the seam of a door seal.

"Here's where you get out." I stopped.

Laurent bumped into me. And then again, harder as my parents ran into him.

I used the lever latch to open the door, letting them out into the bright light of level five.

Leaning in close, I said, "There's a pen of geppa. Use your nose to find them. Beside that pen is a storeroom that no one uses because it smells like geppa shit. There's a staff restroom down the hall and two turns to the left. I keep food and clothes in the storeroom for the orphans who squat on this level. Share with them. They'll help you.

They can show you where the fresh food is out on the rings where we grow it."

"Rita, why are you telling us this?" my mother asked, her dust-smudged face lined with worry.

"Because it's likely I'm going to get caught. I've got to cover our tracks, or they'll know we're here and they'll eventually flush us out. And all the orphans. Those kids don't deserve more aggravation than they've already had in their short lives."

My dad smiled and nodded, but my mother shook her head. "You can't leave us here. You'll figure something out."

Laurent glanced from them to me and squared his shoulders. "How do we get off the station, and where should we go?"

"Stay hidden here for a few days. I'll do my best to get back to you. If I don't, find your way into the social district and talk to Tino. You remember where his place is?"

Laurent nodded.

I reached into my sock and pulled out the credit chip. If I couldn't make it back, they'd need funds to get off the station. We were a bit beyond my daydreaming about spending Ari's credits on frivolous things now.

"Tell him to send Yumi to check the geppa. He knows who you are. He'll help you. Tell him I said so."

He leaned in closer, nearly brushing his lips against my ear. "Thank you, Rita."

Quit being creepy, I wanted to say, but I nodded, enjoying for just a second that the heir to the empire seemed to be genuinely thanking me, an exiled Anduvean who had just thrown her career away and probably much more. But I didn't want to think about that right now. It was only over if I got caught, and I'd do my best to not let that happen.

"I'll see you all soon." I gave my parents a quick hug and then ducked back into the tube and sealed the door behind me.

25

I Don't Need Tools

It took a minute for my eyes to readjust to the total darkness of the maintenance tube. I put my boots back on and slipped out of my shirt, tying one sleeve around my ankle. Time to muddle our smudged tracks and go create some more. Now that I'd had a glance outside the tube, I generally knew where I was. As long as I didn't get turned around again, I'd be alright.

I spent an hour backtracking and also going down every offshoot path I passed. Getting to the downward pole access to level four took longer than I wanted, but whoever had come in after us was now wandering level five. I could see their lights at intervals that were growing too frequent for comfort.

Though I was reluctant to leave Laurent and my parents behind, I didn't want our pursuers to find them. I slid down the pole and ventured into the tubes of the services level. A level that held a lot of supplies and resources. I rested my back against the wall for a minute. I could send a message, something that would make Andover think we had a plan or help coming. Or maybe, that help was already here.

Feeling inspired, I trudged onward, dragging my now bloody and filthy shirt behind me until I came to an access door. This time, I took a few breaths to listen for outside activity and waited for a quiet break to sneak out. Once on the outside, I untied my shirt from my foot and then tied the sleeves around my waist. I'd need it later if I could get back into the maintenance tube to return to level five.

First important stops: the staff outfitter and a bathroom. Wandering around in my undershirt during the burning might not gain me as much attention as one would think, given the crazy behavior of tourists, but I didn't want to take my chances. A quick dip into the first bathroom I happened upon revealed that my undershirt was not what was going to gain attention. My swollen face would do that far faster. No wonder the officers on the lift were concerned Laurent had beaten me into silence. Then again, my headbutt to Andover's man had probably done me no additional favors. From the grimy smudges on my face, it sure looked like I'd been running my hands over dusty walls and brushing stray hairs out of my face for hours. Oh, I had been.

I quickly washed my dirty hands and scrubbed my face. I momentarily considered yanking my braids out to make a rough attempt at the common hairstyle, but given my puffy face and dark circles gathering under my eyes, my hair was the least of my distinctive problems. Using my wet hands, I smoothed the strays back into my braids and then headed back out into the corridor.

Anytime someone walked by, I kept my attention on the wall murals that decorated the services level. The art was dated and faded from the continuous lighting from our hardly-gallery-quality fixtures. The scenes depicted the glamorous life on Harilax that my people had left behind. They provided a glimpse into the past, of those who had come first and created this place to make the best of the punishment Empaetor Iradio VI had handed them.

The mural beside me depicted a grand feast. I didn't recognize most of the food, but it filled tables lined with outrageously dressed men and women. I'd always thought it odd that there were no children or pets in these images. Just wild-outfitted people eating and drinking, and buildings that defied gravity, reaching into the clouds and lined with glass that shone like sparkling rainbows. Lush gardens were filled with deep greens I'd never seen on Anduvea and blue skies artfully dotted with puffy white clouds. These were the fairytales of my childhood. Was this Laurent's reality or had Harilax changed? Were these murals only the idealized memory of a pampered artist or a still frame of history? I doubted I'd have the leisure to bring Laurent here to confer on the subject.

The staff outfitting room was locked. Better locked than occupied, I considered as I went about popping the control panel off and rearranging the wires. As soon as I had the door open, I hurried inside, slipped into a maintenance coverall and then ducked back out to put the door control back together.

I was so fixated on hurrying through the reassembly that I didn't hear the approaching footsteps until they stopped behind me.

"Problems with the door again? It was sticking last week."

"Almost fixed," I said, keeping my head down and acutely aware I had no tools.

Maybe the maintenance crew just knew how to fix things, and they didn't always carry a case of tools with them to be prepared for any spontaneous maintenance emergency. Beyond an occasional brief conversation in passing, I'd never paid much attention to the light blue coverall-clad people that scurried along at the edges of our daily lives, making sure we had heat and water and air to breathe. Hopefully, no one else paid much attention to them either.

The person behind me entered the supply room. Well, dammit. I couldn't leave them locked inside. That would gain attention. Fiddling with the control panel took more time than I wanted. My skin was crawling when they finally left with two uniforms in hand.

Letting out a relieved sigh, I locked the door and headed for one of the public lounges. None of the few occupants turned to look at me as I entered.

Three terminals sat in the corner, only one of which was occupied. Couches and chairs formed a conversation area at the other end of the room, leaving the middle open where a few tall tables with stools usually stood. Today, they were pushed aside while four teens held an impromptu wrestling match in the open space. Despite their whooping and hollering, no one paid any attention to them either.

Shelves lined one side of the long, narrow room. A scattering of low-line datapads joined the dusty assortment of games and a few boxes of art supplies. I hadn't seen anyone creating art in years, not even the kids bothered to try anymore. It seemed like the only hobbies people engaged in were bitching about being exiled on Anduvea, dwelling on how the Empaetor had wronged them, and consuming whatever substances they could get their hands on to cope with being left out of the life they felt they deserved.

A firm believer in 'life is what you make it', thanks to my parents not following the majority sentiments of our people, I had little respect for those that engaged in that lifestyle. Was that even a life?

I shook off my distracted stare at the mostly empty shelves and settled into a terminal seat. The only person I could think of who would gain Andover's attention was Laurent's mother, Marishka Scaavo. Surely, since she was dead, and Andover likely knew that, having come after Laurent by the Empaetor's direct command, communications to her account would be monitored. I didn't have Laurent's security code, but I remembered her address. They knew without a doubt that I was involved now, so there was no need to hide in that regard.

I typed out a quick message:

Ari gave me your contact. I9 is safely on his way to the specified location.

There, let Andover chew on that. Had he already left? Was I just leading his people on a merry chase? Was the heir on one of the ships waiting to depart right now? I grinned, imagining Agent Andover tearing his hair out over not knowing.

Once the message was sent, I grabbed one of the free datapads. If nothing else, the lame games on them might keep us occupied while we were stuck in the stinky closet for days. The roomy pockets in the maintenance coverall came in handy for holding the purloined pad, and as a bonus, it looked like I might have at least a diagnostic scanner on me.

Back out in the corridor, I considered where I could go that I might be seen but could also safely slink away. I needed to be somewhere far from level five because there was certainly nothing to find there. The packed social district seemed a safe bet.

When I got close enough to a public lift, I hung back until a good crowd had guaranteed it would be nearly full. I didn't want to get cornered in the enclosed space if I were recognized.

The lift ride up was uneventful, as were my first few steps into the boisterous late afternoon crowd. If anyone was shouting my name, I wouldn't have heard it. Two men were in the middle of a fistfight just outside one of the bars. Surprising, because these were the nicer establishments, not prone to the drunken fighting crowd. Those were up the stairs on nine, where we had to worry about malicious idiots flinging each other over the railing.

One of the security officers ran toward the fight. I lingered just a second longer than was comfortable, hoping someone might notice me and call the sighting in. When I veered away, I hunched low to blend in with the crowd. I slowly worked my way toward the nearest stairway and went up. Many of the employees of the stores and bars knew my face. They likely wouldn't shout for security, but they would undoubtedly mention seeing me after the fact if Andover was offering any sort of incentive to do so.

It took all of three minutes inside Sector Nine before Tessy swayed her shapely little ass toward me with a smile. "Rita?"

"How's business?" I asked, going with my usual conversation starter for lack of other inspiration.

"Fine. How are you?" She looked me up and down. "I heard...things."

"I'm sure you did."

"Do you know they're offering credits for your whereabouts?"

I shrugged. "Do I need to be worried?"

She glanced around. Today she wore absurdly long purple lashes that fluttered as if her eyelids could barely hold them apart. "A hundred credits, Rita. Just for saying I saw you."

Not a fabulous reward, but Andover had to expect that many people would say they saw me. "Enjoy your credits."

"Payable only if they can verify it with security footage."

She not-so-subtly shifted her eyeballs toward the camera in the ceiling to our left. As if I didn't know where all the cameras were. I'd installed several of them over the years to cover blind spots, for the Maker's sake.

I made a point to look up at the camera, but resisted the urge to give Andover a three fingered wave. My people, well, my former people, would receive that gesture first and they didn't deserve that.

"Thanks." She winked her ridiculous lashes. "Rumor is, the Scaavo heir was seen kissing you? Rita?" She squealed. "I didn't know you even liked men! And well," her eyes widened, and she shook her head, "I thought, him being the heir and all, he would have higher...you know."

"Standards?" Yeah, me too, you fucking bar floozy. Go sway your ass for credits somewhere else.

She looked embarrassed, but that quickly turned into a scandalous grin. "Go, Rita! We're cheering for you, girl."

Don't bother. "Thanks."

I'd lingered long enough. She'd get her credits. I'd get Andover's people away from level five. Everyone's a winner.

I slunk away from Sector Nine, thinking of Ari's unsuccessful visit there. What would he do in my place? Even if he hadn't been killed by the Da'Adio brothers, would he have found a ride out of the empire? We might be on the edge, but the Empire had a reputation and friendly wasn't part of it. How long did the Empaetor have to live, and how long would Laurent have to get back to take his place before factions rose up and tore the whole empire apart with their bids to take control?

I'd worked my way around half of the open arced walkway and was on the center stairs when a hand clamped down on my shoulder. It took a second before my wandering thoughts caught up with the fact that I wasn't still inside the maintenance tube and it wasn't Laurent behind me.

My one saving grace was the rusty orange of a security uniform instead of the blue of one of Andover's people. The hand didn't belong to Yumi or Senio, so I didn't have any qualms about punching first. I'd explain myself later.

I spun, swinging my arm as I went. My fist connected with a female face. She staggered sideways, grasping her cheek rather than retaliating. Amateur. Hadn't she ever been punched before? Taking advantage of her ineptitude, I ran down the stairs, dodging through the crowd until I felt safe enough to slow down and again attempt my vanish into the crowd routine.

"Stop her," someone yelled.

I quickly realized it wasn't a miracle that I heard the command over the ambient cacophony; it was because another security officer was close enough that I could hear through their interface.

Two more security suits crept into my peripheral vision.

"Rita, I need you to come with me."

No. Dammit. I knew that voice. I didn't want to fight Senio.

But I couldn't leave Laurent and my parents in a geppa scented closet for days waiting for me. I turned to face him.

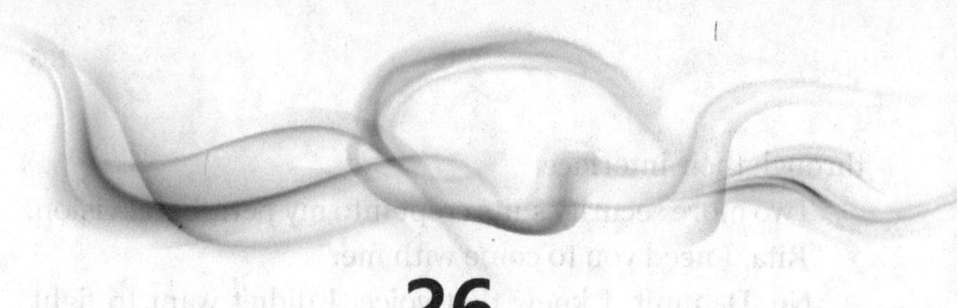

26

Fivers Don't Forget

"Run. Left. Now." Senio said as he reached for a bubble tab on his belt.

I ran, shoving my way through the crowd. All the commotion would bring more security, if not Andover's people, assuming he had them scattered throughout the station.

The press of bodies was heavier down here, slowing my progress. The only consolation was that the team after me had to deal with the same impediments. Except they had the communication interface. They could work as a team and had eyes above me on the second floor. Good thing I ran the drills and knew how poorly they worked together. This one time, that might be to my benefit.

I tried to keep low, to blend, but each time I thought I was making progress, someone shouted, "She's over here!"

Why did they have to pick me as the one thing they could unify against? I hated them all more than ever.

"Rita, in here." A young woman in a bright pink foodservice uniform held open the heavy chain door to her closed workplace. She waved me inside.

Running out of options, and with shouting closing in

behind me, I took the chance and ducked into the empty eatery. Everything was spotless.

I didn't recognize her, but faces were a blur to me until I'd seen them regularly for a couple of years. She looked too young to have been employed for long.

"I'm the only one here. Put the new girl on the shitty cleaning shift," she grumbled. "Go through the kitchen. Use the back emergency door. You know how to turn the alarm off, right?"

"Yeah. Thanks."

"Thanks for taking care of us Fivers. We might grow up, but we don't forget." She winked and shooed me toward the back.

Maybe the Maker's teachings of good deeds leading to rewards had some truth to it. My mother would be happy to hear that her drilling of religious teachings had come to fruition.

The kitchen was as clean as the front end. I ran through it to the emergency door and entered the blanket code to silence the alarm. Swinging my hip into the heavy bar latch opened the thick fire-block door without protest. I'd always enjoyed watching the trainees floundering to get these doors open during safety drills. My sturdy build was good for something.

The back hallway was nothing more than a safety exit for all the social district businesses. There were four wide stairways that led down to level seven, equally spaced along this circular hallway. With no one tailing me and knowing the lack of security cameras here, I ran straight for the nearest stairway without a care for the sound of my pounding feet.

The utilitarian metal gridwork stairs led me down and around in the limited space behind the public side of the station. It was cold here, and the air held a metallic tang. Were this an actual emergency, there would be plenty of warm bodies around me. I crossed my arms over my chest to keep my hands warm and conserve body heat. Steam unfurled before me with every breath.

Praying that I didn't run right into another security officer, I threw the level seven emergency exit door open and entered the public zone. Warmer air hit me immediately. As did the stench of smoke.

My steps faltered at the sight of blood on the floor. Char marks covered the wall to my right. Suite doors hung open. A riot was one thing, but what in the Maker's name had happened here?

"Come back to admire your handiwork?" asked a male voice that made my spine go ramrod straight.

I froze in place. "I didn't do this."

"Oh, I think we both know better." Agent Andover slapped a bubble tab between my shoulder blades.

Encapsulated in seconds, I couldn't see more than blurred shapes as we approached the area where I'd passed through the crowd that had been waiting for the stalled lift earlier. Still shapes lay sprawled on the floor. Bodies. People had been killed here, but by whom and why?

I'd egged the crowd on, but they didn't have access to weapons. Surely, they wouldn't have started burning things. The economy floor, surprisingly, had the lowest crime rate of all the living levels on the station. These weren't violent people. They just wanted equal treatment. I'd been one of them. I supposed I still was.

I slumped against the internal bubble wall, unable to look away from the blurred scene around me even as Agent Andover shoved me inside the now operational lift.

He didn't bother attempting to avoid walls or door frames. In fact, he went out of his way to bounce me off every single one of them.

When my bubble was finally retracted, I found myself back in the same cell as before. Or one just like it. They all looked relatively the same, after all.

At least I wasn't on Andover's ship on a one-way trip to the center of the empire to answer for aiding in Laurent's abduction. Or acting as Ari Leeman's accomplice. Or whatever other charges Agent Andover felt like making up.

I wished it was Yumi's far more friendly face in front of me again, but Andover was taking care of his own business this time around. He did the pre-requisite pat down himself, seizing the datapad and demanding I remove the maintenance coverall so he could do a more thorough search than Yumi had done last time. He indeed did so, leaving no inch of skin untouched.

Mid-gathering my wits after suffering his hands all over me and being rammed into everything between the lift and this cell, I didn't have time to brace myself for being slammed up against the wall with his arm wedged against my throat.

"Where did he go? Which ship?"

He'd intercepted my message. I kept my smile to myself and my mouth shut.

"I don't know what you were told, but this is important. The fate of the empire, the gratitude of the Empaetor is in your hands. Do you understand?"

He leaned in until our noses nearly touched. "What you saw on level seven could happen to all of Anduvea. Are we clear?"

My stomach heaved at the answers provided in that single sentence. I nodded.

"Good." He pulled back, but kept his forearm on my neck. "So which ship and where?"

"I can't tell you that."

"What if I told you that the *Knaldon* left the station and is orbiting Anduvea. The current locked target is your family home."

That would explain why I wasn't on his ship. Fuck.

Andover's lips curled. "So?"

My parents were going to kill me, but I couldn't give Andover information that didn't exist. I also couldn't give him Laurent, not only because the Empaetor's agent was setting off my internal madman sensor, but because my parents would also be in his hands. That would leave me with no bargaining chip to save any of them.

"I still can't give you what you want."

He cocked his head and released his hold. "Interesting. Do you not know, or are you so dedicated to bringing down the empire that you'd let your parents die?"

I peeled myself off the wall and rubbed my throat. "Maybe they're not home."

"The lights are on and the transport is in the dock. No transmissions have been sent to them as a warning. I believe 'blissfully oblivious' is the appropriate term."

I wanted to spit in his face, but my mouth was too dry. "The occupants waiting for the lift on level seven were neither blissful nor oblivious. Just dead. Thanks to you."

"And here you are, adding to your body count. What's a few more added murder charges at this point?"

I shrugged. "I guess I'm just that dedicated." Just not to the cause he'd accused me of.

He activated the comm chip on his collar. "Do it."

Thoughts of my childhood in the house that was being destroyed in that same moment raced through my head. The people who lived there were here, alive, and relatively safe. Everything else could be replaced. Eventually. Except that my father was too sick to work and my mother needed to take care of him. I'd definitely lost my job, my savings were meager, and I'd handed all my extra credits to Laurent before ending up here. My mother might have liked preaching that life wasn't about the material things, but I would dare bet that in the absence of any of them, she'd change her mind.

"I'll give you a few minutes to decide how much your loyalty is worth. Then we'll try this again. And if you're considering pulling whatever trick you did last time, I've left my own guards outside this door." Andover scowled as he stepped out of the cell.

No doubt he'd be diving into an investigation into who else he could try to hold over my head. The joke was on him. I didn't have anyone else. If the threat to my parents' lives didn't get me to crack, surely coworkers with whom I spent a scant amount of free time on rare occasions wouldn't be his next step.

He'd have to go big. And I was willing to bet he'd need more than ten minutes to get clearance for that. Not that ten minutes gained me anything. I was cut off. No one was coming to save me this time.

27

Appropriate Motivation

Andover's few minutes dragged on until I let my guard down enough to slump onto the cot. Maybe that's what he'd been waiting for because he barged in with one of his goons beside him. He was still scowling, and his hands were busy fisting at his sides. That didn't look like a man who'd been given clearance to blow a station or a planet.

"Where is the Scaavo heir?" he demanded.

I sat up and swung my legs over the edge in case I needed to get to my feet for this. "Far from you."

Andover nodded to the man beside him.

I braced myself, but when his fist met my jaw, it still hurt like hell. He hit me once more and then stepped back.

"Watch your tone," Andover said, his fingers still curling and unfurling at his sides.

I wondered why he didn't hit me himself. Did he have delicate fingers? Old injury? Didn't want to get my blood on him? Probably that.

I spat the blood in my mouth at him. It landed on his left leg and dribbled down his pants.

Whatever else he'd been going to say vanished in a

snarl. He muttered something to his goon, who then came at me again, going in hard on my ribs. I got a couple hits in on him, but Andover ended that by slapping a pair of restraints on my wrists. We wouldn't want to play remotely fair.

"Where is the Scaavo heir?"

I had nothing witty left to say. He didn't seem to appreciate my humor anyway.

He muttered something about appropriate motivation and then stood with his back against the door, out of spitting range.

I tried to get to my feet, but found myself thrown on the floor with a loud crack as my head hit first. Even as I tried to squirm out of the goon's iron grasp, he grabbed my shoulders, lifting me upward and then slamming me back down again. Black spots danced in my vision.

He stood up, and I thought I might get a few minutes to catch my breath, but no. His first kick snapped a rib. I was too busy trying to shield my torso to do much about the second and third kicks.

"We'll be back shortly. I'm waiting for a call," Andover announced ominously.

Was he really, or was that a bluff? All I knew for sure was that I hurt. If Andover was convinced Laurent was off the station and he thought he'd killed my parents, they were all safe. Assuming he didn't get that clearance. I prayed he didn't.

If I could keep Andover occupied for a few days, Laurent and my parents would follow my plan to meet with Tino and get off the station. There was nothing more for me to do than be a thorn in Andover's side until he either killed me or left me to my misery while he chased every ship that had left the station around the time of my message to Marishka.

I crawled onto the cot and closed my eyes, determined to make the most of whatever break he gave me. Every breath hurt. I fell into an uneasy sleep, dreaming that my dad was teaching Laurent how to milk a geppa and both of them were getting filthy. My mother was yelling at them to stay out of the house.

Someone grabbed my braids. My eyes flew open to see Andover looming above me. He threw me onto the floor and pulled a boot back, ready to kick me. I curled onto my side to protect my already screaming ribs.

"Where is he?"

Inspiration hit. If he really wanted to haul Laurent back to his father for whatever purpose, he wouldn't want him dead. I winced, which was not at all an act. "He's on the surface. Anduvea."

"See, that wasn't so hard." He kicked me anyway and left.

Getting up was too much work. Curled into a ball on the floor, I closed my eyes and willed myself away to a world where smoke never filled the air.

A warm hand on my freezing, bare shoulders prompted me to open my eyes. Senio shook me gently. My heart leapt into my throat at the surprise of another cell break. Disorienting sleep hung at the edge of my awareness, clouding everything with confusion. In only my undershirt and pants, I was much colder than I preferred to be. Or maybe, I considered as my senses woke up enough to remind me of my situation, it was a combination of pain, exhaustion, and hunger in addition to the wardrobe.

"Let's get you up on the cot. You'll be more comfortable there," he said.

"But..." Was he not going to help me escape?

Senio smiled sadly. "Yumi sends his regards from his house arrest situation."

"His what?" I reached up to rub my face, but when my fingers met puffy, tight skin, I thought better of it.

If Yumi was confined to his suite, he couldn't help Laurent get off the station. Did I want to risk involving Senio too? I studied my friend's face with bleary eyes. I couldn't risk losing another ally to Andover's heavy fist.

Laurent had proven himself to be more than just a handsome figurehead. Surely if he was capable of running the empire, he could figure out an exit plan with Tino.

Senio caught my arms just below the restraints and helped hoist me to my feet. I groaned. The floor had been just fine. In my sleep, I'd forgotten about my bruised and cracked ribs.

"There's no proof of Yumi helping you escape, but Andover has suspicions. There's an active investigation, but it's mostly on hold because he's been hunting you down. Maybe now he'll see that he's wrong about Yumi, and he'll let the old man escape his nagging wife and get back to work."

I nodded, hoping Yumi was cleared soon and suffered nothing worse than a day or two confined with his wife.

"We don't condone violence done to our prisoners," Senio stated loudly, likely for Andover's posted guards outside my door. "As recompense for your treatment, I got clearance for a blanket and pillow for you."

"That's my recompense? I demand two blankets and a

visit from medical."

Senio chuckled. "Glad to see you're still in good spirits."

"I don't think you've seen me in good spirits in a long while."

"Does getting drunk at the harvest party two years ago count? You seemed pretty happy for a few hours anyway."

"Short-lived but yeah."

I grunted as he helped me sit on the cot and then went to the doorway, where he picked up a blanket and pillow. He did not hand them to me, but set the pillow on one end and waited.

I twisted enough to bring my feet up, grunting and groaning my way through settling into a semi-comfortable position. Senio gently draped the blanket over me. He stood back, wringing his hands.

"I'll make sure you get a meal next time the cart comes through."

"Thanks, Senio."

"I wish there was more I could do for you," he said apologetically.

"Thanks for this." I patted the blanket.

He nodded and backed out of the cell.

Once I was alone, I sat up and examined the pillow, every seam and stitch. Then I went over the blanket. There was nothing. No messages, nothing hidden to help me escape. I was truly stuck here.

Hours later, I thought I heard the squeaky wheel of the meal cart, but no food arrived. My stomach rumbled. I forced myself to get up and get water from the tiny toilet sink. It was one thing to be hungry, but I didn't need to add dehydration to my list of problems.

When I woke again, the lights were on their nighttime dim setting. I didn't know how long I'd been sleeping or what time it was. Medical didn't come. Neither did a second blanket or another visit from Senio. When I heard the meal cart pass me by again, I got up to use the toilet and drink more water.

Agent Andover showed up just as I'd broken a sweat getting settled back under my blanket. He stood just far enough inside my cell for the door to close behind him.

"You must be hungry by now?"

He damned well knew that I was. Who wouldn't be?

"If you'd like to eat, perhaps you'd be inclined to tell me where the Scaavo heir is hiding on Anduvea?"

"I don't think so."

"Maybe you'd be more inclined to tell Pitari? The *Knaldon* has returned to the station after my crew finished interrogating the port staff. No one logged anyone matching the Scaavo heir's description."

I turned my head away and faced the wall. Chuey had to have loved that interrogation, as did his coworkers. Would we still be on friendly terms the next time I was on the surface? Assuming I'd ever make it back down to Anduvea again.

There was a moment of warmer air as my door opened. It occurred to me then that my cell had grown colder. That wasn't just me being hungry and tired. He'd screwed with the environmental controls. Of course he'd allow a blanket, making Senio think he was being humane and then cut the heat because he was a bastard.

A second set of footsteps entered, lighter, halting. "Why is it so cold in here?" Seeker Pitari asked.

"Officer Stabinov doesn't deserve your sympathy. Save it for those who do."

The little Seeker approached slowly, one deliberate footstep after another. "She's wounded."

"Just do your job. I need the truth. The Empaetor will accept no less. His heir is missing."

"I've told you repeatedly that I thoroughly examined Officer Stabinov and found no ill intent regarding the Scaavo heir," Pitari said, sounding quite aggravated.

"How's this for ill intent? Officer Stabinov is responsible for the deaths of eight men and women, along with three children and her own parents. She will answer for those crimes, but today, we need to find the Scaavo heir. I don't care what your prior examination revealed, I now have proof she helped him. She knows where he is or where he's going, and we're running out of time."

Oh, were we? I logged that insight away and hoped Laurent was a better man than his father. From what I'd seen so far, he had to be. Then again, throughout history, heirs often offered promises to make things better, but as soon as their asses hit the throne, their good intentions went out the window. Business continued as usual. Maybe there was a good reason for all of it that was shared from father to son, part of the training Laurent had mentioned. Maybe missing that would be in our favor.

If we waited long enough, the old man would die. Hopefully, a horrible death. Alone.

No matter what happened to me, I prayed I'd shown Laurent that we didn't deserve to be exiled out here. That we deserved the same comforts and courtesies the rest of the empire enjoyed. Let Anduvea be a welcome station to the empire instead of a warning to those who angered a fickle Empaetor.

"I'm ready," Pitari said after a long pause.

"Rita, tell me again where the Scaavo heir is," demanded Agent Andover.

I worked myself up onto my shaking arms so I could sit and face the Seeker. She'd tried to clear me, and it wasn't because she was inept at her job. I silently thanked her for that.

Sweat ran down my temples despite my shivering. All in all, I was not feeling my finest. Not wanting to get Pitari in any trouble, I considered how to frame my answer as truth. "He was on Anduvea. On the surface. I didn't say he stayed there."

The Seeker regarded me with a pinched expression, her lips thinned and white at the edges.

"Where did he go?" Andover pressed.

"He boarded another ship and left."

Pitari nodded. That seemed to mollify Andover only to the degree that he stopped glaring as though he could cut me down with his eyes.

"His destination?"

I met the Seeker's gaze, praying she would continue to help me as long as I played by her rules. "He did not inform me of where he would go after he left Anduvea."

Again, Pitari nodded

"Who was he meeting with?"

"That is not information I was given."

After a glance to consult Pitari, Agent Andover came closer, leaning in. "What is the name of the ship he boarded?"

I'd been too busy running for the rising ramp to have

noticed the name of the supply ship Tino had used. "I don't know."

"Did Ari Leeman tell you why he kidnapped the heir?"

I tried to speak but could only cough. Each cough was agony in my ribs. Pitari grabbed my little cup and hurried over to fill it with water. She offered it to me.

I nodded my thanks and downed it. "He was told to do so by the Empaetor's consort."

Andover backed his way to the door, maybe afraid my parched throat was contagious. "Why would she do that?"

"Leeman was not given a reason. He was following orders to protect the heir, as was his job."

"And such a great job he did," Andover scoffed. "The heir is missing and Leeman is dead."

I hadn't known Ari other than to follow him for a couple of hours and the brief conversation after he'd been shot, but I had seen the devastation in Laurent's eyes at finding out his friend had died. The man had gone to great lengths, leaving the comfort and security of the palace and the goodwill of the Empaetor to give his life for the heir. Dammit, that deserved a lot more respect than Andover was giving.

Had I been up for it, I would have had something scathing to say to express my thoughts, but I was exhausted, in pain, and starving. "Enough. Go away."

Andover leaned against the wall, bending one knee like he was settling in to be comfortable for a while. "I'd love not to be in this cesspit a moment longer, Officer Stabinov, but until I get the information I need to return the Scaavo heir safely to the Empaetor, I cannot leave. So, shall we continue?"

Pitari crossed her arms over her chest. "She is telling

the truth. Officer Stabinov does not know where the heir would go after leaving Anduvea. There is nothing more to get from her."

Andover turned his glare on the Seeker. "Did the interrogation of the port workers burn you out? It almost sounds like you're telling me you won't do your job."

The most amazing thing happened right before my eyes. The little Seeker's composure caved inward to reveal a seething rage I felt in my own aching bones. "My job is to see the truth. To help others. To heal. What I see is that your mission does not align with mine or that of my people."

Andover's mouth dropped open. He blinked repeatedly as if it had never occurred to him that this culture exchange might go poorly or that she had the option to quit.

"Your Empaetor is lost in a life of decadence. Those closest to him are nothing more than sycophants. His people are floundering and angry."

Seeker Pitari took a step toward him, and to my utter inward glee, Andover flinched.

"Your people have the ability to help others, to offer a prosperous life to all within your empire, but you ignore all that in favor of serving a tyrant." She shook her bald head. "We had one of those in my star system once. Even he wasn't as far gone as your Empaetor is."

She offered me a quick apologetic nod and then stormed past Andover and out the door. He leaned out after her. "Don't think I'm giving you transportation home, you ungrateful bitch."

"I wouldn't accept it if you did," she yelled back.

Even though it hurt my face to do so, I grinned.

"Don't think this is the end of our discussion," Agent

Andover snarled as he propelled himself off the wall, making a dramatic exit that would have made any cosmetic-ridden Anduvean fashionista jealous.

I had a feeling that it was the end because I didn't plan on giving him anything more, and Pitari had confirmed that to him. I was a dead end that, given a few more days, might just be dead.

28

Don't Piss Off The Mind Reader

I didn't remember falling asleep. Again. Breathing hurt. Water seemed too far away to bother with, given the pain in my side. I shivered continuously even with my knees tucked up to my chest and the blanket tight around me. Something in the room seemed different. The overhead light was off, but dim light shone in from the open door.

The door was open? I blinked upward. The shadow of a man stood over me. I tried to yell for help, but the stabbing pain in my side took away what little breath I had in me. Black spots danced in my vision.

"Rita? Can you stand?"

Stand? I hadn't even sat up since Pitari had told Andover off. Was that yesterday? The day before that? I didn't know.

Wait, Andover wouldn't want me on my feet. He just wanted answers. I could stay on the cot for that.

A warm hand brushed over my forehead. "Rita. Stay with me."

"Senio?"

"Laurent, Rita. It's Laurent." He crouched down beside my cot where I could see his concerned face.

"Why haven't you left? The plan was for you to leave. Where are my parents?"

Panic lit a fire in my gut. If he was here in the prison, did that mean Andover had them too? Why had he put Laurent in here with me? Oh, great Maker, what had he done to my parents when he realized he hadn't wiped them off Anduvea with their house?

"Rita, hey." He squeezed my shoulder like he had when we'd been in the maintenance tube days ago. "They're all right. We're all all right."

"How?"

"Your Seeker friend found me. I told her about the plan to use Tino to get to Yumi, who would get us off the station, hoping she could assist us, but then she told me what Andover was doing to you. With Yumi's help, she used Andover's own authority codes to put a lock on the *Knaldon*. Turns out it's damned handy to have a mind reader on your side."

I stared at him, trying to process what he was saying and only having moderate success. "You shouldn't be here. Someone might see you."

"With Andover contained, it was a risk I was willing to take."

"You shouldn't be taking risks," I grumbled, but I was grateful he was there sitting beside me, all emanating warmth and looking genuinely concerned.

"Medical is on the way. Yumi is sending them as soon as we make sure the rest of Andover's crew is confined to the *Knaldon*."

I really wanted to curl up again and close my eyes, but

Laurent had rested his warm hand on my arm. The heir to the empire was being very familiar. I didn't know what to make of it. Maybe this was all a fever dream.

Even if it was a dream, I couldn't let him make bad choices.

"Don't hold Andover's crew on their ship. They'll know how to hack into the override system and retake control."

He shook his head. "Pitari said the codes would lock everyone out."

"All it takes is one industrious troublemaker to have fooled around with the ship's systems enough to know how to circumvent them."

"You're giving his crew of thugs a lot of credit."

My left side hurt with every shallow breath I dared take. It felt like I couldn't get enough air. Every word came out a raspy whisper. It was all I had in me.

"As an employed thug myself, I'm here to tell you I could pull an override on the station if I had to. Give them a little credit. We're not all just paid muscle."

Was he brushing hair off my bruised face?

Laurent chuckled. "No, you're certainly not."

I wanted to tell him to stop screwing with me and that he should be focusing on Andover's crew and whatever nefarious thing Ari and his mother had been trying to save him from, but given the misery of my past few days, I figured the Maker owed me a little indulgence. If Laurent wanted to pay attention to me for a few minutes, I'd enjoy it. It wasn't like I expected anything to last.

"Where would you suggest moving the crew?" he asked.

"Tell Yumi to bring them here and detain them somewhere they won't cause trouble." I licked my dry lips with my dry tongue. "Better yet, shuffle the majority of them down to surface detainment so even if they crack the lock code, they can't run back to Harilax."

Laurent rested his hand on my forehead and grimaced. "Don't worry about any of that. We'll take care of it."

My eyes begged to close, but I kept them on the man before me. Rumpled clothes, the smell of geppa, and messy black curls, likely from raking his hands through them, were the only signs that he was worse for wear. I was greatly relieved.

"I wish Pitari had found me sooner. She said she had a hard time reading your thoughts about our location, that they were too slippery. Whatever that means." He stroked my forehead gently, lulling me. "Hiding us, even from a mind reader, Rita. That's quite impressive."

Unable to hold back any longer, my teeth chattered. "Can I get another blanket?"

"You got it." Laurent used his most imperiously peeved tone to yell for someone to bring a blanket immediately.

Mostly confident that things were under control, I let my eyes close.

The next time I opened them, I was in the clinic. No one stood over me, and there wasn't a hint of frost in the air.

A warm hand grabbed mine. It wasn't Laurent's, but my mother's. "You're awake. They're getting nutrients into you and fluids. And they fixed the puncture in your lungs."

"Give her a minute to breathe," my father chided. He smiled at me. "My dear girl, why are you always getting into fights?"

A half-laugh, half-sob escaped my throat to hear the words he'd often said to teen-aged me while sitting on the edge of my bed while I nursed a split lip or swollen eye.

"It's what I'm good at," I returned my usual reply.

He chuckled. "You should see the other guy. He's angry."

"I bet." I tested a laugh to find it didn't hurt nearly as much as before, though it still felt like someone had kicked me several times and broken ribs. Because they had. My fingers skimmed my sides, evaluating the tender spots.

"Two broken ribs." My mother tsked. "And your face." She reached over to brush my hair back. "I'll braid it again for you once you're up. It was a mess. I took them out while you were sleeping."

"Thanks." Leave it to my mother to worry about how my hair looked while I was unconscious.

I wanted to tell them about the house being blown off the planet, but they were being so nice. It felt good to have them close. Not smothering, not ragging on me for eating too much or doing something with my hair beyond braids, or dressing better, just here and smiling. But maybe this was the time, while they were in a good mood.

"Sorry about the house. Agent Andover—"

My mother instantly went quiet and withdrawn, like someone had snuffed her candle. She stood and backed away from the bed to sit in the chair that I realized she must have sprung up from when I woke.

My father patted my hand. "Don't worry about it. Laurent said he'd make sure we got a replacement with improvements even, at no cost.

"Where is he?"

"Finally sleeping," my father said. "He hasn't left your side in two days."

"Huh? Why? He should be headed...somewhere."

Back to confront his father? To find out what happened to his mother? Running far away from it all?

My father patted my hand again and winked. "I don't think he's going anywhere without you."

Right. Because I was his bodyguard, and he didn't currently have any of those at his disposal. I vaguely remembered he'd said something regarding that before I'd passed out back in the cell.

If Laurent had offered to replace the house my parents had lost in my covering for him, I'd be happy enough with that. Maybe he'd let me keep Ari's credit chip once I could deliver him safely back into the care of his own guards. If I had anything to say about it, a little something for Anduvea would go a long way toward making up for my broken ribs at his expense.

But first, I had to get him back where he belonged and figure out why he'd been abducted in the first place. Once I knew he was safe, I could leave him to his life and not feel like I was slacking in my duties.

I sighed and rubbed my hands gingerly over my face. When had I gained a conscience about the fucking empire and its heir?

"How much longer am I stuck in this bed?"

"Another day or two," my mother said from her chair. A bit of color had returned to her face. "You had an infection thanks to the punctured lung. The doctor said you'll be short of breath for a while. I'm sure they'll explain everything to you now that you're awake."

My father cast her a worried glance before turning back to me. Was I missing something? My mind was too foggy, and even though I'd just woken up, I still felt exhausted, deflated. The urge to cough hit me hard and sudden. My ribs might have been somewhat repaired, but they still hurt like hell with every deep, wracking cough until I finally caught my breath again.

"We'll let you rest." My father handed me a cup of water. "We'll stop back for a visit tonight. Get some sleep."

I nodded.

Hand in hand, my parents left the room. Just as I closed my eyes, the doctor came in. He ran a handheld scanner over my torso and made notes on his datapad.

"You are fortunate to be here. That lung puncture was serious. In your weakened state, the infection was taking a heavy toll on your body."

Reading between the lines explained my mother's weary face. "I see."

He gave me the rundown on my treatment plan and what had already been done while I was out, ending with the decree that I remain in bed and under observation for two more days. Given that I just wanted him to leave so I could go back to sleep, I wasn't up for arguing.

When I woke next, Yumi and Senio were cautiously approaching my bed. They smiled apologetically.

"Didn't mean to wake you," said Yumi.

I waved off their apologies. "Make it up to me by filling me in. The riot on level seven, Andover's ship takeover, his crew status?"

Senio laughed. "I told you she was going to be in charge."

Yumi rolled his eyes under his white, bushy brows. "I believe I told you that you were on leave."

"Yeah, you and Andover both. Not that it matters. I'm asking as a favor since I'm kind of unofficially sort of maybe employed by the heir to the empire."

Yumi and Senio shared a look that might have been disbelief, or perhaps there was a joke I wasn't privy to.

"Oh, it's official," declared Laurent as he strode in. With his black curls neatly combed back from his clean face and wearing a blue uniform he'd likely commandeered from Andover's crew, he looked very much the heir to the empire. Very much like the still frames of his father when he was younger. I wasn't sure how I felt about that.

And what the hell was he doing openly out in public? "You shouldn't be here. With them." I waved at Yumi and Senio. "People will see you."

"Yes, well." Laurent sighed. "With Andover and his crew contained, I feel fairly confident, after witnessing how much Anduveans despise the Empaetor, that they won't be lining up to do him any favors by handing me over."

"They wouldn't give a fuck about doing your father any favors. They'd be out for the reward!" I tried to sit up more, but my ribs informed me that was a bad idea. "How long have you been walking the station openly? How many people know you're here?"

Great Maker, I was going to need about six clones to keep this fool out of trouble until I could turn him safely over to the care of his own staff. Men like Ari, who were loyal to him.

Senio's lips couldn't have pressed any tighter together.

"Rita, for the Maker's sake," Yumi whispered as he cast petrified glances at Laurent.

Laurent came to stand beside me, looking for all the empire like he was my bodyguard instead of the other way around. He eyed Yumi and Senio. "Not a word to anyone about seeing me here. Is that clear?" he ordered in his father's imperious tone.

They nodded, glancing at each other and then at me. Laurent, they avoided making eye contact with altogether.

Huh, was that what I was supposed to have done from the start? Clearly I'd dozed off during the social etiquette portion of my early education.

Laurent turned to me. "I've stayed sequestered in a suite with your parents or here in this room since Seeker Pitari came for us. Other than my visit to your cell, that is. Some of the medical and security staff know me, I suppose. When your parents said you were awake, I had to see you. I may have gotten a bit ahead of the situation in my hurry to get here."

I was glad to hear he hadn't thrown all caution to the wind. "I'm not up for duty just yet, so could you please get back behind the situation for a little while longer?"

He nodded, his warm smile tickling my memory of him sitting on the cot beside me in the cell. He definitely did not need to be looking at me like he was, especially not considering my boss and coworker, my closest friends, were in the room. I was about to tell him to cut it out when Yumi found his tongue.

"I don't care who you are, you can't steal my one reliable senior employee."

Senio's head snapped to Yumi. "Hey! You've got at least two."

Yumi waved a hand at Senio's outrage. "You've got another five years of service before I'd consider you ready to step into Rita's boots, though I appreciate your reliability."

"You'll have to make do, I'm afraid. The empire has need of Ms. Stabinov's services." Laurent turned back to me. "If you're willing, that is?"

"I'll need to see the job details and the compensation."

Laurent looked worried. "You're already doing the job, Rita. And more. Name your price."

Yumi and Senio's heads snapped to Laurent, all eye avoidance out the window. Guess I wasn't the only one to forgo protocol after a few minutes.

Senio whistled. "Yep, you've lost her, old man. Should have retired when you had the chance. Now you've got to wait, what, five more years for me?"

Yumi groaned. When he met my apologetic gaze, there wasn't an ounce of hope in his, just resolve. "There will always be a place for you here, Rita. You know, if that," he jerked a thumb in Laurent's direction, "doesn't work out."

Everyone seemed to have their minds made up as to what I would do. What I should do. Maybe it was because I wasn't feeling up to even leaving my bed or that I didn't really have much choice in the matter if I wanted my parents to get a new house, my finances in better standing, and the lives of my people improved, but all I wanted in that moment was for all of them to leave me alone until I was feeling more myself.

"Thanks, Yumi."

Senio cleared his throat. "So yeah, I think we should let Rita rest. Glad to hear you're no longer coughing blood and all that."

Grateful that at least one of them knew my moods enough to know when to run, I forced a smile. "Thanks, Senio."

Yumi seemed to get the hint and followed him to the door. Laurent angled himself to sit at the end of the bed.

Senio shook his head. "You probably don't want to do that."

"Do what?"

"Stabby's all done with people for today."

Laurent looked down his nose at Senio. "I just got here."

He shrugged. "Don't say I didn't warn you."

The two of them left, closing the door behind them.

Laurent hovered at the end of the bed. "Do you want me to leave?"

Did I? I opened my mouth to answer, but a round of deep, dry coughs interrupted me. Tears leaked down my cheeks by the time I'd recovered. Laurent hurried to hand me the cup of water from the bedside table.

"Thanks," I said once I'd caught my breath and wiped my face.

He nodded toward the door.

I nodded to the chair.

He pulled it closer and sat. "You weren't kidding about the Stabby nickname."

I shook my head.

He laughed. "I like it."

"I didn't need your approval."

His eyes twinkled with mirth. "I know."

"So, this job…"

The Scaavo heir leaned forward in the chair, planting his elbows on his knees and steepling his fingers under his chin. His gaze fell to the floor.

"Ari is gone. I can never replace him, and I can never recreate the years he stood beside me, behind me, making me feel safe, and laugh, and not alone."

I had a feeling he was never alone in the palace crawling with guards and servants and the host of sycophants that followed his father everywhere. Just like I was never alone on this station, with loud neighbors, months of idiot tourists, and a couple of cherished coworkers who knew when to leave the room.

"I'm sure you have more than one bodyguard," I said, attempting to diffuse the thickness in my throat.

He nodded. "But there was only one Ari." Laurent exhaled long and deep before meeting my gaze. "In the short time I've known you, Rita, you've done every bit as much for me as Ari did."

"I think Ari was not properly challenged in all those years."

"He was fortunate that the palace was a safe place then." He licked his lips. "I fear it's not now."

"It's definitely not. I can tell you that, and I've never been there. People like Andover and the Empaetor live there."

He smirked. "Andover is just following orders. My father is," he waved a hand in the air, "difficult, but that's why I need you."

"I'm definitely difficult. I've been told so by many people."

Laurent chuckled.

"So, you need me because I don't follow orders?"

"Without question? No. You're not afraid to talk plainly. I wouldn't put up with that from anyone else, but with you..." The hint of a smile danced over his lips.

Having seen him interacting with other people, I realized he was not the same with me. He'd had his moments of ranting and nearly exploding, but he hadn't ever looked down on me like he had Senio. More often than not, he was Laurent, not the Scaavo heir, as Andover had been so fond of calling him. As everyone had called him, like he didn't have a name of his own.

"But I don't know the rules there, or the people. Or my way around." I shook my head. "You were in danger here, in the place I know, where I have an advantage. That's entirely different. I'd be of no use to you there."

"I disagree. To you, everyone there is untrustworthy, every room a potential trap. Everything is suspect. You've proved you can't be bought or manipulated."

Would my nerves withstand being on constant high alert? Did I want his life on my shoulders for the foreseeable future? Was I prepared to leave the only life I'd ever known to be surrounded by everything I didn't?

"If you had asked me before I'd known you were in the stasis tube, when I'd first talked to SA Tekka, I would have told you it was my dream job."

Laurent stretched his legs out and sat back, resting his hands in his lap. He looked like someone pretending to be relaxed, but I could see the tension in his shoulders, the stiffness in his spine.

"When I was a child, my only dream was to sit on my father's throne. I couldn't get there fast enough. But now? What I've seen here, overheard..." He shook his head. "What I thought my father's empire was and the reality of it, they are very different."

"Then I'm glad you're here. But we're only one world."

He stared at the blanket covering my legs. "I've traveled a good deal. I knew there were people, whole colonies that needed help, and I've done what little I could, but how many more Anduveas are there?"

"We're not the only exile world, and I doubt we're the most angry about it. Consider how many colonies make up the empire and where they might stand."

"That is a terrifying thought."

I nodded and finished the water in my cup. "Indeed. The people, my level of people anyway, lowly and undistinguished as we are, have been waiting for the chance to overthrow all this empiric bullshit for decades."

Laurent scowled. "I don't approve of your assessment."

"Then do something about it."

He shot to his feet and stalked around the small room, jaw clenched and arms stiff at his sides.

A knock sounded on the door, which must have been more of a warning than a call for permission because a nurse barged in, her attention on her datapad. "Time for your vitals check," she said in a bored tone.

I winced as she adjusted the pillows behind me, setting me up straighter, but giving me a better view of the room. She placed the bed control next to my hand. "Make yourself comfortable, but not flat down, alright?"

"Thanks."

She went about her business, checking me over and tapping on her screen. It wasn't until she turned to leave that she spotted Laurent.

"Oh! I'm so sorry! I didn't realize that you..." She backed away, nearly tripping herself in her hurry to leave.

He watched her exit with a bemused smile before turning his attention back to me. "Why aren't you like that? Like everyone else?"

"They're not supposed to know you're here," I grumbled. "Would you prefer that I was a good little citizen?"

Laurent chuckled. "No. I need you exactly as you are, as much as it may irritate me on occasion."

Why did he have to be charming *and* heir to the empire? If he'd been a simple trader on a ship passing through the station, I would have been interested. Very much so, especially after his performance in the lift, but the Scaavo heir? I wasn't qualified for that.

"Happy to be of service, I suppose."

"If you could help me correct at least some of the, as you put it, empiric bullshit, would you consider taking the job I'm offering you?"

I did like the sound of that, but I wasn't about to get all starstruck again like I had with SA Tekka and not ask for what I wanted.

"I'm not leaving my parents behind. They need me."

"They do, and admittedly, they've grown on me a bit. Done."

Had they? Overcome with a wave of relief and happiness that someone else found value in the people I cared for, I nearly caved and said yes.

But I needed more.

"I don't know what you paid Ari, but his credit chips were impressive. Can you match that for me?"

"I can."

That was easy. I let out a sigh of relief that turned into another bout of coughing. He stood there, helpless and watching with concern.

"I'm not done," I managed to say.

"Coughing or bargaining?"

"Probably both."

He refilled my cup and handed it back to me.

I nodded gratefully and took a sip. "If I can get you safely on your father's throne, will you release the people of Anduvea from their exile?"

Laurent stood beside me, silent for a moment, staring at the cup in my hands. "That's something I intended to do without you asking, so yes."

"Did you?" He hadn't mentioned it first, so it could just be a ploy to seem like a good guy. One thing Laurent was right about without a doubt: I was suspicious of everything. Including him.

"Yes, Rita. I'm not my father, and I hope you'll stick around long enough to believe that for yourself."

Seeker Pitari said I was a good judge of character. I very much wanted to give Laurent the chance to prove that was true. "Alright, I'm in."

He grinned and settled onto the bed next to my legs. "Excellent. The answers we need are on Harilax. We have plans to discuss."

29

Gift Of The Tyrant

Three days later, I was on my feet. Medication had my pain and coughing at a semi-tolerable level. I stood off view of the camera in the spacious ready room with Laurent, who would be remaining absolutely silent and as invisible as possible. Pitari stood beside Agent Andover, who was relaying his report to SA Tekka. Senio stood just out of view on the other side. We both had weapons drawn and aimed at the empiric agent, but it was Pitari who had him under control.

I reminded myself again never to cross a Seeker. Her demonstration of holding control over Andover's mind was chilling. Watching her in action made me second-guess agreeing with Laurent's plan to bring her to Harilax with us. However, he was adamant that she'd be helpful in finding answers, and I couldn't argue with that.

"The Scaavo heir is not here," Andover said, his face strained and sweat on his brow. "We've completed a thorough search of both the station and Anduvea. Ari Leeman's accomplice provided no further information beyond that the Scaavo heir made it to the port on Anduvea and met up with an outgoing flight there." Andover grimaced. "The only flights leaving the surface traveled to the station. Though we interviewed the port staff and searched all the outgoing logs around the day he was there, we uncovered no definitive record of which flight he took or where it went other than the station, which we've also thoroughly searched."

"Next steps?" SA Tekka appeared equally uncomfortable.

I didn't blame him. I wouldn't want to be the one reporting continued failure to the Empaetor either, especially if he was already in a shitty mood from his failing health.

"We have the names of the few outgoing vessels. I've left some of my crew on the surface to investigate further there. Some will be left on the station to monitor those who were on those flights. I am leaving with the rest to search the surrounding area for any residual sign of outbound travel."

That was a thing? I realized I didn't know what the *Knaldon,* or perhaps any of Harilax's ships, were capable of. Having worked alongside Andover, Pitari did.

The Seeker stood silently by Andover's side, her hands clasped together in front of her, legs slightly spread in what looked like a ceremonial stance. Her gaze had the same dazed quality as it had during her earlier demonstration of the manipulative power she was currently utilizing. She'd made Andover announce to his crew that I would be traveling with them and that I was to be treated well. Given my prior treatment, I appreciated the stipulation.

Agent Andover's fingers started tapping against his thigh. I

signaled Senio, who had a voice SA Tekka wouldn't recognize.

"Sir, we may have found something," he called, using the warning phrase we'd agreed on.

Pitari's forehead glistened and the knuckles on her clasped hands whitened as she increased her internal control over Agent Andover.

Hope brightened on SA Tekka's face. "Best of luck on your hunt."

"Thank you, sir."

The vid went dark as SA Tekka cut his transmission.

Andover dropped to his knees, grasping his head with both hands. He wavered there, rocking back and forth. The little Seeker looked like she might throw up. Senio rushed forward and snapped the wrist restraints back on Andover before hauling him up and back to his cell on his own ship.

I tapped Pitari's shoulder. "To bed with you. Rest. You did a great job."

She smiled weakly. "We call that the Gift of the Tyrant and I swore I'd never use it, but in this case, for this cause," she nodded to Laurent, "I don't feel guilty that I did."

"Thank you for your help, Seeker Pitari," Laurent said. "I appreciate you using your gift, even though it clearly is not comfortable to do so."

"It is a painful process for both sides," she admitted. "I would be happy to never do it again." She offered Laurent a head bob of a bow and left to find her bed.

"I'd be happy if she never did that again either. Gives me the creeps," I said.

"You're worried she could do that to me. To any of us," Laurent said quietly, as if Pitari were still in the room to overhear us.

"Who's the mind reader now?"

He smirked. "Go check on your parents. I'll stay out of sight in our suite. You can send Senio to check on me."

Our suite. That was going to take some getting used to.

He'd invited me to share a living space so tactfully and with a hint of childish awkwardness that he'd convinced me this was a platonic work situation and not something out of a gushing girlhood fantasy. Otherwise, I never would have agreed. Separate beds all the way, thank you very much. He'd had the same arrangement with Ari, and he was adamant that they'd been nothing more than friends either. We were the same. End of story.

"Pitari said she'd finish clearing the crew tomorrow. The station staff we drafted have all signed their confidentiality agreements, and she's already vetted them. If we could have gotten away with replacing the entire crew, I'd feel better about you walking around freely."

"Having seen how Agent Andover operates, I shouldn't have been surprised to learn that a quarter of the *Knaldon's* crew isn't loyal to their commanding officer. But it's also disturbing."

I shrugged. "Imagine that a quarter of the empire feels that way about your father."

Laurent's jaw tightened, as it tended to do when I cast his father in a disparaging light, but he didn't disagree with me.

Tapping my comm pin, I summoned Senio back to the ready room once he'd dropped off Andover. I still couldn't believe Yumi had allowed Senio to join us, leaving himself the lone senior security officer on the station. There was some mumbling between him and the heir about gaining favor and upgrading his retirement plans. However, Yumi had made it clear that Senio was on loan, and not to be conscripted, stolen, or bribed to remain in Laurent's service.

He would be monitoring outgoing messages, making sure no greedy bastards leaked Laurent's location or involvement with the station. As reluctant as I'd been to agree to this trip to the center of the empire, I was grateful for the more controlled environment of the *Knaldon* and the minimal crew to deal with.

I leaned against the wall, taking a couple of steady, deep breaths to avoid a coughing fit. They seemed to come on when I talked. Or moved too much. Or tried to sleep, or eat, or... I was so sick of coughing and trying to catch my breath.

Laurent watched me, concern rolling off of him. He needed to dial his intensity down a notch or two.

"The one favor the Empaetor did us was calling you treasure." I poked his shoulder, snickering. "It's so nice of you to come all the way out here to help hunt that stolen treasure down." That was the story we'd given Andover's remaining crew, along with the need to keep Laurent's participation quiet for security reasons. "Perhaps you should check a mirror?"

He rolled his eyes. "You're not going to let that go, are you?"

"Nope."

Senio arrived to save me from being stuck in a room alone with Laurent and his charming smile. They headed for our suite.

Knowing the Scaavo heir was in good hands, I went the opposite direction, taking a leisurely walk to further familiarize myself with the *Knaldon* and get my doctor-approved exercise in. When I reached the little lift on the other end of the ship, I took it down to the second and only other level where the crew quarters were. I passed the large suite I shared with Laurent. The door was closed. Senio stood outside.

I was still getting used to seeing him in a blue empiric uniform. He probably felt the same way about me. We exchanged nods.

Continuing down the corridor, I knocked on the door of the smaller suite my parents had been given. When it opened, they stared at me as though I were a stranger.

"You never wear blue," my mother said finally.

"Never thought I'd see you in that," my father shook his head.

Were they disappointed that I'd defected to what we'd always considered the enemy?

Tugging at the fitted jacket, I tried to find fault with my new softer, breathable, flattering uniform. They might be uncomfortable with it, but I never wanted to wear my station uniform again.

My mother waved me inside. "Out of the corridor, dear. People are talking enough already."

Oh that. Mother had always hated gossip, and I had a knack for ending up on the wrong side of it. As a child, I was the one who didn't fit the proper girl mold, who got into fights. Now I'd somehow seduced my way into this job? The rumor—thanks to whispers about our kiss in the lift and spread thanks to the conscripted station staff now augmenting the crew—was so insanely laughable I couldn't justify it with a response.

My parents knew me better than that. Didn't they?

"For the tenth time, we're not sleeping together," I

huffed as I entered their suite.

My parents shared a knowing look that said they didn't buy it for a minute.

I flopped down in a chair. Out of the public eye, I could relax with my family and pretend that I wasn't wearing the empiric uniform with enormous responsibilities hanging around my neck.

They settled onto the couch, side by side. Two empty mugs sat on the low table in front of them, the dregs of their brewcaf scenting the air. My father reached out and wrapped his hand over my mother's. An awkward lapse in conversation settled between us that had never been there before.

"How are you feeling?" asked my mother.

"I'm taking it easy and doing my breathing treatments, Mom. The medication is helping. The doctor said I'm fit for duty, and my recovery is on track."

"That's good," my father said. He kept his gaze on whatever was behind me.

I turned to see what he was looking at. There was nothing there but the standard minimal furniture and décor. No hints of my parents. Nothing familiar to say this was their home. They had no home. They'd been utterly displaced.

All they owned fit in the two small bags they'd hastily packed when I'd dragged them into hiding with Laurent. And now they were traveling on the same ship that had destroyed their home. I really was a horrible daughter.

My father's color looked better than it had in years. Maybe that was one small consolation.

"Are you breathing easier here?" I asked.

He nodded. "The scrubbers must be even better than

the station. And Laurent sent Doctor Tik to check my lungs. He gave me medication. At no charge." He smiled. "I can see why you like him. He seems like a good man."

"I wouldn't have done any of this if I thought he was like his father."

They both nodded.

"It's just..." my mother glanced at my father and licked her lips before locking her gaze with mine.

I braced myself. If they could just get out whatever they had on their minds, maybe we could go back to the comfortable familial conversation I was used to. That I needed, in light of all the changes around me at every turn here.

"He's the heir to the empire, Rita. We understand that he needs you right now." She side-eyed my father again. He nodded, seeming to encourage her to speak for them both.

I cringed, guessing where this was going.

"Once he gets back among his people..."

"We're also his people, Mom."

"No," stated my father with an unexpected vehemence that startled me. "We're Anduvean. We are as far from *his* people as anyone can get. And no matter what sweet, enticing promises he's whispered in your ear, he's going to suddenly remember that once he's back home and safe on Harilax. In *his* palace. Where *he* lives."

"Honey," my mother said with a sympathetic smile, "we just want you to be careful and manage your expectations. As the Scaavo heir, he has access to the young, beautiful daughters of the wealthiest and most powerful families throughout the entire empire. You're, well," she waved her hand around in my direction, "you."

"I'm well aware." I stood. "And as me, who has worked

as a security officer for twenty years, has it occurred to you that I might be good enough at what I do to be employed by the heir to the empire? I'm doing my job! Which is not warming his bed or ruling the empire beside him or whatever other delusions you're convinced I might harbor." I strode to the door before I said anything further that I might regret later.

"Rita, we just don't want to see you hurt," called my mother from the couch. They hadn't even made an effort to get up, let alone come after me. Like I was a little kid again, running off to my room to sulk.

Lucky for my dignity, the *Knaldon's* doors weren't capable of slamming.

While I too hoped I hadn't chosen unwisely to follow Laurent to Harilax, he wasn't the one who had brought tears to my eyes or sent me running for the quiet solitude of the bathroom in my shared suite where I could get my emotions under control.

This was going to be a very long and emotionally taxing mission without the little pocket of support I was used to relying on. I hoped I was up for it.

30

I'm Not Stupid

"You're decidedly stabby this afternoon. Everything all right?" Laurent asked.

It wasn't his fault I was in a shitty mood, but after talking to my parents, everything rubbed me wrong. I'd wanted to do as he'd suggested and take a nap, but I'd just turned my blankets into a tangled mess and done a lot of swearing at the ceiling. I'd given up and joined Laurent on the bridge.

Pondering the projected navigation map in front of us, I traced our path with my finger. Stars and planets floated over my hand as I moved toward the center of the empire, to Harilax. I'd never seen images of most of the worlds on the map. Although, thanks to the trade ships, I had heard of them.

"Don't worry about me. We've got plenty of other things to concern ourselves with," I said.

"Do you think Pitari is up for puppeteering Andover for the rest of our flight to Harilax?"

"She's resting now."

"I hope she's better at it than you are."

I turned from the map to glare at him, but his smile said

he was teasing rather than chiding. I let his playful jab go.

"One can hope. She's got those relaxation exercises she was telling us about."

Laurent nodded. "She said she'd show you a few of them."

"Excuse me?" I snapped, giving up on holding my mood in.

"Your temper is going to get you into trouble on Harilax," Laurent said blandly, as if my outburst hadn't happened. "I know everything there will be strange to you, but I need you to maintain a level of control over your, well..." he looked pointedly to the other three crew members on the bridge, "tone in front of others."

I pinched the bridge of my nose and took a deep, slow breath. "Right. Sorry."

"I've set up interviews with the members of Agent Andover's crew for you. I'd like you to spend time with each of them. Learn what you can about anything you need to know. Anyone you need to know. Get the latest gossip. Fill yourself in. Do you follow me?"

Get up to speed by socializing with the crew who thought I'd slept my way to the top? Yeah. Great.

"You do know what they're saying about us, right?"

He looked at me blankly.

"Of course they're not saying anything to you. You're... you. You get to do whatever you want with whoever you want, and no one bats an eyelash."

Laurent sighed. "This is because I kissed you, isn't it."

"That certainly didn't help."

"It helped at the time. In that situation, I mean."

"It did." And it hadn't been awful. At all. Was he staring at my face? At my lips? What the hell was he doing? We were working together to thwart whatever had sent Ari running for the edge of the empire. That was the deal. The deal where I wasn't as stupid as my parents were convinced I was.

I shook my head, wanting to forget the whole conversation. "When we get to Harilax, I'm going to your mother's estate to talk to her staff with Pitari. You'll stay aboard and we'll go from there?"

He nodded.

I pulled out the military-grade datapad he'd given me from the *Knaldon's* supplies. It had all sorts of useful information that public-issue pads didn't offer, like detailed imagery of every structure on Harilax. I flipped to the image I'd saved of his mother's estate. Setting the datapad on the control panel in front of us, I activated the full dimensional illustration of the massive estate.

"Are you sure you don't want to find a lounge or somewhere more comfortable to sit while we go over this?" asked Laurent.

"Here is fine. You wanted to be available in case anything popped up we needed to take care of, right? The bridge is the place to be."

It was also where people were. Working. And we were working, being seen together in that capacity, rather than off at a corner table somewhere talking in hushed voices. The fastest way for this crew to take me seriously was to be here.

We spent several hours bent over the floor plans, Laurent explaining about the house, the staff, his mother's hobbies, her few friends, anyone he thought we might be able to talk to. By the time we'd finished, I felt fairly confident about my task. If we needed any on-the-spot clarification, the comm pin would allow me to talk to Laurent.

It would be nine days before we arrived, assuming everything went smoothly and the jump gates were operational. I needed that time for the crash course in all things empiric protocol and royal family related. My brain already hurt from spending the afternoon absorbing everything Laurent shared with me.

By dinner, I needed a break from the man. It wasn't necessarily because he was a chore to be around, but I wasn't used to being around anyone after work hours. And now I couldn't get away from him. He *was* my job.

Pitari approached me as we entered the mess hall. "Would you mind if I borrowed the heir for dinner?"

"Not at all." I offered her a grateful smile and found a small table against a wall in a big pocket of silence that helped me relax. Maybe she'd read my mind about needing space or she actually needed to talk to him, but I drank up every minute of solo time. I could see them from my table, and I glanced up from the book I'd loaded on my datapad every few minutes, but the space...it was heavenly.

Senio plopped a plate down on my table and pulled up a chair. "What are you reading?"

I'd long since finished eating and had no reason to be there any longer other than waiting for Laurent to finish his chat with Pitari. And finish his dinner, I noted with a frown. He was a slow eater when he got to talking.

"A book about minding your own business."

Senio grinned, picked up his fork, and started eating. He gave me just enough quiet time that I dared let my eyes wander back to the History of the Rule of Empaetor Iradio Scaavo VIII. It supposedly covered events up to the last few years. I had a lot of catching up to do in the history department if I wanted a more official take on things. All we received on Anduvea were opinionated word-of-mouth versions of recent events and the officially sanctioned media releases that were merely highlight reels without substance.

"So," Senio drew out the word while wiggling his eyebrows toward Laurent. "Rita Stabinov reels in the big fish. Who knew you had it in you?"

"I don't, and you well know it. Drop it, Senio. I'm not in the mood. Especially today."

He devoured a hard, crusty roll slathered in thick butter in two loud, crunchy bites. When he finished chewing, he smirked. "I don't know. The one date we had wasn't terrible."

I groaned inwardly, recalling that debacle. Poor judgement on my part, agreeing to have dinner with the new guy on the team. Fourteen years ago, when I was going through a try-to-be-nice phase because my mother was ragging on me to find someone and start a family. Thank the Maker, I got over that.

"As I recall, dripping head to toe with tetri sauce was a good look on you," I said.

"Weren't you finding seis seeds in your hair for days afterward?" He threw his head back and laughed.

After that doomed night, we had agreed that we were not meant to pursue that avenue again, but I'd always found his laughter contagious.

"So much awkwardness." I shook my head, chuckling at the memory. "How did we make it back to your room without killing ourselves with stupidity?"

Senio laughed harder, his mirth erasing the strain of fifteen years of low pay and dealing with tourists. For a moment, he was the younger man I'd agreed to have dinner with because I'd really thought we might have a chance.

He pointed his fork at me. "You were the one who ordered the first round of drinks that started the downward spiral."

"You thought ordering a whole bottle would impress me." I rolled my eyes.

"It wasn't me who issued the challenge to finish it before we left."

I laughed, recalling how we'd stood to leave, drunk off our asses, both of us reaching to help the other stay on their feet. Instead, we'd pulled each other onto the remains of our dinner, breaking the table, and sending everything crashing to the floor.

"I wasn't the one who showed up still drunk to work the next day, joking that he slept with me."

Senio winked. "I did. Passing out counts as sleep, right?"

"You vomited on my shoulder."

"You can't prove that. It might have been yours."

"It was down my back."

His shoulders shook with laughter. "That proves nothing."

Suddenly, Laurent stood behind Senio. He caught my jovial coworker in an imperiously peeved side-eye. "Something funny?"

Senio snapped to attention, glancing at me for help.

"Just reminiscing. Are you done here?" I asked, standing and hoping to hell that he was. I couldn't deal with

Laurent being prickly on top of my nerves already being stretched thin.

"Yes, shall we?" He jutted his chin toward the exit.

"Enjoy your dinner, on your plate, and not on your clothes," I said to Senio, lightly smacking him on the head as I got up and left.

"Don't get drunk with him," he called after me.

Laurent waited all of three minutes before taking the bait. "What was that about?"

"We dated. Once. Fourteen years ago. There was a lot of alcohol involved, and it didn't end well."

He was quiet until we reached the lift to go down to our quarters. "And your friend, he thinks we're...together?"

"Everyone does," I snapped. "As far-fetched and idiotic as that is, apparently it's more believable than my possibly earning this position based on performance. Even my parents think so."

He wisely remained silent until we'd reached our quarters. "For the record, their assumption is not far-fetched or idiotic, Rita."

I wanted to hit him, to vent like he was a punching bag of all that was wrong with my life at the moment, but this wasn't the gym and he was the Scaavo heir, and somehow, I'd thrown my livelihood into his arena.

"I'm a grown woman, Laurent. You don't need to soften truths or attempt to console me. I'm fine on my own. In fact, I enjoy being on my own." My temper was bubbling up. An explosion was imminent. The last thing I needed was to piss off the one person who could ruin not only my life, but that of everyone I cared about with a few words.

"Please just give me some space for a bit, alright?"

"Of course." He shuffled in place. "But you'll stay here, with me?"

I sat on the couch, rubbing my temples and pressing my eyes shut. "That is my job, isn't it?"

"I'll just..." His footsteps crept toward the bedroom.

By the time I'd calmed myself enough to apologize, the door had already closed.

31

Like Father, Like Son

Our nine day trip to Harilax passed in a blur of me reading history, learning more about Laurent's homeworld and the palace, and too much chatting with the members of Andover's crew. At least their accountings of the political atmosphere and general gossip were livelier than what I read. Talking to everyone, having to be nice even in light of their giddy questions about my supposed relationship with Laurent, exhausted me. And Laurent, he was in my orbit so much of the day and night that I had little time to myself. I missed my bed back on the station, my suite, my space. My quiet.

It didn't take an empath to sense my mood. Laurent was decidedly professional, both in public and in private. Courteous but not excessively so. Senio accompanied him more often than not when he wandered the *Knaldon*. I slept on the couch. He slept in his bed.

I thought things were progressing productively toward dispelling our mythical relationship until my second interview with the communications officer.

Alessandra had answered all my questions dutifully and

politely, but as we were wrapping up, she leaned across the table in the lounge where I'd been holding my crew meetings. "Are you two all right? Everyone says you've had a fight or something."

"What?" It took a minute for my brain to slip out of business mode to figure out who the 'two' of us referred to.

"The Scaavo heir, he's been sullen. Some of the others say it's just a matter of time until he turns into his father. That temper." Alessandra shuddered. "In such a confined place, it's concerning."

"We're not fighting. He's fine, as far as I can tell. And we're *not* together," I said as forcefully as I could without raising my voice to the point of attracting attention.

"Maybe that's the problem," she said weakly.

"I hardly think so. He's got far bigger troubles than what woman might or might not be in his bed."

"If you say so, Officer Stabinov."

"I do."

I thanked Alessandra for her time and wrapped up the other two interviews for the day before heading off to relieve Senio from heir duty.

We were nearing Harilax, and if my neck muscles wound any tighter, I might snap. I still wasn't sure bringing Laurent this close to the Empaetor without having solid answers as to why his mother and Ari had ferreted him away was a good idea. But he was the heir, and this was what he wanted.

My gut said it was, in fact, a terrible idea. I trusted my gut.

"Are you hungry?" I asked Laurent upon finding him and Senio strolling down the main corridor that led from the bridge to the mess hall at the opposite end.

"I don't think I can eat," he admitted.

"Good. I don't think I can stomach even looking at food."

Senio offered me a friendly nod. "Pitari wanted to see you, Rita. She's with Andover."

"Alright, thanks."

Senio left us and headed into the mess hall.

"Apparently he's not going to let a little feeling of impending doom stand in the way of dinner," Laurent remarked.

"You feel it too?" I'd wondered if he understood how dangerous this was. Apparently so.

The heir to the empire nodded. "We should see what Pitari needs. I heard Andover has been raving in his cell."

"Yeah." I didn't blame Andover for raving. We'd commandeered his ship, imprisoned most of his crew on Anduvea, and had been hijacking his body as needed.

We made our way to the quad of cells that were all the containment the *Knaldon* offered. Pitari sat on the floor with her back against the wall of Andover's cell. He was indeed ranting. At the moment, he was on a jag about demanding his ship back. What intrigued me was that the little Seeker didn't appear to be listening. Her eyes were closed, and her hands lay clasped together on her crossed legs. Was she praying? Sleeping? Meditating? Any of those would be more successful far from Andover.

I cleared my throat, which set off a round of coughing. When none of that elicited a response, I glanced at Laurent. He shrugged.

"You wanted to see me?" I said to her, pulling out my datapad and activating the translator function. Her conversational grasp of our language had been improving, but on important matters, I didn't want any misunderstandings.

Pitari's eyes opened slowly, blinking a few times until she seemed to focus on me. "I did."

The Seeker got to her feet with enviable ease. "I wanted to ask your opinion on our problem," she nodded to Andover, "before I just took care of it to give us all some sanity. Him included."

"I'm listening."

So was Andover. His rant had gone silent.

"While I'm not advocating releasing him, he's going to be a problem once we reach Harilax. And as you heard, he's a problem now."

Laurent nodded. "What do you suggest?"

"I'd like to do a memory balm for him, smooth out some conversations and events."

I wasn't sure what that meant exactly, but calling it a balm sounded like it might be a pleasant procedure.

"Like how you control his body, but controlling his memories?" Laurent asked.

"Not controlling." She thought for a moment. "Dulling? We use a memory balm to soothe patients who have had a traumatic experience. They don't forget exactly, but we dull those memories and put calm thoughts around them to dissuade people from poking into them again."

Andover violently shook his head and backed away from us until he reached the rear of his cell and had no farther to go.

"Is it painful?" I asked.

"For me, a bit. It takes a lot of energy...inside." She tapped her tattooed scalp. "For him, it will be soothing."

"So he'll be quiet?" I was on board with this already.

"And not expose us on Harilax. Specifically, I'd like to keep him from exposing me." Seeker Pitari looked guilty. "Sorry, but I've seen enough memories of the Empaetor to know I should never place myself in his presence. He'd never let me leave."

"You have a valid point," Laurent admitted. "Do it."

I held up my hand. "How much is this going to take out of you?"

"I'll need help back to my room, and I'll probably sleep for a good long while." She looked guilty again.

"What?" I prodded.

"I've seen your memories, Rita. I trust you. Most of the others..." She shook her head. "Can I ask you to see me back to my room?"

"You bet, and I'll lock the door on the way out."

Pitari smiled and settled back into her pose. "This won't look like much to you, but you'll know when I'm done."

"Go ahead. Nothing will happen to you while I'm here."

The Seeker shut her eyes. A few minutes later, Andover's eyelids grew heavy. He slowly slid down the wall to sit on the floor.

Was Laurent standing closer? He sure seemed closer, his shoulder nearly rubbing against mine. I turned to see what was going on with him and was met with a soft smile that made my insides tingle. Since no one conscious was around to see us, I pretended to be too busy observing Pitari to notice and let him continue as he was.

Laurent stuck it out beside me for the first hour, but he settled into a chair nearby afterward. I offered him my datapad to keep busy. From the few glances I made in his direction, I gathered he was playing a game. It amused me to discover that even heirs play games in their free time. I just hoped it wasn't with me.

It was two hours later that Pitari's head sagged back against the wall. Andover also remained blessedly silent, his eyes blinking slowly as he looked around as if waking from a deep sleep.

"Are you finished?" I asked softly in case she wasn't.

She nodded but didn't appear up to moving anything else.

I helped her up, and with Laurent beside me, carried the limp Seeker to her room. Once I had her settled into her bed and locked the door behind me, I rejoined Laurent in the hallway.

He returned my datapad. "Let's go back to our suite."

We walked in companionable silence with a professional distance between us. Thanks to the minimal crew, the corridors were empty, people either being on duty, eating, or occupied elsewhere in their free time. Still, we didn't speak until the door shut behind us.

"You're still willing to stay on the ship when Pitari and I go down to investigate your mother's estate?"

He nodded. "My face is known there. That makes sense."

"Your face is known everywhere. Did you take after your mother at all?"

Laurent looked mildly offended. "I don't look that much like him."

"You definitely do. I might not have recognized you right away, but you were sleeping, and honestly, discovering the heir to the empire in a stasis tube was very unexpected."

"And you hate my father."

It wasn't a question, but the answer was so obvious that it flew out of my mouth. "Yes, of course I do. Everyone I know does."

His gaze slipped to the floor.

"Your father looks too much like the rest of them. Like your great-grandfather, who shunted us all onto smoke-and-fire-filled Anduvea. He ruined our lives. For generations."

"I know," he said quietly. "You'll be careful tomorrow?"

"I try to be careful every day."

"Thank you, Rita. Have a good night." Laurent slipped into the bedroom even though it would be hours, according to the time display on my datapad, before he usually went to sleep.

I settled onto the couch, kicked my feet up on the low table and nestled into the stiff pillows that had been putting a progressively worse kink in my neck with each night I spent there.

It wasn't like anyone knew I was on the couch. They'd know no differently if I went and curled up on my much more comfortable bed. It would be best for everyone if I were well rested and in a better mood from getting a good night's sleep. Who was I doing this martyr act for?

I heaved myself up and approached the bedroom door, picturing the two beds inside with plenty of distance between them. It wasn't as if we were sleeping together, side by side.

Opening the door, I slipped in. Laurent sat on the edge of his bed with his back to me. It wasn't until the bed creaked when I settled onto it that he turned around, surprise plain on his face.

I shrugged. "Got sick of the couch."

"Ari always complained about them too. Too hard. Not enough leg room."

"The pillows suck."

He smiled. "Yeah, he said that too."

"He often slept on the couch then?"

"Like you, he needed space sometimes. I get it. I'm a lot."

"I never said that." Though I had said other things lately that I probably should not have said out loud and quite so adamantly. Guilt poked me in the healing ribs.

"Not in so many words." He shifted back around. "I can take the couch if you want."

"I will certainly not sleep better if you're out there on the couch where someone could walk in and I'd never know."

"Ari said the same thing."

"He was a smart man. Apparently."

"He was." Laurent settled onto his back, still fully clothed, and closed his eyes. "Good night, Rita."

"Good night, Laurent."

32

My Old Friend Ekie

Pitari and I set down on Harilax, a world I'd never expected to visit in person. A world I'd only used as a swear word growing up, the planet was shrouded in all the bad things in the known universe. And now I was here, standing beside a Seeker from a star system far from the empire. Neither of us belonging but both trying to blend in as much as the blue empiric uniforms allowed.

She stood out more, as petite as she was. Though we were similar in age, we couldn't have been more opposite in build.

"You're nervous," she said.

"Do you ever turn that off?" I asked, not trying to sound annoyed, but perhaps not successfully managing to do so.

"Sorry. I'm nervous too."

I turned to face her as we walked. "Your use of our language has vastly improved since we first met."

Pitari flashed an impish smile. "I've been more inclined to learn it. My translator implant," she tapped her scalp just behind her left ear, "mostly does the learning and supplies my brain with the correct words and sounds. I just never bothered to use it in Agent Andover's service."

"Can't say as I blame you. Did your balm work?"

"Yes, and thanks for getting me to my bed. I checked on Andover before we left. He still doesn't like any of us and he's angry, but his memories of whether I can actually see the truth of people are blurred. I added as much blur as I dared to his thoughts of you and the heir too." She grimaced. "Not you two together. I mean, each of you and your actions against him."

"Thank you. We'll all be better off if SA Tekka and the Empaetor don't get many details out of him beyond what he'd already sent. Once we let him go. At some point." I still hadn't figured out that part of the plan.

One thing at a time, I repeated to myself as we walked through the private port that serviced the elite of Harilax. Men and women in fanciful clothing styles that I'd only seen in faded station murals wove around us like we didn't exist.

"We're supposed to turn it off. The mind reading," Pitari said. "We're supposed to ask permission, get consent. But I'm not with my people, and it has sort of been a matter of preservation since I entered this exchange program. There are too many strange thoughts, customs, politics." She shook her head. "I'm doing my best to avoid saying the wrong thing to the wrong people and upsetting anyone. There are stories of these exchanges going terribly wrong. I don't want to be one of them."

"It's fine," I assured her. "I'm used to it from you by now."

She laughed nervously. "Sorry."

The little lander we'd taken allowed us to be mostly generic in the midst of the other incoming traffic. However, the *Knaldon* was in orbit and had registered there. That fact made my gut twinge more than standing here on the surface. If the Empaetor or SA Tekka got wind that Andover was near, would they want to meet with him? And could Pitari puppet the increasingly hostile empiric agent in a convincing enough manner in person? Would she even be allowed in meetings with him?

I also wasn't a hundred percent on trusting the members of Andover's crew that we'd taken with us even though I'd talked with them and Pitari had carefully vetted each one. All it took was one person mentioning that the Scaavo heir was onboard to the wrong person.

"Rita," Pitari nudged me with her elbow.

We'd come to a port scanner. I passed through the ID chip reader. No alarms sounded. I let out the breath I'd been holding.

Seeker Pitari followed behind me, holding the chip card she'd been issued upon joining Andover's crew. The security agent babysitting the scanner waved us over.

Pitari held out her card to him. "Happens at every port. You don't see many of these, I take it?"

"Not every day, no." He held up the card, studying the still frame of Pitari's face on it and comparing it to the woman in front of him.

"Your business here?"

"Visiting a friend," I said. "Ekie Mandalbaum. She works at the consort's home. We're hoping for a tour."

I prayed Ekie, the contact Laurent had supplied, was still employed.

"Good luck. They're pretty strict about who they allow on the grounds there."

"Thanks," Pitari said, plastering a big smile on her face.

Too tightly wound, I didn't have one in me.

She took her ID card from the man and put it back in her pocket. "Do you know the way?"

He pointed north.

We filtered through the rest of the port, trying to look natural by stopping to stare in shop windows. Pitari might have been legitimately window browsing, but I was watching reflections for anyone looking at us twice. No one appeared to be.

There weren't signs to the estate, but once we cleared the port, they weren't needed. The needle-like white spires against the clear blue sky were easy to spot.

We took a public transport to the front gate. Before we got out, I tested my comm pin.

Senio answered immediately. "All good, Rita. Don't worry about us."

I did my best to shunt my concerns to the back burner and focus on the investigation before us. Nothing seemed out of the ordinary when the guard at the gate scanned our IDs or when we gave him our story about visiting Ekie. I expected a more thorough questioning after what the port attendant had said, but supposed they would have record of us if we did anything wrong. He waved us through.

"You'll find Ekie in the kitchen. First floor. The door attendant can bring you to her."

"Thank you."

The kitchen. I wondered if Ekie had served Laurent some memorable treat as a child for him to have her name memorized.

The woman posted at the door regarded us with a

dour stare. "You're friends of Ekie's?" Her grey gaze traveled from my polished boots to my unadorned uniformed shoulders.

Should I have had some marks of rank or perhaps a more feminine appearance? She barely regarded Pitari at all, even though we were dressed the same.

"I suppose it won't do any harm to allow you entry. Consort Marishka isn't currently in residence. But see that you don't make a nuisance of yourselves, or you'll be out the door before you know what hit you."

"Thank you," Pitari said, hurrying inside as though she wanted to make it through before the woman changed her mind.

Remembering who I was traveling with, I hurried to catch up with her. I wanted to ask if she'd seen anything we needed to be alarmed about, but the door attendant followed us. With a few brisk strides, she was suddenly four steps ahead and leading us through a hall with intricately carved walls that looked like wood. The closer I looked, it seemed to be some sort of dense plas swirled with colors from ivory to bronze. I shoved my hands in my pockets, afraid to even think about touching anything.

"This way," our guide said brusquely.

The older woman's determined strides were no challenge for me. Pitari, whose legs were significantly shorter than mine, was doing an admirable job. We walked from the carved hallway to a narrower, green-wall-lined corridor that turned twice before opening into a giant kitchen.

Ekie, at the attendant's announcement that we had arrived, looked up from the bread she was kneading on the countertop with confusion clear on her face. Thank the

Maker I had a mind reader with me and that she had no qualms about using her gift whether she had consent or not. Maybe on her world she would have been an outcast, but here, I could have hugged her for speaking up.

"You probably don't remember us. It's been a while. We're friends of the Scaavo heir?"

Ekie nodded uncertainly. "Glad you could stop by for a visit." There was an unspoken 'I guess?' at the end of that, but the door attendant had already headed back to her post.

Two other women and a teen-aged boy were busy preparing food throughout the expansive kitchen. How did they even reach up to the shelves in the high cupboards that went up to the lofty ceiling? Who had that much stuff to store in that many cupboards? The thick countertops, made of glossy stone colored in ivory swirls that mimicked the pattern in the hallway, had to have substantial cabinetry to hold that weight. Within thirty seconds in the room, my subconscious was adding up the astronomical cost. Long satin drapery hung from ceiling to floor over rainbow-tinted glass. It may have been clearplaz like the average home would use, which didn't shatter and was quite durable, but it had the sparkling quality that was usually reserved for actual glass. I hadn't seen the genuine stuff in person other than in small samples.

Ekie's eyes narrowed as if scanning her memory for our faces. "Would you like to see the gardens?"

"That would be lovely," said Pitari, already heading for the glass double doors behind the wide counter where Ekie was working.

"Can you take over for me, Noni?"

The young man set down the knife he'd been using to

cut up narrow green leaves and hurried over to take Ekie's place with the bread dough.

The tall woman was younger than I'd expected. She had to be younger than Laurent by nearly a decade. Then she took off the smock she'd been wearing before following Pitari. I suspected there was a different reason he remembered her and it had nothing to do with sneaked baked treats.

The shapely young woman wearing a clingy knee-length plain brown dress made me feel like I was back in the social district, surrounded by the fashionable elite, wearing my sack of a uniform.

Ekie wore her brown hair piled in a messy bun. In the sunlight, it shone with a myriad of copper highlights that mirrored the flecks in her big brown eyes. This was exactly the type of woman I expected the heir of the empire to sneak off with for an hour or two. I wondered how many more of them I'd have to stand beside and try not to listen to while still keeping watch.

Did Ari enjoy that part of his job or dread it as much as I was just then? That was one aspect of my duty I'd given no thought to until now. It was annoying enough that people thought I was trading sexual favors for the position. Having to watch even peripherally as Laurent enjoyed those favors with someone else made me snarlier than I'd been all week.

"Are you unwell, Rita?" Pitari asked, saying my name loudly and clearly for Ekie's benefit.

"I'm not used to the bright sunlight, you know, with my homeworld's sky choked with smoke all the time. All the glinting gives me a headache."

"Understandable." Her consoling smile told me she

knew exactly what I'd been thinking. "So, Ekie, the Scaavo heir told us you might have some insight as to the goings on here?" She leaned over to take a sniff of the bed full of waist-high white flowers. "These are lovely."

The garden, yes, now that I tore my eyes from the provincial beauty of the kitchen staff, I took a few seconds to appreciate the gardener's talent. Pruned shrubs that towered over me, beds full of flowers and greenery. Everything was well-kept and orderly. Clean pathways led from the double doors outward along a circular path, crisscrossed with a fountain in the middle. It was something out of a fairytale picture book. We had nothing like it on Anduvea. What gardens we had were inside buildings and mostly hydroponic.

Ekie backed up a step. "How do you know the heir?"

"I'm one of his personal guards," I said, attempting to look friendly even though I wasn't feeling it.

"And I work with the empiric security team as an outside consultant," explained Pitari.

"Is he missing? Like his mother?" Ekie's lips trembled.

"No, he's fine, just worried about her."

Oh, good Maker, she was even adorable on the verge of tears, her perfect round cheeks with high cheekbones daintily pinkening. I hated her so much.

"That's why we're here to investigate," Pitari said, taking the left path at a leisurely pace.

Ekie took the hint and walked beside her. I stayed close behind. "We've read the official report." Andover had a copy of it in his archives. I believed it no more than Laurent did in light of Ari's message. "What can you tell us about the consort's disappearance?"

"It was unexpected. During the night. She never travels at night. Her vision isn't good in the dark. She had the light system of the entire estate designed with dim nightlights so it's never dark in the hallways or public spaces."

It sounded like she was afraid of the dark. And maybe she had good reason to be, considering she was very likely dead.

"And who discovered her absence?"

"Her personal assistant. The consort's bed wasn't made, which she always did upon getting up in the morning. It was the one chore she did herself." She licked her lips and shook her head. "There were a few items missing from her wardrobe and a small bag from her luggage, but the clothes weren't ones she favored. If she was going somewhere, even for a day or two, she packed for a week, never just one small bag."

Someone did a sloppy job of knowing the consort well enough to cover her tracks. Which made me think her absence wasn't all that well planned out.

"There's been no word from her? No one went with her?"

Ekie's long lashes bobbed as she blinked tears from her eyes.

"You don't believe she went somewhere planned?" Pitari clarified. "No emergencies or perhaps a rendezvous with the Empaetor?"

Ekie shook her pretty head. "She hasn't visited him in well over a year. Even when she did, it was only for public appearances. She took several of her ladies with her each time, one or two guards and a few acquaintances or house staff members. She was so kind about taking turns with staff, trying to give all of us a chance to be at her side so we could see the palace and other places we'd never otherwise get to visit. I got to see a play with her once. The heir sat with her too. That's where I met him."

"Ah." I didn't want any other details on that matter. "You like the consort then?"

Her voice quieted. "She's a kind woman."

"Do you suspect the Empaetor had anything to do with her disappearance?" I asked.

"I have no proof of that," Ekie said woodenly.

It was not unexpected that she wouldn't speak out against the Empaetor. This was Harilax, after all. He was on the same world, and who knew what ears he might have where.

"Of course not," Pitari used her mollifying tone masterfully. "Is there anything else you can tell us?"

"We didn't find any blood, if that's what you're asking. The sheets were tangled, but she often tossed and turned. A messy bed wasn't unusual. I think that's why she liked to put it back in order herself. She didn't want anyone else to know what a poor sleeper she was."

"Did she suffer from insomnia?"

"Not as long as she had her nightly drink."

We came to the fountain in the middle of the garden. I peered down to see tiny silver fish darting through the water, moving in a synchronized school like a flashing blade.

"What kind of drink?" asked Pitari.

"Usually tea. Occasionally she'd go through an alcohol drinking spurt. As far as I know, she was on one of those binges before she left."

"Anything in particular she liked to drink on those spurts?" I asked.

Ekie tipped her head back and gazed at the few puffs of white passing overhead. Air transports whizzed by in the distance, none of them being allowed near the estate's airspace. It was almost peaceful here in the garden, surrounded by living things and fresh scents that my nose didn't know how to process. Compared to all this color and life, Anduvea was a bleak, plascrete wasteland.

I wished my parents could see this.

"The consort has a fondness for Ultrusis brandy. So much so that she bought a distillery there. We have quite a supply of several flavors on hand."

"Is it possible her nightly drink was drugged?" I asked.

"Unlikely," Ekie turned to me, rubbing her long, delicate fingers over the light fabric covering her arms. Poor thing probably thought it was cold out. She wouldn't have survived two minutes in the station's back end.

"But I suppose it's possible," she added.

"No new staff members? Anyone acting differently?" I asked.

"There hasn't been any recent turnover. Most of us have been in her employ for years. She prefers to pick staff just beginning their careers so she can mold them to her needs. No bad habits that way, she says."

Pitari watched us, her hands clasped together before her at her waist, confirming my guess that this was her working stance. She didn't interrupt, only observed. I wondered what insights she'd have to share later.

"How long has Nori been working here?" I asked.

Ekie's eyes went wide. "He's my cousin. He would never... I suggested him for hire. Nori wasn't recruited by anyone, if that's what you're insinuating."

She seemed genuinely ruffled. "He's the most recent hire, but he's been here for almost a year now. No one has any complaints about him. He's a good kid."

"I'm sure he is," Pitari smiled reassuringly before glancing at me. "I'll wait for you inside?"

I nodded. If only I'd had her as a partner on my security team, no one would have gotten away with a damned thing. And there were more like her on her homeworld? It must be an amazingly peaceful place.

Ekie's brows furrowed as she watched Pitari leave us. "Do you think she's alright? The consort?"

Laurent thought she was dead, but I had found nothing to confirm or deny that. The only thing I knew was that she appeared to have been taken. The fact that she hadn't returned didn't bode well.

"That's what we're trying to find out."

"If you're here, that means she's not with the Empaetor. Not that she would have wanted to be there, but I was hoping that was the answer."

I walked onward, aiming for the second half of the arc around the garden. "Was there trouble between them?"

She lowered her voice again. "She never forgave him for taking the heir away from her weeks after he took the throne. I didn't know her before that, but others have said she was a vibrant force to be reckoned with when the heir was young and at her side."

"Mothers are like that."

I thought of mine and shook my head. Always sure of what was best for their children. Even when the child in their head and the child in reality were two very different people.

Laurent, if he was to take his father's place, needed to be beside his father, to learn his role, gather his own friends and advisors. If Laurent had remained here with his mother, he would have received none of that. I had to side with the Empaetor on that choice.

"Why doesn't the consort live at the palace?"

Ekie looked at me like I was a clueless idiot. My thoughts went on a mad scramble through my week of intense empiric study but came up with nothing helpful on this topic.

"She doesn't belong at the palace. Her place is here unless she's summoned to perform duties."

Duties. Yep. Got it.

"Theirs was not a romantic match then."

Ekie's cheeks turned the perfect shade of peachy pink that defined the color blush. Not a splotch of red or hint of uncomfortable heat.

"There are stories by the older house staff of how their love match used to be before the Empaetor took the throne. Iradio VII's consort had been dead for years, so Iradio VIII and Marishka were allowed to live here. Risque romps around the estate, laughter at all hours. The moaning was simply scandalous," she divulged behind her hand.

That sounded like a normal day on the station during the burning, except this was a happy couple in their own home rather than a bunch of naked, rich, inebriated assholes in public.

"I'm told they were happy times," she said with a wistful smile.

Until he took her child away.

"They never tried for a second heir?"

"I'm sure they did. Again, before my time. But it never happened. The consort was very against suggestions of artificial pregnancy."

I had more reading to do because I had no clue what that meant. No one on Anduvea had mentioned such a thing in all my forty years. At least not in my hearing.

We passed an opening in the shrubbery that lined the edge of the garden. The space revealed a view that momentarily made me forget my line of questioning altogether.

An expanse of rolling green hills dotted with wildflowers and the occasional tree that was almost too perfect in shape to be naturally formed stood between me and the palace itself. The expansive plasteel and prism glass structure was exactly as the still frames had portrayed. With a single point of entry at the base, the triangular masterpiece seemed to balance on the one point on the ground. The center point jutted east and the apex speared the sky high above. The smooth surface shot up and outward with rainbows dancing off the entire surface.

That's where Laurent lived. Where I would live. Holy Maker.

Ekie halted beside me. "Is there something wrong?"

"No." I cleared my throat. "Just haven't seen it from this vantage point before."

She nodded. "It is a spectacular view. Best on Harilax, I'd say. Rumor is the consort used to stand here every night after the heir was taken from her."

And then she was drinking. I was starting to put her sad life together, and I didn't envy her one bit.

Would Laurent do the same thing with his consort? Would I have to stand around and listen to them romp around her estate, or maybe even this one if he handed it over to whatever gift-wrapped package of shapely thighs and perky tits he chose? I couldn't imagine keeping quiet as I stood behind him while he explained to his own kid that he couldn't live with his mother any longer and why she didn't belong at the palace with them.

Could I keep my mouth shut through any of that? Probably not.

We continued our walk down the pathway, looping back toward the house.

Once we took care of the nefarious plot that had spurred Ari Leeman into action, and got Laurent securely settled onto his father's throne, it would take him some time to find a suitable wife, wouldn't it? He'd surely sample the lot of them first. That would give me enough time to amass a comfortable rest-of-my-lifetime savings. Then, before my tongue got me into too much trouble, I could slink off somewhere quiet to retire and take care of my parents. One could hope anyway.

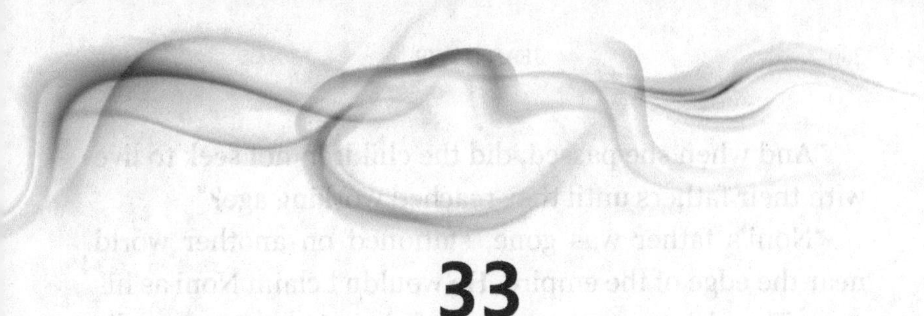

33

Walk With Purpose

When Ekie and I returned to the door to the kitchen, I spotted Pitari inside, sitting on a stool, chatting with the kitchen staff as they worked. Noni was among them, smiling and joining the conversation. I studied the young man.

Similarly genetically gifted as his cousin, Noni had broad shoulders, a trim build, and a visually pleasing face. Nothing stood out about him. He was simply pretty to look at. Whether he possessed a single complex thought in his head was unknown, but working in the kitchen among women who could have been his mother didn't strike me as a lifelong career choice he would have made.

"Why is Noni working here? Other than your putting in a good word for him? Seems like a boy his age would have many prospects on Harilax.

"My aunt fell ill nearly two years ago now. She passed away six months later. She did not live with Noni's father, or the father of her two daughters."

It sounded like Ekie wasn't the only one in the family who was loose and free with their choices in intimate partners. They sounded a lot like Anduveans.

"And when she passed, did the children not seek to live with their fathers until they reached working age?"

"Noni's father was gone, stationed on another world near the edge of the empire. He wouldn't claim Noni as his own. The girls never knew their father. My aunt was a little..."

"Free?"

"Friendly." Ekie shrugged. "I gave them a few extra credits to get by so Noni could take care of his sisters until he was of age. Then I helped him get the job here."

"Do you get many house visitors?"

"The consort often has guests. She likes to entertain. Makes her less lonely."

I could only imagine how difficult it must be to live within view of the center of everything but yet be outside it. To be celebrated and popular, but no one cared about your true name. To be the mother of the heir but rarely see him. And for Laurent to think she'd given him up without a fight and hold it against her. That had to make the few times a year they saw each other fraught with hard feelings. No wonder she drank regularly.

"Did you see any of the more recent visitors paying particular attention to Noni? Before the consort left, I mean?"

"Oh, he's always been one for stories. The more filled with danger and adventure, the better." Ekie smiled. "He often spoke to as many of the visitors as he could, asking them to recount what they'd seen and where they'd been. He hopes to travel around the edge of the empire one day. Do the circumference tour. Have you done it?"

"Not yet." And likely never. I couldn't see Laurent as Empaetor, going on a grand tour of all of his holdings, especially not the entire outer perimeter of the empire. That sounded dangerous, and if I was still holding my position as his personal guard, like hell would I allow it.

Assuming I had any say in the matter. Laurent, the heir in hiding and facing the unknown, was likely far more tolerant of my suggestions than Empaetor Iradio IX would be. Hell, my mother was probably right. Once I helped him take care of whatever this threat against him was, he'd likely kick me back to Anduvea with a pocketful of credits and a thank you. If I was that lucky.

"Thanks for your help, Ekie."

"I hope you find her. She's been good to all of us. And if you see the heir, do tell him I said hello. I'd welcome a visit from him too." She winked.

"I'll do my best."

Ekie bobbed her head in what I was coming to understand was the standard empiric bow of respect. We didn't do that back home.

She excused herself to return to her job. I followed her inside, nodding to Pitari to join me in what I hoped was a quick walk toward the consort's private chambers if my study of the map on my datapad had served me correctly. In my years of service on the station, I'd often found that walking with purpose and a confident appearance got me into a lot of places I wouldn't have been welcome otherwise. Not to say I wasn't chased off, written up, or verbally chastised after the fact, but that hadn't stopped me from doing it again.

The benefits were often too good to pass up. I hoped my excursion into the consort's bedroom paid off similarly.

We passed a few employees going about their business.

They paid little attention to us. It wasn't until we were out of the public living spaces that a house guard stepped into our path. Her long beige tunic hung halfway down her dark-skinned calves. She regarded us with narrowed pale blue eyes set wide over a pronounced nose. Her neatly plucked brows lowered, and her pink lips pursed.

"Your business?" she asked through a strong accent I didn't recognize.

"Investigating the disappearance of the consort," I stated confidently.

"There's already been an investigation."

Cheery Pitari smiled. "We've been hired to do an independent investigation by the family."

The guard pulled out a datapad and looked at us expectantly. "Who specifically?"

"Her father," Pitari answered without missing a beat. "He's very worried."

"We all are," the guard admitted.

"Is there anything you can tell us that wasn't in the previous report?"

"Not that I can think of."

"She was last seen in her bedroom?" I asked.

"Correct. This way."

She led us through a maze of narrow hallways ill-suited for any form of attack. There was only room to walk single file. They may have seemed normal size to Seeker Pitari, but they were claustrophobic to me. Even the maintenance tube offered more space, though I supposed that allowed for tools and repair bots. Here, there were only people.

The halls were lined with dark wood up to my armpits. Pale green paint swirled with gold brush strokes covered the upper walls and ceiling. It gave the impression of walking through a jungle. The feeling was reinforced when we reached the consort's private suite to find the outer room lined with assorted greenery. Carved benches with thick seating pads were scattered throughout the plants. The guard waited outside the doorway, nodding for us to proceed. Maybe she wasn't allowed farther inside.

The second room was a massive closet that resembled a store. Racks of clothes stood in the middle. Shelves filled with folded items and shoes of all sorts, accessories, and bags lined three walls. A locked cabinet with reinforced clearplaz took up the fourth wall with the open doorway to the next room. As we drew closer, lights came on overhead, illuminating the interior of the cabinet. Jewelry glittered inside. I couldn't guess the value of everything in the cabinet, but it had to be enough to buy an entire world. How did one person wear all of that? Certainly not all at once, or even within a lifetime. I owned two necklaces, neither of which I regularly wore, and one ring of blue polished stone that I'd bought off a trader on a whim. I'd worn it once, but it felt weird on my hand at work, like it was in the way if I needed to fight. Jewelry was not for me.

Beyond the massive closet was a bathroom that was the same size as my whole suite on the station. It held a tub resembling a small swimming pool, a second deep tub that would comfortably fit two, several sinks, and counters lined with various brushes, combs and many items I didn't recognize. A reclining chair sat near a tray filled with cosmetics and a shelf full of glass bottles of different colors. The labels led me to believe they were an assortment of scents. A giant rack of towels so thickly plush they begged to be touched. I didn't. This was a potential crime scene.

Everything was spotless. Did she actually use any of these spaces? They looked like showrooms, not like someone lived here. No traces of hair on the counters. Even the brushes were clean. Every towel sat neatly folded. The mirrors were spotless, as were the gleaming faucets.

Pitari glanced at me. I nodded. We opened the next door. The lights came on. The bedroom. She may have normally made the bed, but here was where I knew she did truly exist. Until then, the consort could have been a myth perpetuated by the house staff.

The first thing my eyes were drawn to was the still frame of a handsome boy with curly dark hair on the bedside table. He had Laurent's eyes. Clothing lay tossed over a chair against the wall. A lounge chair held an overturned paper book with ancient yellowed pages. There were no plants here. No windows. No light beyond the two fixtures high above. The room had to be double my height and nearly as large as the bathroom. A bed that could have comfortably slept six stood in the middle, like an island surrounded by open sea but for the bedside table and the two chairs. So much room filled with so little. But what more did a bedroom really need? Maybe she exercised in the open space. Maybe it was there simply because one needed to be opulently wasteful when they were royalty. Or married to it, anyway.

"What do you think?" asked Pitari, her voice quiet in the vast space.

I didn't know if this room was under observation by a security team or if the consort had declared her bedroom private. Likely all of her suite would be if she had a say about it. But did she?

"No signs of blood or even a struggle. Just your average mess."

In fact, it looked like my bedroom back on the station: lived in. It was the only place we'd seen so far that offered a hint of who Marishka might be.

The rest of the house reminded me of the room I shared with Laurent on the *Knaldon*. It wasn't mine. Everything was put away at all times. There were no hints of me there other than skin cells on the sheets, and I couldn't even sleep naked because I shared the space with the man I was supposed to be guarding. All the time.

What I wouldn't give for a night of relaxing. By myself. With no one to watch over. Like the twenty years I'd enjoyed in my station suite, never knowing how good I had it.

I pulled out the small scanner I'd borrowed from the *Knaldon*. Within five minutes of running it over the bed, the chairs and the thick carpet on either side of the bed all the way to the door, I'd still come up with no blood or other fluids that would lead me to think something bad had happened here.

"I have everything I need. How about you?" I asked.

"I'm good. We'll confer later?"

"Yes." This woman was a blessing from the Maker.

Pitari grinned.

Oh yes, I forgot she was still listening to my thoughts.

"Not all of them. Just the loud ones," she said with a hint of apology. "That's what my ancient mentor told me when I was a child. She was always going on about the loud thoughts being the easiest to hear."

If she wanted loud thoughts, I silently voiced the command to shut up. We did not need to spook the staff with implications that she could read minds should they be listening to us. And from the gossip Ekie had been willing to share with me, I suspected that someone was, even if it wasn't in an official security capacity. "Perhaps this is not the right time for this conversation. We should get moving."

"Yes, of course, apologies."

We made it out of the bathroom, the closet, and the sitting room without issue. The guard stood waiting for us in the hallway.

"Did you find anything of use?" she asked.

"Perhaps," said Pitari. "The evidence requires further evaluation."

The guard stiffened just enough to catch my attention. "Is there anything else you can tell us that might be of help in locating the consort?"

"I don't think so," she said quickly. "Best of luck with your investigation. We're all praying for her safe return."

"That's all you can do. Thank you for your assistance." I turned on my heel and started toward the exit.

Pitari walked beside me, a sour look on her face.

It took me two wrong turns to escape the narrow hallway tangle, but we made it back out into the public side of the estate without further incident. We didn't encounter many of the staff. They appeared to be minding their own business. We were halfway to the door when my comm pin pinged.

"Go ahead," I whispered, hoping they got the hint that we weren't alone.

"Andover is being asked to report in. In person," Senio said.

Well fuck. That was going to be a challenge. We couldn't send Pitari with him everywhere. That certainly would be questioned.

"Tell them he's not feeling well. He'll debrief later."

"I tried that. They're insistent."

I checked our progress through the house. Not wanting to chance that any of this was being recorded in any manner, I gave the little Seeker an apologetic grimace and doubled my pace.

"Give me five minutes," I told Senio before tapping my pin.

We reached the door attendant with Pitari outright jogging behind me.

"Did you have a pleasant visit?" asked the woman.

"Yes, thank you." It wouldn't take long for the news that we'd changed our story to reach her. Only a few more steps and we'd be free to run to our transport if necessary.

She stepped in front of the exit. "Did you find what you were looking for?"

I shifted my stance, prepared for whatever came next.

"Yes, I believe we did," said Pitari. Her flat tone assured me the Seeker had indeed picked up on something in her mind surfing.

What I was not ready for was the Seeker to perform a whirlwind spin and kick that landed hard on the woman's throat.

Recovering quickly, I reached for the door panel and activated it. The door remained closed.

My comm pin pinged again. "Not now, Senio!" I yelled at my collar.

The door attendant staggered toward us, still gasping.

If the door was locked from the inside, it had to be from an imprint. All I needed was her palm. She didn't need to be conscious for that. I took a swing at her. She dodged with surprising speed.

It figured that the consort's security staff was actually competent.

Two more beige-dressed employees barreled towards us. Pitari, looking resolute, stepped forward to deal with them. Given her impressive first kick, I left her to it and concentrated on the woman I needed for unlocking the door.

The ping sounded again. "They're sending someone up to the ship. Now, Rita. They're on the way."

I punched the woman in the stomach.

Pitari may have done her memory balm on Andover, but he still had information in his head that would make life difficult for all of us.

"Make Andover unwell. Drunk, violently ill, whatever keeps him from talking coherently."

My attacker landed a hard hit on my jaw that sent me off balance.

"Got it," Senio said.

My pin went silent.

The next thing I knew, the woman had a weapon in hand. Behind me, Pitari grunted. My brain registered the threat was a gun, and the thwacks behind me as three people pounding on each other. Years of experience dealing with breaking up bar fights and taking down groups of unruly tourists switched on like engaging autopilot. The fight slowed a fraction and the sounds dulled.

The woman raised her weapon. With an ungraceful

sliding side-step, I evaded whatever sort of projectile flew from the gun and reached out to grab the weapon from her. Once the hard object was in my hand, I slammed it into her head. She dropped to the floor. Out of habit, I reached for a bubble tab. My hand came up empty.

Right, not on the station. Which meant station rules didn't apply. I could fire the weapon without worry of puncturing anything. Other than flesh, anyway.

Pitari had one woman subdued on the ground. She circled the other, who was maintaining a wary stance and distance.

I shot her in the leg. A projectile buried itself in her thigh. The woman cried out and tumbled to the floor, clutching her leg.

Not wasting any time, I grabbed the doorwoman and yanked her heavy, limp body to the door panel. Slamming her open palm on the control did the trick.

Pitari was right beside me as we bolted from the estate toward the transport we'd left. Once inside, we entered the port address and sat back, breathing hard. A round of breath-stealing coughs chose that moment to attack. At least it had waited until the fighting was done.

Pitari watched me with concern.

"I'm fine," I managed to rasp. "You?"

Her head bobbed as she turned to look out the rear window. No one emerged from the house to chase us. After a minute, she turned back around. Her gaze flitted over me. "You're bleeding."

"Am I?"

Yumi and Senio made fun of me for rarely noticing injuries until after a fight. They claimed I got too into my work.

Like I enjoyed it. Maybe I did. A little. It wasn't so much not noticing wounds, but that I needed to do my job, and the injury, as long as I was on my feet, could wait its damned turn.

If I couldn't disarm someone without getting shot at this point in my career, I probably deserved whatever wound I'd gotten.

I got one sleeve of my uniform halfway down an arm before I felt the sharp twinge of something bad. "How'd I get hit in the back?"

Pitari grimaced. "Sorry. I was tied up with the first one when the second one drew. I knocked her aside, but she still caught you. It's not too serious, I take it?"

Not wanting to probe around blindly, I gingerly turned around and lifted my shirt. "You tell me."

"Looks like just a deep scratch. No entry wound."

"Good, we've got plenty to deal with already. You handled yourself well in there for being a mind-reading priestess."

Pitari grinned. "My mentor, Geva rest her soul, would be pleased that you think so. While our traditional Seekers do not use violence, Seeker Ikeri declared we should have the skills to defend ourselves if we were to go out into the wider universe. Her parents were once assassins, if you can believe that," she chuckled. "She taught us skills she'd seen in their thoughts."

"Sounds like she was a wise woman and an excellent teacher."

Pitari beamed, her eyes glistening. "She was."

Now aware of the blood seeping into my shirt and probably staining my uniform coat as well, the pain came to the forefront of my thoughts. "You had to point that wound out, didn't you?"

"Sorry. Do you have anything to bandage it with?"

"Other than my shirt, no."

"Let's go, remove it then. I'll help. You can wear the coat overtop."

Feeling like a little kid getting help from my mother to undress, I let Pitari assist me. She had my shirt ripped and wrapped around my waist in no time. She even helped me slip the coat back on.

"You're pretty good at that. Another skill from your mentor?"

She shook her head. "Not specifically. Seekers are trained healers too. We also give excellent massages."

"You are officially my new favorite person."

Pitari laughed, then sobered and pointed at my comm pin. "You should check in with Senio."

"Are you picking something up I need to know about?"

"I can only read people who are nearby, so no. But he sounded panicked."

He had. I wanted to think he had things under control, but my gut urged me to follow Pitari's suggestion. I tapped the pin.

"Oh, thank the Maker! Are you both alright?"

"We're fine now. Heading back to the port. We should be back on board within an hour or two."

Pitari called bullshit with a raised brow. I shook my head. Senio had his own problems.

"They'll be here in fifteen minutes, Rita."

Yep, that was definitely panic in his voice.

"Breathe, Senio. Get every actual crewmember out in

view doing their job. Get the station staff out of sight in case they scan ID chips. Tell them they're off duty and confined to quarters until they hear differently. Andover?"

"Unconscious. Doctor Tik suggested he be heavily medicated after suffering a reaction from breathing too much Anduvean air during his investigation on the surface."

"Nice."

"I thought so."

"Keep our charge out of sight as well. But I don't have to tell you that, do I?"

"He's made it quite clear," groused Laurent in the background.

"Good. Senio, you're going to have to be the one crew member they recruited from the station so you can guide the narrative. Can you handle that until I arrive?"

"You're going to stay hidden too, right? Andover's reports mentioned you and provided your visual ID."

"Yes, but Pitari will join you."

"Thank the Maker." He let out a heavy sigh of relief. "Stay safe, Rita. See you soon."

"You too." I tapped the pin to end the transmission.

Now all I had to do was get back aboard the *Knaldon* undetected. Pitari could help Senio get rid of our unwanted guests. Once that was accomplished, we could get back to figuring out Laurent's future.

34

Wisdom Is Overrated

Once we were aboard our lander and rising safely away from Harilax, I got down to business with Pitari.

"What did you get from Noni?"

"He received a large payment and was happy about it. Good intentions—he needed the credits for his family. Where he got them from was unclear, but I think it's safe to say it was a bribe for some sort of service."

"Nothing specific?"

"Only that he's the one to prepare her nightly drinks."

"Drugged her most likely then."

Pitari nodded. "That aligns with the missing body and lack of struggle."

"And the guard we met outside the bedroom?"

"She didn't want us finding anything. Her thoughts centered on the consort's rooms after the disappearance and putting items back in order."

"She was in charge of the coverup. And the door attendant?"

"Wanted us dead," Pitari said without hesitation.

"One of us anyway," I grimaced. "I'm guessing she'd

pound on you until she learned who really sent us."

"I'm glad we deprived her of that." Pitari gestured toward my face. "Looks like she had a lot of force behind her punches."

"She did." I rubbed my cheek to find it warm and swollen. It had just finally gotten back to normal. Dammit. "What about Ekie?"

"Nice woman. Loves gossip and her family. I didn't pick up anything that led me to believe she was involved."

"Well, there's one honest employee on the staff."

I couldn't imagine living in a house filled with people who were willing to drug me or sell me out. If the consort really was as well-meaning as Ekie made her sound, it was pretty rotten of her employees to treat her that way. My previous research had shown them to be favorably compensated for their work, but I supposed, like my view of the Empaetor, it was easy to hate those set high above us.

"No clue who has the consort or where she might be?"

"Sorry, no."

That trip didn't answer nearly as many questions as I'd hoped. The only good thing was that I couldn't definitively say she'd been killed.

Feeling Pitari's gaze, I glanced up from contemplating my thoughts with a silent question.

Her face scrunched up for a moment before she came out with it. "Are you going to be able to sit this out? Stay out of sight with Laurent, I mean, while Senio and I handle this?"

"Why wouldn't I be?"

One brow quirked. "You tend to turn up in the middle of things."

"I do not," I said weakly. "Not every time."

"Try this time."

"Yeah, fine." Sitting awkwardly forward in my seat to avoid further irritating my back made me cranky, but that wasn't her fault.

With nothing more to say, I gathered my thoughts on my datapad for future reference and then anxiously awaited our arrival on the *Knaldon*.

Pitari voiced the request to dock and gave her clearance code, which was quickly accepted by Alessandra, the communications officer who wanted me to jump into Laurent's bed to make him less moody. I glared at the speaker. Thankfully, the Seeker was occupied and didn't seem to notice.

Once we docked, I waited inside while Pitari exited. A stranger greeted her, and then the two of them walked away. When I ventured out, two of our crewmembers subtly nodded to me and went about their jobs as I scampered by.

Moving through the corridors was more of a crapshoot, but I kept my datapad in hand. The one time I passed someone I didn't recognize, I pretended to be engrossed in it, keeping my face down as much as possible.

I reached Laurent's suite and ducked inside as quickly as the door allowed.

"You made it," Laurent announced.

I nodded, tucking my datapad into my pocket. "We didn't find your mother, but we also didn't find any evidence to indicate she is deceased, so there's that."

He cocked his head and looked me over. "What happened to..." He waved his hand at my face and torso."

"We ran into some trouble. I should find a clean shirt." I reached into the drawer under my bed for one of the other two white uniform shirts I'd been given.

"Is that blood on your jacket?" His voice rose. "Are you wounded?"

"Just a scratch. I'm fine. Pitari took care of it for me. I'll just go change, and I'll be right back."

My comm pin pinged. What now? I was supposed to be hiding, for the Maker's sake. "Go ahead."

"Can I see you on the bridge?" Senio asked in a strained voice.

Laurent shook his head, his eyes wide.

"Everything alright?"

"Yes." The waver in Senio's answer said no.

"I'll be right there." I tapped the pin.

"You will not!" Laurent decreed.

I didn't have time for decorum. Gingerly slipping out of my jacket, I ignored Laurent's concerned gasp behind my back and ran my hands over the bandage Pitari had created. I didn't feel any wet spots, and it seemed to be holding in place. A minute later I had the new, intact shirt around my shoulders. Fastening it was easier to accomplish when forcing myself to pretend I wasn't in pain for Laurent's sake. With my uniform jacket back in place, I started for the door.

"Stay here." I drilled that into him with the sternest stare in my arsenal.

"Rita, don't go."

"You'll be fine. Just, please, stay here."

"I'm not worried about me," he growled.

"I am. Kinda my job, you know? Do *not* leave this room. Unless you have to, in which case, you know where to go?"

He nodded, looking like he might make a lunge to grab me.

I walked out before he could. Senio and I had worked out a secure hiding spot for him. He'd be cold, but his heat signature would be masked if anyone did a scan. Damned needy heir. Couldn't he just let me do my job instead of throwing concern for me into it? My mom was probably right. He just didn't want to be alone in all this. Once he was settled on the throne, the compassionate act would end.

If I was going to the bridge where I could only assume someone of Andover's rank was waiting for me, there was no use in hiding.

I strode onto the bridge as if I had every right to be there. My weapon wasn't drawn in case I was totally over-reacting, but I kept my hand on it just in case.

My stomach plummeted as I recognized SA Tekka standing beside Senio. Pitari sat nearby at a workstation—one my scattered brain couldn't put a task to at the moment. Another security agent stood beside her, his weapon drawn and aimed at her head. Five other agents approached me from all directions.

This wasn't going to go in my favor.

"Rita," Senio said, by way of apology.

I nodded. No more words were needed between us.

"Rita Stabinov. Nice to finally meet in person." SA Tekka smiled in a way that implied nothing nice at all. "You may not be used to the ID scanning capabilities built into the Empaetor's fleet, being from, well, Anduvea," he sneered, as if the very word tasted like dirt. "But we noticed your arrival, along with Andover's pet."

Inside, I was shaking. If they could trace me by my

ID chip to know I was aboard, did they also know exactly where I'd been? Did they already have people on the way there? Was Laurent already in hiding, or would he wait a while to see if Senio or I came back for him? Fuck.

Scattered as I was, my brain short-circuited on a snide retort, but I maintained my composure. At least, I hoped I did. Wisdom said I should remove my hand from my weapon and go along peacefully because my ribs were still healing from Andover's interrogation tactics. But hell, wisdom was overrated.

Hoping to create enough chaos that Laurent might hear something was wrong and hide, I drew and fired at the nearest unknown body. I had no awareness of Senio or Pitari's responses, and no regard for the gun aimed at the Seeker. Laurent was my priority. If he remained safe, one day, the empire might be too.

I got three more shots in and several punches before the room went black.

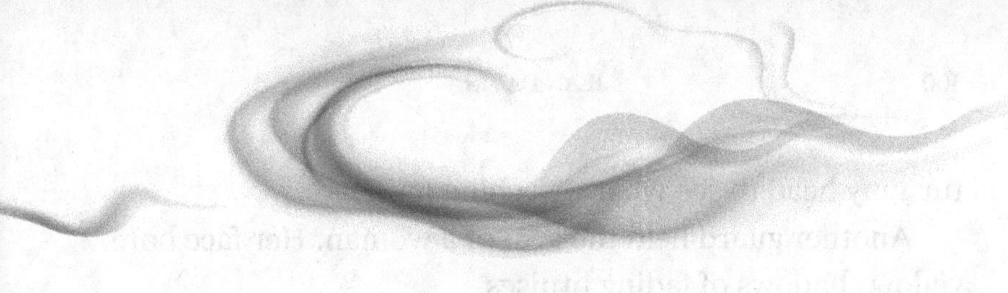

35

A Concerned Party

When I came to, I opened my eyes to a glaringly bright cell. I hurt everywhere, and I wasn't alone.

"So nice of you to rejoin us," SA Tekka said.

"I wouldn't have left if you hadn't knocked me out."

He sneered. "Let's revisit your opening of the stasis chamber and what you did with the body inside."

"It was empty." I gave him the same story I'd given before.

"That sounds like the same rehearsed garbage you gave Agent Andover. He's been debriefed, by the way."

I had to wonder how that had gone in light of Pitari's mind balm and whatever Doctor Tik had given him. SA Tekka's ominous tone didn't instill confidence in our measures to muddle Andover's clarity of events.

He stared down at me. "I know the Scaavo heir was with you on the Anduvean station, Rita. I'm going to need a more detailed answer."

"I don't have more details to give."

"We'll see about that." He snapped his fingers.

Rustling at the opposite end of the room prodded me to

turn my head to see what was going on.

Another guard held the arm of a woman. Her face bore yellow shadows of fading bruises.

"She didn't have the answers I required either."

Got it. More pain in my near future. Laurent was going to owe me. A lot.

The one thing I clung to was that if SA Tekka was about to beat the hell out of me, he didn't have Laurent. Secure in that, I turned back to the ominous figure standing over me.

I gestured to the bare-bones cot I'd been placed on. "How hospitable of you."

SA Tekka seemed more annoyed than he had already been. He pointed to the woman with a forceful jab at the air. "I did not have clearance to kill her, but I have no such restrictions for you. The only way you'll limp out of here is by offering your full cooperation in the recovery of the Scaavo heir."

"I can't help you."

"You better hope that you can." He gave me one swift kick in the ribs before leaving. The second man followed, leaving the woman behind.

When the watering in my eyes subsided and I'd caught my breath after a round of side-splitting coughs, I noticed the woman now standing beside me.

She held one hand out tentatively. "Are you thirsty?"

I nodded, still clenching my teeth from the rib kick I sorely hadn't needed. Andover would be gratified to learn that SA Tekka had in fact read his reports. He sure knew right where to cause the most pain with the least amount of effort.

Water ran somewhere nearby. A plas cup appeared

near my face. I took it and drank, washing the taste of blood from the fight on the bridge out of my mouth.

Feeling somewhat more alert, I worked myself up to sitting with only a few grunts. "Who are you?"

"Consort Marishka Scaavo."

Twenty-some years my senior, she stood, favoring one hip over the other. Her greying brown hair hung loose around her face, covering her shoulders. She wore clean clothes, loose and casual, but not what I would have imagined she would have chosen, having glimpsed her cavernous closet.

"Glad to see you're alive. I represent a concerned party on that matter."

She smiled warmly. "One of my son's personal guards?"

"Yeah."

The consort settled stiffly onto the floor next to the cot, looking me over. "Rita, is it? You appear to have had a rough go of things."

From the way she was moving, I guessed she had as well.

"Is he safe?" she whispered.

All I knew for sure was that Laurent was not in SA Tekka's hands. Was Senio safe? Pitari? Were they able to help him? Worry twisted my guts into knots. If he stayed in that hiding spot too long, he would freeze. He knew the time limit. I'd drilled it into him. But what if Tekka's men were waiting there to seize him the moment he emerged, chilled and blinking from the darkness? Not knowing was gnawing at my nerves.

I wasn't inclined to trust that the consort wasn't working a deal for her release or whatever other royal machination she might be up to. Maybe she was a genuinely worried mother. Maybe not. I avoided her question.

"SA Tekka, is he involved in the threat that spurred you to send Ari off with the heir?"

She shook her head, eyeing the door.

Other than the cot and the same toilet setup we had on the station, the room was empty. We were just two prisoners bonding. Except I was the battered one on a cot and, given the lack of a second cot, who knew what accommodations the consort had been enjoying these past weeks. Her bruises were old, likely from an interrogation shortly after her abduction. She was stiff, but was it because of injuries or simply her age and a hard bed she wasn't used to?

"Where are we?" I asked.

"In the palace." Her tone implied I should know this.

I supposed if I were one of the heir's guards, I would be familiar with the security and layout of the palace grounds where he lived. Sadly, all I had was what I'd gleaned from the detailed maps on the datapad. The location of secure cells wasn't on the maps. That would be a security risk.

Were we underground? Behind a public room? In a distant tunnel or another location that was fairly accessible to the rest of the palace? If I were to escape, how the hell would I know where to escape to?

She whispered even quieter than before, "At least tell me if he's safe? He's not injured?"

I'm not giving you a damned thing, woman. At least that's what I hoped my glare told her. Maybe I looked just as tired and defeated as she did.

The consort dropped her head into her hands. "They say Ari Leeman is dead."

"He is." That was no secret. "You sent him on a danger-ous mission knowing that was a possible result."

She stared me down for a moment. "Ari was a good man, a good friend to my son. I never meant for him to come to any harm."

"Why did you send the heir to the edge of the empire?"

"Please tell me he's still out there, that he's safe."

No matter her allegiance, she was his mother. Guilt prodded me to give her something. "He *is* safe."

"Is that all you can tell me?" she asked the floor.

"That's all I'm willing to tell you. Unless you can tell me exactly why you sent him away?"

Ekie might have vouched for the goodness of the con-sort, and her mourning the absence of her son did tug at my heart. However, in all the years of obligatory family appear-ances, she'd had to have had plenty of opportunity to speak honestly to Laurent about their nonvoluntary parting.

Consort Marishka met my gaze with a sudden fierce-ness. "I sent him away to protect him."

"From what?" I prodded.

She eyed the door again as if I should know what she was trying to tell me. That we were under observation was a given, but other than that, I could only blink like an idiot and hope she gave me something more.

She didn't. Instead, she stood. "Thank you for your ser-vice to my son. May the Maker bless you and keep you."

Consort Marishka walked to the door to knock on it twice. It opened seconds later.

If she was leaving of her own volition, she was a far freer prisoner than I was. Even in confinement, royalty had perks.

36

It's All A Misunderstanding

The lights went out after a while with no movement in the room. At least in the blackness and safely alone, I could sleep.

Shuffling noises outside my cell prompted me to open my eyes. I expected to see either the consort again or perhaps one of my crew at gunpoint when the door opened, but it was only SA Tekka. He stepped in and shut the door behind him.

"Normally, I would reward your tight-lipped performance." He came around to stand at the end of my cot.

I didn't bother to sit up.

He crossed his arms over his chest and regarded me thoughtfully. "Not being from Harilax, perhaps you do not understand the gravity of the situation."

My curiosity was piqued. I propped myself up on my elbows.

SA Tekka seemed pleased, his scowl easing a fraction. "Given where you are from, you distrust us. You don't know us. You're out of touch with the inner workings of running the empire."

"I'm listening." That's all I was doing, but I really didn't want another round of beating.

"There is no conspiracy against the Scaavo heir. Whatever Ari Leeman told you, whatever loyalty you're aligning yourself with, it's based on a misunderstanding between the Empaetor and his consort. Don't let a marital spat cost you your life. More importantly, don't let it continue to put the heir in unnecessary danger."

That sounded scarily logical. As much as I was only intending to humor him, I sat up. From what I had learned so far in my studies of the workings of the empire, both in reading and in the interviews with Andover's crew and the consort's staff, the Empaetor was prone to his whims. He only offered semi-explanations to those required to carry out said whims. If he'd had something planned for Laurent, as a surprise or a gift for taking his turn on the throne, had it simply been blown out of proportion and misunderstood by the consort? Did she think she was doing the right thing but was instead putting Laurent at unnecessary risk? Was that what I was doing?

Ari believed the Empaetor's guard was rampaging over the empire to retrieve the heir for some nefarious purpose. However, their rampage to recover the second-most important person in the empire because he'd been *stolen* made far more sense.

"You've been obstinate, but I'm willing to admit that we may have misunderstood your intentions. Being from an exiled world, it tracks that you'd be against the empire, that you'd conspire to take it down by taking the heir."

"I didn't *take* him."

How dare he make me sound like some empiric terrorist? That was an instant death sentence, and I wanted no part of dragging my parents into that shame. They wouldn't find peace within the empire for the rest of their lives.

SA Tekka held up a hand. "However, the crew, along with Andover's pet and that station guard friend of yours, are under the impression that you're a logical person, Rita. That you're smart. That you mean the Scaavo heir no harm."

He'd interrogated them all. My instant panic at the realization leveled out seconds later when his tone caught up with me. There was no menace in it. Was this a benevolent tactic, and attempt to befriend me for cooperation? Or was he actually understanding, having more pieces to this conundrum than I did?

"I wouldn't harm him." That wasn't an admission that Laurent was in my possession.

SA Tekka nodded. "The consort believes you are loyal to her son. If you were to cooperate, fully, and are able to deliver the heir safely to us, I'm willing to dismiss the charges for the injuries you caused to our people on the station, the unjust imprisonment of most of Agent Andover's crew, the conspiratorial intent with which you arrived on Harilax, and the attacks on the consort's staff and my own men. Do you understand the offer that I am extending to you?"

My pulse pounded in my ears. My parents were on the *Knaldon*, but he'd not mentioned them. Did he have them contained somewhere? Was that the next level of torture he had in his pocket if this offer of clarity didn't do the trick? Or had one of the crew hidden them away somewhere where their ID chips couldn't be scanned? Had it only been mine that had been flagged? Great Maker, there were too many things I didn't know.

"I understand your offer."

His eyes narrowed. "But you're not accepting it."

"Can I have a little time to think?"

Somewhat mollified, he nodded. "Please consider that with every minute that passes without the heir safely ensconced in the palace, the empire is in danger. Civil war is behind every shadow without a strong leader at the forefront. You're obstructing the security of the empire, Rita Stabinov."

When he put it like that, I was not at all sure of my place in the scheme of things other than a minor bump everyone wanted to smooth out by any means necessary.

"I don't know who to trust." The words slipped out in a wave of frustration and worry.

SA Tekka's face softened. "If I were to allow you a few minutes alone with the Empaetor himself, would that convince you we mean the heir no harm?"

This was the same man who'd kicked me when I was down, but if he'd thought me a terrorist, I would have kicked me too. Even Andover's treatment, extreme as it was, if it resulted in preventing the collapse of the empire, was understandable. Was I the one in the wrong? Was I keeping Laurent away from the throne and the training he needed from his father for no reason?

I realized the consort, after talking to me, had been a part of this offer. I hadn't gotten the impression that whatever threat to Laurent she'd imagined had been resolved. Yet, she'd been relatively calm, given that her son had been missing for almost two months. I considered SA Tekka's suggestion that it had been a misunderstanding, a marital spat. Was she simply worried that Laurent was missing because of her overreaction and not a continued threat? Was all her door glancing because she felt foolish for her actions?

If Ari Leeman had died because of an overreaction between two of the most elite, that would truly be a tragic loss of a loyal guard and friend.

The floor seemed to go out from underneath me. There were so many unknowns.

"I'd like that meeting, yes."

"I'll arrange it. In the meantime, eat and get cleaned up. We can't have you meeting the Empaetor like this."

I didn't know how I was supposed to do any of those things considering my situation, but SA Tekka nodded to the ceiling above the doorway, confirming my assumption we were under observation.

"Someone will be here for you once the meeting is arranged. Please see that you are cooperative. I wouldn't want us to lose the progress that we've gained."

"Understood."

"Good."

He left. Though the door lock did click behind him, I felt less of a prisoner than before he'd arrived. The promise of clarification lifted my spirits. If Laurent was indeed safe, if he could go home and slip back into his elite life, would he still want me around?

Laurent would still honor the job offer, wouldn't he? He was still the man I'd spent the last two weeks with, the one who'd seemed genuinely concerned when I'd walked out of said quarters to face SA Tekka. Or would he become the man with the imperiously peeved expression he'd let slip now and then in my presence?

For that matter, would Laurent just adopt the Empaetor's personal security upon taking the throne and not need me at all anyway? Even if his father was truly gravely ill, once he passed away, his personal guards would become Laurent's by default, wouldn't they?

Tangled in my thoughts, I started when the door opened a short time later. A female security officer entered with her arms full. Another stood in the doorway behind her, armed and ready. SA Tekka may have offered peace, but he wasn't taking chances. Given my behavior since meeting Andover, I didn't blame him. He'd read the reports after all.

The officer didn't talk to me but did set down a clean uniform stack and a covered plate. She backed away, never taking her eyes off me, like I was some rabid, violent criminal.

I considered what had gone down on the *Knaldon* bridge with SA Tekka's men. Alright, fair.

When the door closed, I uncovered the plate and picked up the thick slab of juicy meat to take a bite. They hadn't trusted me with utensils. Yeah, I probably deserved that too.

My stomach rejoiced over a mound of cubed baked squash and a wedge of hearty bread slathered in butter. If SA Tekka was trying to win me over, he was making a good effort.

Once I'd cleaned the plate down to the last tangible crumb, I stripped down to my underclothes, noting the new assortment of bruises along with the fading remnants of the previous ones. What a feminine sight I was, as far from Ekie's natural beauty as one could get. I laughed, wondering what kind of freak whoever was watching my cell thought I was.

Considering I was going to meet with the Empaetor, I got dressed, washed my face, and rebraided my hair as neatly as I could in the small, plas mirror over the toilet. My distorted reflection wasn't at all flattering. Given what the mirror was working with, that wasn't unexpected.

Hours had slogged by with no knock at the door. Eventually my full stomach convinced me to return to the cot and get some rest. I must have really been out because I didn't wake until someone shook my shoulder.

I was dismayed to find it wasn't Laurent, as it had been at the tail end of my dream. Instead, it was an aggravated-looking young man with a black eye.

"That looks like it hurts."

"So does yours," he said with a grim smile.

Oh, he was one of the men from my altercation on the *Knaldon*. Wouldn't want to send a friendly escort. Gotta keep me on my toes. Thanks, SA Tekka. Like meeting with the Empaetor wasn't enough to rattle my nerves into a slurry of uncertainty.

"I hope you're worth the strings he's pulling for you," he grumbled.

SA Tekka was pulling strings on my account? Well now, didn't I feel privileged. "I didn't ask him to."

All I got was a glare. "On your feet then. Hands out. Palms up."

"Yeah, I know the drill."

Even though I complied, he slapped the wrist restraints on with far more force than necessary. His eye must have really hurt.

I smirked. "Feel better?"

"No." He grabbed my elbow and aimed me at the door. "If you make any questionable moves, I'm authorized to shoot you."

"I notice you didn't say kill." I did have information they needed, after all.

He glared again and propelled me forward.

The trek to the meeting involved a host of corridors that all looked the same, two sets of stairs, and a lot of bruising on my arm where the overzealous idiot felt the need to channel all his aggression towards me.

"I get it. Next time I'll aim for your gut so I don't mar your pretty face."

He squeezed even harder.

Fine, be a dick. "How's Agent Andover doing?"

"After you poisoned him?"

"Such a victim. Maybe if he had been a little more forthright with the truth of the matter, we wouldn't be in this situation."

He spun me around and shoved me toward the wall. "Fucking Anduveans. They should have exterminated the lot of you."

I caught myself before falling, though not without a significant amount of wincing. "You know what? Just bring me back to my cell. I'm not feeling very cooperative."

His ire flashed into uncertainty within seconds. "I can't do that. The Empaetor is waiting."

"Then shut your mouth and get me there before I throw away SA Tekka's goodwill and any hope you have of finding the heir."

I started off in the direction we had been going. He

caught up two steps later but didn't touch me as he again took the leading position.

A blast of fresh air, cool and clean on the other side of a locked door confirmed the moment we exited whatever area the prison was in. I turned to make note of the door—a simple, unmarked door that matched the others across the wide, pillar-lined corridor. Massive windows on either end let in enough sunlight that the lighting fixtures on the walls and hanging from near-invisible cables high above us were irrelevant.

Breathtaking vistas that put the view from the consort's garden to shame spread out before me. Even on a clear day, the hazy Anduvean air didn't allow for seeing more than a mile out.

"First time?" My escort asked, looking annoyed at my being frozen in place.

"Yeah."

"Enjoy it. Probably your last."

I turned away from the view of the city at the center of the empire, full of shimmering air transports, towering trees, and buildings not as splendid as the palace but certainly in stiff competition for the title. "Only if you're lucky."

He put a step of distance between us. "Down to the end, last door on the right."

It wasn't that he didn't escort me, but he was definitely thinking twice about touching me or getting too close. His trepidation put a little energy in my step.

We reached our destination. My escort stood outside the door before a security panel that put what we had on the station to shame. It took him three different scans before the door slid open. He nodded for me to proceed.

After making a cursory examination of my immediate surroundings, during which he made impatient noises, I went in.

"You're late," chided an elderly woman, her pale blue eyes sunk so deep into her face behind wrinkles, it was a wonder she could see at all. She wore a jeweled tunic that covered her from neck to feet. Her thin white hair was piled on top of her head with sticks. Strings of jewels dangled from their ends.

She tapped her skeletal fingers on my restraints. "Are those required?"

"Yes," said my escort.

The woman frowned, her pale thin lips getting lost in her saggy jowls. "SA Tekka did not think so. He will be along shortly to supervise this meeting himself."

"Then he can remove them. I will not be held responsible for this prisoner without them."

The woman nodded. "Very well. Please wait over there."

"What are we late for if we have to wait?" I asked my escort.

"Pompous antics. Happens all the time around here," he grumbled, seemingly forgetting we were enemies amid his irritation.

Like whatever antics had led to Laurent getting smuggled out of the palace, off world, and out to the edge of the empire? Maybe I didn't want to subject myself to that sort of drama on a regular basis, no matter what the pay might be.

We waited until my back and legs were stiff. I very much wanted to sit, but there weren't any seats.

My escort smiled slyly. "Sore?"

"A little. There were five of you, and I started with two freshly healing ribs going into it."

His smile vanished.

SA Tekka burst into the room, his demeanor blatantly flustered. He hurried over to us.

"Sir?" my escort asked.

Tekka shook his head and waved the young man off. It took him another minute before he noticed my restraints. "For the Maker's sake, I told him…"

I shrugged.

He entered the code to release them, and after retracting the set, shoved them into his pocket.

"I don't need to tell you to be on your best behavior?"

While I had several choice replies to that, I held my tongue. "It was implied."

"Good."

"You do know the protocol for meeting with the…" He swore under his breath. "Of course you don't. Follow my lead and don't get us both killed."

Was the Empaetor really that volatile? I studied SA Tekka's unsettled, jerky movement and the twitch under his eye. Yes, apparently, he was.

"Are you alright, sir?" I asked, now wondering if I needed to worry about him more than myself.

He paused a moment, watching me watching him before letting out a beleaguered breath. "The consort was being difficult. You've got your own skin to be worried about."

I wondered what difficult meant in regard to her. Was she complaining about the temperature of her food? Had he beaten her again? Was she demanding to be present for this meeting about her son? SA Tekka did not enlighten me.

"You're up," announced the ancient woman. "Chins up, spines straight. There you go." She waved us impatiently through the door.

My steps faltered. We'd entered what I could only call a throne room. A massive chair sat against the vast windowed wall at the midsection point of the triangle that was the palace. The arms of the throne were covered in what appeared to be controls, including a sizeable vid screen on the left side. The seat itself was empty, as was the room, other than one man who stood with his back to us. He wore no obvious adornment on the deep blue uniform jacket cut similar to ours, but longer, nearly to his knees, to declare him Empaetor. None was needed. I knew him from his posture and his silver, loosely curled hair. Rounded shoulders suggested the weight of the empire had taken its toll after all his years on the throne.

The Empaetor stood with his hands clasped behind his back, looking out onto the city below. "This is the one?"

"Yes, sir," said SA Tekka.

"I'm told you know where my missing heir is."

Not his son. Not Laurent. No hint of concern, only business.

Much like my first dealings with Pitari, I tread delicately with the truth. "I have no doubt that's what you've been told."

Outside, clouds sped across the sky, casting moving shadows on the city and countryside. It was almost mesmerizing.

"I'll talk with the prisoner now. Wait by the door," the Empaetor ordered.

SA Tekka gave me a look of warning before retreating

to the door where we'd entered. The room was vast and cavernous, making me feel very insignificant. That was probably the point. I waited, trying like hell to keep my breathing even and not give in to panic.

"Anduvean, I hear."

"Yes, sir."

"And is my glorious empire prospering there?"

Didn't he know where or what my homeworld was?

"No, it's definitely not."

His head cocked, almost enough to side-eye me over his shoulder, but not quite. "You've been left to your own devices for generations. Provided with everything my empire has to offer. Perhaps you require more stringent oversight."

Keeping my tone as respectful as possible, I proceeded with the truth. "What we require, sir, is an environmental alteration team to correct the volcanic disruption that is endangering the health and wellbeing of the Anduvean people. We were never given access to that benefit of your empire. It also wouldn't hurt to send some of your more current wonders because everything we have is generations old."

He turned then, his face so familiar, but much older and harder, all sharp edges, as if a hurricane of hostility were barely contained beneath his flesh. To be caught in the Empaetor's gaze was to be trapped, as if a net had fallen from the ceiling to hold me in place. There was a power there, a knowing that defied his age, as if he were ancient and encapsulated the entire history of the empire.

Would Laurent look like this? Carrying the weight of the empire not on his shoulders, but heavy in his soul?

The Empaetor bared his yellow teeth. I couldn't decide if it was a smile or a grimace. His gaze was hard, direct, without the cloudiness of age.

"Insolent one, aren't you."

"I've been called worse."

He huffed. "I imagine you have. I can see that leaving your world to rot in exile has not improved the stock of its citizens. You've learned nothing, even in four generations."

"We've learned plenty, sir."

His long neck craned forward as his head swiveled eerily, much like a snake. I suppressed a shiver.

"I do not like you."

"I get that a lot."

He bared his teeth again.

"My heir, where is he?"

If SA Tekka had expected me to be more at ease with sharing information after or during speaking to the Empaetor, he'd sorely misjudged my reception to the Empaetor's charm.

"I'm sure, given your own understanding of personal security, that you can appreciate that I'm not prepared to answer that just yet."

"You are not in my employ."

If there were any time to make my place in the scheme of things known for better or worse, I supposed this was it. "But I am in the employ of the heir."

A spark lit in his eyes. Perhaps it was a trick of light and shadow from the massive window. "Is that what he told you?"

"That's what Ari Leeman told me."

"Leeman. A weak bloodline, that one. I should prune it."

"He's dead, sir. Already pruned."

"The rest of it," he snapped.

"Seems unnecessary. Ari did his job admirably, protecting the heir even out on the lawless edge of the empire on an exile world."

"So, my heir is safe."

"I can confirm that the last time I laid eyes on him, he was safe."

His head did another snake dance, giving me the creeps. "And when was that?"

"Recently."

"You would do well for your people to answer my questions fully and to the best of your knowledge."

"My people being who exactly? Agent Andover already obliterated my family and my home."

"Impatient fool."

"Agreed. You can see how this makes me less in awe of your glorious empire."

His hand sprang forward with unexpected agility, grabbing me by the neck. His fingers might be thin and spotted with age, but they were still strong as they dug into my skin, grasping my windpipe and squeezing tight.

I didn't raise a hand to the Empaetor, not even to attempt to pry him off. Cocky as I might be, I fully understood that any threat to the man would compel SA Tekka to shoot me without hesitation. As it was, I could see a gun in his hand and his incoming intervention as he raced towards us.

"Sir, if she's dead, she can't tell us where he is."

The Empaetor threw me backward as he released me. I gasped, refilling my lungs as I staggered away.

"Interrogate the *Knaldon* crew again. Kill a few if you need to."

"Sir, they are your people. They've done no wrong."

"They've aided this woman in abducting my heir," he yelled, waving his claw-like hands.

"I9 was not abducted," I corrected. "He was evacuated by his personal bodyguard from a perceived dangerous situation in this very palace." I coughed and rubbed my throat. "Neither of you has explained what that situation was or how it was misunderstood."

The Empaetor snarled, "I do not have to explain myself to you. You will answer, or I will make your existence very unpleasant."

"That's already been accomplished. It didn't gain my cooperation for anyone else, and I wouldn't bank on a different result now."

SA Tekka opened his mouth to surely fling censure my way, but the Empaetor stalked toward me, silencing him.

"I require my heir to take my place. He has a limited time to do so, and those days are growing shorter. There is much I must share with him before that day comes."

"He has said the same thing, yet he is not eager to walk through your door. Why is that?"

"I should kill her," the Empaetor muttered.

SA Tekka's gaze darted from the Empaetor to me and back.

"Not me, I'm guessing. The consort," I clarified before SA Tekka took any initiative.

"Yes, that soft-hearted twit. She spooked him, no doubt."

"She never spoke to him about any of this, only to Ari Leeman." I straightened my uniform coat and back-burnered my unease in the hopes of getting answers. "If you can give me a straight answer about what she would have shared with Leeman, I will pass that on, and your heir can choose whether to come to you or not."

"Choices," the Empaetor cackled. "He has no choices. He will do what he is told until the day I'm gone."

"Sir, could we not just share what the consort misunderstood so we can resolve this situation?"

Even SA Tekka was on my side at this point? Was the Empaetor's over-the-top reaction due to medication from his terminal condition? Did SA Tekka know about the Empaetor's impending death? It wasn't my place to ask, but I was considering doing it anyway.

The Empaetor went still, eyeing us both with deep suspicion. His nostrils flared. "She was worried he would no longer be himself."

"After he became Empaetor? That is a lot of responsibility," SA Tekka said to me. "He will give up his free time, his hobbies, the carefree personal time he spends with anyone of his choosing."

That made sense. As a mother, she'd want her son to be happy, to have all the things he enjoyed. Even if she wasn't directly a part of his life, she would still care about him.

"Are you saying that in favor of keeping her son's access to carefree trysts with the kitchen staff, afternoons of rock hunting, and endless hours of fingerpainting clouds, the consort would ship him off to the edge of the empire in a stasis tube with only one man to guard him?"

SA Tekka grimaced. He turned his attention to the Empaetor as if he were also waiting for the answer.

"I do not understand the mind of that woman. That's

why I've had little to do with her since taking the throne. She was making my heir weak in the head."

"And you were also unable to beat the logic of her decision out of her during her captivity?" I hazarded to ask, since I seemed to have Tekka on my side.

"I would never harm my consort!" his voice rose as if the suggestion was outrageous.

"Oh? Who did?"

SA Tekka's mouth fell open as if I'd just betrayed his deepest secret.

I turned to him with raised brows and my heart in my throat, but I hoped no one else saw how desperately my wits were treading water. "That wasn't information to be shared? Sorry, I missed that in our briefing prior to this enlightening meeting."

That spark I'd seen earlier resurfaced in the Empaetor's eye. "You dared lay a hand on my consort? Without my knowledge? Without my leave?"

SA Tekka stammered incoherently.

"I asked you to procure her. To bring her to me for a conversation, to contain her until further notice. Interrogating her yourself, laying a hand on her in any manner, was never discussed or implied," the Empaetor roared.

"He mentioned he didn't have clearance to kill her," I interjected.

SA Tekka backed away.

"I can't help but notice that there aren't any other guards present. Would you like him detained?" I offered.

The Empaetor seemed to suddenly remember that I was in the room. "Yes."

I liked how the tide was turning in my favor. So much

so that I opted to overlook the semi-mad Empaetor, who had been choking me a few minutes ago and run with the opportunity to turn the tables on SA Tekka, who had kicked me and locked me up the day before. Doing me a favor by meeting the Empaetor himself, indeed.

SA Tekka ran for the door.

A burst of adrenaline helped fuel my sprint after the security advisor. I caught and tackled him just before he reached the exit. Thanks to his removing my wrist restraints, I knew where he kept them and their code.

With the man secured, I hauled him to his feet and immediately winced at the strain on my midsection.

"You'll regret this. I was trying to help you," he snarled.

"You are helping me." I grabbed his arm, turning him toward the Empaetor. "What would you like done to him, sir?"

"Whatever he did to my consort."

"Yes, sir." I happily aimed SA Tekka at the door. "Off we go."

"Stabinov," the Empaetor snapped.

"Sorry, sir." I turned back around. "Was there something else?"

"My heir. You will have him in front of me by morning or you'll find yourself back in a cell. Permanently."

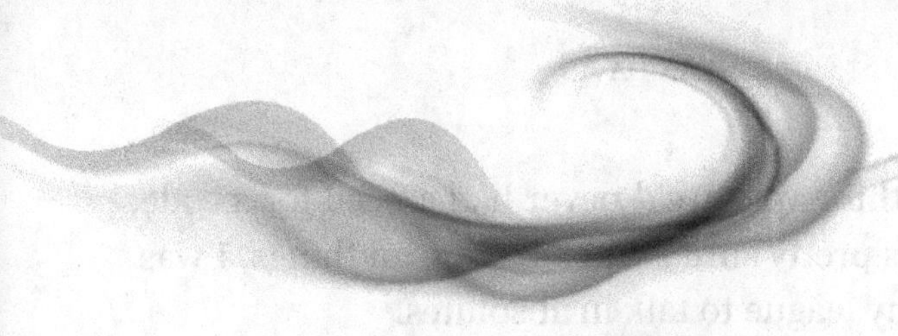

37

You Should See The Other Guys

I boarded the *Knaldon* to a quiet welcome. That may have had something to do with my escort of four of the Empaetor's guards.

Senio and Pitari greeted me with open hesitation. Six other crewmembers stood close behind them. Everyone appeared to be armed except me.

"I've come for the heir," I announced, making my thoughts as loud as possible as I ran through my conversation with the Empaetor in my head.

"Have you?" asked Senio.

"Is that a problem?" Was there something I was missing?

"You umm..." he gestured at my face, "look like there's been a problem."

"That was a yesterday thing. Today is all good."

"Are you sure?"

"Mostly, yes."

He seemed to be waiting for me to offer some secret code conversation wherein I would tell him what was really going on. The thing was, we'd never had a need for a code, and while I was pretty sure I had a handle on things, I was too far out of my league to talk in absolutes.

"So, we're letting them take him?" Pitari asked with every bit of skepticism that was written on Senio's face.

"No, I'm going with him to meet with the Empaetor so we can clear up some things."

"As…" asked Senio

"Not as prisoners."

He shared a look with the Seeker. She nodded. They both stepped aside, waving to their backup to do the same. My escort and I proceeded.

Senio stuck close while Pitari lagged back a few paces to chat with my escort. In our time together, I'd noticed she had a knack for engaging people in conversation by working from what she saw in their thoughts. She'd done it with me a couple of times even after I knew what she was capable of. She was so subtle that it felt natural.

Senio cast me a worried side-eyed glance.

"I'm sore but on my feet."

"And we're doing this?"

"Unless Laurent has a major objection, yes. Is he alright?"

"He was pretty chilled, but safe, yes."

"Good." My neck muscles eased a bit.

"He's where you last saw him. Do you want company?"

"No. We have some things that need to be discussed in private."

He nodded. "Doctor Tik is keeping those patients in quarantine like you asked."

The what now? I let that knock around in my head while we walked to the lift. Oh, this was an attempt at the code we didn't have. My parents were safe.

"Good." I finally said.

He seemed satisfied that I'd understood. He left it at that.

"Andover?" I asked.

"He was transferred off the ship after you were... removed."

"That's one way to put it."

"Two of the others were also removed. Another limped his way to the door." He grinned.

"I missed all the fun."

"You *were* all the fun."

I laughed and held up my bruised wrists. "They didn't think so."

"You kinda deserved that. You know, had I been on the other side."

We waited for the others in the lift and then proceeded down to the living quarters. Seeker Pitari gave me a nod that seemed to confirm an all clear with the situation and then left.

Senio stayed. "We'll wait out here," he heavily suggested.

My escort took the hint. Threats had already been issued, after all. I knew what had to be done and so did they.

Taking a deep breath, I palmed the panel and walked inside. The main room appeared empty, and the lights were on standby mode. The door closed. I waited, letting my eyes adjust.

"Rita?" Laurent whispered from the bedroom.

I went inside and turned on the light.

He gasped, his hand going to my cheek before I even

got my bearings. "They said you'd been wounded."

"You should see the other guys."

He made a half-hearted effort at a smile but concern dulled it. "Your ribs?"

"Sore." I realized his hand was still on my face. I pulled away enough to put a few inches between us. "Your father wants to talk to you. I also found your mother. She's alive, though she also endured what I'm coming to understand is a standard empiric interrogation at SA Tekka's hand."

"He dared beat my mother?" he asked with righteous fury.

"Yeah, your father had the same reaction." Except now seeing it on Laurent, I realized how different the two men were. Maybe Laurent would also be all sharp edges and erratic rage after ruling the empire for thirty-one years, but I hoped not.

"And you're here," he said after he'd calmed down a moment.

"And SA Tekka is not."

"I see."

Since it was just the two of us, and I'd admittedly had a rough few days, I sat on the edge of my bed. It might not have been my bed on the station, but it was a hundred times more comfortable than the cot in the Empaetor's cell. My eyes wanted to close, and my body wanted to enjoy a little comfort for even an hour or two. But my escort and the Empaetor were waiting.

"Your father claims this supposed threat was all a fig-ment of your mother's imagination, a misguided attempt to maintain your personal freedom. He said that he doesn't understand her. Is it possible that there was a misunderstanding about your upcoming obligations or about what this training might entail? I don't know your parents. Does that track for you?"

He let out a heavy sigh. "They don't get along. At all. When we all lived together at the estate, we were happy then. Then he took the throne, and he changed. He never went back to how he had been. I kept waiting for a quiet day when he might relax, when he might smile or crack a joke like he used to, but he never did."

"I can only imagine what a massive responsibility running the empire must be." Why the fuck was I making excuses for the lunatic who'd had his hands wrapped around my throat? Oh yes, because he was Laurent's father. Because hopefully, we wouldn't have to deal with him much longer.

I cleared my throat. "What I'm asking is, do you think your mother would go so far as to evacuate you from the safety of the palace simply because she didn't want the obligations of taking on the empire to end your enjoyment of... Whatever it is you enjoy doing with your free time."

Laurent settled on the edge of his bed across from me. He bowed his head, studying his hands on his lap. "I'd guess it was more than that, but if she thought getting away from my father's influence at the end of his life would help me be a better Empaetor, that's a reason I can accept Ari dying for."

This was not the time for my heart to do its warming toward him thing, but it sure was doing it anyway. "You're not him. You *will* be much better."

He glanced upward hesitantly, but then locked on to me with an intensity that warmed a lot more than just my heart. Maker save me, we needed to get back to the palace.

"What do you think I enjoy doing in my free time?" he asked.

I gave the question a little serious thought, more so than when I'd been spouting off to his father. "Reading dry old books like your mother does, enticing the beautiful, wealthy daughters of your father's dignitaries into your bed as Ari insinuated, and rock climbing because you pretend to like danger. Or maybe collecting exotic animals or obsessing over bird figurines from ancient civilizations. I don't know. Things rich people do when they have too much time on their hands."

He snickered. "Reading yes, but history, and on my datapad, thank you. I gave up chasing snitty, fragile-egoed, rich girls years ago. And it's fish. Not collecting, but observing. Preferably in their natural habitat, which does involve a good deal of travel. So yes, I suppose that is something rich people with too much time on their hands do."

"You travel around the empire looking at fish." I prayed he was kidding.

But he nodded.

"Do you have a favorite?"

Laurent grinned and held his hand out for my datapad. "Here, I'll show you." He busied himself flipping through pages of underwater creatures as if we didn't have an escort outside waiting for us. All his concern for me and rage over his mother vanished into an energetic, boyish smile.

He held up the pad to show me a chubby, bright orange fish with a gauzy tail and fins. It wasn't flashy or particularly stunning, just a plain old orange fish.

"Why do you like that one?"

"It was a gift meant for my father from the representative of a poor world on what used to be the edge of the empire. Before his last expansion." He tore his gaze from the fish to look at me. "If it doesn't shimmer, glimmer, or shine, my father has no use for gifts. He tossed it out with the other unwanted things. I rescued it and put it in a bowl in my room. I'd just moved to the palace, and for years, that fish was my only friend. It knew all my secrets."

I wished I had Pitari there to tell me if he was making this all up. But he looked and sounded sincere. I couldn't think of anything he'd have to gain by making up a heart-warming fish story.

"What happened to it?"

"Oh, it lived a very good life, had the best of everything my father's credits in my hands could buy. It was this big." His hands spanned fourteen inches. "Sadly, it died eleven years ago."

"You didn't get another one?"

He shook his head. "I went looking for other fish that might be overlooked. People gifted me all kinds of fish, knowing I liked them. Don't tell them, but I let their gifts go if I could get away with it. Before leaving their worlds, of course."

Laurent handed the datapad back to me. "The empty bowl still sits in my room."

"And you've never found another orange fish?" With his resources, that wouldn't be hard to do.

"I never needed another orange fish." His eyes took on a mischievous glint that was nothing like the dangerous spark in his father's. "At seventeen, I came into my own staff and funds. I adopted that poor world my father didn't care about and showed off my favorite fish to anyone who would listen, so they might want to buy one. That world now has a stable economy thanks to its pet fish exports."

"Does your father realize what you did?"

"He's too busy to notice."

I stared at the picture of the fish in my hands. "When you say you travel to look for fish, you're not looking for literal fish."

He winked. "No."

I really wanted his father to train Laurent as fast as possible so we could get this much better man on the throne. "In that case, I would really like to travel with you."

"I was hoping you might. I'm particularly interested in Anduvea's fish at the moment."

Was I the fish or was he talking about my homeworld? My brain was too busy melting over the man before me to work properly. "I could probably answer some questions if you have any."

He leaned forward. "Do your lips hurt?"

"Umm, what?"

He kissed me. Not in a lift for cover, not as a distraction, but behind closed doors where there was no one to put on a performance for. I allowed myself a minute of enjoyment before kicking my stupid brain back into action. It had been bad enough living with *Knaldon* crew rumors. I didn't need a palace full of them. Especially not when I was just beginning to feel my way around on Harilax. I pulled away.

"Did you and Ari have this sort of relationship too?" I asked, half joking but half not. I might be new to Harilax, but I'd had a lifetime of dealing with the frivolities of the rich and bored.

Laurent chuckled. "Uh no. No offense to those who do, but that's not the pond I swim in."

"I see we're sticking with fish."

"Sorry, I may have gotten a little too deep with my metaphor."

I laughed, unable to keep my amusement contained. "Can we not confuse this new job situation in the midst of the, umm, situation we're already in with your father?"

"At a loss for words?"

His grin made me seriously regret pushing him away. But I had a job to do.

"There's an escort outside," I pointed to the outer door, "that is likely getting very antsy right now. Let's get you safely in front of your father and sort out the throne and whatever is between your parents before we discuss this. Deal?"

His grin grew larger. "You're willing to discuss this?"

"If there is actually anything to discuss." I did not match his smile, wanting him to know I was serious. "I have zero interest in being toyed with, and frankly, this entire planet and everyone on it is not in my comfort zone."

"Understood," he said sincerely. His smile remained.

Great Maker, I was going to have to keep any hint of this from my mother. I'd never hear the end of it.

38

Multiple Choice

I walked beside the heir to the empire, not as relaxed companions surrounded by a crew vetted by a mind reader as I had on our flight to Harilax, but as his personal bodyguard walking into an unknown situation. One where I didn't fully trust anyone, including Laurent, whom the little voice in the back of my head said was pulling a cruel prank that he'd reveal to everyone else at any moment.

Two of the Empaetor's guards marched before us and two after. They'd seized my comm pin, cutting me off from the *Knaldon*. No one was willing to give me a weapon, so all I had were my eyes, wits, and hands. None of which were at their best, given how sore and tired I was.

"You're going to implode," Laurent said under his breath. "Relax. You said this was under control."

"I said no such thing. And I can't. When do we meet up with the rest of your security team?"

"If Ari didn't trust them, I certainly don't. My father likely fired them all the moment I went missing. You're all the security I've got."

"You're not helping me relax."

"You'll be fine."

"Have you seen me? Do I look fine?"

At least in the pocket of guards as we were, all I had to do was move forward and try not to trip over my feet. I highly doubted his father's guards would let anything happen to Laurent since the Empaetor was so concerned with getting him back home.

"You look like you've handled every situation that has been thrown at you for the past two weeks. Once we get this meeting with my father over with, we're going to my wing of the palace where you're going to sleep while I don't leave the room. I can get medical in to look at you after you sleep."

I kind of really liked him just then.

"I should go check in with Doctor Tik about his patients. We wouldn't want them to break quarantine. He can check me over while I'm there."

"Absolutely not. The *Knaldon* crew can manage that situation. I'll let Doctor Meldorn—he takes care of me and my father—know you'll check in after you've slept."

Even though it sure seemed like he was trying to be kind, being ordered around annoyed me. It had been years since anyone had been inclined to do that as long as I was doing my job. Yumi knew how to phrase things as suggestions. I didn't mind suggestions.

"Is that an order?"

Laurent gave me a look that said he was weighing his answer. "Does it need to be?"

I could accept that as a suitable response, given who he was. At least it hadn't been a definite yes without hesitation.

"It does not."

"Maybe also something to eat before you sleep. For

everyone's benefit," he added with a wink.

He'd spent too much time with my parents, but I liked him for that too. Not that I was supposed to be liking him right now. I shook off the warmth that was softening my defenses and refocused my attention on everyone around him.

The walk from the port to the palace was twice as long as I remembered. By the time we got through the palace entry security and up onto the first floor, I was sure my shoulders were so tight that they rode up to my ears.

"Rita, relax."

"Easy for you to say. You're not the one responsible for you."

Laurent chuckled. "You and Ari would have been best friends."

He might have been right. But if Ari hadn't died, I wouldn't have his job or even have been looked at to join Laurent's team. Thank you, Ari.

I was glad our escort knew where we were going because my scrambled mind was too busy running scenarios where everything went wrong: where I died. Laurent died. Someone murdered the Empaetor and framed me. My parents were discovered and used to blackmail me into betraying Laurent. Laurent and the Empaetor sat side by side on the giant throne, rehashing the whole escapade, ending with pointing and laughing at me for thinking I might have a place here.

We had entered the staging room before I realized how far we'd come. Shake it the hell off, Rita. Pay attention.

The old woman was gone, and in her place stood a young man, probably in his early twenties. His midnight skin seemed to absorb all the light in the room, but his wide smile radiated it back.

"Are you surviving your promotion?" Laurent asked him.

The boy grinned. "Yes, thank you, sir. It's much cooler here than at home."

"You look happy."

"I am." He performed a head bow and walked to the doorway, cracking it open to speak to someone inside.

"One of your fish?"

"Yes."

The way he watched the kid reminded me of how I felt when I walked one of the Fivers into their own suite for the first time. I found myself smiling and relaxing a little.

We'd made it safely to the meeting. Laurent was home and talking to his father. I'd fulfilled my obligation to the Empaetor and was no longer in danger of being thrown back into a cell. At least, I really hoped that was the case because the tiny optimistic part of me was very intrigued with how comfortable a bed in Lauret's wing of the palace might be.

"Don't you get a free pass to see your father without the gatekeeping?" I asked.

"I found it's best for everyone if I follow the rules. He doesn't like surprises or unanticipated interruptions. They don't end well, not even for me."

"Got it."

He watched the young man by the door. Whatever the signal was, I did not see or hear it, but the kid nodded to Laurent.

I didn't know what was expected of me here. "Do I go with you?"

"Yes, please."

I hadn't anticipated his pleading tone.

"I hate this room," he said.

"Why? It's breathtaking. Well, the view outside, I mean. That monstrosity of a throne, not so much."

Laurent's fingers fidgeted at his sides. "Try sitting in it. No, don't. I'm kidding. He'd have you killed. But yes, it's not at all comfortable, and it *is* hideous."

The Empaetor's guards stepped aside to allow us access to the door. They followed us inside. Despite his unease and pleading, Laurent strode confidently toward his father, who now sat perched upon the throne.

The footsteps behind us halted. I glanced back to find the guards had lined themselves against the wall just inside the room. No private meetings today. Though I supposed they were out of earshot of the throne, unless it had amplifiers in it. With all the tech shit dripping off the thing, it wouldn't have surprised me if it did.

The old man's hands rested on the arms of the throne. Seemingly, there was some area on them for that functional purpose without activating anything. He literally had everything within arm's reach.

Laurent marched ahead of me. I didn't know how close I was supposed to get. To either of them. When he stopped ten paces from the throne, I also stopped, leaving a few paces between us. If anyone wanted me somewhere different, they were going to have to speak up.

I'd assumed the Empaetor would smile at his son, who had returned from a harrowing journey he hadn't gone on intentionally. That he would perhaps get off his ass and embrace his heir—that he'd been willing to rampage around the empire looking for. But he did not.

He looked past Laurent and addressed me. "Ms. Stabinov, you have delivered as promised."

I thought it best to keep my smart mouth shut for once and went with a head bow in favor of retaining his goodwill. Assuming this was leading to goodwill. One of those buttons near his fingertips might open a trap door that would drop me into a pit of spikes for all I knew.

"What would you have for your reward?" he asked.

My mind went blank at this unexpected question. I'd wrongly assumed that if there were some grand reward, he'd name what it was and I'd take it with a smile, be it fake or genuine. Barring that, maybe a multiple-choice question—a few options to pick from at the very least.

I was keeping the Empaetor waiting, and I could sense his goodwill meter ticking out quickly. "Absolve the citizens of Anduvea," I blurted.

The Empaetor scowled. "Why would I do that? They did nothing. One more chance, Ms. Stabinov. What would you have as *your* reward?"

Laurent had already offered to release Anduvea when he took the throne so that would happen eventually. He'd also offered to replace my destroyed home and pay me well for my services. I might have asked for a monetary sum, but my gut told me putting a price on Laurent's head wouldn't sit favorably with his father.

My parents were here on Harilax now. They couldn't wait for him to take the throne and as much as they'd gone through recently, I didn't want to send them home empty-handed. "Lift the exile restrictions on my family."

His eyes narrowed. "You must be third generation, yes?

Free to leave as you will."

"My parents are not. The Anduvean air has not been kind to them."

"It wasn't meant to be." His eyes narrowed. "You said Agent Andover killed your parents."

Fine memory for a terminally ill old man. I shrugged. "In case he missed."

The Empaetor cocked his head and stared me down for a long minute. I stared right back.

"Fine. Parents only. No other extensions of your bloodline."

Specific bastard. Luckily, there were none or I would have haggled for a better deal. At least this way, the record showed him as benevolent and still victorious over my request.

"Thank you, Empaetor." I offered another bow and wished I could leave before he changed his mind, but I had a job to do. Not that I anticipated Laurent would come to harm in his father's vicinity with four of the Empaetor's guards in attendance.

With our business completed, the Empaetor tapped on the arm of his throne for a moment and then turned his attention to Laurent. "Why didn't you return home immediately upon being released from the stasis tube Ari Leeman used to trap you?"

Laurent stood tall and steady, but I noted his thumb rubbing his forefinger at his side. I wasn't the only one who was nervous.

"I didn't know why Ari had snuck me out of the palace. Whether there was a threat to me or to you or the entire empire. It seemed better to get more information before running home and possibly into the exact danger I'd been saved from."

The Empaetor studied him for a long moment, his lips pursing and relaxing in what may have been pondering or uncontrolled spasms.

"I suppose that was wise. Why didn't you contact me to ask those questions?"

"How could I know if you had been compromised from out on the edge of the empire with no current news or anyone I trusted to confirm what you might say?"

"That damned Leeman made you needlessly paranoid." The Empaetor sneered. "He was a simple-minded fool, drawn in by your mother's lunatic ravings. My men wasted thousands of hours hunting for you, fuel, resources better used by the worlds who need them for survival."

The Empaetor's face flushed. "You could have been hurt or even killed! Then what would I do? This was inexcusable. I needed you here. Weeks ago, you irresponsible fool! You could have sent a message with your location. You could have ordered a ship to take you home. But no, you hide? Coward!" he ranted.

I'd never seen anyone mad enough to spit teeth before, but what was before me perfectly matched what I'd imagined that would look like.

Part of me wanted to see the Laurent I knew square his shoulders and boldly point out that he hadn't left the palace of his own volition, or that he'd been abducted from the Empaetor's own supposedly secure palace. Or even that he blamed me for advising him against racing back home or sending his father a message to confirm his safety. But Laurent merely bowed his head and remained silent. Given the rage-filled man before us, I didn't blame him. He knew his father's temper, as did I. I rubbed my throat. From the rumors I'd heard in my crew interviews, submission was always the wisest choice.

I was really sick of rumors.

Seeing Laurent disassembled flipped some insanity switch inside me.

"He wasn't hiding voluntarily, and he would have sent you a message. That was on me. I didn't have all the information needed to know if that was safe."

Yep, I'd just said that out loud. To the Empaetor. I'd be back in that cell in no time.

The Empaetor's dark gaze snapped to me. So did Laurent's far more aghast one. My feet begged to depart from the room with all haste. I gave them one backward step before regaining my resolve.

The man who ruled the empire motioned to the row of guards along the wall. The ones who had escorted us here, who were probably advancing toward me right now to drag me back to the cell I'd been in before. I'd yet to wrap my head around the layout of the palace. Maybe that was one mystery I'd unravel before I was permanently locked away. Assuming I remained conscious while in custody this time.

My ears itched for the sound I was sure was coming. But no footsteps approached.

The Empaetor scowled at me for several more breaths before he focused back on Laurent. "An exile station guard? Who had no information? That's who you took advice from? Not only took, but followed? You are just as empty-headed as your mother, as Ari Leeman. Simpletons, all of you," he roared.

In light of his spindly fingers tapping on far too many controls on the arms of the throne that I also had no information about, I kept my mouth shut and followed Laurent's bowed-head preservation technique.

"Rita Stabinov."

I hazarded a glance upward at the forceful use of my name.

"You brought the heir home, and so I will forgive this one outburst. This one." The old man drilled his warning into me with an iron glare. "You will see my heir to his room, where he will await his indoctrination first thing in the morning."

He tapped another button on the throne and turned the vid screen towards us. The still frames from both of my parent's ID chips were on display in vivid color.

"If anything should befall my heir while you still breathe, I will hunt down those parents you so thoughtfully mentioned. And I will not miss. Am I clear?"

"Yes, Empaetor."

"Be gone." He forcefully pointed to the door where his guards waited.

I knew my way to the door and to the room beyond it, but after that point, I had to walk beside Laurent. He avoided me as much as physically possible. Like two opposing magnets held in one hand, we made our way through the wide central corridor to one of the doors at the end. It turned out not to be just a door, but a stair entrance.

The stairs were only wide enough for two to walk side by side, not that we were. I was trailing three steps behind, considering how I should approach apologizing for making the Empaetor's tirade even worse. The view up the windowed stairway was as grand as the one from the throne room. Better really, because the irate old man wasn't there with us.

Laurent's steps were just short of stomping as he made his way up the stairs, up a turn to another flight, and then through a doorway identical to the one we'd entered. The corridor, however, was different. While the lower levels of the triangle structure that I'd seen were more utilitarian in design, and the throne room section opulent, this part of the palace was decidedly less grand. Like it had been let go.

We'd entered a corridor as wide as the one outside the throne room, but there was no fancy lighting, no lighting at all other than what came through the windows at both ends. But unlike two levels below, the sunlight wasn't as bright here. The clear surface had a brownish tint. Having not recalled any color variation when I'd seen the palace from the consort's estate, I gathered the tint was on the inside. I supposed it would keep even distant air traffic from seeing into the palace.

The corridor was devoid of any ornamentation—no pillars, plants, tables or seating, no artwork. Just plain green walls and a serviceable carpet to cushion our steps. No one else was in sight.

"Where are we?" I asked.

Laurent didn't answer. He didn't even turn to look at me. It was safe to say he was angry and not just with his father. His determined steps brought him to one of the doors along the corridor. It looked no different from the rest.

Slamming his palm on the panel was not enough to open the door. As he stood entering a code and a scan, his entire body shook. Noted, his father was not the only one with a temper. I braced myself for an epic tongue-lashing like he'd started in on when I'd taken him to stay with my parents. And that was before he'd been dressed down in front of me.

If we hadn't been in a strange place where I knew no one and had nowhere nearby to go, I would have given him some time alone to cool off. Unfortunately, the *Knaldon* was a long walk away, and I didn't know my way out of the palace or if I'd be let back in.

I kept quiet when the door opened and followed Laurent inside. The lights came on slowly, almost reluctantly. Before me was a poor imitation of the receiving room two floors below. No attendant stood inside. No hint of finery, just a dusty open space with a slightly less dusty trail across the tile floor leading to an ornate door like the one leading to the throne room.

Curious to see what was behind it, I stood back and gave Laurent time to open the second door. The lights came on more energetically here. Sensing that Laurent knew where he was going and wanted no interference from me, I gave him a minute on his own while he was still in sight.

The windows here were also tinted, giving the interior a dingy impression. However, the furnishings were what I expected: high end, clean, and plentiful. The room had a somewhat maze-like appearance with partial walls scattered around to break up the space. Some were shoulder high, allowing me to keep Laurent in sight. Others, like the one he walked behind that prompted me to get my ass into the room, were taller. There were no fully enclosed rooms within the space, no drop ceilings, just spaces defined by short walls and tall walls. As I wove my way through to find where he went, I was met by a closed door. One with an antique knob, not a panel. I took that as a solid hint that he wished to be alone.

With the heir contained and surrounded by silence, I took the opportunity to explore. The throne room had been an open expanse of light and a show of wealth. Laurent's space was more of a curated collection of furniture and maybe souvenirs, perhaps items he'd picked up on his fish explorations. The only cohesive themes I could identify were that he liked blue and a sandy shade of beige, things that were made of natural substances, and very little sparkle. Pretty much the opposite of his father.

There were three nooks near the room Laurent had sequestered himself inside. If I'd really been inclined and not already sore everywhere, I could have jumped up onto the half walls around them to peer over into his room. I wasn't eager to get my ass verbally handed to me, so I didn't.

Each nook contained a bed that was twice the size of the one I'd had on the station. All of them appeared deserted. If other guards had lived here, they'd packed up and left. A quick search confirmed that even Ari's things must have been taken away. Which was a shame. I would have liked to get to know my predecessor a little better. He'd been important to Laurent and might have left some insights on the job or the man that would have been helpful. Sadly, I really was on my own.

Claiming the nook farthest from Laurent's room, I pulled back the covers to discover sheets and two thick blankets. I stifled a gleeful squeal. As tired as I was, I didn't care if someone else had slept in them. I pulled off my coat and stretched out on the coverlet. As I'd suspected, the bed was amazing. I could feel it forming to my body, supporting everything perfectly. I let out a sigh. If Laurent could let me get a twenty-minute nap right here, he could yell at me all he wanted.

I must have closed my eyes because I woke to Laurent standing over me. He didn't look any happier than before. "That was reckless," he snapped.

Falling asleep? I wanted to say, but I kept my mouth shut, knowing I owed him a target to vent upon after my performance with his father. I sat up and gave him my full attention.

"He could have sent you back to a cell. Would you like that? What am I supposed to do if you're in a cell? For the Maker's sake, Rita, learn to keep your mouth shut."

I nodded, doing exactly what he said.

"Not now." He let out a frustrated snarl and raked his hands through his hair. It was a mess. I gathered he'd been doing a good deal of that before coming out to face me.

"Your father was being unreasonable."

"He's the Empaetor. He can be unreasonable if he fuck-ing wants to!"

"Do you plan on being unreasonable?"

Laurent pinched the bridge of his nose. "Hell if I know."

I moved to sit on the edge of the bed. "He's not much of a father, is he?"

Laurent caught me in an incredulous stare. "He's the—"

"Empaetor, yeah, I know. But come on, if I was missing and in potential danger, and gone for months before mak-ing it home, my father would hug me. He would be relieved and show it. He would use my name, call me his daughter, a nickname. Something. He might be angry, but he would want me back safe and keep the berating to a minimum."

I couldn't sit a moment longer, no matter how much I wanted to remain calm for Laurent's benefit. I stood and paced my nook. "At least your mother was concerned. She was clearly worried about you. I don't trust her, but she was a real person about it, not a tyrannical asshole."

His mouth dropped open.

"Sorry, that was probably too much, wasn't it? It was. But I'm not wrong. Has he always been like that?"

"You realize we're in his palace? That someone might be listening to you? That you could end up back in a cell, and I could do nothing about it?"

I paused my pacing to glance at the distant door and back to Laurent. "Do I really need to worry about one of your father's guards busting in here to drag me out?" I shook my head. "If this is your space, I'd like to think that you're competent enough to keep your father's eyes and ears out of it." I waved my hand around the vast suite. "I don't see any hint of him here, only you."

The heir to the empire deflated, crumbling to sit on the bed that I'd slept in. His head dropped into his hands.

"Don't push it, Rita, alright? He let it go today, I promise you, that's a rare thing. Very rare."

"Come on," I said, trying to make him smile. "If I talk my way into a cell, you'd release me once you took the throne."

He looked up at me balefully. "You're assuming you'd still be alive."

I considered the treatment I'd received so far from the Empaetor's staff. "Oh. Good point. So, behaving then."

Laurent nodded. "How is my mother?"

I settled onto the bed beside him. "Sore but healing, on her feet. Her estate is gorgeous. Her staff is not. Other than the Ekie woman, and really, Laurent? She's a vacant twit."

He managed a chuckle. "She's a pretty twit, and it was a while ago."

I waved his excuses aside. "Not judging. I've had a few escapades with pretty myself." I gave him three seconds and then couldn't contain my snort any longer. "Yeah, not so much."

He laughed more heartily. "I could see you enjoying a few pretty boys."

"Now you're just being cruel. To those boys and to me." I shook my head. "So, your father—"

"You're not wrong. But—"

"Yes, keeping my mouth shut outside this room."

He nodded. "Are you hungry?"

"Very. You have to be too, I would think."

"After that meeting, and with whatever tomorrow holds? Hardly, but I should eat. You definitely should eat. In fact, for your own safety, you should have a hearty meal before facing the Empaetor for as long as he lives."

I snickered. "You've definitely spent too much time with my mother."

"Is there such a thing as too much? She's a good cook."

There went that flush of warmth rushing through me again. At least we were in a relatively safe place where I could enjoy it.

"If nothing else," he said, blissfully unaware of my pondering both of us being on my bed in the damned palace, of all places I'd never thought to be, "my life with you and your friends has taught me to eat when food is available because who knows when it will be again."

"Not a bad takeaway from all of this. I hope you'll remember that when you're on the throne. There are oceans full of fish out there."

"I will," he said solemnly. "I ordered two meals. They should be ready about now."

Whatever magic he'd used to make food magically appear was much appreciated. He walked over to a cabinet that stood by itself in one of the open spaces. When he opened the top two clearplaz doors, a wonderful aroma hit my nose. Led by the scent, I joined him by the cabinet to take one of the covered platters. He nodded toward a nearby low table surrounded by thick pillows.

"There are drinks on the side." He pointed at the cabinet.

I found a tall door that opened to a selection of chilled beverages. Picking one for me, and one Laurent often chose on the *Knaldon*, I returned to the table.

We ate in companionable silence. I quite enjoyed it. The view of the sun setting outside from up this high in the palace was amazing, even through the tinted windows. I caught Laurent smiling at me smiling at the view more than once.

"I'm not looking forward to these sessions with my father," Laurent said once his plate was nearly empty. "As a kid, I dreamed of him wanting to spend time with me, to teach me about running the empire. But now that the time is finally here, I'm not ready."

"Your mother felt the same way, I think."

Doubt rushed over his face. "That I wasn't ready?"

"Let me rephrase that. That she didn't want you to have to give up what you enjoy doing to run the empire. Which seems a frivolous concern given that this is what you were born for. However, I'm not looking forward to you spending time with your father, especially if it means I also have to spend time with your father."

"I'm guessing that was more her concern too. He's not exactly a friendly man."

I couldn't hold back my snort.

"He was. It was just so long ago. I've always thought that maybe he forgot how and hoped that I would be the one to remind him. Seeing him today, I know that was a stupid dream."

I had the urge to hug him, but I kept my ass planted on the pillow. "It wasn't a stupid dream. A hopeful one that I don't see panning out, sure, but not stupid."

He chuckled softly. "If she's being kept here in the palace, I'll talk to my mother. We might not be close, but I do want to make sure she's cared for. And that my father makes up for whatever she suffered at Tekka's hands. But first, I need to sleep. In my bed. Good Maker, I've missed my own bed."

I pointed to the bed I'd slept in. "I can see why. That's fabulous. And to think you've been slumming it with us common folks and our brick-like beds for so long."

Laurent stood, snickering. "I've missed you, Rita. Get some actual sleep. The bathroom is over there." He pointed toward the rear of the room where he'd gone before.

Visions of the consort's private bathroom danced in my head. I couldn't contain my excitement. I ran to check it out and was not disappointed.

The main area of the bath space was open: a giant tub, several sinks, counter space. Racks of towels and cleaning cloths. Shelves of soaps and bottles filled with the Maker knew what. Three half doors lined one wall. Two opened to toilets, fancy toilets that I looked forward to using because my ass had never been so pampered. The third opened to a larger deep tub, suited for at least six. Did Laurent bathe with his security staff, assuming that's what the three beds were for, or did he entertain women there? Someday, when we had the leisure to discuss the situation between us that Laurent had suggested might exist, I'd have to ask. Bathing with the heir to the empire had just found a spot on my things-to-do-on-Harilax list.

I used a sink, sampling sweet soap and a soft cloth to wash with and then made my way back to the bed I'd claimed. Laurent had retreated to his room, but the door was open.

I stripped down to my underclothes and folded my uniform, setting it on the shelf beside the bed and glanced over to the still open door. He had to hear me out here. Was this an invitation to see what his bedroom looked like? An invitation to it for more than looking? Was he just leaving the door open for security reasons? The only way to know was to blunder my way through an awkward finding out when I went too far.

Taking a chance, I poked my head through the doorway. "Do you need me for anything else?"

Laurent stood facing the corner, silent.

I stepped inside to realize he was standing in front of a small altar and apparently in prayer. Well, shit. Making a quick retreat, I sought out the light controls and dimmed everything. The light over his space remained bright, confirming my assumption that he had his own controls inside.

Once back in my bed, I thought back to the last time I'd actually prayed. Like, officially. It had been a long time. Years, for sure. Maybe Laurent was the wise one here. Who knew what tomorrow held with the meeting with his father. I bowed my head, not to anyone, but in the traditional prayer pose, mustering a few words. Protection and guidance for Laurent, for myself, for the ability to keep my mouth shut, and lastly to keep my parents safe. Content I'd done all I could for the day, for better or worse, I settled into someone's bed and prepared for the best night of sleep of my life.

39

Stink-eyed Glances

I woke feeling rested, which was a miracle at my age. My body still ached in too many places, but that was to be expected for a while yet. You can't rush healing, according to every doctor I'd ever talked to.

The unfamiliar surroundings took me a minute, but my brain quickly aligned itself with my current situation. Laurent's door had remained open all night, which I still found curious, but after interrupting his prayer session dressed only in my underclothes, I wasn't about to barge in again without asking him for some ground rules first.

While I waited for him to show his face, I used the bathroom, finding everything I could need within reason, as it seemed to be set up for male use. Exploring, I found uniforms hanging in the closet across from the bathroom entrance. The one plus of having a not super feminine physique was that the uniforms fit me just fine. There were also underclothes that at least suited the needs of the lower half of my body. I'd have to ask about getting a few female-oriented items brought in if Laurent expected me to stay in this part of the palace with him. If he didn't, I would beg for one of those mattresses to take wherever he'd be sending me.

Still not seeing him, I walked close enough to his door to catch a glimpse of his legs on the bed.

Secure in the knowledge that he hadn't wandered off without me, I went to investigate the food situation. The cabinet he'd pulled food from last night turned out to be a food delivery system with an order screen on the opposite side of the cold drink area. I ordered us breakfast and waited for it to show up.

I was sitting down at the table with the two plates when Laurent emerged. He ate with a single-minded purpose.

"Am I supposed to attend these lessons with you or just escort you there? I'm going to need a little guidance since I seem to be the only one of me around and have no one else to ask."

Laurent smiled nervously. "We'll fill the other team positions soon. Honestly, I don't trust a soul here other than you at the moment."

"No pressure." It was my turn for the nervous smile. "Your parents are," I waved my hand in the air. "I'm still not a fan of your father, and your mother isn't high on my list either. However, the one thing I do feel safe in saying as that they are both concerned for your safety."

He pushed his empty plate aside. "It's been drilled into me since I came to live at the palace that my life was constantly in danger."

"Were there frequent attempts on you?"

"Not frequent, but there were some. That's the point of having guards, isn't it? For you to neutralize the problem before I even know about it?"

"That's true. I'm surprised that your father let you do all your traveling if he was so worried about your wellbeing."

"I had my own guards. And six of his when I left the palace. Precautions were taken at every step. Being with you, on the station," he shook his head, "I've never experienced that level of being alone."

I chuckled. "You mean freedom?"

He shook his head. "It was, frankly, terrifying at times."

"You can take care of yourself, you know. I saw it when you shot Andover's man in the lift."

"Ari helped me," he said sheepishly.

"Ari was smart. And you're not as helpless as your father thinks. Don't let him get in your head."

Laurent smiled warmly. "Thanks. I should get ready. I'd appreciate an escort if you're feeling up to it?" He froze. "I meant to get medical in to check you over. One of my father's guards can take escort duty."

"I'm fine."

I tentatively pressed on my newly bruised but still healing ribs to find them tender but at a tolerable discomfort level. According to my glance in the mirror in the bathroom earlier, the deep scratch on my back was scabbed over. Also sore, but past the point of needing immediate attention as long as I kept it clean. And my face, well, there was nothing to be done about that. My nose was sore but still operational. The black eye would fade in a few days. The rest of the swelling would work itself out in a day or two.

"Mostly fine, anyway. Don't worry about the medical visit."

"You're sure?"

I nodded. "Like I'd trust your safety to your father's

guards without me keeping an eye on them?

He chuckled. "Can you at least avoid getting punched in the face for a while? For a long while, preferably."

I might have read too much into that request, remembering him asking if my lips hurt just before kissing me, but given my current condition, I nodded. "I'll try."

"Good. I'll be ready in ten."

I took care of our dishes, placing them inside the cabinet and pushing the return button. No wonder Laurent hadn't known what to do with plates when he'd been in my suite on the station.

When he was ready, I followed him out the door. "Why does this area look so deserted?"

"My father figured it was the best deterrent from the average person finding me. For my protection, it looks like there's nothing important here. There's not even a lift. Surely the heir wouldn't live in this area."

And yet he did and had for most of his life while the Empaetor and everyone else in the palace were surrounded by luxury and beauty. For a man who seemingly had everything my wildest dreams could imagine, I was starting to feel sorry for him.

We walked down the stairs and retraced our steps from the day before. Instead of going to the throne room as I'd expected, we went through one of the other doors. Three guards, ones I recognized from our escort duty, milled around inside.

"Go on through, sir," said one of them, addressing Laurent.

"Wait for me here," Laurent said to me.

I found a seat while the other three guards returned to

their wandering around. The Empaetor arrived ten minutes later with three more guards. Jumping to my feet, I realized why they'd been standing when we arrived. We were supposed to be waiting for him. I'd thought he was already in the room where Laurent had gone. Assume nothing, I reminded myself.

The Empaetor paid no attention to us as he strolled past. Today he wore a white shirt and grey pants with knee-high black boots. Everything masked by the long coat he'd worn before was on full display. While the cut of his clothes was stylish and would have been flattering on Laurent, they clung to the older man in all the wrong places, highlighting his too thin arms and a paunchy belly. I could see why he preferred to meet people on his throne, elevated and seated.

He went into the next room where Laurent had gone, leaving us to our own devices. The three guards that had arrived with the Empaetor exchanged a few words with the three I'd recognized, and then all but two guards left. The three of us stared at each other awkwardly.

"So, I'm Rita, and you are?" I tried to coax them into some sort of polite conversation while we waited.

They both uttered names, neither of which I remembered three minutes later, gave me stink-eyed glances, and went off to a corner near the door to talk quietly with one another. So much for camaraderie to pass the time. Seeing that there was nothing to be done in the immediate future, I returned to the seat I'd vacated.

My nails were only so interesting, though definitely a mess. And dry skin everywhere. The change in water from the station to the *Knaldon* and now on Harilax wasn't doing my skin any favors. The seat was too short, cutting off circulation in the backs of my thighs and too straight, making my back ache, though my ribs ached less. An hour into my boredom, I'd catalogued every ache and pain in my body and was reminiscing about the chaos of the social district. At least there was always something to do there, to see, to hear, people to police. People sort of liked me there, maybe two or three of them anyway. My mind wandered, drumming up names of people who might be missing me. Maybe that was extreme. More like wondering why they hadn't seen me in a while. They were all probably glad for that and up to no good because of it.

By the third time I'd yawned, I pulled out my datapad and occupied myself with more reading of the not-so-enthralling history of Harilax and its palace. I was in the middle of a chapter about the engineered environmental alterations that had been accomplished to create the land and weather as it was today when Laurent and the Empaetor emerged. Both looked unsteady on their feet. Maybe they'd been sitting for hours in deceptively uncomfortable chairs like I had. I did not jump up. It was more of a half-disguised stretch and stand in place until my ass and legs had regained feeling. Looking at the time on my datapad, I realized we'd spent half the day here.

Laurent blinked and rubbed his temples. "Rita?"

"Are you alright?" I looked from him to the Empaetor, who was exhibiting a similar sleepy, dazed demeanor.

"I'd like to lie down. Headache."

I nodded. Did he have a schedule? Were there things he was supposed to be doing that a nap would interrupt? I had no clue if the heir had daily obligations. If he did, was it my job to make sure he got to them, or did he have an administrative assistant I'd yet to meet? There was so much I didn't know, and was it Laurent's place to tell me, or was there some household overlord that should have given me an orientation that I'd missed while in a cell?

Knowing now that the whole escape from the palace was a paranoid motherly escapade, I should have just handed him off to Agent Andover at the beginning. While I had enjoyed getting to know Laurent, and that wouldn't have happened had I handed over his sleeping body, I didn't belong here. There was an endless contingent of guards on staff who knew the routine, where they were supposed to be, and the protocols for everything. I was just faking my way, and not very successfully, given their disdain.

There were no other guards to help me now. They'd left with the Empaetor.

Laurent did not lead the way. He walked beside me, missing an occasional step and shaking his head. Thankfully, one of the few things I did know was the way back to his bed.

"Are you alright?" I asked again.

"The procedure, the transfer of knowledge, it's disorienting to have the thoughts of eight generations of Empaetors overlaid in your mind."

"I thought you two were just going to talk. It's a whole medical procedure kind of thing?"

He nodded. "Nothing is left to chance that way, no omissions from one generation to the next. And in case he'd died before we arrived, I would still have all the knowledge of the generations before to guide me."

"But not his? If he wasn't here? That seems like a big omission of knowledge you'd need, being current events and all."

"He does periodic updates. I wouldn't have lost too much."

"Then why does he need to be there? Wouldn't he just wait until you needed his piece of the puzzle?"

"He wanted to be in the loop, to help ease my transition into the knowledge bank."

Maybe the old man did care a little. He'd looked not much better off than Laurent when they were done.

We reached the top of the stairs and entered the dusty corridor. Laurent halted to place his back against the wall, shoulders sagging.

"This used to look like the floors below." He blinked slowly. "I can see the memory of it clearly. Iradio I had it decorated for his children. Their mother lived here," he said with wonder. "In that room." He pointed to one of the four doors farther down the corridor on the other side. "Her name was Andriel. I...remember her."

No wonder the poor man had a headache.

"Come on." I held out my hand, inviting him to get into his suite before he collapsed. "You look like a bed is where you should be."

His hand grasped mine. Alright, I hadn't been expecting that, but I offered him the support he needed to get to the door panel.

"I'll set up an entrance sequence for you." He let go of me to rub his forehead. "Maybe later though."

"Sure."

Once the inner door was open, he headed straight for his bed. No pausing to turn on any lights or remove clothes or shoes, just straight under the covers. I let him be and went to one of the far more comfortable chairs near one of the windowed walls to pull out my datapad to reach the *Knaldon.*

Everything felt too uncertain yet. I wasn't ready to send Senio home, to cut off the quick exit if I or my parents needed it. Though I missed the ease of working beside Pitari, I definitely didn't want the Empaetor to fully understand what she could do. She would become another accessory for his throne. And my parents, I missed them. There was so much here I wanted them to see, but my gut was still doing nausea-inducing shimmies over the Empaetor's threats.

I settled for sending each of them a quick voice message, confirming that we were safe and well and to hold for now. I also messaged Doctor Tik to let him know quarantining my parents was no longer necessary. We would all be in touch soon.

With that accomplished, I flipped back to my history reading. If no one else was going to brief me, I'd have to do the best I could on my own.

40

Pink Tissue And Warm Jelly

The next three days passed in much the same way. We got up and went to the room where Laurent met with his father. They both emerged looking worse for wear, and I got a lot of reading done. I saw very little of the rest of the palace, but the brief contact I had with the guards and passing public surprised me with the lack of Anduvean-like behavior. Maybe the spite and absence of actual responsibilities brought out the worst in my people. Or maybe I just hadn't ventured into the more salacious areas of the palace yet.

Laurent slept a lot, ate when I urged him to, and generally left me to my own devices. There was no more hand-holding, endearing conversation, or questionable bedroom invitations. He didn't revisit the idea that there might be something between us.

Given all he was going through and me getting used to living in the palace, I was grateful for the reprieve from any romantic entanglements. There may have been a shadow of disappointment, but logically, his overtures had likely been fueled by his terror of being alone in an unfamiliar situation with one consistent person.

I really enjoyed my bed, despite the lack of full walls and a ceiling, but since I was alone other than Laurent in his mostly enclosed room nearby, it was an acceptable compromise. The air was clean. The bathtub was amazing, as was the selection of lotions. And the view was fantastic. When Laurent stayed in bed most of the day, my job was simple. I really couldn't complain.

I did, however, worry about everyone we'd left on the *Knaldon*. When I urged Laurent out of bed for breakfast, I asked what we should do with my parents, and with Senio and Pitari, who had been so helpful to us.

He blinked at me blankly. "Who?"

"My parents? Do you think it's safe to let them leave the *Knaldon*? In spite of his threat, the Empaetor said they were free citizens. I'd love for them to see Harilax."

"Parents." He seemed to mentally chew on that word for a moment while his mouth worked on a piece of fruit. "Right, yes, I said I'd find them a home. I suppose if you're to stay with me here, they should live on Harilax too?"

"You could do that?" The idea of having them close by where I knew they were safe brought a smile to my face.

"I am the Empaetor." He caught himself. "Or will be soon. I think I can manage finding two people a place to live."

"I would really appreciate it. Thank you."

He nodded.

"Speaking of parents, were you able to speak to your mother?"

"My father assured me she was given a comfortable room here and Doctor Meldorn was seeing to her recovery."

"But you were going to ask—"

He cut me off with a flick of his hand. "She will have to wait until after our sessions are complete. She'll need to be on hand when I take the throne anyway. Ceremony and all that. She's not going anywhere."

I nodded and picked at the remainder of my meal, having lost my appetite.

Not only had whatever misguided budding affection between us vanished, but we also seemed to have lost the familiarity we'd had before. He didn't make any silly remarks about me smiling or comment about my parents that he'd lived with for a few days, that he'd been in hiding with on the station, that he'd admitted enjoying being around before we'd arrived here. He'd been friendly with Senio and Pitari, but now he acted like they didn't matter one bit. If he could turn that all off, move on so quickly, would he do the same to me?

To cover my spiraling thoughts, I asked, "How are the memory overlay sessions going?"

"Well enough."

"And how many more do you need?"

"Four. Once we do that last session, the empire will be fully in my hands. My father will advise me for a short time before fully retiring."

"Are you looking forward to that?" I wasn't sure how I felt about it yet. I was barely holding up my end of my job with him as the heir who spent most of his days behind closed doors.

He went quiet for a moment, and then an unfamiliar smile slithered over his lips. "Yes, I think I am."

"Are you feeling alright?" He'd been sick after his session the day before, and I was pretty sure I'd heard him talking in his sleep last night.

"I'm fine. Looking forward to being done with this. It's a lot to take in."

"Hundreds of years' worth of memories? Yes, I imagine so. But I understand why you're doing it." That didn't mean I liked it.

Out of concern, my recent reading had veered from history and Harilax to memory overlays. A lot of reading. I rubbed my eyes.

"I was under the impression memory overlays were problematic and had been discontinued a hundred years ago."

Laurent scowled. "If you understand why I'm doing it, then that answers your question. Think before you speak."

"Right. Sorry."

How would Ari have traversed this transition from supposed friend to Empaetor's sole personal guard? In the middle of finding my footing here, losing Laurent's camaraderie was a blow I was struggling with. Maybe Ari would have retained that relationship, having been beside Laurent for years instead of months.

I took care of my plate and settled into a chair near my nook to give him some space. This overlay business could not be finished soon enough. Not that I imagined his mood would improve with his father supervising his first few days on the throne, or even after that, while he found his own footing.

When Laurent announced he was ready to go, I walked beside him out into the corridor. "Where would I go to get a few things that I need? Your supply shelves are decidedly geared toward men."

"See the outfitter."

"And where would that be?"

Laurent let out an exasperated sigh. "You have a map on your datapad. Use it."

He was especially testy today. It occurred to me this was fate paying me back for treating him as my trainee back on the station. I wasn't fond of the tables being turned.

For self-preservation, I needed a break before I talked myself out of a job. "Do you mind if I do that while you're at your session? I assume this one will last as long as the others?"

"Yes, fine," he said impatiently.

"Thank you."

My politeness earned me nothing. I hoped whatever he'd been paying Ari was worth my putting up with this or I wouldn't be staying on Harilax very long.

Once I had Laurent safely delivered and was assured that the other three attending guards would be standing around as usual, I pulled up the map on my datapad and navigated my way to the lift and down two floors. There, I discovered, was where the rest of the guards lived, except for the select few that served the Empaetor himself. I assumed they had a similar assignment to mine, never leaving him fully alone. Would the old Empaetor be moving out of the palace or to another area once Laurent was installed on the throne? More questions I'd have to find answers to without further trying his already thin patience.

Was this how he'd always been here in his comfort zone on Harilax? He'd mentioned Ari continually trying to get him to relax and smile. He was a braver man than me, or maybe he'd just been on more solid footing.

Was it only outside the palace, far from home, and in an unknown situation with no one else to trust that he'd been forced to be more easy-going and personable? If that was the case, I might be inclined to kidnap him myself.

The outfitter was much like the supply room on the station, stocked with everything members of the staff might need. Except this one was attended, names were taken, and inventory was tallied—a far more well-oiled machine. Not that I expected different, being that we were at the literal apex of the empire.

Along with my requested supplies, I was offered a weapon and restraints, which I gladly accepted. After running my heavy box up to Laurent's suite and successfully using my new suite access codes for the first time, I found I still had a couple of hours left. If I hurried, I could make it to the *Knaldon* and check in with everyone there before Laurent would be done. The idea of seeing a few friendly faces held an allure I couldn't ignore.

Setting a near jogging pace, I made it to the landing zone in twenty minutes. Pitari greeted me just inside the ramp.

"I saw you coming from the bridge," she explained. "We've been waiting."

"Sorry. This is the first chance I've had to get away."

She studied me. "You're unsettled. What's wrong with the heir?"

"What do you know about memory overlays?"

"Memory what?"

"Yeah, that's where my knowledge was five days ago. Maybe I should speak with Doctor Tik. I need to see my parents too."

"I hope you find the answers you seek." Pitari shooed me off.

"It was good seeing you," I called over my shoulder.

What little crew native to Harilax that we had arrived with had gone on leave. Doctor Tik caught sight of me as soon as I entered his clinic. He seemed to be in the middle of something, so I joined him at the counter where he was working.

Having limited time, I skipped the small talk. "Are you familiar with memory overlays?"

He pursed his lips and squinted his eyes. "Only loosely. The practice was discontinued after studies showed it produced uncertain results and complications."

"What kind of complications?" I leaned against the counter where he was taking samples of pink tissue from a jar and separating them into small, shallow dishes.

"Psychotic disorders mostly, but some carried over into physical manifestations. In rare cases, a complete disconnect between mind and body. It was popular a few hundred years ago with deep space explorations, used to transfer memories from one caretaker crew to the next to ensure no knowledge was lost."

"Sounds like there was plenty of opportunity for things to get lost. Including people."

"Sadly, yes. The most successful overlays were between genetic matches. But when cloning was outlawed, that nixed that. Deep spacers returned to using stasis and good old-fashioned logs for those who came after."

I supposed the father-son link boosted the success rate since they'd been doing this since Iradio I. The whole psychosis angle concerned me though. Was his demeanor due to stress and dealing with the onslaught of memories or something deeper? I'd have to keep a close eye on Laurent.

"Thanks. I'll let you get back to...whatever it is you're doing."

Doctor Tik smiled and turned his attention back to dissecting the pink tissue. Not wanting to give any thought to what that might be, I left quickly and went to the suite my parents had been using before I'd left.

The door opened seconds after I'd touched my hand to the panel. "Rita!" My father barreled out and wrapped his arms around me.

My mother tucked herself into our embrace. "We've missed you." She stepped back, tugging at my father's arms. "She's hurt. Remember? Let the poor girl go."

"I'm feeling much better. It's fine." I wasn't. I was sore and tired and stressed the fuck out, but it was habit to keep my discomfort to myself.

"I can still see bruises." My mother shook her head, tsking. "Why couldn't you take a nice job at a terminal somewhere on that station? Something where you don't come home with bruises every visit?"

"Come on, you're exaggerating. Outside the burning season, I've got a fairly cushy job. During, yes, I come home with bruises."

"Is it burning on Harilax too"? my father asked, one brow raised.

"That was mostly from an altercation here, before I was carried to a cell in the palace. Or under the palace? I'm still learning the layout."

My mother's voice rose. "A cell?"

"As you can see, I'm free now. Things are fine. Better

than fine, actually. As I said in my message, you're out of exile."

I took a deep breath and consulted my gut. The Empaetor seemed just as out of sorts as Laurent. Well-occupied with the memory overlays and ignoring me. He'd be far too busy installing his son on the throne to bother with harassing my parents. As long as I did my job, they'd be safe.

"It's been a few days and nothing has come up to make me think you won't be safe here. You're free to leave the *Knaldon*. You can go wherever you want. If that's here with me, Laurent has offered to provide housing for you here on Harilax."

My parents looked at each other. Grins burst out on their faces. They hugged one another with so much enthusiasm that if they were ten years younger, I imagined they'd be jumping up and down. A lump formed in my throat as I grinned beside them.

I handed them Ari's credit chip. "Don't go crazy with this, but find a nice place to stay for now until Laurent can set you up. It will probably be a week or two. He's tied up with briefings before he takes his father's place on the throne."

"So exciting! And you're in the center of it all," my mother squeezed my shoulders. "We're so proud of you, Rita."

Those words brought a rush of emotions that clogged my throat and turned my insides to warm jelly. Everything with Laurent might be uncertain, but I was back on solid footing with my parents. A sense of relief swept through me as I hugged my mother, keeping her in my arms a few moments longer than usual while I blinked tears away.

"I've got to find Senio and then get back. Sorry, I can't stay longer."

After relaying my new contact details to them, I found Senio in the lounge where I'd done crew interviews. He was talking to Alessandra. The two of them were smiling and chatting. She laughed at something he said just as he noticed me approaching.

"Rita!" He jumped up to greet me.

"I didn't mean to interrupt."

Senio waved off my apology. The disgruntled look on Alessandra's face said I was definitely interrupting. I snickered inwardly. She turned around but didn't leave.

"I'm as settled as I'm going to get, I guess. Neither the heir nor the Empaetor has thrown me out yet. No need to keep evacuation plans in place."

"You're staying out of trouble?" he asked.

"Does it look like I'm staying out of trouble?"

Senio looked me over. "No fresh bruises, so maybe?"

"Maybe is a safe answer." I cleared my throat. "No need to keep you away from the station any longer. Yumi has to be going crazy without both of us by now."

"He is. He left me a message yesterday." Senio groaned. "You're sure you're good here?"

"It's been a rocky start, but I'm hoping things will smooth out in a week or two. The empire is much bigger than one station. The learning curve is steep."

Senio slapped my shoulder. "You'll have it all down in a month. Just give it some time."

"That's the plan."

We said our goodbyes. I left Senio to his conquest of

the communications officer and hurried back to the palace, hoping I would reach the waiting room before Laurent's session ended. Being late would certainly not put him in any better of a mood.

41

Your Mother Is Crazy

When I stepped inside the palace entry doors, I did not expect to have my arm grabbed by a woman with fading bruises.

"I need to speak to you. Now. Come on."

Consort Marishka hauled me after her into a room down the first hallway. She glanced both ways and then closed the door, backing us into the room. The auto lights activated, illuminating a round table and six chairs, muted purple walls and a pale grey tiled floor. Nothing to see here, just a couple of bruised women hiding out for a clandestine conversation.

"Good to see you out of the cell," I said, shaking my arm free. I was also relieved to learn that the Empaetor had followed through on what he'd told Laurent. I didn't have to like him, but I wanted to be able to trust him with Laurent's wellbeing.

"You too," she said. "Where is my son? Is he safe?"

I pointed upward. "He's with his father. Doing another one of their memory overlay sessions."

She groaned. "All the effort to get him away, and he gets

sucked right back in!" She flexed her fingers, each tipped with a long, manicured nail.

I backed away. "What did you expect him to do?"

"Kill the Empaetor! He's insane. He's old and unwell. It shouldn't be that hard," she hissed, eyeing the closed door warily.

Laurent's mother was going to get us both killed if anyone overheard her. She wore clean clothes, and she didn't appear to be nursing any fresh wounds. If she was being cared for and the miscommunication resolved, why was she sounding like a raving lunatic now?

Had she approached Ari like this, begging him to get Laurent away from the palace? Were I not already jaded by her needless dramatic abduction of her son, I might have taken her more seriously. As it was, and as much as I didn't like the also-raving Empaetor, I could see his point. Laurent's mother was unhinged. Maybe her breaking point had been losing custody of Laurent as a child, or years of drinking her sorrows had weakened her mind.

"Look, I've only known Laurent for a few weeks, but he doesn't strike me as the type to kill his own father, and the Empaetor, no less." I took another step toward the door, half wishing someone would bust in and take her off my hands before she said something else that might implicate me in her wish to kill the Empaetor.

Sweat glazed on my forehead. Not only was my life on the line, but those of my parents if the Empaetor thought I had nefarious intent of any sort.

"The Empaetor is under constant guard. He's safe. No one can get to him," I declared in case anyone was listening to our conversation.

Her face contorted. "You should have killed the Empaetor when you met him with that Tekka bastard. It would have been easy enough then. That's your job, isn't it? To protect my son?" Her hands curled into fists. "I did what I could. Now it's your turn."

"Are you trying to get me killed here? Don't say another word." I backed up to the door, not taking my eyes off her and reaching blindly for the panel. "I have no reason to harm the Empaetor. Neither does your son. These sessions will allow for a seamless transfer of the throne from father to son. Within a week, I9 will be the new Empaetor," I said.

"Laurent is a good man. Kind." Tears welled in Marishka's eyes. "He doesn't deserve this."

My hand finally found the panel, but I didn't palm it quite yet. I didn't trust the consort not to burst out into the hallway shouting her murderous plans for all to hear.

"Deserve to rule the empire? That's kind of his job, isn't it? What he's been groomed for his entire life?"

She broke down sobbing.

I didn't smell any alcohol on her, but who knew if she was on something else. Or just plain not right in the head. Resorting to my calmest talk-the-crazy-off-the-social district-railing voice, I said, "Why don't you go home and relax? I'll make sure Laurent is safe, and when he is past all this taking the throne business, I'll see that he pays you a visit."

"Once he's on that throne, he'll never leave this place." She started to wail.

What the hell was she going on about? My mind raced over the history I'd been slogging through, searching for examples where the Empaetor visited worlds or took a tour of the empire. I came up empty. Alright, that was a little peculiar.

Laurent enjoyed traveling. He'd said so, said he wanted me to travel with him. If he traveled with some of the palace guards with him before, he could take as many as he wanted now. For the Maker's sake, he could take an entire fleet on tour. Unless there was something I was missing.

"Why don't Empaetors leave the palace?" I asked.

"It's not safe. The people hate Iradio. They've always hated him."

"Not everyone, only those who don't benefit from his actions. The Scaavo empire wouldn't have reigned for eight generations otherwise. Besides Laurent traveled before. It seemed important to him, from what he said. I don't foresee him giving that up."

"They always give it up," she said between sobs. "They exchange their freedom for power and a prison filled with paranoia."

If anyone sounded paranoid, it was her.

I gave deescalating with the calming voice one more shot. "Laurent seems like a logical man. We talked quite a lot on the way here. I really think he'll be fine once this all settles down."

"You're a fool!" she spat in much the same tone as the Empaetor had used on Laurent. Maybe that was a royalty thing. I didn't like it.

"Maybe I just know your son." I left off the 'better than you' that wanted to sneak out with the rest.

"In a few more days, he won't be my son. He'll be Iradio all over again."

Had she been missing doses of medication while down

in the cell?

Calming wasn't working. I wasn't exactly loyal to the Empaetor, but neither could I let her leave the room knowing her intent to see him dead. Laurent wasn't going to like either way this ended. I let go of the door panel and reached a hand out slowly, gauging her reaction.

"Yes, as Empaetor, Laurent will take his full name," I said, subtly lining myself up to subdue her.

Did that mean I was going to have to remember to call him Iradio now instead of Laurent? Or would he require that I call him Empaetor at all times? That was going to be weird.

Marishka waved her hands forcefully in the air like she'd rather be ripping my braids out of my scalp. "No, you back planet idiot, he'll *be* Iradio. Again."

Yep, definitely missing some meds.

"Why don't we get you to your estate? I'm guessing you could use some medical attention from your stay in the cell."

She slapped me. Hard. And those pink lacquered nails were like claws on my barely healed cheek. I swore loudly.

The one thing Laurent had asked me to do was keep my face free from damage, and within days, I'd gained a handful of gouges. Thanks, Marishka.

As if she could sense that I'd lost my patience, she backed away. "I'm not going back there. Ever. He thought he could keep me sedated! Keep me trapped in my pretty prison like he is?"

Alright, this had gone on long enough. I pulled a pair of wrist restraints from my back pocket and grabbed one of her flailing arms. The second arm pounded on my shoulder until I grabbed it and added it to the restraint.

I wrestled her in front of me, securely grasping the restraint with one hand and palming the door panel with the other. "Your estate didn't feel like a prison to me. Granted, the staff could have used better vetting, but it's a beautiful home."

"You don't know. You're making a mistake. A big mistake! Please. Don't let him do the last session. You'll never see Laurent again." Her shoulders shook with wracking sobs. "Don't let him kill my son."

"I won't let that happen," I assured her. "Let's go get you settled somewhere comfortable."

She dragged her feet, making me work for every step forward. If only I'd had a bubble tab, but I didn't. I swore under my breath all the way down the hall until we reached the security post to go upward.

The three guards on duty regarded me with raised brows.

"The consort is unwell. Could you see her to a doctor where she can get medication to calm her down?" I handed her over. "Be careful. She's feeling hostile."

The female guard came forward to take Marishka from me, her gaze taking in the scratches on my face.

As much as I didn't want to cause Laurent's mother any further grief, given SA Tekka's earlier interrogation tactics, my conscience wouldn't allow me to just leave her with medical. "She'll need a cell afterward. Threats were issued."

One of the two male guards gave me a skeptical once-over. "What kind of threats specifically?"

"To the Empaetor's life. Is that specific enough? Do they not teach you to read between the lines here on Harilax?"

He glanced back at the other male, who was mouthing

something to him. When the guard turned back to me, he'd taken on a more respectful tone. "We'll take it from here. Thank you."

Maybe I was finally getting somewhere with establishing myself. "Good. I'm late."

Marishka seemed more subdued now that I handed her over. Defeated almost. It saddened me to think that this same woman had run laughing through the beautiful estate with the young Empaetor, that her scandalous moans had echoed through the hallways. Hopefully, a doctor could get her meds straightened out so she could get back to herself and go home.

I'd just reached the lift to head upward when it occurred to me that none of the three guards at the security station had scanned my ID chip or asked their requisite questions. While I was in a hurry, the lapse in procedure was hardly something I could let go given my position as the heir's personal guard. That was damned sloppy and not acceptable.

I jogged back to the station and reamed the two male guards out for their negligence. The woman was fortunate to have taken the consort to medical. With that situation resolved, I again hurried back to the lift. By the time I arrived in the main corridor, I was wound tight, knowing I was very late and how volatile Laurent was after his sessions.

Running down the mid-floor corridor didn't do me any good, but it felt necessary. I was still late. When I entered the room, breathless, not so much from exertion as trepidation, I was not at all surprised to see Laurent waiting. The lingering guard from his father's retinue nodded to me and left just as speedily as I'd entered. That didn't bode well.

I smoothed my braids back over my shoulders and took a deep breath. "Sorry I'm late. I ran into your mother downstairs. She required assistance."

Whatever he'd been going to yell dried up instantly. His demeanor flipped to concern. "How is she? I'd like to see her."

"The Empaetor was not entirely wrong about her mental state. She's in need of help."

"Where is she?"

"I left her with the guards at the first checkpoint. One of them escorted her to a doctor to get some medication. She was very upset."

Laurent clutched his hands in front of his waist, fingers twining through each other restlessly. "I should go see her."

For all his trusting his father to have the situation under control, I was glad he was finally taking the time to care about his mother.

"You're the heir. I'm sure you can do that." I said, giving humor a try to check his mood.

His face brightened. "Yes, you're right."

At least he didn't appear so sick this time, and he wasn't biting my head off. Maybe the overlay sessions were getting easier.

His attention focused on me again. Just when I thought the delayed rampage was going to surface due to the scowl forming on his face, he reached out to brush his fingers over my cheek. "Who did this?"

Surprised by his unexpected return to familiarity, the truth slipped out of my lips before I thought to edit it. "Your mother."

His scowl deepened. "I need to see her now."

"Alright then. I'll take you down to where I left her. Someone can point us in the right direction from there."

"There's no need for that. I can scan the palace for her ID. You should be able to do that too." His brow furrowed. "I guess I haven't facilitated your full clearance yet."

"You've been busy." I passed him my datapad.

He offered me an apologetic smile. "Once I get through these sessions, I promise I'll get you properly settled in."

"Sure." I had a feeling the whole taking the throne thing would derail him for a while longer, but I supposed having an easy excuse for not following proper protocols wasn't a terrible thing.

He had her ID and location pulled up in just over a minute. This technology would be game-changing for the station. I added that to my list to ask him about once we had all this behind us.

We headed off to find his delusional mother.

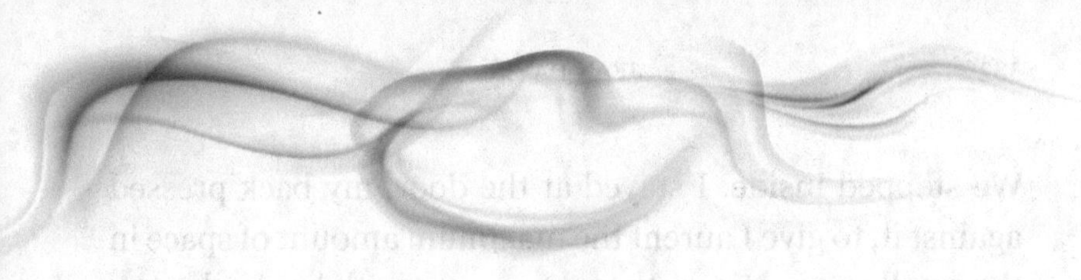

42

So Many Iradios

The prisoner holding area was indeed underground. Level two of three, to be exact. The guard who had guided us to the correct area left—after bowing to Laurent, of course.

"Why is my mother back in a cell?" Laurent asked.

"She isn't well." That sounded better than admitting she'd had a mental break.

He stopped in front of me, blocking our progress down the corridor of closed doors and solid walls. "Rita, why is my mother in a cell?"

I sighed and then whispered, "She was ranting and raving, telling me to kill your father, saying *you* should kill your father."

He grimaced but turned to continue walking. We stopped in front of the specified door.

"I'm sorry that she hurt you," he said.

"Her demands would have hurt me a lot more. And my parents. I know you don't want her in here, but if word got to your father that I might try to kill him..."

Laurent nodded. He took a deep breath and exhaled slowly before entering the lock code our guide had given us.

We stepped inside. I stayed at the door, my back pressed against it, to give Laurent the maximum amount of space in the small room. His mother sat on a cot with her back to us.

He approached her slowly. "Mother?"

She turned as if in a daze. They must have sedated her somewhat. From what I could see, she'd been treated well. She was free to roam her cell, no new bruises, no restraints.

"Laurent?"

"Yes, Mother. It's me." He knelt down beside her, taking her hands in his. "What happened? Why are you here?"

She frowned, looking around. "Here? Your father put me here."

"I think you're confused, Mother. Rita suggested you be held here."

Thanks for that clarification. I wasn't sure your mother hated me yet. I glared at him, but he wasn't paying any attention to me.

"Confused?" She shot up from the cot, her face contorted into a vicious snarl. One hand went to her hip, the other toward Laurent as if to hug him.

My gut when on high alert, spurring me into action.

I darted forward, placing myself between the two of them just as she raised her other hand in a stabbing motion. A sudden sharp pain hit my side. Not a stabbing motion. An actual stabbing. Fuck, that hurt.

Grabbing her wrist and yanking backward, I dislodged the scalpel from my side and her hand. I spun her around, pulling her arm up behind her back. When I reached for my restraints, I remembered that I'd sent her off with them last time. Frustrated and in pain, I spun her around to face Laurent.

"What do you want to do with her?" I asked.

"You're not my son," she screamed.

He glanced down at the knife at my feet. "She tried to stab me?"

"Iradio, you need to die!"

"Mother, it's Laurent. The Empaetor isn't here. It's just us."

She shook her head wildly before slamming it backward into my nose. I held on tight despite the throbbing pain and blood dripping down my chin and onto my jacket.

"You're a vile creature. I loved him, and you took him from me!"

My patience was leaking down my face and from the gash in my side. "Get someone in here to sedate her before I do something you won't like."

Laurent tore his gaze from the writhing woman in my grasp and noticed my face. He winced and ran to the door, yelling for help.

A guard showed up just as I spat a glob of blood onto the floor. He shook his head and regarded me as though I were an idiot trainee. "Why don't you just—"

"Knock the Consort out?" I suggested. "Yeah, I don't think the heir would appreciate that. Apparently I need to carry two sets of restraints from now on."

He dug into his pockets and pulled out a set of restraints.

I thrust the consort forward to put enough space between us for the guard to get one hand secured and then snap the other side onto a metal loop on the wall just behind the cot.

"Thank you." Now that my hands were free, I pulled my jacket open to check the severity of the stab wound.

"You're hurt," Laurent announced, having just noticed the lower spot of blood on my shirt.

I nodded to the scalpel on the floor.

"Sit, for the Maker's sake," he gently pushed me down onto the cot. "I'll try to make this quick." Laurent turned to the guard. "Get medical in here to look at Rita."

"Yes, sir." The young man dashed out of the room.

I didn't trust the woman even in restraints, not with Laurent there. I started to get up, but Laurent placed his hand on my shoulder and pressed firmly. As if sensing the need for compromise, he stepped around my knees to stand on the other side of me, effectively placing my seated body between him and his mother.

"Mother, what are you going on about?" His voice was calm except for the slight tremor beneath his words.

"She knew. Isharat, she found you out. You thought you could contain her too, keep her docile with your poison. She wrote it all down, Iradio. All of it. Her handwritten pages were at the bottom of a drawer waiting for me in my beautiful prison. Now I know."

"Know what, Mother?"

The pleading in his voice was so genuine that it tugged at my heart.

"What you are, old man." She spat over my head into Laurent's face.

Aghast, he stood there as the gobbet of spittle slid down his cheek.

"Perhaps we should..." I motioned to the hallway.

"Yeah." He reached out to help me up.

"I'm fine," I snapped. The pain in my repeatedly half-healed ribs and nose was making me as irritable as he'd been for the last few days.

We adjourned to the hallway to await medical, closing the cell door behind us.

I leaned heavily against the wall, trying to keep my head tilted back and pinching my nose shut to stem the flow of blood. "Has she always been like this?"

"No, she's usually calm. Sedate."

"Sedated, you think? She was going on about that earlier too, saying she was drugged."

"I... I don't know."

He eyed the cut on my side like I should care about that more than my nose. He was probably right. I applied pressure to the second wound with my other hand. Hopefully Laurent stayed out of harm's way because I was out of hands.

"Why would she think I was my father?" he asked.

"She went off when she learned you were doing the memory overlays. Does she think getting your father's memories will turn you into him?"

He stared mournfully at the closed cell door. "There are so many memories, Rita. So many Iradios. It's hard to keep them all straight. They flow together, merging and combining." He rubbed his temples.

"That was one hazard of the overlay technology—losing yourself in the memories. Subjects became catatonic."

"Some of them," he corrected. "I read the studies when my father explained what the indoctrination meant.

"Do you think that's why you've all continued with the same name—to keep the memories more coherent and cohesive?"

"Maybe."

Where the hell was medical? I could have bled out by now if the wound were more serious. I checked my shirt again. Blood was still flowing, but not excessively. I didn't feel faint yet, so that was one thing in my favor.

"Who's Isharat?" I asked to distract myself from worrying about where the knife she'd grabbed had been. Was it clean when she'd stolen it? Visions of Doctor Tik and his tissue dissection kept popping into my head.

"My fifth wife. I mean, our fifth consort?" He shook his head. "This is confusing. How do I speak of them when their memories are my memories?"

"I don't think there's a proper term for that. A previous consort. Got it."

A female member of the medical staff finally arrived. She set her supply case down and looked at me. "Oh! You were stabbed!"

"I noticed."

"And your nose, that looks broken."

"Feels like it too. The weapon is inside the cell. The occupant is restrained. Can you please retrieve the scalpel and let me know if it's contaminated, beyond sitting on the questionably clean cell floor, I mean?"

She looked at Laurent. "Could you... Oh! You're the heir. So sorry, sir. I'll, umm, get someone, and a seat, and..." She tapped the comm pin on her shirt and voiced a rapid string of requests.

An hour and a half later, I was safely ensconced in my bed in Laurent's suite, comfortably propped up on several pillows. The pain medication lent me a pleasant distant and dreamy feeling.

"Are you hungry?" Laurent asked, fussing over how the

blanket was covering me.

"Maybe something small." I blinked slowly, the room alternately blurring and focusing. "What did your doctor give me?"

"Medicine for the pain. Doctor Meldorn said you'd be fine now that you're stitched up, but you need to rest."

"Send someone to your mother's house. To her bedroom. Contact Ekie. She's not in on anything. Pitari cleared her. Have her search the drawers in the bedroom. And the closet." There were more words I wanted to get out, but there was suddenly a lot more blur than focus, and my head wouldn't leave the pillow. My eyes drifted closed.

When I came to, Laurent wasn't in sight. I carefully got up and used the bathroom, checking his bedroom on the way back. He wasn't there either.

The time display showed midday, which made me think he'd gone off to another memory overlay session. Without me. I swore under my breath. He better have ordered up an escort. If he was wandering the palace solo and anything happened, the Empaetor wouldn't hesitate to follow through on his threats against my parents. Who were now legally registered at a hotel somewhere nearby, and I'd yet to check in on them. Fucking knockout medication.

The one plus in all this was that Doctor Meldorn had left ten more of the powerful pills sitting beside my bed. At least at the end of whatever this day brought, I'd have pain-free sleep. Until then, I couldn't afford to be a zombie on the job.

I found my datapad on the table beside my bed. Laurent must have put it there. Sure enough, there was a message saying he'd gone to a session. And yes, he'd taken not one, but two, house guards so I could rest without worrying. It was the last line that I read several times over.

Please don't ever get stabbed again. You scared the hell out of me. I can't lose you, Rita. My heart couldn't take it. -L

That sounded like something pre-Harilax-arrival Laurent would have said directly after having the conversation about our potential situation that we still hadn't gotten around to talking about.

That I never expected to actually discuss, because I was quite sure he was just lonely and making do with whatever friendly and willing female was at his disposal. Mostly sure.

I shook my head. Don't be stupid. You're reading too much into a quick note.

I was currently his only trusted personal guard. He was still grieving over Ari. It made sense he wouldn't want to lose another guard, perhaps a friend, if I were to go that far, so soon after that.

Tossing the mention of a heart at the end of the message didn't mean anything.

Resolved that I had my emotions under control, which were only at the surface because of the medication, surely, I changed into fresh underclothes and a blood-free uniform. All the bloodstained and dirty clothes went into the magical chute to be taken care of by someone or something automated. No laundry, yet another perk of living in Laurent's proximity.

To pass the time, I grabbed a quick meal and then sat down at the terminal that was nicer than any I'd ever used in my life. Everything on it was spotless. I contacted my parents to see how they were faring on Harilax.

"Rita, what in the Maker's name happened now?" My father asked.

"I met the consort yesterday. It didn't go as well as I'd hoped."

My mother's face took over the vid. "Oh my, honey, you need to sit down. Get in bed. Rest. Look at those dark circles under your eyes! Is your nose broken?" She let out an exasperated sigh. "Get that man over here. I want to talk to him."

"Laurent?" I could only imagine how he'd take getting a lecture from my mother. Let alone being referred to as 'that man'. Given his current overwhelmed state of mind, he'd either laugh it off or launch into a tirade my mother would never withstand.

Thank the Maker she couldn't see the stitches.

"Mom, I'm just doing my job. No different than on the station."

"You didn't work alone on the station. You had a team," my father said from behind her.

"There are countless guards here. Laurent is with some of them right now. I am resting. Now, I called to see how you were doing?"

They proceeded to relay a high-speed tag-team rundown of everything they'd done and seen and eaten since leaving the *Knaldon*. Seeing that I had nothing else to do while Laurent was gone, I let them ramble on, enjoying their excitement. They looked so happy. While seeing worlds like this one had been a dream for me, they'd never even dared go that far, thanks to the exile rules hanging over their heads. Freedom looked quite lovely on them. My eyes started to tear up.

"I gotta go," I said before any of them escaped, giving my parents further cause to worry about me. "I'll talk to you soon. Have fun."

"Take care of yourself, Rita," my father said.

"For real this time. And put some ice on that swelling. It will help. And rest!" my mother added.

"I know, Mom. This isn't my first broken nose." I forced a smile and ended the call.

A vague memory reminded me that the doctor had left me with a cold pack. With the first dose of medication wearing off, that seemed like a good idea. A check of the cold cabinet yielded gratifying results. I broke one pill in half, swallowed it with some refreshingly chilled water, and went back to bed with the cold pack and datapad in hand. If everyone was harping on me to rest, with Laurent occupied, I supposed I could listen. This one time.

I queued up the history text I'd been boring myself with, set the datapad to read aloud, and then settled back to enjoy the cold pack relieving pressure on my face.

Someone sitting on my bed brought me back to the waking world.

"How are you feeling?" Laurent carefully took the now warm pack from the side of my face where it must have fallen when I'd melted into the pillow pile.

The half a pill had taken the edge off everything and was still doing its job. "Well enough. How was your session?"

"Tiring." He rubbed his hands over his face. "I was going to take a nap. There are only three sessions to go. Thank the Maker. I can't wait to be done so I can have time to sort through all of it." He looked around at the ceiling high above as though he could see the onslaught of memories that were not his own.

"Do you need help getting up?" he asked.

"I can manage. The cut was deep, but not wide. It's tolerable." With pain meds. But he didn't need to hear me whining.

"I don't mind helping if you need it. You did take a knife to the gut for me and all."

"Ribs, not gut, and it was a scalpel. Thank you for the offer, but it's kind of my job."

He stood beside me, staring at my torso for a long moment before crossing over to the empty side of my bed. "Would you mind?"

"Mind what?"

"If I slept here for a little while."

Was he kidding? "With me? In my bed? I suppose it's not really my bed, is it?" I waved at the expansive suite. "This being all yours."

He cracked a nervous smile. "It's your bed, Rita. It's just that I slept so much better when we shared a bedroom on the *Knaldon*, and right now, with all this," he squeezed his eyes shut and shook his head. "I could really use that."

I noted the slump of his shoulders and the exhaustion on his face.

"You, Rita, I mean, I could really use you right now. If you don't mind."

What did he mean exactly by use and did I mind either way? In the grand scheme of things, this felt like the beginning of a joke I'd tell Senio years later, after I'd retired back to the station. I'd say I'd turned down sleeping with the heir and the punchline would be something about the fact that he snored and that it had never been about sex to begin with because really? Look at me.

"Sure, yeah, I guess," came out of my mouth even as I realized how stupid that sounded if he meant something other than actual sleep.

The heir to the empire took off his coat and draped it over the end of the bed next to mine. He kicked off his shoes and settled himself onto the bed with a relieved sigh. His head nestled into the thick pillow beside mine. Laurent closed his eyes.

"I could kiss you for this," he said dreamily beside me.

"Could you?" my smart mouth said.

He opened one eye and turned to me with a playful smirk that admittedly made my heart flip. "I could, but it would probably hurt you right now, and that's the last thing I want to do."

Oh.

Oh shit, he was serious. I watched as he closed his eye and turned his face back to the ceiling.

Or was he fucking with me because I was being a smartass? I watched out of the corner of my eye as the smirk melted away and his breathing went soft and steady. One of these days, once we were past getting him on the throne, we needed to have that clarifying conversation.

It was one thing to sit here while he entertained whatever woman had caught his eye behind his closed door, but quite another if I'd once been that woman and then had to endure all that came after me. I didn't like the idea of that at all.

43

Delivery

"**E**kie says she's found something," Laurent announced.

I blinked sleep away to find I was in dire need of another half dose of painkiller. "Something like what? The papers your mother was talking about?"

"Exactly that. She's having them delivered to you."

"Why not to you?"

"Because that's what I asked her to do." He paced at the end of my bed. "I have too many memories in here." He tapped his forehead. "I remember Isharat. How she smelled, her smile. All of it. I don't think I can read her words objectively."

That had to be confusing as hell. "Yeah, alright. I'll get dressed and go down to see about picking that up."

The medication would have to wait. I couldn't very well wander around the palace with confidential information while half-sedated.

He nodded. "Be careful. Meet the messenger at the door if you can. Don't let anyone take that package from you. This might all be mad ravings, or it might be important. I don't know what to think."

"We'll figure it out."

The walk down to the ground level was uneventful. Everyone was clothed. No one was openly drunk or high. There wasn't one fight, not even a lewd conversation or rant of obscenities. All in all, the palace was downright orderly and peaceful except for the familiar feeling of whispers following me. I hadn't noticed those since leaving the station, and I hadn't missed them.

Waiting around outside the palace entrance had been my goal, hoping to avoid catching any additional notice by meeting up with Ekie. As luck would have it, it was raining. Hard. So I waited inside the entry vestibule, and the only other people near the entry doors were two whispering palace guards. My intent focus on the doors and wondering if what Ekie had found was anything of merit distracted me initially. However, after forty-five minutes of waiting, I didn't need Pitari to explain what loud thoughts felt like.

I turned toward the murmurs behind me. "What in the Maker's name are you two going on about?"

They both jumped, eyeing each other with trepidation.

"Out with it before I inform the Empaetor that his staff can't keep their mouths shut when on duty. Gossiping like a couple of teenage girls."

One of the two men cleared his throat raggedly. "Is it true you imprisoned the consort?"

"For her own safety, yes." Fucking rumors.

"You cuffed her to a wall in a cell," said the other one.

No truth was going to go over well, and I had a feeling that neither Laurent nor the Empaetor wanted the details of the consort's imprisonment or her mental health made public.

"I may be new here, but I have read the employee handbook. Repeating rumors is cause for termination. Are you interested in being terminated?"

They shook their heads, mouths clamped shut.

"Good. The Empaetor and his family thank you for your discretion."

Where the hell was Ekie? Maybe the rain was slowing her down, but the consort's estate was not that far away, and I was regretting not taking the half dose of painkiller before I left.

It was another awkward hour of standing in the vestibule with the cowed guards before the consort's baker finally arrived. Ekie appeared decidedly flustered and wet.

"You'll see this information gets to the heir?" she asked, handing over a sealed brown packet. "He said no one could touch it but you."

"Yeah, he told me that too."

She nodded. "Is he well? I was hoping to see him."

I bet she was. Probably hoping to get a little payment of one sort or another on the side.

"Sorry, he's very busy." I pointed upward. "Business and all, you understand."

"I've never been inside the palace," she said wistfully. "What's it like?"

"Full of guards and rich people. Not much different from the consort's estate. Maybe someday you'll be able to visit."

Ekie laughed lightly. "No one visits without being invited."

Oh yes, I'd made a joke. How charming of me. I faked a chuckle. "Thank you for bringing these over. The heir appreciates your discretion."

"He does. The deposit has already been made. My lips are sealed."

What the hell was she going on about? He'd paid her? That didn't seem like Laurent. Or maybe it was now that he was home.

"I should get this to him. Safe travels." I headed inside before she rubbed my pain-wracked patience any further in the wrong direction with another attempt at a hookup invite with Laurent.

Following the usual protocols, I let the checkpoint security scan the package. It didn't set off any alarms. That was a good sign. No one looked twice at it other than to ask what it was for logging purposes. They made sure to scan my ID and ask their questions. I smiled grimly, thinking ironically that this time, in pain and with this packet, I would have appreciated them skipping it all and just letting me through.

"A delivery from the consort's estate for the heir." That's all they needed to know. I hoped that a delivery from mother to son would seem safe and maybe even mundane enough to bypass any further interest. Half the staff here was aware by now that the consort was in some sort of care on the lower levels. But her son sending for a few items for her should be normal. Hopefully.

The guard held the package. "We were told not to relay anything to her."

"It's not going to her. This delivery is for the heir. I'll pass along that stipulation to him."

She nodded. "You're all clear then."

Package in hand, I made it to the lift before three familiar faces of the Empaetor's guard cornered me. They backed me into the vacant lift.

"What's this all about?" I asked.

"We're going to need to see what's inside that package," the tall, stern one in the middle informed me.

"What business is it of yours? This is for the heir."

"Empaetor's orders," said the man on my left.

If their orders came from him, they knew the consort was imprisoned and probably that she was out of her mind. No need to hedge with them.

"I'm sure the Empaetor has more important things to deal with than the consort's insane ramblings."

The one on my right held out his hand.

Laurent wasn't going to like this, but even as the heir, he was subject to his father's ruling. I handed over the package.

He broke the seal with exuberant glee and reached inside to pull out a thick stack of yellowed paper covered in black symbols. The text, if that's what it was, wasn't in any language I knew. That was entirely unhelpful. Thank you so much, Isharat.

"What is this?" the Empaetor's guard demanded.

"No idea. I was told to retrieve the package supposedly containing some text from the consort. I was expecting a datapad, not whatever that is."

He held up a page, shoving it in my face. "Read it."

"I can't. I don't think that's even actual text. Like I said, insane ramblings." I shrugged. "I hope she's getting the care she needs. Is she feeling better?"

"I wouldn't know." He put the page back with the others. "We should destroy this."

"The heir is expecting this delivery."

"Empaetor's orders," repeated the tall one.

I leaned in to read his name badge, knowing how annoying that was from twenty years of tourists doing it to me.

"Be that as it may, Jerrod, the heir will be irate if I show up empty-handed. Why don't we let the two of them work this out so we can all avoid getting screamed at?"

They appeared interested in my proposal.

"How about I deliver this with the provision that the heir must talk to the Empaetor before he opens the package himself?"

They mulled this over, but Jerrod shook his head. "I'll accompany you to convey this message. Then we are both assured that their meeting will happen, and we're all safe from censure."

I didn't think I'd get a better deal than that, so I nodded.

The other two guards left, and we headed up in the lift. At least he let me lead the way up the two flights of stairs to the heir's suite. That gave me time to think about what I would say to Laurent when I arrived without the package in my hand and one of his father's guards behind me.

As I used my code to unlock the outer door and then traverse the empty receiving room, I made a note to set up some sort of emergency signal in the near future. In the absence of that, I was left to open the suite door and shout, "You have a visitor."

I kept my body in the middle of the doorway so the Empaetor's guard couldn't pass.

"I told you to get the delivery, not bring anyone up," Laurent snapped from his bedroom.

Great. He was back to being irritable. That's just what I needed.

"The Empaetor is concerned about this package. He'd like to speak to you before you open it."

That got his attention. Laurent arrived in front of me, shirtless and looking every bit as annoyed as he'd sounded. "He can—" Then he caught sight of the guard behind me.

"The Empaetor does not wish to wait," Jerrod said.

Laurent let out a disgusted growl. "Fine. Rita, help me dress so I can look presentable for the Empaetor."

"Yes, of course." I turned to Jerrod. "Please wait outside. We'll be with you in a few minutes."

He looked as annoyed as Laurent. "Let the heir's attendants see to him."

He was used to having attendants help him dress? He'd never mentioned it. Surely that wasn't in my job description.

Laurent had already headed back to his bedroom and was nowhere nearby to order the guard to get the hell out. I tried to win him over with sympathy.

"He doesn't have any. It's just me. All me. All the time."

Jerrod grimaced. "Don't be long."

"Not really under my control, but I'll do what I can."

He nodded and stepped back into the vacant receiving room. The door closed.

I hurried to Laurent's bedroom.

"What the hell is this?" he asked, pointing at the suite door.

"Your father must have intercepted your request to Ekie. Or he was notified that someone from your mother's estate was on the palace grounds? He's got a directive to inform him if anything arrives from the consort for you?" I shrugged.

"What's inside? Did you see?"

"Paper? Like real paper, old and yellow. With black symbols on it."

"They still used paper sometimes in Isharat's day. For personal use, not official." He gazed at nothing on the wall. "She enjoyed writing with her own hands. Beautiful, long, delicate fingers. With lacquered nails. Soft blue was her favorite color."

"That's all very nice, but how are we going to get those papers from your father's guard, or his own hands? If they're even worth getting. Like I said, they're just symbols, not even recognizable words."

"Family cipher. She invented it. Made me learn it." He smiled wistfully. "We used it to write each other messages no one else could read."

"Love notes. Wonderful. Do you think that's all these are? Love notes from Iradio V to his consort?"

"From Iradio..." Laurent shook his head. "Sorry, what?"

"Love notes. Is that what these are? Saved mementos from generations past?"

"Mother said she read them all, that Isharat had written everything down. There's got to be more to it."

"I'd like proof of that before we do anything we'll regret. Grab a shirt, stay in here, and start yelling at me. Loudly."

Laurent nodded, grinning far more than I liked for this task, like he relished the idea. A chill ran up my spine as it struck me that this was his father's face. Younger and sometimes solely Laurent as I'd come to know him, but this, this was all the old man leering down at me from the throne. I backed away.

Laurent launched into a tirade that exceeded my expectations for his performance. It was like getting chewed out by Yumi all over again but now ten times worse. Here, I was alone, with my parent's health and happiness held over my head by the Empaetor's threats. My only friend was the one screaming about the incompetence of a frigid backwater bitch with a tongue that didn't know what it was meant for in a full imperious rage.

I backed out of his bedroom and pulled the door mostly closed behind me. By the time I reached the suite entry door, my cheeks were burning and nausea swirled in my stomach.

How had I not seen Laurent for what he was—a mirror copy of his father? Now I was stuck here with my only escape option being grabbing my parents and running somewhere outside the empire. Assuming we could get off Harilax alive. Great Maker, I was Ari Leeman all over again.

I had little doubt that my merrily oblivious parents were under observation while they enjoyed all that Harilax offered. The *Knaldon* was likely also under watch, since the Empaetor knew we had ties with the crew. Senio was on his way home on whatever ship had been headed that direction to pick up the rest of the *Knaldon* crew we'd detained on Anduvea. Pitari, even after Andover's memory balm, was keeping a low profile, lurking on the *Knaldon* with the maintenance crew to avoid the Empaetor's notice. I didn't trust anyone else not to betray us. I was stuck here.

My shaking hand opened the door to the suite. The heir's tirade barreled on in full force, only slightly muffled by the ajar bedroom door. Jerrod blanched, peering over my shoulder as if he could spot the heir breathing fire somewhere close behind me.

"Could I have a few pages? Please? We can put them back before seeing the Empaetor." I glanced over my shoulder, half expecting to see Laurent's red face. Something hit his bedroom wall and shattered. I winced, and it was no act.

The guard grimaced, glancing from me to the room beyond.

"You can pick them. Make them random. I don't care. Just give me something to mollify him."

"Rita! You can't hide in the bathroom forever. You're going to regret this. I'll make sure of that." The heir let out a chuckle that made my stomach seize.

"Please," I begged Jerrod. "We'll give them back as soon as he realizes they're nothing. The Empaetor doesn't have to know a thing."

The guard shifted uneasily, his fingers gripping the package.

"If he sees the Empaetor like this, just think of the mood he will be in. You'll be bringing this," I waved behind me, "on yourself."

He chewed his lip for a few seconds before pulling the package open and tugging out a few pages from the middle. He kept a finger in the spot. "Don't be long. The Empaetor is waiting."

"Thank you." I offered him a heartfelt head bow and closed the door before scurrying back to Laurent's bedroom.

The heir held onto the back of a chair, his head down, breathing hard.

"Laurent?" I kept my back against the wall beside the door and one hand on the knob just in case I needed to bolt.

He held up one hand. "Stay back. Too many memories.

I enjoy doing this too much."

"Yelling?"

"Humiliating others. Because I can. I'm the Empaetor."

"You could try not enjoying it. Maybe be a better man than your father and those before him."

He took a shuddering breath but didn't look at me. "I didn't mean any of that. You know that, right?"

"You sounded very convincing."

"Rita," he peeked up. "I didn't mean it."

The chill in my gut didn't go away, but I hoped it would in time. Forgetting all the terrible things that had just spewed from his mouth was a big ask.

My hand was still trembling as I held out the six pages the guard had given me. "Best I could do. This is only a few of them. And we still have to meet with your father in a few minutes. Read fast."

Laurent eyed my hand, offering me another silent apology before taking the pages. He skimmed over them, his eyes following his finger that trailed along the lines. His lips moved as he read, but he remained silent until the fourth page.

"My beloved Radeceio is becoming more like his father every day, losing the parts of himself that I love. Prone to tirades and fits of violence ever since he began those cursed memory overlays."

Laurent glanced up from the pages with an unspoken question.

I nodded, noticing the glass on the floor and the missing fishbowl from the bedside table. "You too."

Laurent followed my gaze and shook his head, running over to the shattered glass. His trembling fingers gathered up the shards as if he could reassemble them.

"You need to meet with your father. The longer he waits, the worse this is going to go."

He swore under his breath and dropped the glass.

"Did you cut yourself?" I asked.

He sprang to his feet and rushed at me. I braced myself, not knowing what to expect but not willing to strike him. That would certainly bring retaliation on my parents.

One arm wrapped around me. The other hand went to my cheek, caressing. "Rita, I didn't mean any of it," he said again.

I stood stiff in his embrace. "You sounded like you did."

With only a brief glance of apology, he kissed me. Like he had in the lift on the station and later in the *Knaldon* bedroom we'd shared. I wanted to block out what he'd said so I could enjoy this, but his brutal words were too fresh.

I pushed him away. "Please don't."

He stared at me, regret clear before it vanished into something else. Something darker.

"Not convincing enough? You realize that any other woman would be overjoyed to kiss me?"

"I wasn't kissing you."

That vile chuckle returned. "You most definitely were."

Laurent clamped a hand over his mouth and turned away.

Holy Maker, his mother wasn't as crazy as I'd thought. If she'd watched her Iradio suffer through this memory overlay nightmare, it made sense that she'd do anything to keep her son from going through it too.

Laurent stood facing the wall for a few breaths. "I'm sorry. That wasn't me. I swear."

What the hell was he trying to pull? "Your voice. Your lips."

He shook his head. "I didn't... You've got blood on your face. Here." He grabbed a tissue from beside his bed and held it out to me. When I didn't take it, he started forward, reaching out.

I backed away. "Leave it. It will look convincing to the guard."

"I don't want it to," he said adamantly.

I shrugged. "We need to go."

Laurent grimaced. He used the tissue on his hand, and then straightened his shirt and ran his fingers through his hair. As he strode past me, he leaned in close. "I will make this up to you. I promise."

If there was one thing I put little stock in, it was the promises of the Empaetor.

44

Just Pick One

Laurent shoved the pages at Jerrod. "Take them. Worthless trash."

Given his mood, I wasn't sure if that referred to the pages or the guard. From Jerrod's bowed head and averted gaze, I gathered he wasn't sure either. Not taking any chances, we fell in line behind Laurent. He set a speedy pace toward the throne room.

We arrived in the receiving chamber in record time to find the old woman back on duty. She took in Laurent's flushed face and scowl and maintained her distance. No cheery welcome, not even a forced smile. She merely opened the door to the throne room and bowed her head as we streamed past.

The Empaetor sat upon his throne, glaring. Yet, he said nothing until Laurent stood six paces away. I stopped beside Jerrod, several steps back, doing my best to appear invisible.

"Where have you been?" the Empaetor demanded.

"Waiting for a delivery that you felt necessary to intercept. I would like to know why."

"They are the words of a disturbed woman. They will only confuse you. Given your stage in the indoctrination, you've got enough on your mind. Your focus should be on sorting and assimilating the knowledge you've been given."

"Have I not correctly answered all of your test questions before each session?"

The Empaetor chewed on his answer a moment before saying, "You have."

"Then what is the problem with these pages? Wasn't it you who kept preaching that all knowledge is worth having during our sessions?"

The Empaetor heaved himself up from the throne and stood. His face softened. "You have a lot of responsibility with this knowledge I'm sharing with you. Look how unhinged your mother has become since reading these pages of another disturbed woman from our past. Let me deal with her care and the cause of it. You need not worry."

"She's my mother. Of course, I'm worried," Laurent spat, wholly unmollified.

The Empaetor strode toward us, holding out his hand. Jerrod edged forward, extending the package, now again sealed, as far ahead of him as his arm would reach.

The old man plucked it from Jerrod's hand. "You're dismissed."

Jerrod hurried toward the exit. I followed him.

"Not you."

Keeping my head down, I maintained my position, now several paces from where I'd stood. I'd been so focused on the Empaetor when we'd arrived that I'd not checked to see if other guards were in attendance near the entrance as they'd been before. I hazarded a glance over my shoulder now to find two there, one being Jerrod. That seemed like slim staffing given that Empaetor was in the room.

Unless he didn't want an audience for this. My muscles tightened even more.

"Has this one lost favor so quickly?" The Empaetor asked.

"Still learning her place," Laurent answered without missing a beat.

My mouth dropped open for a second before I caught myself and clapped it shut. If hearts were truly involved, I wanted to believe this was all an act, but he was too convincing at times.

"I see." The Empaetor stalked closer, the stink of old man preceding him. He halted two steps away and pondered me like a geppa up for auction. "She serves you well?"

"Yes, quite."

Even with my head down, I glimpsed Laurent turning towards us and the confusion on his face.

"Sturdy stock, this one. Able to take a beating without breaking. I approve," the Empaetor announced.

"I wasn't looking for your approval," Laurent snapped.

"She'll serve well. A change of pace from my usual entertainment."

Laurent was suddenly beside me. "She's not yours and never will be."

"Fond of this one, are you?" The Empaetor bared his yellowed teeth.

"I have no others at the moment, so yes."

Way to make me feel special, Laurent. I wanted to glare at him but kept my head down.

"That is a problem we need to remedy, and the other

reason I called you here today. You're missing several key people around you."

I'd been saying the same thing since we'd arrived on Harilax. It was about time someone noticed the lack of staffing in the heir's wing.

The Empaetor cleared his throat with a raspy cough. "Before you take the throne, you must take a consort. I've been patient, giving you far more years than necessary to find your match. Yet you are here before me, empty-handed. Heirs do not appear out of thin air."

So not the staff opening I'd been anxious to have filled. Sure, I agreed it was necessary, but right now?

Laurent sputtered. "I'm well aware of how children are made."

"Then why haven't you done so? I was quite clear about the requirements for taking the throne. You've been offered more daughters than I can count. You've even been offered sons with willing surrogates. Yet, you've done nothing. The time for waiting is over. You will decide now."

"I'll do no such thing," Laurent declared.

The Empaetor pointed at me. "Then she will choose."

I couldn't keep my gaze lowered any longer. It was all I could do to keep my lips pressed shut rather than tell the Empaetor where he could shove his choices. Laurent must have known me well enough, because he shot me a warning glare. Or maybe it was a warning not to pick the worst match out of spite. I was entirely out of my league here. Good Maker, Yumi and Senio were going to eat this up if I lived to tell the tale.

Laurent stepped into the Empaetor's personal space. The old man didn't back down.

"You also said I'd need to have an heir to take the throne. What if the chosen woman is infertile? We might not know for years."

"Your heirs need not be of natural birth, only of your blood. The bloodline of the consort is irrelevant."

It was hard to believe that he and the consort had once been a fun-loving couple. Maybe age did that to people, drove them mad and apart.

"There are surrogates or labs. Either can create a healthy child, no matter your age or that of your consort."

Laurent paled. "But that means you could have created another heir at any time."

"You are alive and well-formed. Why would I create another drain on my patience or my treasury?"

I found that exceedingly cocky, though I supposed having a handful of guards with the sole duty of protecting your offspring from birth could make one that complacent.

Laurent sputtered something about a greater responsibility to the empire, but the Empaetor clapped his hands and called out, "Bring them."

A line of twenty-five women filed in. They varied in skin tone from porcelain to ebony, and in height from barely to Laurent's shoulder to equal, not a single one taller. Their ages ranged from mid-twenties—I hoped because one looked to be in her mid-teens—to close to his age. As they lined up before us, all had good posture and were dressed in finery that would have bankrupted all of Anduvea. Their hairstyles were as varied as their hair color. Every single one of them appeared healthy and smiled with perfect teeth.

The Empaetor had truly amassed a wide selection from what the empire had to offer. No two of them were alike.

Some were slim, others shapely. All were beautiful in the ways one would expect an elite of the empire to be. I could easily see any of these women as the next consort. From the batting eyelashes and giddy grins, any of them would die to live at the estate. They all appeared willing and ready to spread their legs for the heir right here and now.

I hated them all.

To my surprise, Laurent appeared no more thrilled than I was. I remembered him saying that he'd given up the twit market ten years ago, but having to pick one of these beautiful women to visit whenever the urge hit, didn't seem too much of a hardship.

He would need an heir if he wanted to keep the empire at peace. The Empaetor wasn't wrong in calling him out for not getting down to business. Laurent wasn't getting any younger. It wouldn't have surprised me to learn that the Empaetor may have stepped down sooner, considering his health, if Laurent had been married and had an heir or two in the wings. Being in control of the empire might be fun, but sitting back and maybe enjoying a tour of your life's work while one could still enjoy it might also have an allure.

The Empaetor clapped his hands loudly, the sound echoing through the vast room. "You have one hour. Choose." He turned from us and strode up to his throne to oversee the picking of the new consort.

Laurent approached me. I had nowhere to go. I gritted my teeth and let him.

He leaned in close. "I don't want to do this."

"You only have one choice, and it's one of them." I gestured to the line of women. "Did he really offer you men at one point?"

"Yes, even after I made it clear that wasn't an option I was interested in." He sighed. "He tried blatantly offering and more subtly, just in case I was being coy about my preferences."

"I may not have known you long, but I wouldn't say you're coy about anything."

He chuckled, but then sobered. "I wish you'd washed your face. I don't like seeing you like this. Even more, I don't like him thinking that I did that to you."

"He seemed happy about it, as I guessed he would."

Laurent scowled at his father. "I like that even less."

He appeared to be back to regular Laurent. I let myself relax a fraction so I could focus on the task at hand.

"You've got less than an hour to pick your consort. That seems like an important decision you should be focusing on."

He cast me a look filled with regret. You and me both, pal.

"Walk with me," he said.

Laurent started at one end of the line, talking just loud enough for me to hear. With each step, he relayed how he knew the woman and what he didn't like about her. He'd been with some of them, and he hid nothing from me. I rather wished he would. Even if he had been the heir to the empire in the prime of his life, enjoying the willing company of the empire's elite, I didn't need to put faces to names.

My occasional dalliances with visitors to the station over the years made me downright chaste in comparison.

"Just pick one," I ground out before we'd made it to the end of the line.

"Let me finish," he snapped.

I did, though I didn't like it. When we reached the end, he pulled me aside.

"I have no desire to pick any of them, but he's forcing my hand."

I nodded. The Empaetor watched us with a distinct lack of patience.

Laurent nodded toward the line. "Given what I told you and what you know of me, you choose."

I glared at him. "I most certainly will not."

"Yeah, that's exactly how I feel about it too." He grumbled. "The memories I've been given so far are from before each Iradio took the throne. From when they found their consorts either earlier in their lives or in preparation for taking the throne. None of them were forced as my father is doing to me."

"Because all of them picked a consort before they were forced to," I pointed out. "How hard is it? You have every woman in the empire throwing herself at you. I mean, come on, just pick one."

"They don't *all* throw themselves at me," he grumbled.

The Empaetor stood and started towards us.

"His health is failing, Laurent. He can't wait on your whims any longer. This is it. Pick one, or you're going to leave him no choice but to make the decision for you."

Laurent regarded me with a calculating gaze. He perused the line twice, steepling his fingers before him as he turned from one end to the other and back.

"Well?" the Empaetor rasped.

"Rita," Laurent said.

"You're letting her pick?" The Empaetor focused all his

attention on me. "Alright, who will be the next consort?"

I went over all the information Laurent had given me and narrowed the selection down to two. My debate was between a thirty-something brunette with hips and an ass I'd die for and a forty-ish woman with vivid green eyes. Laurent's only criticism of her had been that he didn't like her brother from some childhood prank he'd pulled. I was about to make my choice when Laurent took my hand in his.

What the fuck was he doing? I subtly attempted to pull my hand away. He held on tight.

"No, my choice is Rita."

"No, it's not," I heard myself say.

The Empaetor laughed. "See, even she has enough brains to know how careless that would be."

"You asked me to choose a consort, and I have. There will be no further discussion." Laurent tugged me after him and started for the door.

Twenty-five beautiful women and one fuming Empaetor burned holes into me with their eyes as we walked out of the throne room.

"What are you doing?" I whispered.

"Making things better for the empire, just like you asked me to do."

"No, I'm pretty sure you just made everything far worse. Your father will never approve of this insanity, and twenty-five elite families will be out for blood."

"Twenty-four of them would be no matter who I picked. What's one more?"

"They would not. They would accept that you chose one of them and move on with their social clawing at one another until the next cycle comes around."

He squeezed my hand. "See, you're good at this. You're exactly what I need."

"Not even remotely." When we reached the door, I turned to face him and tugged my hand out of his. "Get your ass back over there and pick a suitable consort. You can't afford to make a joke of this. I understand not wanting to be forced into making a choice, but if you want to rule the empire, you need to play by the rules."

"I'll be the one making the rules as of next week." His lip curled when he looked back at his father. "I'm not joking, Rita. I'm not picking anyone else."

"I won't be a pawn in your rebellious game against your father."

"Rita, I'm serious. I want you to be my consort." He reached for me.

"You're being fucking ridiculous." I shook my head and stormed out of the throne room.

I didn't know where I was going, but wherever it was, it was away from the man intent on throwing the entire empire into chaos. There were trillions of lives at stake, and I had no intention of being the reason any of them ended before the Maker's intended time.

45

Prospective Consort

"**H**e said what?" asked my mother for the third time.

I couldn't even look at my parents after I'd barged into their hotel room and shouted the whole mess at them while stomping around and waving my hands in the air. Now planted on the spongy couch that was upholstered in some sort of stiff stain-repellant fabric that crinkled with my every movement, I could only hold my head in my hands and stare at the worn spot in the yellow, low-pile carpet between my feet.

My father settled onto the crinkling couch beside me and wrapped an arm around my shoulders. "You did the right thing."

"The right thing?" my mother's voice rose so sharp and high I was amazed she didn't shatter the chipped glass bowl on the table in front of us. "She swore at the heir. In the presence of the Empaetor!"

"I'm sure the Empaetor was laughing his ass off, if that's any consolation," I muttered.

"It's not," my mother said, still utterly aghast.

"What are you going to do?" asked my father.

"What is *she* going to do? She's going to march back over to the palace and accept what has been offered to her," declared my mother.

"Seriously? You were the one who pointed out that he wouldn't need me once we got here. That he'd cast me aside. That I shouldn't get attached."

My mother thrust her fisted hands onto her hips. "Clearly, I was wrong."

"You weren't," I said firmly. "He's only doing this because his father is forcing him to choose. Laurent is making a mockery of it all. Like a three-year-old pitching a fit. I don't want any part of it."

My father's hand rubbed over my back, calming, bringing back memories of my childhood. "You're already part of it. All you can do is make the best of it."

"There is no best." I stood, needing to be on my feet. Needing to do something, to be somewhere. Yet having no clue what or where, and my nose and the stab wound were fucking throbbing.

There was a knock at the door.

"Who is that now?" My mother tsked her way across the room.

I heard enough murmuring at the doorway to give up avoiding whatever it was. My father called after me, but I was already on the way over when Jerrod entered.

He confronted me with a nervous smile. "I've, umm, been sent to retrieve you."

"Retrieve?" I started at how much my affronted voice matched my mother's tone. "You can all fuck off. Get out."

He put his hands up. "Before you start swinging, I've been sent for you and your parents."

"That's all the more reason not to cooperate."

The guard glanced behind him. "Can we shut the door, please? And maybe keep our voices down? Everyone wishes to resolve this quietly. Without rumors."

"I'm sure they do." My mother waved him in, closed the door, and gestured for us all to return to the sitting area.

Once we'd all gathered in the small space, Jarrod faced the three of us.

He offered a quick bow. "The heir sends his apologies for my intrusion."

"Maybe he should have intruded himself if he wanted to convey that convincingly, Jerrod," I muttered.

The guard smirked. "He intended to. The Empaetor stopped him, citing his concern for the heir's health in your presence while you were angry."

"Fair point," I conceded. "I'd send for my things, but I have nothing of value at the palace."

"Send for your... Why?" he asked.

"If you think my raised voice here is going to ignite rumors, you're missing out on the twenty-five angry women with access to the gossip pool on at least twenty worlds. I'm the least of your worries."

"They've all been detained with no access to outside media."

"How did you manage that?" I asked while coming to grips with the fact that it had already happened.

"Standard procedure. Can't have the news get out before the Empaetor and heir are ready to make an official announcement."

"Good, then he can choose again from someone who wants the position."

"Would you consider taking it?" Jerrod asked.

"In the Maker's name, why?

"If you do, there's hope for the rest of us," he said earnestly.

"I have no desire to be the face of a cause. No one even likes this face. I mean, seriously, look at it." I waved at my broken nose, scratched cheek, and black eyes.

My father cleared his throat.

"No one outside of this room likes this face," I amended. "A guard, sure, fine. I'll figure out how the palace protocols work eventually, so everyone stops whispering about everything I'm doing wrong. But act as consort? Hell no."

Jerrod shook his head. "You're not doing anything wrong."

My brows shot up even though it hurt seconds later.

"The whispers are because they're intrigued. You're new, interesting. The heir has never had a female personal guard before. He's also never stood up to the Empaetor, but after you stormed out, which was glorious by the way, the heir exploded in ways I've only seen the Empaetor go off on people. They were both yelling, and the next thing we knew, the Empaetor was gasping for air and on his knees."

"Is he alright?" asked my father.

"He's under medical care now in his private suite. We should know in a few hours if there are any lasting effects."

If the Empaetor's health was in danger, would Laurent be subjected to a rush memory overlay session? His mood swings were already a problem. I didn't want to consider what piling on back-to-back sessions might do. What if he ended up with issues of his own? I'd read enough to have a good idea of what he might face. All of it made me anxious.

It was one thing to cause chaos by accepting a place beside Laurent, no matter the trivial reason or consequences, but if he ended up catatonic or suffered memory damage or permanent mood disorders, the empire would be in serious trouble. There was no backup heir, only hundreds of people who would fight for the chance to become Empaetor in his place.

There was one thing I needed to know before I agreed to anything.

"Why were you asked to bring all of us back?"

"Same reason that we detain the prospective consort pool."

"No one is a prisoner?"

He shook his head. "Guests of the palace until an announcement can be made."

"If I agree to go with you, I want to be clear that I'm not agreeing to be a part of any announcement."

Jerrod held up his empty hands. "That is between you and the heir."

"Alright then. I want to check on the situation with the Empaetor and what cautionary provisions are being made."

He grinned. "The palace has been much more interesting since your arrival."

"*Interesting* is not a word my coworkers have ever used. Aggravating and overbearing came up a lot in my reviews."

My father snorted. "Short-tempered."

"I believe brusque came up repeatedly," my mother offered.

"Love you too, guys." I let out a heavy sigh. "Fine. Would you like to see the palace? Maybe stay for a couple of days?"

My mother didn't answer. She was already packing. My

father joined her, tossing everything they'd brought into their bags.

Jerrod and I stood, alternately watching them pack and glancing at each other. Finally, I couldn't take it anymore.

"What?"

"That was all an act when I came up to his suite, wasn't it? There's no cut on your face."

"You are correct, there is no cut on my face."

I couldn't elaborate on the act part. While I wanted to say that it was, there was something bad going on with Laurent. I didn't want to dwell on the horrible things he had said. He'd apologized, but the memory of it all was too fresh, especially when he'd worn his father's face. I shuddered.

"Alright. What were those papers about?" he asked. "They looked old."

"I wouldn't know. I was only sent to retrieve them."

He pulled the steady interrogation stare. I returned it.

Finally, he nodded. "You'll do just fine. Don't mind the whispers."

"Easy for you to say, but thanks."

He pulled a tiny packet out of his pocket and handed it to me. "Now that you might be open to the idea that I'm not here to poison you, the heir thought you might want this."

I opened it to find a half dose of my pain medication. I swallowed it on the spot.

"As rough as I'm feeling, I probably would have taken the chance it might have been poison."

Jerrod chuckled.

While I waited for the pill to take the edge off, my parents finished packing. We used the room terminal to check out and pay and then left. I might have had plenty of energy to burn when I'd walked eight blocks from the palace to the hotel, but now I was grateful for the transport Jerrod had left outside. The four of us piled in and returned to the prism glass triangle that towered over the city.

Jerrod had notified the palace of our arrival, including the addition of my parents and their need for lodging. We were met at the entry by four attendants and a host of guards.

I glared at Jerrod. "What the hell is all this?"

He winked. "We wouldn't want to chance harm or offence to the prospective consort during her first reception."

"Fuck you. Get rid of all this attention. It's unneeded, and if anything, it's begging for disaster. Understated and invisible has always been my objective in both security and my personal life."

Jerrod let out a loud guffaw. "I love you already." He waved to the fawning attendants. "You heard the lady, go. Someone grab their bags. You," he pointed at one of the confused attendants, "show our guests to a suite suitable for the consort's parents."

"Prospective," I grumbled.

"Right, the *prospective* consort's parents," he corrected with a smirk. "And where would you like to go?"

"I can't believe I'm saying this, but back to Anduvea?" I groaned. "I came here to safely deliver the heir. I stayed to assure he remained safe, but I had no intention of fully integrating myself into this nightmare."

Jerrod walked beside me to the first security checkpoint. "It doesn't have to be a nightmare," he said quietly.

"Your life on Harilax can be what you make it."

"How blissfully optimistic of you."

The guards on duty scanned our ID chips and waved us through without question. I'd let it go today.

I could see my parents up ahead of us. Three attendants fussed over them and their two pitiful bags containing all they owned. This might not be my dream, but I had a feeling my mother was having the time of her life. From the wide smile on my father's face as he spoke to the attendant beside them, he was enjoying himself too. They deserved to be spoiled a bit. Or a lot, considering what they'd gone through at Laurent's expense.

Jerrod was busy with a darting conversation through his comm pin that I only caught snippets of. I waited until he was quiet for a moment, which happened to be in the lift where reception was dodgy.

"Does the prospective consort get a personal guard?"

"Yes, of course. And attendants. A private suite. If memory serves, also a small staff to manage public appearances, purchase clothing, run the consort's estate and transportation. There's also a generous stipend, of course."

"Of course."

The consort's estate. I'd forgotten about that. As beautiful as the place was, I couldn't see myself living there. Or even wanting to. I didn't see myself doing any of this shit.

It was temporary. I'd play along until I could talk some sense into Laurent and make sure he emerged from his memory overlay without his brain scrambled.

The lift came to a stop on the throne room floor. I pressed the button to pause the doors from opening. "Alright, here's the deal. I don't plan on being anything more than prospective. I'll help sort out the heir's role during the Empaetor's recovery, talk some sense into him about declaring a suitable consort, and then get him settled on the throne when he's ready. After that, we'll figure out if I'll still be his personal guard or if I'm going home."

Jerrod looked like he was about to interrupt me. I shook my head.

"Until that time, I'm stealing you from the Empaetor. No arguments. I don't like anyone else here. In fact, I barely like you, but I'll take it for now. All that other shit can wait for the actual consort to come to light."

Jerrod offered me a grin and a deep bow. "At your service. Where to then?"

"I'm assuming the Empaetor is under whatever care he requires. The heir is my priority. I'll check his suite, unless you know if he's elsewhere?"

"He sent me after you," Jerrod said, already touching his comm pin. "One moment."

He entered into a quiet conversation. Then he scowled and looked nervous.

I swore under my breath. "What?"

"No one has seen him since the Empaetor was taken away to undergo medical care."

"Then Laurent is with him?"

"I'm not getting any confirmation of that. Or where the Empaetor is, actually."

My gut knew where they were, and I didn't like it one bit. "Fucking memory overlay. The Empaetor must not be doing well, or they wouldn't push him to that right now. Come on." I hurried down the corridor to the room we'd both been in before.

46

Deathtoller

Several guards milled around the waiting room. They formed a barrier neither of us dared rush into.

"What's the meaning of this?" Jerrod asked.

"No one enters," one of them replied, standing firmly in our way.

"The heir has asked that you await him in his suite," the spokesman informed me stiffly.

That didn't sound like Laurent. He normally wanted me close by. It sounded like his father.

"I'll wait here."

The three of them bristled, stepping forward as if to back us out of the room. I looked at Jerrod and planted my feet. He responded with a raised eyebrow but followed my lead. As the three guards continued to approach, we didn't move. Two paces from us, they faltered, glancing uncertainly at one another.

One pointed to a bench near the door. "You can have a seat over there."

Jerrod consulted me with a glance.

"I have no intention of sitting here idly while who knows

what is happening in there."

"The same thing that has been happening all the times you sat here with us," one of them said with forced calmness.

"Funny, you've never blocked me from entering before."

"You never attempted to enter before."

I took a step forward. "I don't have time for this. Stand aside, or I will move you."

The three of them conferred silently and then resolutely stood their ground.

I'd warned them. Jerrod might help or not, but I figured I could make a decent go of it on my own. Whatever the outcome, at least I was doing something. Besides, I had a healthy stash of pain pills at my bedside for later.

Maybe being too combative would disqualify me from being the consort. That was all the incentive I needed to dive in.

The first punch thrown was mine, but Jerrod's was second. The three guards defended themselves with impressive skill. We were all bruised, sore, and bleeding by the time two guards went down and stayed there. The third one held up his hands and backed away.

"Whatever happens in there is on your head."

"Noted." I strode through the door with Jerrod on my heels. "Have you been in here before?"

"Never. No one other than Doctor Meldorn is allowed in here."

My side hurt like hell. I lifted my shirt to see that the stitches had torn. The wound was bleeding again. I put pressure on it and prayed that it would stop quickly.

The room we'd intruded upon was long and narrow,

with a partial wall standing between us and the majority of the space. All I could see of the room beyond were flashing lights, shadows, and someone's arm. A series of quiet clicks and hisses came from unseen equipment. The entry area where we stood offered deep shadows. We stayed in them. I crept forward to peek around the edge of the wall.

"I'm pretty sure, as your guard, I'm supposed to be going in first," Jerrod whispered.

"Shut up and stay behind me."

He listened. We may have had a rocky start, but I decided he was alright.

Beyond the wall lay a long space with two standing tables. The Empaetor stood in front of the nearest one, tilted back just enough that his feet were off the ground. Wide fabric straps held him to the shiny metal surface, fastened at his hips, waist, and shoulders. Tubes ran from his arms to bags on hooks at the top of the table just above his head. His face hung slack, and his eyes were closed. Limp and asleep, he appeared far older than he had in the throne room, devoid of animation.

Just behind him, Laurent was attached to the second table. His face was pinched, jaw tight as though he was clenching his teeth, and his hands were in fists at his sides. Whatever memories he was being fed did not appear to be peaceful.

Doctor Meldorn stood just beyond them, monitoring a long table full of controls, his eyes locked onto a vid screen.

I don't know what I'd imagined the memory overlay to look like, maybe a vid playing recordings made by each ruler at important times in their lives for the incoming heir to watch and absorb. But when I spotted the nest of wires sprouting from a web-like device on the old man's head that were connected to a mirror copy on Laurent's, I revised my grasp of what was going on. Were they pulling the shared memories from the old man and feeding them to Laurent?

He didn't appear to have any other connections to anything beyond the web of wiring. That was promising, but also concerning as to the Empaetor's health.

"What do you see?" whispered Jerrod.

I motioned for him to be quiet. The doctor was entranced by whatever he was monitoring. Laurent let out a keening noise that set my nerves on fire. His body went taut, his back arching, straining the straps at his hips and chest. The doctor paid no attention to him, walking calmly over to the Empaetor to take his vitals.

Whatever was going on needed to stop. I took half a step, nearly exposing myself before second-guessing my actions. What if interrupting the overlay caused more harm?

Laurent's head shook from side to side, held firm to the table by the forehead strap. The Empaetor's body sagged further. Doctor Meldorn scowled. He applied an injection to the Empaetor's arm. Whatever his intention, the result didn't appear to be happening because he started swearing and looking frantic. He dashed back to his terminal and stared at the vid, swearing louder.

Deciding that not deciding wasn't doing any good, I threw caution out the door and darted into plain sight.

The doctor yelled, "You can't be in here!"

"What is this?" I pointed to the web of wires.

"Get out," he yelled, running to the Empaetor's side. He injected a swirl of deep yellow into the clear fluid running into his arm.

"Jerrod, help me get the heir out of here."

"You can't move him. Not now," screeched Meldorn.

One of the machines connected to the Empaetor beeped fast and loud.

I didn't think Laurent would want the memory of his father dying firsthand. That certainly seemed like something that would mess a person up for life.

I hurried to his side and started tugging the wire web off his head. Doctor Meldorn screamed at me to stop. Jerrod released the strap on Laurent's forehead and then the one on his chest. It was at that point that I realized there was also a thick wire connected to the base of Laurent's skull.

"Stop. Keep him on the table," I said to Jerrod.

Brushing Laurent's hair aside, I discovered a port where the wire was jacked into his skull.

"What the fuck is this?"

"Don't touch it." Meldorn grabbed my hand, trying to pull me away. "The fate of the empire lies in completing the transfer."

"Laurent has enough memories. He'll be fine." I tugged on the cable, only to find it firmly lodged in the port.

"Stop!"

The beeping of the Empaetor's monitors grew more insistent.

The doctor let go of my hand and took a step back. I got a firm grasp on the cable and leaned in to better examine the port, looking for a release mechanism. Out of the corner of my eye, I glimpsed something in Meldorn's hands. It wasn't an injector.

It was a deathtoller pistol.

Fuck, was the only thought I had when the shot went

off. Jerrod spun and lunged for the doctor, knocking him to the floor.

I remembered to breathe and looked down to verify that I was whole. Thank the Maker, Laurent was too. My fingers felt the release. I yanked the cable free. Laurent went limp, but also blessedly silent. Or maybe silent was bad.

I shook him gently.

"Wake up. Come on." I prayed my interruption of the process hadn't caused lasting damage.

The beeping at the Empaetor's side became an endless whine.

Laurent did not respond.

"Restrain the doctor. We need answers," I said to Jerrod.

He didn't respond either.

I tore my attention from Laurent to the guard atop Meldorn. Jerrod shook his head, looking dazed, while holding the doctor down. Jerrod also appeared amazingly intact.

"Hey, are you with me?"

The doctor, seeing Jerrod wasn't focused, struggled harder.

He nodded before muttering, "hit my head on the fucking table."

Laurent wasn't waking up. The doctor was the only one who knew what was going on. I grabbed Meldorn's arm and pulled him out from under Jerrod. The guard groaned. Thank the Maker, he was still alive after that close call with a deathtoller.

The wall beyond where Jerrod had been hadn't fared so well. Whatever had been there was now a shattered mess of clearplaz and metal. Doctor Meldorn might be a skilled doctor, but he was an exceptionally terrible shot.

"Make that fucking machine stop." I shoved Meldorn at the Empaetor.

The doctor shook his head. Terror that had nothing to do with me yelling at him flooded over his face. "No, this can't be."

He shook the limp old man, but got no response. The doctor grabbed the injector and pressed it to the Empaetor's neck again. The high-pitched whine remained.

"Turn it off," I demanded.

Doctor Meldorn did as I asked, his head hanging low and looking like the world had just ended.

"He's gone?"

The doctor offered the barest hint of a nod.

"And the heir?"

"Let's pray the full identity transfer was complete."

My heart stuttered as his words repeated in my head. "The what? It was a memory overlay. That's what he said."

Doctor Meldorn skirted Jerrod, who got to his unsteady feet and was blinking at the blood on his hand from where he'd touched his head. I gave him a nod, but couldn't spare him more than that at the moment. Laurent had top priority.

"Memory overlays form the groundwork, yes." The doctor examined Laurent's port and then took his vitals.

"Groundwork for what exactly?" The niggling, creeping feeling in my brain knew the answer, but I needed to hear it for sanity's sake.

He frowned at his findings and lifted one of Laurent's eyelids, examining his eye. "To become Iradio. To become the Empaetor. To assure an uninterrupted rule of the empire."

I looked from Laurent to the old man and back again. "And what happens to Laurent in this whole 'becoming Iradio' scenario?"

"He's overwritten. The heir is merely a host body." Meldorn hurried to the terminal. A few seconds later, he let out a sigh of relief. "He had a good life, little responsibility, many years of leisure and pleasure. It's their reward for maintaining the line."

He picked up a new injector and pulled a labeled vial from a lit clearplaz-faced cabinet on the wall. Once he had it loaded, he tapped the injector on Laurent's wrist. "That ought to do it."

"Maintaining the line. Of Iradio? As in Iradio I? In body after body?"

"Exactly. A smooth transition. No random changing of policies, no lost knowledge—everything remains on an even keel. The empire remains strong. Our people are safe and cared for. Business goes on as usual."

"I don't feel particularly cared for. I feel I can speak for an entire world on that, as a matter of fact. And I'm sure there are others like Anduvea that feel the same way."

He typed on his terminal and then scowled at me. "There are always a few casualties. It's the majority that matters."

"Rita!" Jerrod yelled a second before I realized the doctor was making a lunge for the pistol Jerrod had knocked out of his hand when they'd gone down.

Caught between shielding Laurent from Meldorn's inept aim and protecting myself, I watched with relief as Jerrod caught Meldorn before he'd gotten halfway to the fallen pistol. He restrained the troublesome doctor.

While part of me wished Jerrod had just shot the

man, we needed answers. The empire, as a whole, needed answers.

I strode over and secured the damned pistol once and for all, shoving it under my jacket through my belt. Then I slapped a pair of restraints on Meldorn's wrists. He could still work, but that would slow him down in case he had any other weapons stashed around. I did a quick scan of the room, but didn't spot anything beyond medical tools, and we needed those available.

Keeping a close eye on Meldorn, I checked Jerrod's head. "You'll be fine. It's not deep. You're going to have a good lump and a headache for a few days though."

"I'll take it over being blown to bits." He rummaged through Meldorn's cabinets for first aid supplies.

I returned to Laurent's side, dragging the disgruntled doctor with me.

Laurent appeared relaxed. His coloring was normal. I examined the port again. From the healing still forming around it, I gathered it was a recent addition. Likely something inserted during one of these sessions while he was out. No wonder he'd been cranky and not acting entirely like himself.

Was he himself anymore?

"Wake the hell up, would you?" The not knowing made me more anxious than I'd ever been in my life.

Pounding erupted on the door.

"Sounds like he brought reinforcements," Jerrod said.

The guard who had given up had come back to haunt us. I gave Laurent's sleeping body one last look, hoping for a hint of who he was. When I didn't receive one, I drew the pistol and propelled the doctor toward the door.

47
The Strong Ones Remain

I hurried to the door to find Jerrod had locked it behind us when we'd entered. He was a handy man to have around, competent and able to think on his own. Skills I thought most people had until I'd worked with enough of them to realize the error of my assumption. Now that the Empaetor was gone, I'd keep him close no matter what my future role here would be.

After making it clear to the doctor that I knew how to aim the deathtoller, I addressed whoever was outside.

"State your business," I demanded through the door.

"By order of the Empaetor, you will come out and submit yourself to his judgement."

"Seeing that the Empaetor is currently unconscious, I know he ordered no such thing. We're in the middle of a medical emergency. Remove yourselves, or at the very least, conduct yourselves quietly. We can't afford further distractions."

The voices on the other side of the door muttered among themselves. "We will leave if we can speak to Doctor Meldorn or the Empaetor," their spokesman offered.

Meldorn gave me a questioning glance. I jabbed the pistol into his back. He nodded.

I unlocked the door and opened it far enough for him to stick his head through. He wisely kept his bound hands inside.

"You're interrupting an important procedure," he said.

"Sorry, sir. All is well?"

"No, it is not. Pray and leave us in peace so I can work." He ducked back inside.

I locked the door and waved him over to Laurent. "How much longer will he be out?"

"Because you interrupted the procedure, I'm not sure. He should have awoken once the transfer was complete, and the identity was free of the old body."

"The Empaetor would have died either way?"

"The old body." He returned to the terminal and consulted the readings there. "Iradio lives on."

Indeed he did. That explained why he held such long grudges and favorites. Why the heir's best intentions before taking the throne always fell by the wayside. If a single session of memory transfer could lead to multiple kinds of mental illness, it stood to reason that an identity that had hopped eight bodies would act erratically on occasion.

Fuck, Laurent's mother wasn't crazy at all.

If it was always Iradio who was Empaetor, that explained how the men Isharat and Marishka had come to love had dramatically changed upon taking the throne. How Laurent would change. My heart sank.

While we'd not defined what was truly between us, it hurt to think that we'd never get to have that conversation. That we'd never get the chance to find out.

It had all been a silly daydream anyway. One I'd barely allowed myself to even consider as a possibility. So why were my eyes watering?

This was no time for tears.

Doctor Meldorn seemed to be managing his tasks despite his hands being bound in front of him. I returned the pistol to my belt.

"Watch him," I said to Jerrod.

Looking more himself now, he nodded.

I left Meldorn to his work and went to Laurent's side. Peering down at the younger variation of the dead man on the table four steps away, I shook my head. Business first. Feelings later.

"When will we know what identity now controls this body?"

"When he wakes. I've studied the notes from the past procedures extensively. Brain activity will be too difficult to map for confirmation until a few days have passed. The body and mind will need an acclimation period. This is socially excused as a time of reflection and final briefing from the outgoing Empaetor."

"And no one has questioned that every Empaetor dies the day the new one takes over? Isn't it suspicious that none of them have simply handed over the throne and retired?"

The doctor shrugged. "According to the records, we've done that routine twice, the retirement with I3 and I7. Grown a clone body, filled it with a partial memory transfer and sent it off to parade around Harilax as a failing old man."

Jerrod leaned against the wall, arms crossed over his chest, watching the doctor's every move. "That leaves a lot of room for coincidence with the rest."

"We vary their ends. Three of them remained on their sickbeds for weeks after the transfer."

That couldn't be right. "You said they died when that was complete."

Meldorn smiled coldly. "They did. Bodies can be kept alive once the mind is gone."

Jerrod looked as mortified as I felt. All of it, it was disgusting. I shivered, thinking of all the men with dreams of a better empire who had died in this room.

"What if the sitting Empaetor has no heir?" Jerrod asked.

The doctor's lip curled. "That's never happened before. They've all sired one, if not two or a whole gaggle of heirs by their middle years. This one is a failure in that regard."

If the heir's personality changed significantly after taking the throne, it made sense that the consort would be kept at arm's length and relegated to her own estate other than for...

"That means every visit between a new Empaetor and his consort was Iradio I enjoying himself with his ancestor's spouse?"

The doctor nodded.

I threw up a little in my mouth. So gross.

Jerrod also grimaced, glancing at me and then away.

One thing was for certain, if I'd lost Laurent, I had no intention of getting involved in any manner with the new occupant of his body. Zero. None.

My stomach heaved. I frantically darted to the nearest trash receptacle and threw up.

"Maybe you should sit down," Meldorn said offhandedly. "I see you've ripped your stitches."

I glanced down at the dark stain. Yeah, that could just bleed for a while. No way was that man touching me.

"Shut up and wake him so we know what we're dealing with," I said.

"You'll be dealing with the Empaetor either way. Neither man will have time for an Anduvean pet. Your novelty has worn off. Go home."

Home, even filled with smoke and tourists, sounded blessedly peaceful just then. With the Empaetor down, this would be the time to grab my parents and run.

"Like you'd let her leave after divulging the truth about the Empaetor," Jerrod scoffed.

He had a point, and that illustrated how much I wasn't thinking clearly. I glanced at Laurent again, still sleeping and giving us no hint of his identity.

It came down to how much I could trust Jerrod. He seemed loyal, but to who? Me, who he'd spent a few possibly honest hours with or the Empaetor who employed him?

He had tackled the doctor and warned me. I went with my gut and hoped the Maker was on my side.

"Once Laurent is awake, for better or worse, the only one who knows my part in what happened here is you, doctor. Perhaps it's you who will no longer be needed."

Jerrod grinned. "About time we have an intelligent consort."

"Her?" Doctor Meldorn scoffed. "The Empaetor will nix that idea in seconds. If that was your plan, you should have sealed it before today, woman. A publicly announced consort is more difficult to do away with. Though accidents happen, even here in the palace."

"Yes. You could get caught in the crossfire when the distressed guards outside break in," I pointed out. Except I needed him alive for now, and he knew it.

He glared at me but shut his mouth, diverting his attention to the readings flashing in front of him and twisting his bound hands together. It was half an hour later that he announced, "He should wake soon."

"Thank the Maker," said Jerrod. "Rita, why don't you take a seat for a bit? It might be wise if you're not the first person he sees until we know who we're dealing with."

I didn't like the thought of not being right there to deal with whatever situation we found ourselves in but agreed with his logic. I took the seat beside Meldorn's table and kept an eye on the doctor as well as the new Empaetor.

Great Maker, we had a new Empaetor. Or maybe the same one but now in a younger body. My stomach twisted again.

"After this identity imprint, how much of the heir's memories remain?"

"The strong ones, though they will no longer be at the forefront. This helps Iradio more smoothly integrate into the host body without raising too many questions," said the doctor.

"How will we know which one is controlling the body now?"

"The transfer was nearly complete. Iradio is there. The question is how fully integrated he will be."

That vile old man would be in Laurent's body. No question. No doubt.

If only I'd arrived sooner.

48

There's A Code

The Empaetor's eyes opened. I watched, breath held, from across the room.

Doctor Meldorn, his hands still bound in restraints, stood by his patient's side, waving a scanner over his body. "Physically, everything checks out," he announced.

Jerrod stood on the Empaetor's other side, the bed now lying horizontally to allow for waking recovery from his sleep after the identity transfer.

The transfer I was silently praying did not take.

"How are you feeling?" the doctor asked.

"I'm not sure." Laurent sounded shaken. "What happened? This feels different from the previous transfers."

"It was a more thorough procedure this time, multiple sessions condensed into one. More arduous than I prefer to do, but necessary."

"Necessary why?" The new Empaetor tried to sit up, only to discover he was strapped to the table.

"Please rest, sir. Confusion is normal after this stage. Relax and give the memories time to settle. Same exercises as before."

"Yes, alright." His body relaxed back onto the table, eyes half-closed. His eyelids fluttered. He gasped. "Too many memories. I can't sort them all." His voice took on a panicked edge. "Too many. I... Who am I?"

Meldorn's demeanor lost its calm blandness. I stood. He shook his head. Jerrod did too. Well damn, I didn't like feeling powerless to help. Not one bit.

"You are Empaetor Iradio IX, sir."

"The ninth. Iradio. Yes." He settled back again, eyes drifting closed.

That's when the seizure started. The Empaetor's body contorted and shook.

"Do something," I shouted.

"This shouldn't be happening." The doctor ran to the clearplaz-fronted cabinet and scanned the contents. I darted to his side, freeing his hands in favor of getting Laurent whatever treatment he needed. Meldorn pulled out another vial, snapped it into his injector and inserted the drug into Laurent's arm.

Four long, agonizing minutes later, his body went slack.

"Help me get him onto his side," the doctor said to Jerrod. "Release the straps."

"Will he be alright?" I asked.

"Time will tell. If you were so concerned with his health, maybe you shouldn't have interrupted the transfer."

"I interrupted it because I was concerned for Laurent's health. The Empaetor's time was over."

"Sabotaging the entire empire," he spat. "You will be held accountable for this."

Jerrod snapped his fingers. "Concentrate on your job and leave her alone."

Giving me one last disgusted look, Doctor Meldorn went back to his terminal. "He seems stable, but he'll be out for another hour now. Hopefully that additional time will allow his brain to adjust to the new identity."

"Let's hope not," I muttered. "Can we move him to his room?"

Even Jerrod's face said I was nuts.

"Right, so he stays here under observation then." Unfortunate, since this room gave me the creeps, now knowing what went on here.

"How's your head?" I asked Jerrod.

"Pounding. How are you holding up?"

"I'll live."

We'd both suffered a few hard hits when taking the guards out to gain entrance to this place. Sitting quietly for an hour wasn't unwelcome, even if the location and company sucked. If anyone else had gathered outside the door, we didn't hear them.

There may have been a limited audience in the throne room, but enough people would have seen the unconscious Empaetor being taken away that word of his collapse had to have made its rounds by now. People would be wondering about his condition.

I gestured to the dead man. "What do we say happened to him?"

"The truth," said Doctor Meldorn. "The Empaetor suffered from a weakened heart due to his age. It gave out. Long live Iradio IX."

"That seems too easy," said Jerrod.

"That's why we have an heir. Empaetors don't live forever."

"One can hope," I said under my breath.

The hour passed with me pacing and watching the new Empaetor's sleeping face with trepidation. Jerrod popped half a painkiller and leaned against the wall. He offered me the other half. I shook my head, wanting to be fully alert.

The doctor made regular scans, alternating with staring at the readings on the vid. When the new Empaetor's eyelids flickered again, we all raced to his side.

He blinked up at me. "Rita? Why are you here?"

"I was worried about you."

"You shouldn't be in here. The Empaetor will be furious," he whispered, oblivious to Jerrod and the doctor on the other side of the table.

"You're the Empaetor now," I said.

He blinked several times, mouth gaping. "That can't be right. I…" He picked up his head to scan the room. His gaze locked onto his father. "That's me. My body." His head cocked at an unnatural angle. He blinked again, eyes not syncing their motions. "This body is mine. Now mine."

The new Empaetor scanned my face as if taking in every pore. "Rita Stabinov. Anduvean station security."

"Yes."

Meldorn wiggled his hand in an encouraging gesture.

"You were there, on the station. Do you remember?" I prompted.

"Ari Leeman. Stasis tube. Yes, I remember. We walked in a dark tunnel. You and me."

"On the station, yes. And we flew back to Harilax on the *Knaldon* so you could begin your memory transfer sessions with your father."

"My father." He nodded, eyes losing focus. He stared at

the lights overhead. "The Empaetor. Me. Iradio IX."

"Yes," confirmed the doctor. "Do you remember the identity confirmation code, sir?"

"A code. Code. There's a code," the Empaetor said in a singsong voice.

Dear Maker, had he lost his mind?

"Don't worry about that for now," I said. "Let's get you sitting up. Maybe that will help clear your head."

Jerrod helped me tug on the Empaetor's arms until he was seated on the table. He looked around, blinking and not seeming to focus.

"Rita?" He reached out with one hand.

I took it, hoping I was talking to Laurent and not the ancient man. "I'm right here."

His voice trembled. "My body isn't listening to me. I don't like this."

The doctor scowled. I took that as a promising sign.

I prayed that he might have a chance. "You need to take control of your body. Look at me."

Jerrod stepped in front of Meldorn before he could insert his annoyed self between us. The doctor tried to side-step Jerrod, but that only made the guard back him further away.

Laurent blinked again, his head slowly turning toward where our hands were joined. When his eyes met mine, they were focused. Finally.

"Laurent?"

"There is no Laurent. Only Iradio," he said firmly.

I dropped his hand and jumped back. "Get out of him!"

"I *am* him." The Empaetor slid off the table and stood. He took a few tentative steps and then grinned. "I forgot how good it feels to walk in a healthy body. Meldorn, you did it."

The doctor clapped his hands and grinned. "I'm glad to hear the transfer was successful, sir."

"Quite." He walked over to his old body. "What are we doing with this husk?"

"The staff knows you were in a health crisis. I'm thinking a coma for a couple of days before we let it go."

"Very well."

"The code, sir?"

He listed off a rapid-fire stream of what sounded like nonsense words, but when he finished, the doctor looked victorious.

"Well done, sir." Doctor Meldorn approached me confidently, holding out his hand. "I believe you have something of mine."

"Do I?"

He eyed the deathtoller pistol.

For a second I considered taking Iradio out once and for all, but Laurent might still be in there somewhere. Somewhere I might reach him given enough time.

"Rita," Jerrod urged, shaking his head subtly.

Fine. The whole reason I was here was to prevent the empire from falling into chaos. But I couldn't hand the pistol back to the man who likely just killed Laurent.

The Empaetor watched me and Meldorn with what appeared to be amusement. He must have been quite confident of Jerrod's allegiance.

As if proving my point, Jerrod slowly reached out and took the pistol from me. He set it on the table the Empaetor had vacated.

"Well then, we're all set here," the doctor announced.

"I'll be on my way to my suite then. Jerrod?"

"Yes, sir?" The second of hesitation as he glanced at me first confirmed our one-day alliance wasn't entirely an act.

"Let's be off."

If they were leaving and Iradio had control, that meant Laurent was gone. I had no desire to remain anywhere near this body inhabited by another man.

"Am I free to go then?" I asked.

Iradio looked me up and down, frowning. "What horrible taste. Of all the women in the empire, he named you as his consort? Ridiculous."

"I know. How about you call it off and I go on my way?"

"That won't do. You were here. Where you shouldn't have been." He waved his hand around the room. "That leaves you with three options."

My heart plummeted. If he had access to Laurent's memories, he knew that my parents were right here in the palace.

"You remain my consort and your parents remain alive as long as you keep your mouth shut about what you've seen here."

That would mean letting Iradio touch me. Hell no.

He held up two fingers. "You join my previous consort in a cell below the palace for the rest of your lives, and I kill your parents."

Definitely not an appealing option. I waited anxiously for what had to be a better choice. Something enticing that he knew I'd agree to given the other two options.

A third finger rose. "I kill you, Jerrod, and your parents now. Then I find a far better consort and don't worry about anyone saying anything about what they've seen today."

"I don't like any of those."

He shrugged. "The only one where Jerrod and your parents live is if you remain my consort. Knowing that if either of you says a word, I'll kill you both for conspiring something treasonous. Being Anduvean makes this all quite simple."

Jerrod silently begged me to opt for the first choice. Given the shitty alternatives, I couldn't disagree. At least we all got to live. Sort of.

I really should have just stayed on the Anduvean station. And I'd thought my life sucked there? I laughed to myself. It entire-empire-sized sucked now.

"Consort it is then," I muttered.

"You're sure?" He looked me up and down like something he'd found clogging his shower drain.

"You're not exactly a catch either, pal."

He smiled tightly. "I look forward to taming that mouth of yours."

My stomach heaved again, but I pressed my lips firmly together and begged any remaining contents to stay inside. He didn't need to know that I was actively drowning in dread. Though from the sympathetic look on Jerrod's face, I wasn't doing as good of a job at masking that as I'd hoped.

Iradio peeled his attention away from me. "Meldorn, please see to the husk. Your services will be well rewarded."

"Thank you, sir."

I couldn't believe Meldorn got to go about his day, that he got to remain free after he'd just wiped Laurent from his own body. That wasn't fair at all. My vision blurred as I started for the doctor.

Jerrod grabbed my arm, halting my progress. He whispered, "We'll find a better way, Rita. Accidents happen, remember?" He nodded toward Meldorn.

"Yeah." But I wanted them to happen right now, like the deathtoller pistol accidentally going off in his face.

"Another day." Jerrod gently tugged me toward the door. "Come on."

With little enthusiasm, Jerrod and I followed Empaetor Iradio IX out of the room and into the eager gazes of the amassed silent guards that awaited us.

Iradio commanded the room, just as he'd done in his elderly form. He gave a brief but moving—for those who didn't know he was waxing poetic about his conceited-ass-self—speech about his father falling deathly ill and how he'd taken on the mantle of Empaetor at his father's behest. He asked them to pray for the man—who'd now been dead for two hours—to make a recovery.

During all this, Jerrod and I avoided making eye contact because I didn't know about him, but there was no way I could keep my emotions off my face if anyone offered me even a hint of sympathy.

As it was, I was barely keeping myself together. Torn between sobbing uncontrollably and tackling Iradio to the floor, I kept my hands firmly pressed against my legs so they didn't get me into trouble.

When Iradio finished, he excused himself to go pray for his father and begin his briefing so he could take up the business of the empire in the coming days. He walked out into the wide corridor and turned back toward the throne room instead of heading for the stairs.

"Where are we going?" I asked.

Iradio regarded me as if I were an idiot. "My suite."

He wasn't wrong. I should have stayed on the fucking Anduvean station.

"Your suite is up the stairs."

"I'm the Empaetor now," he said in the same condescending tone.

"Moving right into your father's suite while he's still alive,"—I had to resist sarcasm—"would be rather disrespectful, don't you think?"

His steps faltered. "But all my things are there."

"And you can go back to them after a death is announced. For now, it would be better for your public image to go back to Laurent's suite."

Iradio didn't appear pleased, but he reluctantly nodded. "At least you've got a head on your shoulders. For now."

Fuck you, old man. I wanted to punch him so badly. Jerrod's subtle headshake helped convince me that the middle of the main corridor, in public view, was not the ideal place. Sadly, there was no ideal place. How was I supposed to live with him? Let alone let him touch me? I swallowed another surge of warning saliva. Would throwing up on him be in bad form?

The three of us marched up the two flights of stairs to Laurent's suite. He stood at the door controls, face twisted in concentration, one hand nearly touching the panel but not bridging that final inch gap.

I let him struggle for a couple of minutes, wondering if Laurent was protesting his father's invasion of his suite or if, more simply, the code sequence was so ingrained that it wasn't a strong enough memory for Iradio to easily pluck and use.

"Would you like me to get the door?" I eventually offered.

"Yes, be useful, would you?" He stepped aside.

When the door opened, he eyed the dim and dusty receiving room with disdain while I entered the code at the inner door. Within seconds of entering the suite, he turned with a sneer on his face. "This is how he lived? In this," he waved his hands around wildly, "mess?"

Everything seemed as tidy as usual. "What mess would that be?"

"This austere collection of castoff pieces. The man had adequate funds. Why wouldn't he spend them on beautiful things?"

I smiled at the memory of the fishbowl, even though it was now a pile of shattered glass. "He did. Just not here."

"Here is where he lived. That should have been his priority."

Jerrod hung back by the door while Iradio and I moved inward. The new Empaetor picked up Laurent's things, examining them with a scowl and putting them back, but never in the same place he picked them up. His blatant disregard of his son's belongings pissed me off. Somewhere in the back of my mind, I could hear Yumi, Senio, and even Laurent's voices telling me to calm down, that my mouth fueled by anger was going to get me in serious trouble. I clamped my lips together and tried not to watch Iradio.

"How comfortable is my bed? Did he at least get something worthy of an heir in his own bedroom?"

"I wouldn't know."

Iradio threw his head back and laughed. "He named you his consort just to needle me, not because of any feelings or connection to you. Oh, that's priceless."

For a moment, I couldn't breathe. Was he pulling that from Laurent's memories? Was he just being his asshole Empaetor self?

Jerrod was suddenly right next to me. "Rita, let's allow the Empaetor to settle in on his own for a bit, shall we?"

"What?" Had it really been a ruse all along? All my thoughts collided into a tangled jumble. If there was a way I could have ceased to exist just then, I would have leapt at it.

"This body is hungry," called Iradio from the bedroom. "Order me something to eat. Whatever these tastebuds prefer. Surely you at least know that."

"Yes, sir." Jerrod nudged me toward the dining area. Once we were out of earshot of the bedroom, he pointed to the chairs by the table. "Sit before you say something that will get you killed."

I nodded dumbly.

Jerrod took the seat across from me. He rested his elbows on the table and leaned inward. "He's full of shit, if you're doubting the heir."

"Iradio has all of Laurent's memories. He would know the truth."

He shook his head. "Iradio only has immediate access to strong memories. Remember what Meldorn said?"

"Wouldn't actually caring about someone be a strong memory?" I heard myself say, even though I meant to keep that thought to myself.

"If it were a memory the heir wanted to share, I would think so, yes. But consider what we've seen so far. He isn't fully stepping back. Let's give him a little time to see if he can break through this identity overlay before we give up hope, alright?"

"I thought being here, in his own suite, would help," I said quietly, another thought I wasn't sure I wanted to admit out loud.

"That was well done, by the way." Jerrod went to the order screen and pulled up the history. He pondered the past few meals Laurent and I had shared, and then made a selection.

"Nothing for me." The thought of eating with the invading old man made me shudder.

"You need to keep your strength up."

"I'll take that advice at the next meal, but leave me out of this one."

He nodded.

"I need some time to process all this. Are you good with taking a shift with him?"

"Yeah."

I stood.

"Rita?"

Why couldn't he just let me be? I pressed my lips together so tight I was afraid I might bite through them to trap the tirade begging to break free.

"The heir sent me after you, not because he was worried that you would say anything to the public, but because he cared about you. Don't let the old man get in your head."

I nodded, wanting to believe him, but the Empaetor's freshly uttered words were loud and at the forefront of my thoughts. Even worse, they matched the tone of the vile words Laurent had spewed at me.

I made my way to my bed with tears swimming in my eyes now that I was relatively alone. Facedown on my pillow despite my aching face, no one could see me cry.

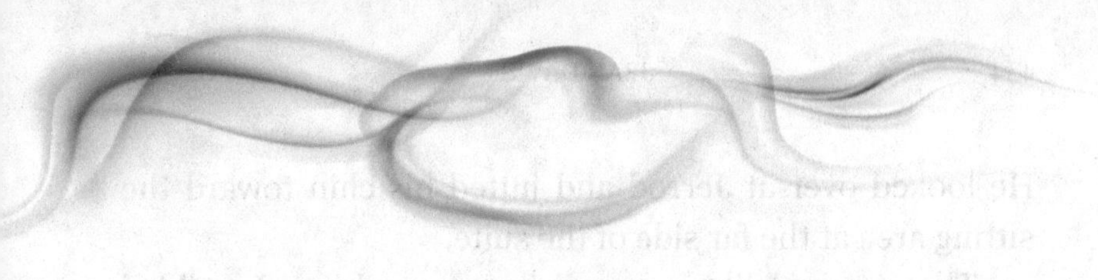

49

Sorry About Your Face

I woke with a hand covering my mouth. Another hand pressed down on my chest, holding me down. Wild thrashing took care of that in a matter of seconds. On my feet and with a gun in my hands, I focused on my assailant.

"Rita, stop. It's me."

Laurent's voice. No, my waking awareness reminded me, Iradio's voice now.

"Get the hell away from me."

He held up his empty hands. "It's Laurent. I swear."

"How do I know it's you?"

"Your mother's melon salad is salty. Why the hell is there salt in it?"

That definitely didn't seem like a strong memory unless Laurent had a major aversion to salt. I allowed a sliver of hope to take root.

"What color are the walls in my bedroom?"

His lips quirked. "Pink. Rita, why?"

"A cruel joke. My mother hoped that surrounding me with a feminine color would do some good."

He chuckled. It wasn't Iradio's condescending laugh.

He looked over at Jerrod and jutted his chin toward the sitting area at the far side of the suite.

That seemed like a promising proposition. I nodded and followed him. Droplets of rain ran down the thick, tinted plaz of the giant window.

Laurent spoke quietly. "He was sleeping. He might be in my body, but taking over is exhausting. For both of us. Help me stay in control."

"How?"

He shrugged helplessly.

"I interrupted the last minutes of the identity transfer. Maybe that weakened his hold?"

Laurent's gaze darted around the dimly lit suite. "I don't like him in here. Touching my things."

"Me either. I've wanted to punch him since he stole your body."

He smiled. "Thanks for not doing that. For both of our sakes."

That smile was his own, lighthearted and genuine. There was none of his father in it. All the vile things that had come from those lips were not him. They were Iradio, lifetimes of his personality flooding Laurent's brain. None of that was him.

Relief surged through me.

"Can you wall him off? Flush him out?" I pondered what little I knew of the process, what I'd seen over Meldorn's shoulder among all the readings. "It's like an advanced version of the memory overlays, right? They were the groundwork for this nightmare?"

Laurent scrutinized me as if I were the answer to the puzzle he was trying to solve. I hoped he didn't think too hard and accidentally wake Iradio in the process.

"Doctor Meldorn had to shove the last sessions into you all at once. Did that weaken the foundation in any way?"

Laurent settled into an armchair aimed at the window. "Everything feels jumbled. I know my own memories. They're clear as day. The others from the past sessions are mostly integrated, organized by Iradio and age. The newer ones—everyone's memory post-identity transfer—that's what's scrambled. There's so much. Eight lifetimes of one man on the throne."

"I'm guessing Iradio was in such a hurry to take hold of your body that he didn't bother sorting those out yet. They're his memories, so it would be easier for him."

My breath caught in my throat. "If those last sessions would have revealed the truth to you, does that mean you wouldn't have left that table until the transfer was complete? Would I have lost you in that room even if he hadn't had a heart attack?"

"I have a feeling you would have barged in and tried to save me just as you did today." A bemused smile broke out on Laurent's face. "Why, Rita, it almost sounds like you care about me."

"You're integral to maintaining peace in the empire, and you still owe my parents a house. Besides, I'd be doing a shitty job if I let you die. I'd never find another job in security," I said as lightly as I could past the lump in my throat.

The twinkle in his eyes called bullshit, but he let it go. I appreciated that he knew me well enough not to press for a more definite answer.

Rain beat down on the window overlooking the city, blurring the buildings below. The view was still breathtaking, even in the grey haze of rainfall.

A haze. Was that the answer?

"Would it weaken him if you not only didn't sort those memories, but ignored them for as long as you're able, like to the point where you could forget them?"

"Like with a memory balm?" Laurent's eyes grew wide. "Pitari. Is she still on Harilax?"

"She's hiding on the *Knaldon* until you can send her safely home."

Guilt shadowed his face. "She did so much to get us here. I've neglected not only to thank her but to even consider that she'd have to remain hidden from my father while we were happily going about our lives here." He gestured to the suite.

"I don't know what drugs you're on, but there hasn't been any happily going about anything since we arrived." I shook my head. "She understands. I've talked to her."

"Thank you, Rita." He started to stand but then sat back down. "With my father gone, mostly," he chuckled weakly, "do you think it's safe to ask her to come to the palace to try a balm?"

It was a risk. "Do you have control? Can you hold on to your body?"

The uncertainty that flooded over him made me want to hug him, but we both needed Iradio gone before I was willing to entertain close contact.

"I'll try. Having you close helps. Can you ask her? Let her decide."

I hurried over to the terminal. The connection to the *Knaldon* was nearly instantaneous. Not wanting to put pressure on her with a vid call, I typed up a quick message to the Seeker, outlining our request, the risk, and the urgency. I left it open for her to decide, letting her know an escort would be waiting at the palace entrance if she chose to come.

Then I contacted the first security checkpoint, clearing Pitari for entry and through the checkpoints up to Laurent's suite. I prayed the Seeker trusted me enough to come.

She wasn't even part of our empire. She was a guest. In hiding. Who had been treated like shit by Andover for however long they'd been together. I begged for her cooperation as loudly in my thoughts as I could, even knowing she couldn't hear me.

Last on my list was waking Jerrod.

He groaned as he rolled onto his side.

"Sorry to make you move."

"Sorry about your face." He waved toward my head.

"What?" A sudden wave of paranoia took hold, paralyzing me.

"The Empaetor, after you were asleep, demanded Doctor Meldorn come up here and fix you up. Said he couldn't have his consort looking like a pit fighter."

I ran my hands over my face tentatively, but the swelling in my nose and the scabs on my cheek were gone. Nothing specifically hurt. I'd been too distracted with Laurent to notice.

"There's still a little lingering discoloration, but even the Empaetor's prized doctor can't work miracles. He swore the rest would fade in a day or two. He had to sedate you for the treatment."

So that's why I'd slept longer than I'd expected. As far as unpleasant things Iradio could have done to me in my sleep, this was at the bottom of the list. In fact, I could have even found it within myself to thank him for it if pressed to. Other than the lack of consent and the fact that creepy fuck Meldorn had touched me.

"I thought you were supposed to be on my side, not letting people perform medical procedures on me while I'm unaware."

Jerrod winced. "It was the Empaetor, and honestly, it was kind of a favor in the grand scheme of things. The fixing, not the sedating you in your sleep part. He restitched the wound on your side too. Thanks to the painkillers, I was also kind of out of it," he admitted.

"Never again?" I glared at him until he nodded. "Good. Now get up. I need you to escort a friend up here. I don't want to leave Laurent alone."

Jerrod's brows shot up.

I explained how he was in control for now but that I didn't know for how long. He dressed quickly, darted in and out of the bathroom, and was out the door in less than ten minutes. I could have told him he had an hour before Pitari would arrive—if she chose to arrive—but I was ticked about the whole sleep procedure. He could stand around for a while.

An hour and a half later, a cranky Jerrod stood at the door to Laurent's suite with the Seeker at his side. She barely stood halfway up his chest, making him look like a giant.

"Open the damned door, Rita." He grumbled into the camera.

I added getting Jerrod an entry code to my to-do list and let him and Pitari in. He gave me a questioning glance.

I nodded toward his bed, and he gratefully returned to it.

Pitari entered with awe clearly written on her face, taking in the vast windows that comprised two walls of the suite. Her gaze finally landed on me.

"Thank you for coming." I conveyed my gratitude with more thoughts than my few words.

She gazed at Laurent for a moment and then back at me. "I agree with your assessment of the benefits versus risk."

"The balm for Andover that you did, that encapsulated memories, right?"

She nodded slowly. "Sort of, yes."

I briefly explained the identity transfer process and the memory overlays as I understood them. "We need Iradio gone, or at the very least, walled off from taking over Laurent's body again."

Her mouth dropped open. "What an invasion of privacy! Did you consent to this?" she asked Laurent.

"The overlays, yes, but I didn't realize that they were the groundwork for the identity imprint. I thought it was just a memory database to provide knowledge of those who came before me. Not that I'd be hijacked by Iradio I himself."

Pitari gasped. "It's such a violation of everything we believe in. I can't imagine."

"Exactly," I muttered.

She stared at him intently, her face growing paler and more strained by the second. "He's there, just below the surface. I can almost hear him. What kind of twisted science is this?"

"One that should never be used again," Laurent said.

I nodded.

Pitari tore her gaze from Laurent and rubbed her hands over her face and then her bare, tattooed head several times in what looked like some sort of cleansing ritual. When she finished, she said, "Balming Iradio would be the equivalent of killing him."

Laurent scoffed. "He's already dead. Eight times over. He's an abomination."

"I see your point." But despite all her seeing, Pitari still looked uncomfortable. "There are limits to violating the rules of my training. My mentor encouraged expanding our knowledge and being flexible, but let me consider if there is a less abhorrent solution."

This wasn't the time for deep meditation. "Consider quickly. Laurent is on stolen time in his own body."

Pitari nodded and stepped away to find a quiet spot. She stood nearby looking outward but with her eyes closed and her hands clasped before her at her waist.

"I feel we're asking too much of her," Laurent said. "This isn't her problem. Andover was taking advantage of her, and then we upped his game. Does that make us worse than him?"

I glanced at the Seeker, wondering if she was listening to us or deep in her own thoughts. "We've never forced her. She helped of her own accord. You asked if she wanted to return home before we left Anduvea, but she came with us. You've given her choices. She's been the one to make them."

He uttered an agreeable sounding grunt.

We both looked at Pitari, but she wasn't ready with an answer yet. It felt like a timer was counting down over our heads, but neither of us could see how much time was left on it.

While I had Laurent in his body, I grabbed his arm. "Go to the terminal now and issue the order to release your mother. Maybe to medical, but not to Meldorn. Assign her to someone you trust. Laurent, she wasn't crazy. She was legitimately trying to save you from this."

His eyes went wide. He sprinted to the terminal and pounded out the commands with thunderous fingers. When he finished, he walked back to his seat with hunched shoulders. "I can't believe she was right. It seemed so..."

"Insane?" I nodded. "I appreciate her good intentions," I rubbed my healed cheek, "but her execution leaves a lot to be desired."

Laurent sat silently for several minutes, staring at his hands in his lap. He finally turned back to me. "Are your parents safe?"

"Iradio has been too busy with you to do anything more than hold their lives over my head and threaten to kill me and Jerrod. He's made a lot of threats."

"He enjoys them. Makes him feel powerful."

"Have I mentioned that I hate him? Is that a deal-breaker in this consort thing?"

He smiled. "Does that mean you're considering it?"

"That means I still think you're an idiot who makes terrible choices."

"I respectfully disagree." He leaned closer and tentatively raised one hand toward my newly healed cheek.

Pitari cleared her throat. I nearly jumped out of my skin.

"Sorry, you seemed caught up in something there." She winked. "I wouldn't have interrupted, but I think I have a better solution."

Laurent settled for standing directly next to me so that

our arms rubbed together. It was too damned close if Iradio took over, but this was Laurent, and he looked so hopeful. I didn't have it in me to crush that. I remained beside him.

"Oh?" he said.

"The doctor... Meldorn?"

I nodded.

"He knows this process, the identity part of it, as well as the rest. What if I take control of him like I did with Andover and have him siphon Iradio out?"

"I have no issue with this plan, but wouldn't that have the same result as the one you didn't like—effectively killing Iradio?"

The Seeker's gaze dropped to the floor. "I won't be the one doing it."

But she was, in a roundabout way. I was about to point that out when I noticed Laurent's subtle head shake. Right, not the time to argue logic with the Seeker.

"I do like the idea of removing Iradio. Then I wouldn't have to worry about him possibly taking over every time I let my guard down," Laurent said.

"Agreed. When do we make this happen?" I asked.

Laurent rubbed his temples. "As soon as possible. There's not enough room in here for both of us."

I rested my hand on his shoulder before I realized what I was doing. Once it was there, it felt more awkward to pull away rather than to roll with it. "Can you feel him? Is he awake?"

"Yes," Laurent said through clenched teeth.

"Is he aware of our plan?" Pitari shuddered. "I don't want to touch your mind any more than I have to. It was like he could feel me in there."

"I don't know." Laurent rested his hand atop mine, still on his shoulder. "I couldn't hear when he had control of my body. It was like being deep underwater, only dimly aware of anything going on around me. It was exhausting to fight for more sensory control."

"That's good," said Pitari. "We should return to the room where this process took place. Quickly."

Reluctantly pulling my hand away, I said, "Summon Doctor Meldorn to his lab so we can get this done."

Laurent sat at the terminal, rubbing his temples.

I went to his side. "How are you doing?"

He reached for my hand and held it tightly. "I need you. The outside physical connection makes it easier to maintain control of my body."

Considering my possible limited time with Laurent, I took what affection I could get. "Just keep this out of the call. It will give you away."

Laurent leaned closer to the vid while initiating the call to Meldorn. His face filled the view when the doctor answered. He did such a convincing job conveying his need for Meldorn to get his ass to his lab immediately, that I was scared that I was holding hands with Iradio. I froze, wanting to pull away, but knowing I'd mess up the call if I did.

"I'll be right there, sir. We'll subdue him more fully so you can enjoy the use of your new body."

"You better. I'll not stand for a minute longer of this struggle for a body I've spent thirty-eight years paying for."

My heart thudded heavily. He sounded just like Iradio. What if he was? What if Laurent had slipped below the surface and there was nothing I could do? Panic rushed over me.

Laurent squeezed my hand. Or was it Iradio holding me tighter?

"Of course, sir. I'll meet you there right away." Meldorn ended the vid call.

The pressure eased. "Hey, Rita. It's me."

I nodded, doing my best to tuck my panic back under wraps, but everything Iradio had said, all I knew he'd done—it swirled inside my head, making me nauseous. Having almost lost Laurent once, I desperately didn't want to go through that again.

He stood but kept his fingers entwined with mine. "I can feel him. We need to move fast."

Pitari shooed us toward the door. Jerrod popped up from his bed, and seeing us fleeing with all due haste, rushed over to join us. I figured one more body couldn't hurt.

My mind spun as the four of us hurried down the stairs. "If Iradio had died while you were in hiding on Anduvea, do you think that Meldorn would have sedated you upon your return to implant him in your head anyway? Could he have saved the identity data outside of Iradio himself?"

"That's a terrifying thought." Laurent looked at me as though I was the monster.

"What I'm saying is, if we can remove him from your head, should we destroy Meldorn's lab so that Iradio remains dead now and forevermore?"

Both Laurent and Pitari nodded emphatically.

"Alright then, we'll do that after we stomp the body-snatching asshole out of your brain."

"Leave the destroying to me, Rita," said Jerrod from the rear. "You focus on the stomping."

"Deal."

The four of us rushed single file down the stairs. We gained a few concerned looks from those in the main corridor, mostly staff. I gathered they knew to keep their mouths shut when it came to the Empaetor's whims and temper.

As the Empaetor's consort, though not officially announced, holding his hand in public wasn't too odd. He did, however, reluctantly let go when we entered Meldorn's lab.

The doctor already had the lights on and was at his terminal. "Let me just get the heir's brain pattern brought up so we can dial him back. That should subdue him enough to allow you full control while still maintaining his recent memories. Normally, I could have pulled him entirely and simply done an overlay to supply you the necessary integration memories. Unfortunately, his months of absence from the palace disrupted our regular physical schedule. Our most recent memory log was outdated."

Recent logs? How often did this creep siphon memories from Laurent, and did he know about this?

The few seconds of shock and sudden pallor on Laurent's face told me that no, he did not realize this had been going on. I silently thanked Ari for getting Laurent away. Even though we'd come back too soon, the heir's absence had still screwed with Iradio's scheme.

I turned to check on Jerrod, who was locking the door behind us, to verify that it would be safe to give Pitari the signal to slip into Meldorn's thoughts when Laurent's tone of voice took a sudden shift.

"What's going on here? Meldorn?" Iradio caught me in a disdain-filled once-over and then jumped his gaze to Pitari.

"You? What is Andover's pet doing in here?"

No, this couldn't be. Not now. Not when we were so close.

I couldn't punch that face. I couldn't leave with my parent's lives at stake. And as much as I tried, I couldn't will Laurent back to the forefront of his own mind. I hated Iradio so much, but there wasn't a damned thing I could do about it.

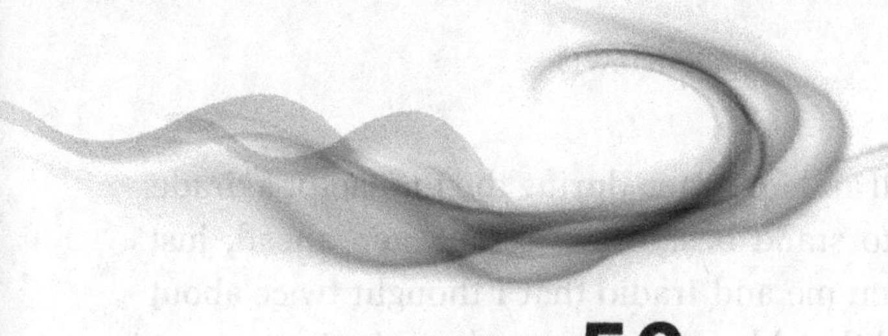

50

Crush Him

Meldorn chewed his lower lip, looking worried for his own wellbeing. "Sir?"

"Why am I here?" Iradio demanded, slamming his fist on the table he'd left yesterday.

"You said the heir was struggling to take his body back, that you wanted him further subdued."

"That ungrateful fuck. I gave him thirty-eight years of wealth and leisure, and this is how he repays me?"

The near-mirrored wording from what Laurent had used scared the hell out of me. Had Iradio been that close to the surface when Laurent had been on the vid call? Or did the two of them think that much alike?

"If you could please sit here, sir. I'll get you hooked up and dial him down."

Iradio glared at me. "You were part of this, weren't you? I'll see that your parents pay for your betrayal."

Not if we could get Laurent back in control of his body. But could we do that now that Iradio was again at the helm? I sent Pitari a silent plea.

She stepped behind Meldorn, against the wall, in the

shadows, small and forgotten during the Empaetor's tirade. Jerrod came to stand beside me, a half step ahead, just enough between me and Iradio that I thought twice about leaping toward the old man and strangling him into unconsciousness so we could maybe get Laurent back.

Focused on his task, Meldorn picked up one of the wire webs from his desk and began applying it to Iradio's head. "The preparations won't take long. I'll just need to run a few brief test rounds to verify the heir's brain activity so I can accurately separate it from your own."

"Skip it. Just crush him."

"Sir, that's not recommended. The procedure is too fresh. Your personalities are difficult to separate at this stage."

"Are you saying you're too inept to manage this procedure you've spent years researching and training for?"

Meldorn swallowed hard. "No, sir, but if I don't do the base tests, I could accidentally erase parts of you instead of him. Your patterns are too similar, as all of your line has been. That's what makes you such an excellent subject for this procedure." He fussed with the wires. "Other people, when overlayed with someone else, do not have the nearly seamless integration that you do. Keeping this all in your direct genetic line has helped your success rate tremendously. Though I'm sure other doctors before me have explained this to you."

"Yes, you all proudly prattle on about the science. Just get on with it."

"Of course, sir." Finally satisfied with the wire net, he returned to the terminal. "I will now ask you a series of questions. Please answer with the first thing that comes to your mind. Don't ponder your responses."

Meldorn did indeed prattle on for ten minutes, asking questions and logging Iradio's responses. Through it all, I wondered if Laurent would have answered differently. Was he staying in the background, not fighting this, so we could make sure we pulled the right person from his head?

The lives of my parents rested on Laurent staying hidden until we were ready.

"I want him gone, Meldorn. Scrubbed. I have her to fill me in on anything vital during the heir's absence." Iradio loosely gestured at me.

"Sir, I don't recommend a complete removal."

"I feel him pounding at the walls as we speak. I can't stand at the helm of the empire with all this internal racket going on. Delete him."

I thought as loudly as I could at Pitari, screaming for her to do something. She was too far into the shadows for me to see if she caught my silent plea. Jerrod slid directly in front of me, blocking my view of the Empaetor.

"As you wish, sir." Meldorn scowled but tapped away at his terminal.

Movement behind the doctor caught my attention. Pitari stood beside Meldorn, her face twisted in concentration. She'd never appeared this strained when holding Andover's mind during our travel to Harilax. There had been headaches and she'd been tired, but nothing had visually given her away. This was different. I didn't like it.

Was Pitari's hold on Meldorn working, or was Laurent being scrubbed before our eyes? My fingers itched to rip the damned wire net off Laurent's head again. But I couldn't see what was going on inside. The battle was taking place before me, and there was nothing I could do.

My mother's voice told me I should pray. I couldn't even remember the words to invoke a prayer at the moment. My thoughts were running emergency simulations and discarding or altering them for better results. If Laurent was gone, I'd have Jerrod to help me rescue my parents. I'd have Pitari to help me sway the *Knaldon* crew to get us away from Harilax. Then we'd go where? Somewhere outside the empire on a ship the Empaetor could likely trace? My brain scrambled for a list of outside worlds that I had enough information on from traders. Were there colonies of prosperous people beyond the empire? Were those colonies from the wild stories about cannibals and drug havens, criminals and fugitives my future home? What would I be able to trade for food and supplies?

All these things flew through my mind in seconds before my hand met warm flesh. I realized I'd side-stepped Jerrod and had gone to Laurent's side to take his hand. A hand that was limp. My vision swam. I fought to focus on his face, to find any hint of who was in control or of the battle raging inside.

His face remained vacant, eyes staring off at the wall toward the exit. There may have been someone yelling, or the room may have been silent. All I could hear was the pounding of my pulse in my ears.

Fingertips twitched in my grasp. I blinked away the blur in my eyes to scrutinize his face. Lips in a grimace, eyes pressed shut, jaw tight. None of that told me whose hand I was holding.

I glanced at the terminal. Meldorn lay still, crumpled on the floor. Pitari sat slumped in the chair, her head tilted back like after she'd done the memory balm on Andover.

Whether she was staring at the ceiling or also unconscious, I couldn't tell.

"What happened?" I whispered.

"I don't know," Jerrod whispered back.

The only thing bolstering my nerves at that moment was that Iradio was used to being an old man. He might not have a full connection to Laurent's more agile motor skills yet, and there were two of us built for combat. If all was lost, we could overpower him and end Iradio's rule in a more permanent manner. Maybe we could restrain him and get Pitari to puppet him through naming an alternate heir with a few impartial witnesses on hand. At least then we could avoid a mad scramble for the empire. Maybe.

"Rita?" Warm fingers squeezed mine. "Are you with me?"

"Laurent?"

"I think so, yeah." He pressed on his temples with his other hand. "This hurts. All of it."

Pitari's chair creaked, making me jump. She slid off and onto her feet, closing the gap between us in slow motion. "One of them was purged. I did my best to direct Meldorn, but he was very stubborn and very devoted to Iradio."

She yawned, blinking blearily. When she stopped beside us, she pondered Laurent and then smiled. "I got it right."

I exhaled, feeling tension flood out of my lungs. "Thank the Maker. You're a miracle worker, Pitari."

"Just a very exhausted Seeker, but I'm glad I could help. This," she waved her hand at the room, "is what I was sent on this program for. To learn from others and experience challenges outside our star system so I can better prepare the next generation of Seekers for their time in the known universe."

"Your efforts will be rewarded," Laurent vowed.

"I'll settle for two days of uninterrupted sleep."

"You're welcome to stay here at the palace. I'll have a room prepared for you."

Pitari nodded. "That would be appreciated."

I gave him my datapad so he could tap out the appropriate commands.

"Someone will be outside in a moment to guide you," Laurent said.

I pointed to the door. "Go rest before you keel over. Do you need me to carry you?"

"You have your hands full here. I'll manage." Seeker Pitari offered a small bow and headed to the door.

I studied the face before me. Soft lines, even in pain, the crinkles around his eyes. None of it was sharp or hard. If Pitari said this was really Laurent, I trusted her.

The old man was really gone.

"I think we all need some rest," Laurent declared. "Except Meldorn. He can rest in a cell. Jerrod, can you see to that, please?"

"Gladly." Yet, he looked to me before carrying out the Empaetor's order. "Are you good here, Rita?"

"Yes, thank you. Your destruction part of our deal will need to wait until we can better evaluate the contents of the terminal and anything else Meldorn may have hidden away. Seal the room for now."

Laurent squeezed my hand and chuckled. "Which one of us is the Empaetor?"

"I sort of emergency drafted Jerrod as my personal guard while we were maintaining the ruse that I was going to be your consort."

"Ah."

Jerrod hoisted unconscious Meldorn onto his shoulder with a grunt and followed Pitari out.

Laurent cautiously felt his way to the edge of the table and tested his footing on the floor. Wavering there for a moment, he maintained his grip on my hand. "You realize that it's not a ruse, right?"

"You've had a rough day. Several of them. We all have. How about we table this for now and do that resting thing you suggested?"

"Only if you'll walk me back to our suite."

"Your suite."

He grinned. "I said what I meant."

While I enjoyed his playfulness, the tremor in his grip couldn't be ignored. He was exhausted.

We made it out of the lab and a short way down the main corridor before a crowd accumulated around us. They clamored for news about the previous Empaetor. It occurred to me that everyone else in the empire was under the impression that the old man was in a coma.

"Iradio is dead," he whispered in my ear before stopping to address the gathered people. My efforts to subtly urge him along instead were just as subtly thwarted. I gave up and let him do his Empaetor duty.

"My father served the empire well, but his time has passed, as has his spirit from this realm. He rests with the Maker now. Today we will mourn. Tomorrow we will celebrate the beginning of a new empire."

He took a moment to wave and nod to those in attendance before finally following my lead and making for the stairs.

"If you're standing by the story that Iradio is gone, shouldn't you move to the Empaetor's suite?" I asked when we were out of earshot of the others.

"Hell no. I have no desire to ever set foot in that suite. This is our home and it will remain so."

I did like the sound of that. Specifically, the 'hell no' part, but also that no matter what my role here, I'd remain in Laurent's space, a space I understood and felt comfortable in.

"Do you approve of remaining here?" he asked as he opened the door to the suite.

"Yes, not that it matters what I think."

He gave me a skeptical side-eye. "My consort will live with me, not at that damned estate. So I ask again, do you approve of remaining here?"

"As your personal guard, I approve. As for the other, we're tabling that, remember?"

He went inside, making an annoyed sound. I followed but gave him space. My efforts at space were foiled when I saw him waiting at the foot of my bed.

"Please see that your parents attend the accession dinner tomorrow as my guests."

"I will. They'll love that." Far more than I would, surely.

What the hell was I doing here? Laurent was safe. Iradio was gone for good. Jerrod said I was doing well here, that people liked me, but was that just one man trying to be nice? And now I was going to be in front of more than just a handful of guards at this momentous ceremonial dinner. Surely everyone in attendance would be of the same ilk as the prospective consort pool. They'd all give me the same contemptuous look Iradio had.

Maybe I could stand behind Laurent in the shadows as his guard. Or he could enlist any of Iradio's personal guards now that they were at loose ends. Could I get out of this?

His raised eyebrow said he knew exactly what I was thinking. "You'll be attending with me," he said firmly.

Dammit. "I've never attended a royal function. What will be required of me?"

"Be yourself, Rita. And the only tabling we'll be doing tomorrow will involve eating."

"Can I at least sleep on this mad proposal of yours?"

"Most certainly. Whether you wish to solely remain my personal guard or be my consort, there will be a place here for you and your parents. Anduvea will be pardoned. Your station will receive upgrades. None of that will rest on your decision. Am I clear?"

"Quite." My brain said he was still being stupid, but in that moment my heart was quite full. "I'll give you my answer tomorrow."

Laurent nodded, plainly disappointed over not having one immediately, but he let me be. Now, knowing my people were taken care of, I had to decide what my future looked like. I went into the bathroom and took a long look at the woman in the mirror.

51

Same Assholes.
Different Station.

After a long night of thinking and a couple hours of sleep, I'd finally worked up the gumption to talk to Laurent. Except I couldn't find him. For a moment, I panicked, but then I noticed Jerrod was there, as well as another woman in a guard uniform.

"He went to oversee plans for the accession dinner and the interment of the former Empaetor's remains," Jerrod informed me.

"Shouldn't there be some sort of ceremony for that too?" He was the Empaetor, after all. Wouldn't Iradio want a full spectacle over his death?

Jerrod shrugged. "Not usually. The Empaetor lives a life of service to his people. In the past, we've always focused on the new Empaetor and let the old one fade away."

That made perfect sense now that I considered it. Iradio would have wanted all the attention on himself, not on the body he was finished with.

Resolved to wait for Laurent, I went to the bathroom to take a long, hot shower and find a fresh uniform for the damned ceremonial dinner. I'd gotten as far as stripping down to my underclothes and washing my face when the new female guard came in.

She hung just inside the door, shuffling her feet.

"What?" I finally asked.

"Can I ask you something?"

"Only if I get your name first. I'm assuming you've been recruited to round out our personal guard team?"

"Mende. Juana Mende," she said with a friendly smile. "Yes, Jerrod asked me to join. If that's alright with you? He said it was up to you. Do you have a title I'm supposed to use? Are you the next consort?"

Juana was a solid woman like me, not too pretty, not exactly plain. Solidly average. Her nose was nice and straight, like it had never been broken. The thin white scar on her light brown cheekbone lent a little interest to her otherwise generally pleasing face. Other than her apparent nervousness in my presence, which I was used to from every trainee I'd ever worked with on the station, I couldn't find anything immediately objectionable. I trusted Jerrod to know the palace staff far more than I did.

"If Jerrod says you're in, you're in."

She grinned, clapping her hands together and then catching herself. "Sorry. I've always dreamed of having this job."

"Me too," I admitted. "Though I'm guessing you were far more on the right path for it than I was."

Juana chuckled. "Never doubt the Maker's plans." She grabbed a cloth from the stack and set about washing her face at one of the other sinks.

Plans... I had those—dinner, and the loaded conversation with Laurent. I sighed. The one consolation to all this was that I would be part of a team of competent guards. No more bottom of the barrel trainees. Just like on the station, the elite would whisper and cast their snide looks at me, but they couldn't stop me from doing my job. A job that allowed me more freedom and benefits than they had.

Same assholes. Different station.

Juana wrung her cloth out and then idly twisted it in her hands, looking me over, in all my underclothes glory, with open curiosity. "So...are you the consort?"

I couldn't very well give her my answer before Laurent. "Nothing has been made official yet. Just call me Rita."

Juana nodded. She traded her well-wrung cloth for a brush, smoothing her short black hair back from her face with determined strokes. She smiled nervously into the mirror at me. "I couldn't tell you what the last consort's name was even though I've been on duty near her several times over the years. My sister is going to be so jealous."

"Why?" And then it occurred to me what she was implying, and again, I couldn't correct her. I should have just declined when he'd asked instead of putting my answer off until today.

I attempted to cover my stupidity by asking what her sister did for a living. Twenty minutes of conversation unfurled from Juana's excited lips. Not wanting to miss the opportunity for a shower, I excused myself and stepped under the water in blessed silence.

Washing quickly, I enjoyed the last few seconds of steam and hot water beating down on my neck. When it didn't turn off at the usual allotment, I was momentarily confused. Right, no allotments here, just endless water looping through the palace filtration system. Feeling reckless, I lingered for another ten minutes, removing my braids and testing out an assortment of available hair products before finally drying off.

Juana had left the bathroom, so I took the time to sniff the various lotions and picked one. Once my skin was blissfully moisturized, I slipped into a clean uniform.

I was mid-toweling my hair when Laurent ducked in.

His gaze seemed fixated on my hair, making me self-conscious of having it down and loose in his presence. I gave him an expectant stare in the mirror.

The new Empaetor didn't look away but finally said, "Doctor Meldorn's lab has been sealed. I'll have to carefully consider who I can trust to examine everything there and deliver an unbiased report."

I picked up a brush and pulled it through a section of hair, expecting my usual tangled mess. To my amazement, the magical combination of indulgent products had left it soft, shining, and tangle-free. Brushing for the pleasure of it had never been a luxury I'd enjoyed, but I sure was now.

Even if the Empaetor was watching with that soft smile I liked on his lips. Not that I was looking at his lips.

"I can go over the lab tomorrow. Assuming you can spare me for a few hours. I'm sure Jerrod can recommend someone otherwise. You'll probably have your hands full with simpering, well-wishing representatives from around the empire."

Laurent chuckled, a cheerful sound Iradio would never have made. A sound that made me warm all over.

"No one else can sum up my reality quite as boldly as you."

"I'm sure they can. They're just smart enough not to."

He outright laughed. "That sounds exactly like something Ari would have said. I'm sorry you never got to work together." He sobered. "And also, I'm not sorry."

"Why's that?" I set the brush down and started braiding. He watched my fingers with rapt attention.

"We'd be fighting over you."

Now I was the one laughing. "Never in my life has that been said." I gestured to the bathroom. "Thank you for this. This was the best start to a day I've had in a long time. Speaking of, what's on the agenda other than this dinner where I'll be enjoying a comfortable wall and as many shadows as possible?"

"Is that what you'd prefer? Not a seat next to me?"

That question sounded very loaded. Despite my resolve to remain here solely in the capacity of his guard, my tongue and my heart went to war. Neither one produced an answer in a timely manner.

He pondered my reflection in the mirror as my fingers worked. "The wall it is for now."

"Thank you," my tongue managed to eke out.

His pale blue eyes locked onto mine in the mirror, giving me chills in the best sort of way. I was mortified to watch my cheeks flush.

"As long as you'll be behind me?" he asked in that low soft tone that didn't help matters in the least.

"Of course."

"Good. I want my legacy to be a peaceful, flourishing empire. It's going to take a lot of work to fix everything Iradio did over eight lifetimes, but I think, as long as you're with me, keeping me safe and offering your bold truths, we can make a solid start of it."

"I'd like to see that." And behind or beside Laurent, I'd have a front row seat. No more reading glossed-over summary headlines out at the edge of the empire.

"Me too." He seemed lost in thought for a minute. Whatever thoughts they were must have been good because he was grinning. "I have more preparations to oversee. We'll meet here later so we can enter the dinner together."

As his guard, I repeated to myself, searching for the resolve I'd had earlier. Not trusting my voice, which was feeling decidedly breathy at the moment, I nodded.

Laurent lingered for a minute, but he didn't push for more.

By the time I finished my hair, he had left with Juana to oversee his preparations. I used the terminal to find where my parents were being housed and left Jerrod to sleep.

My step started as a springy jaunt until I was halfway there and the giddiness of Laurent's attention had worn off. The covert whispering from nearly everyone I passed helped to ground me. By the time I arrived at the door to the guest room my parents had been given, cold logic had settled back in. Don't be stupid, Rita. You're a mature woman, not a love-sick teen.

"Come in," my father gestured me inside, grinning widely. "Look at this place. It's bigger than our entire house on Anduvea."

And fancy. Opulent even. On par with the design and furnishings in the consort's estate.

"The view!" My mother exclaimed. "I'll never get sick of this. It's amazing. The sky is so clear. You can see everything from up here."

Their suite was two floors above Laurent's, and the windows were very clear. A little voice in the back of my head said that if I took the role of consort, they could stay here. They *could* enjoy this view for the rest of their days.

We settled into the seating area overlooking the city below. No worn, crunchy couch. Every piece of furniture appeared immaculate, and if it was all as comfortable as the chair I now sat in, my parents would never want to leave.

"You're being taken care of? They've fed you?"

My father laughed, patting his stomach. "Rita dear, I've never eaten so much amazing food in my entire life. Tino's meals were good, but this, this might be from the Maker's own table."

I hadn't been so enamored with the cuisine Laurent had ordered thus far, but I'd also been injured, exhausted, and occupied with all of Iradio's shit. Maybe I'd get a chance to actually enjoy a meal after my shift at this dinner. There were sure to be leftovers.

"Laurent invited you to his fancy schmancy accession dinner. Were you made aware of that?" I asked them.

"Oh yes," my mother gushed. "He invited us personally. The Empaetor, Rita. He invited us *personally*."

Yes, Mom, I sleep in the same suite as the Empaetor, almost made it out of my mouth. Maybe Laurent's talk of restraint was sinking in.

If he was making rounds to proffer personal invitations, he was already making strides to set himself apart from Iradio. A smile escaped my hold on neutral logic.

"The start of a new Empaetor's reign. Exciting times," I said. "Who would have thought we'd be here to witness it?"

My mother leaned forward to squeeze my arm. "All

because of you, dear. He owes you so much."

"The entire empire does," my father added. "Who would have thought our Rita would be so important?"

"I don't know about all that." I shifted uncomfortably in the very comfortable chair.

"The Empaetor is such a wonderful young man," my mother said, grinning from ear to ear.

I wondered how Laurent would take being called a young man. Compared to my parents, sure, but neither of us were exactly young. He'd probably smile and nod and not think twice about it. He was good at that, not picking apart everything like I seemed to do.

Not that he was oblivious to what was said as much as what wasn't. He'd picked up on my nonanswer smoothly enough. An answer he would want from me tonight if not before.

"Wonderful, huh? I seem to recall you sending me a message about him causing havoc when he stayed with you on Anduvea."

My father shook his head. "Having the heir to the empire as a houseguest was unnerving. Not only did we not know how to deal with him, he holed up in your room and barely came out."

I pictured Laurent sitting on the very pink bedcover in my very pink room and stifled a laugh.

My mother tsked. "We thought he was being inordinately difficult, but after seeing him with you, I think he was scared to be on an unfamiliar world, with us, without a guard. Without you."

Not that I thought she was wrong, but I couldn't help but raise an eyebrow. "This heartwarming revelation from the same woman who told me not to get attached to Laurent because he was going to toss me aside as soon as he no longer needed me?"

It was my father's turn for a disapproving cluck.

I returned it, remembering how miserable their comments had made me.

My mother patted his leg and cleared her throat. "You'll be at the dinner, dear?" asked my mother.

"Yes, I'll be on duty."

My parents exchanged a look that immediately sent my stomach into a knot.

"What?"

"Nothing. We're looking forward to it," my mother said sweetly before launching into a conversation about the colors the designer had chosen for their suite, furniture styles, and what her Anduvean friends had said when she'd done a vid call earlier.

It was nearly three hours later when I escaped to return to Laurent's suite to check in with Jerrod. With Juana still on duty, it turned out we had some downtime before the big event.

Jerrod and I sat sharing a plate of crusty bread slices and an assortment of cheeses I'd never heard of.

"Anything in particular I need to be aware of tonight so I don't inadvertently piss someone off?"

He stuffed a thick slice of pungent cheese into his mouth. "Just stick close to the Empaetor. You'll be fine."

"The whispers, Jerrod. What can I do to make them stop?"

He chewed and chewed. "Nothing that I can think of. You're a novelty, new. They'll whisper until they find something else to whisper about. Ignore them."

"Easy to say for the one not being whispered about."

He raised a slice of bread coated with a thin layer of creamy yellow cheese to me and grinned. "You kind of stand out. But they'll move on eventually."

"Stand out how? That's what I'm asking you, dammit. How do I better blend in?"

"Why would you want to?" Jerrod set his half-eaten bread slice down to study me. "You're here at an important time, a historical time, as a few of us know. You've saved the life of the Empaetor. More than once, if the rumors are true. You delivered him safely home from the edge of the empire." Jerrod shrugged. "Rita, your deeds are the stuff historians love to wax on about. No one wants to sit through the recitation of the edicts the new Empaetor laid out during his first week on the throne."

The history of Empaetor Iradio VIII and his predecessors was a sore topic during any educational year. I wondered if Iradio IX would be different. Would one of those initial edicts he planned to announce tonight really be a pardon for all of Anduvea?

I hadn't known Laurent to not keep his word. Not yet, anyway.

I picked at a crumbly orange cheese, tossing a few small nuggets in my mouth to test it. Savory and slightly tangy, I approved. "I suppose you're right. It's just disconcerting to be on the inside of a historical event."

"Yes, I can see that. For what it's worth, I'm enjoying being inside it with you," he said with a smile. And cheese stuck to his teeth.

I wagged a finger at the offending view.

While he sorted that out, I said, "Juana also seems to be enjoying the promotion."

"Between you and me, I'm not sure what she was more excited about, the promotion to the Empaetor's guard, or working with you."

"I highly doubt that."

"I'm not kidding," he said earnestly. "You're one of us, Rita. Proof that good things can happen to the people usually stuck behind the bright lights that history remembers. And Laurent values your opinion. We've all seen it."

He took a long drink of water and set the cup down, fussing with the condensation dripping on the outside. "I hope that as consort, you'll use your sway to benefit us, the ones in the shadows. There are more colonies like Anduvea, plenty of them. I want to think that our new Empaetor will be different than the others, but with you beside him, he'll have no choice."

Torn between an unexpected burst of pride and annoyance that everyone assumed I was definitely Laurent's consort, I sat there gaping.

"You're a force to be reckoned with. Even for him."

I mulled over what he'd said and the sincerity with which he'd delivered it. "Thank you for that."

He nodded, pointing to the last two pieces of cheese. "Are you going to finish those?"

"All yours." I pushed the plate toward him and went to the bathroom to do a final freshen up. Laurent would be arriving shortly.

Staring into the mirror, I tried to see myself as the Empaetor's consort. A woman of style and grace, wearing the latest fashions and dutifully bearing an heir or two.

Even if I wouldn't be banished to the consort's estate, he'd expect those things of me. They went with the role.

Style and grace had never been my forte. My mother may have remarked on my 'wide child-bearing hips' more than once, but it felt like those years were behind me. I liked my new uniform, and I was at peace with how my body looked in it. The last thing I needed was a giant distended belly to screw with my balance and leave me covered in stretch marks. As far as I was concerned, the lack of stretch marks was one of the few things I had going for me.

But Jerrod had made a good point. A point that my gut had formed a deep instantaneous attachment to.

"Are you ready?" Laurent asked from just outside the bathroom door, reminding me of our time there that morning. A time I had quite enjoyed, and could have many more of depending on how the evening went.

"Yes," I said, lying through my teeth.

52
Five Minutes

The accession dinner turned out to be even more terrifying than I'd imagined. We walked in, Laurent first, me following right behind, flanked by six other guards, one of whom was Jerrod. They spread throughout the room, staying close enough to maintain a direct line of sight. I quickly realized that they were looking to me, not to the Empaetor, for any additional instruction. No pressure.

Rows of tables filled with the empire's elite, including—to my immediate gut-writhing terror—the twenty-five prospective consorts, made enough noise to compete with an average evening in the social district. They all fell silent as we entered, shooting to their feet and effecting an obligatory head bow.

Laurent wore a white suit that fit his form impeccably well. He wore no jewels or other ornamentation to mark his new rank as Empaetor other than an air of dignity that Iradio hadn't managed in the few times I'd been in his presence.

We made our way down the center aisle to a table raised above the rest. My parents sat at one end of it. Laurent's mother—who was looking fully recovered—sat at the other. A few dignitaries and advisors sat between them and the seat in the middle that Laurent took. His chair was the same as the others. No magnificent throne, as I'd imagined Iradio would have demanded.

The seat beside him remained empty. I eyed it with trepidation and then stepped behind Laurent. There was no wall, comfortable or otherwise, to rest against. No shadows to disappear into. Just bright lights, the sweet scent of twenty giant flower arrangements tickling my nose, and mouth-watering aromas sneaking out from under massive platter covers, making my stomach growl. That cheese plate had nothing on this dinner.

I scanned over the guests, recognizing a few faces that I'd passed in the corridors since my arrival. My heart leapt to see Pitari sitting beside members of the *Knaldon's* crew. She was deep in an animated conversation with one of the crewmen. As happy as I was to see her, I was grateful that she was tables away and occupied. I had many thoughts, and they were very loud.

Laurent picked up his glass and held it aloft. "Eat. No one likes long speeches on an empty stomach."

A great roar of approval filled the room that was only mildly overpowered by the clanking of covers being removed from the platters by a rush of staff. I watched with jealousy as they blended back into the décor, awaiting their next cue.

"It sounds like you're hungry," Laurent said over his shoulder, just loud enough for me to hear.

Stupid traitorous stomach. "I'm fine."

"Of course you are." He chuckled.

Laurent ate his meal neatly and without a rush, but neither with leisure. He did have that speech to deliver that he'd alluded to. I watched the staff handling the massive platters as if they weighed nothing, smiling as if there was nowhere they'd rather be than serving the elite of the empire. 'Our people', Jerrod had called them.

I leaned in close to Laurent's ear. "You're wasting that empty seat and a lot of food."

He turned to give me a wry smile. "You could sit in it."

"I might, but you could better use this as an opportunity to set the tone for your time on the throne."

Laurent turned back to the table and took a drink before again leaning back. "I like the sound of *might*. What do you propose?"

"The one thing your mother did right with her employees was to treat them like people. The honest ones loved her for it. Pick one of the attending staff as a representative. Give them the seat and let them enjoy this feast. Ask questions. Listen to them. Not just tonight. The listening, I mean. And not the seat, after tonight. I might be in it, after all."

He laughed, glancing up over his shoulder at me. My heart stuttered.

I eyed the empty chair and then caught sight of Jerrod. His brows were raised, eyes darting between me and the chair as if daring me to take it.

I'd already offered it to someone else. I gripped the back of Laurent's seat, pretending to do my job instead of wishing I'd kept my mouth shut and just sat down.

Laurent leaned forward, taking his cup in his hand. He gazed over the chattering crowd before him. Then he stood.

I didn't know what to make of that, but I stepped back to get out of his way. Laurent caught my arm with his hand and pulled me beside him.

He leaned in close, conspiratorially, like it was the two of us against the entire room. "Do you trust me not to be my father?"

I studied the face I'd come to know. Other than the physical family resemblance, no sign of Iradio's sharp and volatile edges remained. Laurent was asking questions, not ordering. The mischievous gleam in his eyes brought a smile to my lips.

"Yes. However, I won't wear any of that." I nodded to the host of elite women in their designer finery. "And I have zero desire to give birth to an heir."

He turned to face me, his light grip on my arm sliding down to my hand. His warm fingers intertwined with mine. I distantly became aware that the level of chatter had diminished.

"I like how you look in that uniform, though perhaps an upgrade will be required."

"I could live with that."

He grinned. "There are external means of bringing an heir to life. I was thinking that would be wise anyway, considering—"

"Our workload? Our age?"

"Never one to soften the blow, are you?"

"Nope."

All I could think about in that instant was how happy my parents would be to have a grandchild. Or children. I wasn't feeling nearly as cocky as Iradio.

The room had gone quiet but for a breath of whispers.

I was used to those, yet I couldn't bring myself to drag my gaze from Laurent's face, and peripherally, his fingers twined around mine. There were plenty of other guards in the room. I was busy just this once.

"Rita, will you take the seat beside me?"

"Now?"

"Maybe in five minutes. I think I can squeeze everything that needs to be said into that timeframe."

"Business before pleasure?"

Laurent laughed, the loud guffaw permeating the hall.

"Exactly that," he said more quietly, also seeming to notice the sudden silence.

"I still think—"

"Five minutes, Rita."

He looked quite earnest, and everyone was staring raptly at us now. Fine. Fuck it. I was going all in and praying to hell and back that this moment didn't come back to bite me in the ass.

"Sure. Yes. I'll take the damned seat."

He grinned. "Not exactly the spirit in which I'd hoped that answer would be delivered, but I'll take it."

Laurent turned around, facing the crowd, which meant I also had to face them. I swore under my breath. My comfort level with crowds was more of the dispersing a riot or breaking up a group fight variety. Facing a wide-eyed room full of elite assholes scared the shit out of me. Laurent squeezed my hand.

Right. Breathe in and out. I tried to smile, but my face seemed frozen.

Thank the Maker, Laurent spoke because I'd forgotten how.

"Though we mourn the loss of my father, Empaetor Iradio VIII, care for the empire has fallen into my hands. I take this responsibility seriously and hope you will offer me the same patience and cooperation that you have given my predecessors since the beginning of the Iradio line."

A polite round of applause fluttered through the room. Many eyes were still on me, specifically the women from the proposed consort pool. To my surprise, they weren't glaring daggers in my direction, nor were they muttering spitefully. If anything, they appeared wistful. The muscles in my neck relaxed slightly.

"As to the Iradio line..." Laurent cleared his throat. "While I may have been named Iradio Octao Laurent Scaavo IX, I have been known as Laurent by those closest to me." He glanced at me and smiled shyly.

My memory scrolled back to when we'd first met, when he'd told me to use his name. When he'd admitted that Ari and his mother were the only other people to use it. Everyone else had always referred to him as the Scaavo heir. I nodded my encouragement, liking where I hoped he was going with this.

"I will take my oaths as Empaetor Laurent I."

A cheer erupted, led by, to my surprise, Laurent's mother. She stood at the table, clapping her hands, looking every bit as proud as my mother had looked when I'd gotten my first job on the station.

An officiant stood, a man in a long grey suit coat from the first table to our left. He approached us. Once the crowd quieted, he administered the oath of Laurent's appointment as Empaetor. Thankfully, it was short, because as much debate as I'd had over taking the seat beside Laurent,

I now very much wanted to sit down and not have every-one so blatantly staring in my direction. If they could all go back to covert whispering, that would be fantastic.

Once the oath was taken and the officiant had returned to his seat, Laurent again addressed the room.

"Tonight is a celebration of a new direction for the empire, for all of us. I won't take up too much of your time, but there are a couple items of business that need to be addressed immediately."

Laurent turned toward the end of the table where my parents sat. "Would the representatives from Anduvea please stand?"

A murmur passed through the crowd.

"Yes, representatives. Anduvea is now a free colony world. The exile restrictions have been removed. They now have a seat on the council just like every other free colony world."

My parents both wore radiant smiles, and I joined them. This was the reward I'd wanted for my people when I'd set out to help Laurent. If only Agent Andover or SA Tekka could have easily granted it and then let me go about my job. Of course, then I'd still be on the station, annoyed and alone, no matter how free. I rubbed my thumb over Laurent's palm.

"Speaking of representatives," he glanced meaningfully at me before returning to the crowd. "Could we get another chair up here? It seems there is a faction of the population whose voice has been overlooked."

A middle-aged male member of the staff appeared with a chair and stood uncertainly. Laurent pointed to the spot next to his, opposite the empty one, urging the men and women at our table to make room. He studied the staff member. "That seat is for you. Someone get him a place setting."

"Me, sir?" The man stood gaping.

"You're not in any trouble. We'll talk shortly. Please sit and eat."

Another staff member darted forward with a place setting. I noticed many of the staff at the edges of the audience were talking quietly and gesturing at me. They were smiling. Maybe Jerrod was right. Not all whispers were bad.

"You may have heard rumors of my travel from Anduvea and the ship that brought me safely home."

The seated audience nodded.

"While I will not go into details about that adventure, members of that crew will be rewarded for their service in my time of need, as will several staff members of the Anduvean station."

The table where Pitari sat with the *Knaldon* crew broke out into a momentary cheer before quieting to wide grins.

"I would also like to invite my mother, who has fulfilled her role as consort, to retire here, to the palace with us if she so wishes."

Laurent's mother's smile nearly eclipsed my mother's. I wondered how the two of them might get along. The bragging my mother would be doing to her friends back on Anduvea was going to be stupendous.

"Speaking of consorts," Laurent again glanced at me.

For better or worse, I nodded.

"I would like to introduce my chosen consort, Rita Stabinov. From the moment we met, her skill and tenacity have protected me. I hope she will continue to do so until we take our last breaths."

It seemed I would get my dream job and the wistful position all in one. We may not have spent months in some eye-roll-worthy romance, but he did know me and what I wanted. I had a pretty good idea about him too.

My tongue finally thawed. "I will."

A cheer spread through the crowd, both those seated and standing.

"Now then, we have a celebration to get back to. Enjoy yourselves. Tomorrow, we will begin to bring the empire into a new age."

Laurent let go of my hand to pull my chair out. "Sit and eat. No one wants to see you hungry. Besides, I think the rest of your team can handle security for the evening."

"My team?" I settled into the chair and slid it closer to the table, surveying the remaining food options.

"You didn't strike me as the sit-around-holding-ladies-meetings-and-hosting-dinners sort. Frankly, that would be a waste. Overseeing palace security seemed like it might be a better fit. I would love to see what you discover here, secret passages and all."

My hand froze mid-serving myself a slab of meat. "There are secret passages?"

"I don't know. Promise you'll let me know if you find any?"

"More than promise. I'll take you on a private tour."

Laurent laughed. "Look, I know we haven't had much time to explore this relationship, and I'm rushing you into this. From here on out, you set the speed as long as I have your cooperation on the external creation of an heir."

"Heir creation aside, I was hoping for something a little

more personal than a medical exam to seal this deal."

He finished his drink while I chewed a few bites. With a mischievous smile and sparkling eyes, he said, "More personal can definitely be arranged."

I sighed dramatically. "You undoubtedly have a packed schedule tomorrow with this whole new age of Empaetor Laurent I to launch into action."

The new staff representative sitting on the other side of Laurent coughed loudly.

Laurent glanced from the man to me. "Five minutes, Rita. Eat all you can. I don't want you going all stabby on me while we have an in-depth security evaluation of my bedroom."

Laurent launched into a conversation with the new staff representative. I left him to it. As someone who was used to grabbing a meal on a short break, eating fast was a skill I'd long ago perfected.

"One minute," I whispered a countdown warning into his ear.

Laurent shook his head and snickered, but kept his attention on the staff representative's passionate speech.

"I've heard you and will keep this in mind when we start our work tomorrow. Please let me know if any other concerns come to light before our next meeting."

"Thank you, sir." As genuinely grateful as he appeared, I almost regretted rushing Laurent off. Almost.

The new Empaetor stood and reached a hand out for me. Rather than take it, I wrapped my arm around his. We made a dignified exit through the crowd, unrushed but not stopping to chat either.

"I'm looking forward to this new age," I said as we

entered the corridor, where I paused to nod to the guard who had escorted us out. He handed us over to four more who were waiting.

"I'm looking forward to having you beside me as we bring it about."

"My first suggestion is a private lift that goes directly to your suite."

Laurent grinned. "*Our* suite. If you can make it secure, consider it done."

"Not done fast enough," I muttered as I started up the stairs.

"Change takes time, Rita."

"Tonight was a good first step."

We sped up the rest of the stairs, through the outer door and receiving room, and entered his inner door code.

"I can't wait to see what we can accomplish together."

He opened the suite door and pulled me inside. "Tomorrow."

"Tomorrow," I agreed, laughing.

We nodded to Juana on our hurried way to the bedroom, where I discovered the best mattress the wealth of the empire could buy was even better with someone to enjoy it with.

**If you enjoyed this book,
please consider leaving a review.
They are much appreciated.
Thank you!**

About the Author

Jean Davis writes an array of speculative fiction and plays with chickens. She has written short story collections, a space opera series, stand-alone novels, children's books about her chickens, many projects that aren't yet finished, and a lot of pages that you will never see.

When not ruining fictional lives from the comfort of her writing chair, she can be found devouring books and sushi, weeding her flower garden, or picking up hundreds of sticks while attempting to avoid the abundant snake population that also shares her yard. She lives in West Michigan with her musical husband, an attention-craving terrier, and a mostly friendly flock of fluffy fowl.

Read her blog and sign up for her mailing list at www.jeandavisauthor.com. You can also follow her on Facebook and Instagram @JeanDavisAuthor, and on Goodreads and Amazon.